Out of the Comfort Zone

Copyright © 2006 Frank Agin
All rights reserved.
ISBN: 1-4196-5791-7

To order additional copies, please contact us.
BookSurge, LLC
www.booksurge.com
1-866-308-6235
orders@booksurge.com

FRANK
AGIN

OUT OF THE COMFORT ZONE

2006

Out of the Comfort Zone

THE COMFORT ZONE

We live in a zone of comfort -- situations that threaten us, we tend to avoid.

When we're hurting, we seek consolation; when we're tired, we rest; and, when we're outmatched, we concede.

But still somewhere within us, we have the concentration to ignore the deepest pain; the strength to endure the most exhausting fatigue; and, the means to conquer even the impossible challenge.

In essence, through courage, hard work and discipline, we have the ability to leave this zone of comfort.

Only here can we discover our true potential.

Although testing the limits of our potential doesn't guarantee fame, fortune or championship status, it's Out of the Comfort Zone where winning begins.

AUTHOR'S NOTES

During four falls in the early 1980s, I had the wonderful privilege of playing football at Beloit College (Beloit, Wisconsin) for Coach Ed DeGeorge. Despite playing for an average team, in a mediocre league (Midwest Conference) at the lowest level of college football (Division III), this was one of the most inspiring times of my life. It was such a moving experience, that during the summer of 1986 I wrote *Out Of The Comfort Zone* – a story based on my experiences playing college football.

It is important to state, however, that this is a novel. Yes, 95% of the book is comprised of events that did happen and statements that were made. However, these events and statements were taken from 4-plus years of involvement with the Beloit College football program (as a recruit, player and ultimately a recruiter for the program) and then re-assembled into one tumultuous and ultimately magical season.

What is real, however, are the characters in *Out Of The Comfort Zone*. There is someone behind pretty much every character I developed in the novel.

While I clanked out this story in 1986 on a Macintosh 1M, it has sat largely untouched for the last 20 years. Getting in the way of its publication was life. Since the summer of 1986, I focused my attention on obtaining a law degree and MBA, having a career and starting a business, marrying a beautiful woman named Linda, helping to bring three great kids – Lucas, Logan and Chase – into the world, and umpteen other distractions.

In the fall of 2005, however, I was invited to return to campus for Coach Ed DeGeorge's final game as head football coach of the Beloit College Buccaneers. Once back in Beloit, I was reunited with many of those who became characters in *Out Of The Comfort Zone* as well as 29 years worth of others who shared a similar experience at Beloit College with Coach DeGeorge.

As dozens and dozens of loyal ex-players formed a gauntlet to welcome Coach DeGeorge onto the football field at Strong Stadium one last time, it all came rushing back to me. There was a reason why I devoted 40 hours per week over a 10-week summer in 1986 to authoring *Out Of The Comfort Zone*. It was not to just write a novel. It was partially for Coach DeGeorge, the right mentor for me at the right time.

But more importantly, it was a tribute to those I had the wonderful privilege to play football with …Zepper, Joe, Bruno and Hubs … Beaver, Heisman, Simba and Porky … Doc, Stubby, Bertso and Scooter … Wilk, Mead, Bobby, and Pete … and countless others that wore the blue and gold of Beloit College.

Whether or not anyone other than those who were part of these events reads this story, is not important. What is important is that it is finally written. In a certain respect, this is a very long-winded thank you.

Go Bucs!

Frank Agin
October 15, 2006

Dedicated to

Ed DeGeorge
Head Football Coach
Beloit College Buccaneers
1977-2005

Thanks for helping to
Strengthen our bodies;
Develop our minds; and
Instill a desire to succeed in our hearts.

1

In Beloit, Wisconsin, the weather is always hot and sticky in middle August, especially during the mid-part of the day when the sun is at its high point.

Despite the uncomfortable heat and humidity for this small Midwestern town, Mark Stubner struggled to carry a heavy box of his textbooks along the sidewalk between the Main dormitory and the Sigma Rho Fraternity house. He stopped and shifted the weight onto his hip long enough to wipe the sweat from his balding forehead. He studied the sidewalk that he walked along and remembered how the steam pipes under the sidewalk always kept the walkway clear of snow and ice all winter long. He suspected that those steam pipes were probably responsible for some of the heat he was experiencing.

Mark had spent the entire summer working for the Beloit College Building and Grounds Department. It was difficult for him to make this decision. He had to weigh Mom's home cooking against a summertime of macaroni and cheese, the comfort of his waterbed against a standard Residential Life super single bed, and a high paying job with his old girlfriend's father against the average pay of a student supervisor on campus. Thinking back Mark wasn't sure why he decided to stay. His memories of the previous year weren't very fond. The football season was, at best, so-so, and his grades seemed to be stuck around 3.0. Worst of all, his relationship with the woman he cared about most was highly questionable.

Deep down inside, though, Mark knew that the reason he forfeited all the comforts of home was the opportunity to work out with a couple of the guys he played football with during the school year at Beloit College. It just so happened that these guys were able to enjoy the comforts of home because they grew up and went to high school in Beloit.

But because Mark had to sacrifice and others didn't, he wasn't concerned. The sacrifice paid off. Or at least for right now it had. He was in the best shape of his life. For the first time in years the skin was tight around his shoulders, and veins began to surface on his biceps. However, the most noticeable benefit of this summer of driving himself hard in the weight room was that the inner tube he had developed via late night pizza and beer was almost gone. He was ready to play his last season of collegiate football, and just maybe, if all went well, to have a shot at a pro try-out somewhere -- anywhere (NFL, AFL, CFL) would be fine.

Stubby, as Mark was known among the guys on the team, put the books down on the front porch of the Sigma Rho fraternity house. He squatted his six-foot-five, two-hundred-sixty pound frame down to remove the key for the door from his shoelace. Stubby was surprised that despite all the problems the football team had caused on campus, the Residential Life office allowed him to move in a day before everyone was supposed to report for preseason camp. Maybe it was because the Director of Residential Life was a great guy and could relate to all the fraternity's mischievous activities or maybe it was because Mark had gotten to know everyone on the tiny Beloit College campus so well. Stubby didn't question the Residential Life Office's reasoning in saying yes to allowing him early entry. He was smart enough to take what he could and go.

He propped the door open with a crushed Diet Coke can, picked up the heavy box and entered the empty fraternity house. As he walked in, a strand of spider web caught him across the nose. He moved his head to free himself of the invisible nuisance. The idea that the house had to be crawling with spiders didn't bother him in the least.

As Stubby pushed his way through the second doorway leading from the entryway to the main living room area, the terrible stench he expected hit him. The house smelled of the party the fraternity had at the end of the last year. Of course, none of the seniors who threw the party after graduation took the responsibility to clean up after themselves.

Mark put down what he was carrying and picked up a glass of beer which was sitting on top of the grand piano. Almost like a scientist, he examined the glass. He slowly tipped the glass upside-down and laughed with a disgusted look on his face when none of the contents poured out. From a distance it appeared to be a trick glass, but Stubby knew different. Before the beer could evaporate, a film of mold had sealed off the top of the beer line. Stubby put the glass down and walked to the front double doors. He opened them as wide as he could, hoping to air out the smelly living room.

He grabbed the load he had brought with him and proceeded to his room in the back part of the South wing. The hallways were not in much better condition than the living room -- piles of garbage, used notebooks, unwanted furniture and clothing lined the hallway. He had to step cautiously the entire way.

Again, he put the books down to get another key off his other shoe. A gentle turn of the key revealed a room that was immaculate. This was one of the benefits of working on campus all summer. One day he was able to sneak off for about a half a day and clean out the mess that the previous person had left. Naturally he didn't touch the mess anywhere else. He would have been more upset about the mess if the previous person had not happened to be a fraternity brother.

The walls were completely bare except for one poster which Stubby had found in the garbage while cleaning. Big blue and yellow letters said: "FOOTBALL IS MY LIFE; EVERYTHING ELSE IS BULLSHIT." The sign was so appropriate to his state of mind that he had to have it. And by the laws of this Sigma Rho fraternity house -- anything left in the hallway at the end of the year is considered unclaimed -- it was his, and it hung proudly above his door.

Mark slid the box of books across the carpet over to the corner closest to the door. There he let them rest. There was no sense in unpacking them until he got his waterbed and shelves set up. He leaned against the wall and slid his large body down until he was sitting on the floor. He seemed to daydream for a minute in the stifling heat -- then something in the box caught his eye. He reached in and pulled out a card.

It was an any-occasion card with a cute picture on the front and nothing printed inside it. He knew from the beginning that it was from Sue, the girl he dated up until last May, but it wasn't until he opened it that he remembered the exact day he got it. It was the day after their first date. The card was tacked to his door when he came back from class. He remembered the feeling he had when he first read about the wonderful time she had and that she was looking forward to more of the same. He smiled as he re-read the card. Putting it down, he thought about that night again. Then he went out to get another load of stuff.

2

Just north of Madison, Wisconsin, U.S. Route 51 pours into Interstate 90. Among the many cars and trucks was a blue Chevy adding to the early afternoon traffic. From in front, the Chevy appeared to be just another car on the road, but as it sped by well above the speed limit it was obvious that it wasn't: the license plates -- 035-JEC – were from Michigan.

Inside the Chevy, Foster Addison was wearing a pair of pink hospital scrubs, given to him by a previous girlfriend, and a sweat-stained gray T-shirt. This was Foster's standard dress for long trips.

With his right hand he steered the car and with his left he quickly wiped the sweat that dripped down both sides of his face with the front part of his T-shirt. He opened the vent down by his left leg and then grabbed for a Diet Coke off the seat to his right. The sun was positioned over the top of the car, causing the interior to heat up. Normally Foster would have rolled down the windows, but with such a long trip it was important to hear the radio and with the windows down at this speed that would not be possible. Besides, he reasoned, the August heat made him tough.

The sun had been hidden behind the clouds for most of the trip. But now the sky was beginning to clear and it was definitely a hot Wisconsin day, a lot hotter than his home in the Upper Peninsula of Michigan, where Lake Superior had a cooling effect on the area. Foster wiped the sweat again and wondered if the relatively hot climate would have any effect on him in football. In his three previous seasons at Beloit College it didn't seem to bother him at all, except for making his appetite bigger than normal. He decided he wasn't going to let it bother him.

This trip was Foster's first drive back to college by himself. In previous years he wasn't as fortunate to have a car. But this year, his senior year, his father allowed him to take the car back to school. This was also the first time that he traveled down from Houghton, Michigan, through the extreme northern part of Wisconsin. In previous years he was either brought back to school by his brother or his father via the traditional route that passed through Green Bay, then Milwaukee, and then across on Highway 15 to the city of Beloit. The reason for the change was that Foster intended to stop and see a girl he had met at a track meet the spring before. She was working at a resort in northern Wisconsin. However, when he finally arrived at the town where she worked, he lost his nerve, talked himself out of stopping, and drove right through town.

As he continued down the highway, past a sign that read, "Beloit 60 miles," he thought back to exactly how he ended up a Beloit College. He remembered the Christmas before he graduated from high school when his Uncle Jim asked whether he planned to follow in his father's footsteps and go to the same small Midwestern liberal arts college. Foster politely said no, but thought to himself, 'hell no.'

Not long after Christmas vacation Foster's father received a call from the Admissions Office at Beloit College inquiring about Foster's plans for college. At that point he had none. Foster's father, a Beloit grad himself, was flattered that the college was keeping such close track of his life, but he never pushed any of his three children toward anything. He told the Beloit recruiter that he wasn't sure where Foster was leaning. However, he knew that wherever it was, Foster was interested in playing college football.

His father was correct. Foster really didn't care where he ended up going to school, as long as he could still play football. An education is an education, he reasoned. It wasn't that he was a dumb jock. So in his search for an acceptable school, Foster searched for one where he could play football. This goal bordered on the impossible because Foster was only a five-foot ten, one-hundred-seventy-five pound defensive tackle, from a high school with a one-and-eight record his senior year.

Despite his chances, Foster sent letters to football coach after football coach, concerned only with getting a chance to at least walk on. Much to Foster's disappointment, there was only one reply -- the college in his hometown -- and they didn't seem too enthusiastic. However, once the football coach at Beloit knew of Foster's interest in his college, the outlook changed.

From the instant Foster received the initial contact from the Beloit College football coach, his attitude toward the college went from 'hell no' to 'maybe.' This change was due in part to Coach Bonaventure's recruiting philosophy, which he spelled out for Foster: "Beloit is looking for men who love the game of football, who aren't necessarily Big Ten in size, but Big Ten in heart." Foster immediately identified with that philosophy.

Aside from philosophy though, for once someone out there was paying some attention to him. His ego, deflated from not receiving any responses to the dozens of letters he had sent out, was beginning to recover. Coach Bonaventure did a great sales job. He would make an inspiring phone call and then follow it up with a letter or postcard which in essence said, "It was nice to talk to you the other day." Then he would call to see if the letter arrived, while giving another inspiring speech. The cycle continued until Foster was finally saying 'hell yes' about Beloit College.

When the Madison radio station gave the temperature, Foster stopped thinking about his history with Beloit College. Foster felt his body begin to sweat more at hearing the words "ninety-five degrees." The heat in the car was too much to bear. There is a fine line between being tough and being stupid and he was crossing it. Foster took a quick swig of Diet Coke and then placed the can between his legs. He leaned forward and shut off the radio. 97-WZOK out of Rockford, Illinois (Foster's favorite station) wouldn't be in range for another half-hour. Once Foster had taken care of all that, he quickly rolled down the window. Feeling the air from that one wasn't enough. He carefully leaned over to the passenger window and rolled that one down too.

He took another drink of Diet Coke and then placed the can between his legs again. The pop was quickly warming, but the wetness was satisfying. Foster quickly finished the can and reached for another. As he opened the second can he let the spray from the carbonation hit him under the chin. It felt cool, for a minute.

The last hour of a long trip usually seems the longest, and this trip was no exception. It was an eternity between the sign that read: "Beloit 60" and "Beloit 49." Foster was getting irritated with the trip and started to press harder on the gas pedal. The speedometer moved from 65 to 70 to 75.

Foster locked his ankle at the position needed to stay at 75 miles per hour. He stuck his hand out the window and either let air rush through his fingers or else curved his hand so the wind would blow through his hair.

With his right hand on the steering wheel tapping out the beats to a song that was stuck in his head, Foster reached down to his crotch to grab the can of Diet Coke. As he raised it to his mouth he sang out a line from a song. The Diet Coke flowed smoothly down his throat as he continued to tilt the can. He was determined to finish it as he peered around both sides of the can to see where he was driving.

Just as Foster had three-quarters of the can down, he spotted a Wisconsin State Highway patrol car parked about a quarter of a mile ahead trying to hide among the trees. Foster immediately slammed on the brakes. The jerk of the car caused diet Coke to spill out all over the front of his shirt. "Shit," he said, as he sat the can down between his legs. He was still pressing on the brakes.

When he passed the patrol car he had slowed down to about 62 miles per hour. That was only a little faster than anyone else on the road. But then again this was the Wisconsin Highway Patrol, notorious for holding to the slogan, "FIFTY-FIVE MEANS FIFTY-FIVE." And besides, Foster's car had Michigan license plates -- another strike. But as Foster looked out the corner of his eye he noticed that the officer was doing some writing on a clipboard -- no doubt completing paperwork from the last ticket. Foster sailed by unnoticed.

Feeling confident that he was out of range and that there would be no patrol cars again for a while, Foster began accelerating. As the speedometer pushed past 70 miles per hour, Foster sang again.

3

It was a typical weekday afternoon for the McDonald's just off Wisconsin Route 15. The few diners left from the lunchtime rush were just finishing up, and the work crew, consisting mainly of high school girls, was busily trying to get the all-American diner back into shape. Summer was nearing an end for the crew. Soon they would no longer have mid-afternoon shifts, but rather evenings and weekends.

Since there was a lull in the day, a short blonde girl was given the task of making price changes to various items on the intercom board's menu. Her co-workers uttered the usual jokes and obscenities at her through the intercom.

While she carefully made certain that each price change was correct, she blocked out her joking friends. Because she was engrossed in her work, she didn't notice the powder-blue VW Bug that came coasting around the corner to make a drive-through-window order. The Bug came to a stop behind her and the driver patiently waited until he realized she would be there for quite a bit longer than he was willing to wait.

"Excuse me," the driver said calmly and politely, "Do you mind if I make an order?"

Startled, the girl turned and jumped back at the same time she said, "Oh, you scared me."

"I'm that ugly," the driver said as he grabbed the one-day's growth on his chin. "Does that mean I can't order?" he said with a smart-ass tone as he removed his tortoise-shell sunglasses.

She stopped and gazed, then stared. Behind his glasses was a pair of captivating blue eyes to match the car he was driving. All the light brown hair on his head was neatly combed and his smile was extremely sexy. Without any question, he was the cutest guy she had seen come through Elkorn, Wisconsin this summer. That included everyone who resided there, or had a summer cottage in the area, or was just passing through. Not even the guy her older sister had dated this summer -- whom she idolized. She jerked herself back to reality.

"No. I mean yes." She became flustered. "No, you can't order and yes, you are ugly," she stammered.

"Oh, really?" he exclaimed, knowing what she meant, but teasing her. "Isn't that sort of discriminatory?" He gave her a very deep and serious look.

At that point she realized what she had said and quickly became embarrassed. As her face began to turn red, she blurted, "No, you aren't ugly and yes, you can order." She nervously added, "I'm so sorry," as she quickly placed her hand on his left arm which was resting on the open window.

The driver, feeling bad about embarrassing the girl, turned sideways in the front seat so as to extend his right hand to the bewildered girl. "Hi, my name is Todd, but my friends just call me Doc -- what's yours?" He flashed his smile again.

She was slow to respond. Wanting to say the right thing this time, she carefully enunciated, "Lisa," as her right hand slowly met his.

"No nicknames?" Doc quickly fired another question back at her. She didn't dare chance saying another thing, but she managed to nod her head 'no', the whole time keeping an eye on how cute Todd, or Doc, or whatever he wanted to be called, really was.

As Doc's attention switched to examining the intercom board's menu, Lisa slipped around the rear of the building and rushed through the door bearing the sign, "EMPLOYEES ONLY." She knew that with all the screwing around that usually happened with the post-noontime rush, no one would be paying much attention to the drive-thru window area.

As she quickly ran up front she caught everyone's attention. In her excitement she could not utter a single word. However, it was evident that she did have something to say. Her co-workers eyed her with concern as a distressed look covered her face. Then all at once, like a volcano, she let loose:

"HE'S SO CUTE!" she screamed, bending over at the waist as she clenched her fist by her knees.

Customers waiting to order looked on with amazement as the entire lunchtime crew began laughing at Lisa. It was something certainly never seen on a McDonald's commercial. Once the crew calmed down enough to listen, Lisa was able to quickly explain what she was talking about as she hustled a high school girlfriend over to take the drive-thru order.

"Welcome to McDonald's; may I take your order please?" Lisa's friend was extremely formal.

"Sure," Doc said and then paused. He still hadn't made up his mind. After a short time, he said, "Just give me a chocolate milkshake and a large order of fries."

Lisa stood in the background and grabbed her heart as she leaned up against the wall. His voice sounded as good as he looked. She gazed up at the ceiling.

Her friend held the microphone away from her mouth and registered the order. Unable to make any association between Doc's voice and how cute he was, she looked at Lisa as if she were weird.

"Will that be all?" the girl said, still staring at Lisa.

"Yes," Doc said with certainty.

The girl responded: "That will be three dollars and fifty-seven cents."

Doc pulled up to the window before his order was ready. As he produced a five-dollar bill and extended it up toward the window, the four or five girls who worked there peered over the counter to catch a glimpse of Lisa's newly found idol. The girls concurred with what Lisa had described and they dropped back out of Doc's sight to giggle. All the customers were entertained by the drama behind the counter.

The girl who took the order was also there to greet Doc. She was captivated by his blue eyes and looked deeply into them as she counted the change from the five dollar bill. "Three-fifty-seven," she said as she handed him the receipt, "and one forty-three, makes five dollars." She handed him a dollar, a quarter, a dime, a nickel, and three pennies. Then she quickly pulled her head back in the window and said, almost as flustered as Lisa, "Where is his food?"

Two girls fought to complete the order. The girl who then completed the order had to struggle with the girl who took the order to give the bag to Doc. Doc sensed all the attention he was receiving and merely turned his head away and smiled. The girl who took the order, after a quick, nonsensical debate, won the right to give Doc his food. As she moved toward the window she used her hips to box out the other girls who were trying to catch one last peek at the cute guy in the powder blue VW Bug, as he would be referred to for the rest of the summer.

"Here you go," the girl said as she handed him the bag. "Sorry for the wait." She put her best foot forward, smiling and trying to look sexier than she ever had before.

"Thanks," Doc said as he grabbed the bag, quickly opened it, checked the contents, snatched two fries and put them in his mouth. As he chewed and swallowed he put his sunglasses back on and looked straight ahead. Doc then began to push down on the accelerator and make the VW sputter. Just before he released the clutch he turned to the window again and noticed five or six pairs of eyes watching his every move. He only recognized one pair and addressed them. "Have a good summer, Lisa," Doc said as he waved and drove off.

All the girls huddled around Lisa for a split second and envied her. She was in a wonderful daze as she looked up at the ceiling and let her mind wander. She took a deep breath as if she were going to continue to daydream, but then all at once she pulled herself back to reality and pushed through her co-workers to the drive-thru. She grabbed for a piece of paper and a pencil, and shouted, "Get his license number," as she looked down the street. But it was too late. He was too far down the road.

Lisa moved away from the window area with a disappointed look on her face. Everyone was quiet. He might as well have been a dream because he was gone forever. "Why can't just once, a guy like that not just be passing through," Lisa said almost to herself.

From the back part of the kitchen a male voice broke the chatter of female ones. "Oh, what's the matter with the guys here in town?" Ralph, a guy from their high school who had been cleaning the grill, spoke up. His hair was grease covered and complexion poor at best. "You girls are always looking elsewhere for Prince Charming to come sweep you off your feet." He spoke again, this time waving a grease scraper in their direction.

The girl who had taken the order stepped in front of the rest of the girls and boldly said, "Why don't you get a real life, Ralph?"

Ralph had nothing to counter with. He simply waved back at the girls as if to say 'never mind.'

Doc, or Todd David Wallace as his parents named him, finished all the French fries before he got his trusty VW Bug back on Highway 15. He was extremely hungry as he hadn't eaten since he had breakfast three hours earlier at his home in Green Bay, Wisconsin. He knew he only had about a fifteen- to twenty-minute drive left, but he figured that once he got to Beloit he would be too busy unloading to get something to eat.

As the powder blue Bug accelerated on to Highway 15, Doc pulled the chocolate milkshake out of the McDonald's bag. He had to suck hard at first to get any of the shake up the straw. After a lot of effort sucking on the straw and very little shake, Doc got discouraged and placed the shake between his legs.

He looked out the window to both sides of the highway and saw nothing but farmland. He rolled his eyes and then yawned. It had been a busy past couple of days. His last day at work was yesterday, and so along with going to work he had to work out, spend time with his family, and also get packed for school. There wasn't much time for more than the minimum amount of sleep. Not helping his tired state was the fact that he had traveled this route dozens of times before and the only thing that ever changed was the seasons.

Doc was glad that the summer was over. Although he didn't like class as much as the spare time the summer had to offer, he was getting a little fed up with working the swing-shift at Fort Howard Paper Company. Since this was his last year in school, he would no longer have to work there.

But more than getting away from the Fort Howard swing-shift, Doc wanted to get going on his senior football season. He looked forward to this season more than any before, because this year he, along with Foster Addison, would be serving as team co-captain. It was a great honor for him, an honor which he was hoping for ever since Coach Bonaventure called him aside two years ago to tell him that he had received six votes for captain as a sophomore. But now the dream had come true.

Being captain was more than just an honor to Doc. It meant that his teammates had enough confidence in him as a football player and a leader to elect him. He wasn't about to let them down. This past summer he worked harder than any other before. He was primed to be a serious contender for All-Midwestern Conference quarterback honors. He felt he had a lot to prove, mainly to himself, and this would be the year he would do so.

He reached down for his shake, hoping that the warmth of his thighs would have melted some of the thick shake. It had. However, the melting process had caused condensation to form on the outside of the wax-covered cup. Most of this condensation soaked into his navy blue shorts and made it look as if he had wet his pants. He looked at the wet spot with disgust and shook his head. Doc quickly turned the VW's vent that had been hitting him in the face down toward his crotch hoping that the air would dry up the wet spot.

As he rounded the next corner he could see the outskirts of the city of Beloit. Off to the left where Highway 15 meets Interstate 90, the city had established an industrial park where Freeman Shoes, Frito-Lay, and Hormel signs were visible. Straight ahead was a multitude of motels, gas stations, and truck-stop diners to serve the thru traffic from the Interstate. Doc was anxious about being back. He began to suck hard on the straw. This time he got plenty of milkshake.

4

Foster took Interstate 90 down until it met with Shopiere Road. From there he followed various streets until he found Church Street. From here it was only a matter of a block or two until he was able to take a right down the alley by the Zeta Kappa Zeta house.

This alley led to a strip of College Street that was isolated between Emerson and Clary streets. College Street ran north/south and was one-way north. This portion of College Street served as Beloit College's fraternity row. To the north the street was blocked off by residence halls, and to the south by the college's main library. The only access to this part of College Street, other than the alley Foster had taken, was Emerson Street, and the only exit was Clary. Driving around campus was confusing, but it was even more confusing to try and follow someone's directions because it seemed that all streets were named "Street" and none "Avenue." It was impossible to make any kind of north/south -- east/west distinction.

As Foster approached College Street, he could see Doc's car. Parking was prohibited on the left-hand side at all times. Despite signs to that effect being posted about every 100 feet Doc had his car parked snug up against the left curb right in front of the Sigma Rho house. He wasn't in his car, but the driver-side door was wide open. His hazard lights were flashing as if to indicate that he was unloading.

Foster parked his car on the right side of the road about twenty feet ahead of where Doc's was. He got out of the car and closed the door behind him. He didn't bother locking the door or even rolling up the window because nobody but football players and residence assistants, R.A.'s, were due to be on campus for a couple of days. Besides, anything he had of value was packed well below everything else, at his father's insistence, so before someone could get at his limited valuables, they had to dig through three or four layers of towels, socks, sheets, and notebook paper.

Foster walked back toward Doc's car. Looking inside the VW Bug, he had to smile as the car was loaded to the maximum with CDs, plaques, tapestries, a stereo, and clothes. Foster looked around to see where Doc was. No sign. Foster then moved quickly towards the two double doors which Stubby had opened to air out the living room. The doors were closed now. Nonetheless, Foster headed toward them. As he reached the porch, just outside the doors he heard someone come around the side of the house. He didn't know who, but he could hear the sound of flip-flops clicking through the grass. Foster stepped off the porch and saw that it was Doc looking for an entrance into the fraternity house. Foster leaned up against one of the Sigma Rho house's big white pillars and waited for Doc to notice him.

"Where is Stubby?" Doc asked Foster. "He was supposed to be here with the house open at three o'clock; it's almost three-twenty-five." Doc looked around for Stubby's car.

Doc had been racing around campus in the heat looking for Stubby for over fifteen minutes, which made him a little upset. Foster understood why a more congenial greeting was not given, but replied as if one were. "Just fine, thanks. How was your summer?" Foster smiled, waiting for a response.

Doc realized his rudeness and the serious look on his face turned into a smile. They both laughed. Doc extended his hand to Foster and they shook hands using the secret fraternity grip.

"I'm sorry, but I've been out here for a while and I'm about to fall over because of the heat." Doc wiped the sweat from his forehead.

"Don't feel bad. At least you've had all summer to get used to this heat." Foster showed the sweat-stained armpits of his shirt. "Christ, I spent my summer up in the snow country where I had to wear gloves biking into work in the mornings. It snowed the day before my sister's graduation."

"You're kidding," Doc replied with his head tilted to the left.

"No shit." Foster wanted to seem credible. "That was June 6th." Doc had nothing to compare with that experience so the topic of weather died.

"So what do we do? Wait for Stubby to show?" Doc asked.

"Well, we've got one of two choices," Foster responded.

"What are they?" Doc looked curious.

"One: we could get into your car and turn on the air conditioner and wait." Foster said this with a serious look on his face.

Doc laughed. They both knew that on a good day Doc's VW barely had an AM radio. "I can hardly wait for number two," Doc said as he continued to chuckle.

"Number Two." Foster held up two fingers and stepped on to the porch and pushed the front doors open. "We go in the house and wait." Foster knew that even when these doors were locked, a gentle push could open them up. Foster stood just outside the house holding his arm out into the doorway as if saying, 'you first.'

"Let me close my car door first." Doc took two steps toward his car and then turned while running backwards and said, "Hey Foster, do you want a can of Pepsi? They are semi-cold." Doc continued to hop backwards while he waited for a reply.

Foster thought twice because he had already had a six pack that day, and then responded, "Yes." He thought it was too damn hot to be picky about what kind of fluids to put in his system. Besides, the water in the house would probably have a rust color for the next day or so.

Doc again turned toward his car and began to open up his stride. He reached into the cooler his mother had stocked with a six-pack of Pepsi and grabbed two of them. He put the cover back on the cooler and closed the car door. He didn't bother moving his car because he figured that the police would come warn him before he got a ticket since his hazard lights were on.

When Doc got into the house he, too, noticed the moldy smell left over from the party, but he didn't mind because the house was cool. He took a quick look around for Foster. After not spotting him, Doc called out. "Foster!"

Foster quickly replied, "I'm in here trying to get some windows open."

Doc went from the living room to the dining room and saw Foster straining to push open the last window. The summer humidity had caused the wooden frames to swell. Immediately a breeze filtered through the house. The two of them went back to the living room where they sat on the couches that faced one another.

Foster opened his Pepsi and took a long drink. The cool wetness was much better than the warm Diet Coke he had been drinking. As he pulled the can away from his mouth he inquired about how Todd's girlfriend, or at least the girl he had been seeing, was doing. "How's Carli, Doc? Did you get to see her at all this summer?"

"She's fine," Doc said with a smile. It was evident that he really liked her. "We talked on the phone a lot -- neither of us is any good at letter writing." Doc paused to take a quick swig of his Pepsi and then continued to talk. "One weekend I came down and we went to a concert and then one day we met each other halfway between Green Bay and where she lives, which is just about thirty minutes outside of Chicago, and had a picnic." Todd broke into a really big smile. "You'll love this." Todd sat up as if it would help him say what he had to say more effectively. "I went to go see my grandparents in Florida in July -- hell of a time to be in Florida. Anyhow, on my way back I had a five-hour layover in Chicago." Doc quickly took another sip of Pepsi. "Carli said she would meet me at the airport, you know O'Hare." Foster nodded and he paid close attention. "So I thought I would be sweet and get her something while I was down in Florida." Doc started to chuckle as he continued, "So I bought her a pair of pierced earrings." He started to really laugh hard when he said, "But she doesn't have pierced ears."

Foster chuckled a little bit out of politeness, but didn't quite find it as funny as Doc did. However, Foster wanted to show his interest and so he acted curious. "What did she do?" Foster asked.

Doc, still laughing, replied, "She thought it was funny. She said that she would wear them like a stickpin." Doc pointed to the breast area of his polo shirt. "I just thought it was so classic that with all the time we've spent together that I still didn't notice that her ears weren't pierced."

Doc chuckled for a little longer. Soon his chuckle turned to a mere smile and then the smile faded altogether. He put his feet up on the coffee table that separated the two couches and appeared to daydream as he watched his toes wiggle. The living room became quiet. Foster's mind began to wander also.

Doc broke out of his trance abruptly. "What's happening between you and Marianne, Foster? I never really did catch the full story of what was happening between you two before we left last spring."

Doc caught Foster's eyes and could see that he had named the one person Foster was daydreaming about. "Well," Foster said and then paused. He was reluctant to answer. He had hoped that this topic would not come up at all this year. It still hurt too much. "Not much."

"I'm sorry," Doc said, as he could see the hurt on Foster's face.

"No, that's all right," Foster said as he tried to hide the pain. "It'll probably do me good to talk about it." He, too, sat up as if the prone position would make what he had to say less clear.

"Marianne and I got in a conversation about our future last year just about the time school was getting out. She knew that this year she would be going away to that college in Illinois and that I would be coming back here. Anyhow, to make a long story short, she was trying to get me to give up my last year here to finish school down in Illinois." He shifted his weight and took another drink of Pepsi, which was now becoming warm. Setting the can down, he began to elaborate.

"She says she couldn't understand why football was more important than being with her, or how it had any importance at all. Basically what it came down to was her or my last year here." Foster's analogy made some sense. "The decision was no contest; I liked Marianne a lot, but I love football." Foster made the joke to clear the seriousness that had developed. But the truth of the matter was that the decision wasn't all that easy. The decision he made, the one he felt he had to make, broke his heart.

Just as Foster finished, the South entryway door flew open and hulking Stubby came running into the room and yelled, "What the fuck are you guys doing in here?" He knew that Doc and Foster were there and so he snuck into the side door and was hoping to scare them into believing, for a moment, that they were in trouble. It worked a little bit. Both men jumped. They weren't scared about being in trouble, however -- just plain surprised. Doc then swung his head around quickly to see what the commotion was all about. However, both quickly surmised what Stubby was up to.

"Christ, nothing like scaring the living shit out of us," Foster said, as his heart rate returned to normal.

"Nothing like," Doc checked his watch, "being forty-five minutes late."

Stubby just chuckled. He knew he was late and he didn't have an excuse, but there was nothing he could do now. He walked behind the couch where Doc was sitting and dropped to his knees, crossed his arms and rested them on the back of the couch. He smiled. Addressing both of them, he said, "How's it going?"

"All right," Foster reflexively answered.

Doc, who still hadn't looked at Stubby, turned to return greetings when Stubby's balding head caught his attention. The expression on his face showed that he changed what he had to say. He reached up and rubbed his hand on the exposed skin on Stubby's head. "Good God...nice baldhead," Doc said rather loud.

Stubby quickly grabbed Doc by the face as if he were palming a basketball. "Nice face, Doc," Stubby said in a joking manner.

Doc grabbed Stubby's wrist with both hands and tried to pull the hand off his face. He couldn't move it. Slowly, Stubby, with his tongue slightly out of his mouth as if he were concentrating, powered Doc's face down into the arm of the couch. He held it there for a split second and then released it. Doc tried to make it look as if his strength pulled the hand away. When Doc finally put his head up it was a purple-red in color and one vein was prominent on his forehead. Along with the strained look were indentations where Stubby's fingers rested. Doc rubbed these while a pained look crossed his face.

Foster, confident that he was a safe distance away, joined in the fun. "Oh man, the reflection is blinding," he said as he put on Doc's sunglasses.

"Okay, nose," Stubby countered.

The football team was back. Constant teasing about peculiar or defective physical features was a favorite team activity. Stubby's was excessive hair loss, which had really come on strong over the past summer. Foster's was a slightly oversized nose, as he put it (he claimed that it was the reason he flunked gym class in grade school because he could never do a good push-up). Others got teased because they were overweight, too smart, or a little slow. For the most part all this teasing was taken in fun.

Before Doc's face could regain its normal color he was talking as if nothing had happened. "When is everyone getting back here?" Doc asked about the rest of the players on the team. "I know that Bert will be here about noon tomorrow, but what about everyone else?"

"How about Simba?" Foster interjected before Stubby could answer. "In a way I sort of miss that crude mouth of his."

Focusing on the most recent question, Stubby answered, "Simba just called last night. He is supposed to fly into O'Hare early tomorrow morning and then I've got to pick him up at the Holiday Inn."

Students who lived too far away to drive had to fly into O'Hare Airport in Chicago and then take a bus up to Beloit. The bus ride wasn't all that long or very expensive and the practice was well established so no one ever thought much of it.

"Where the hell did he go this summer anyway?" Doc asked.

"Seward, Alaska," Foster answered.

"What for?' Doc countered quickly.

"I guess his grandmother got him a job on a fishing boat up there," Foster speculated, and then turned to Stubby who affirmed the answer with a nod.

"Nice life," Doc said with a chuckle.

"It is," Stubby contradicted Doc's sarcasm. "He's making close to $18 an hour up there, paying nothing because he lives with his grandmother." Stubby laid out his rebuttal. "There isn't shit to do up there so he will have saved a whole bunch of money. He's going to be loaded when he comes back."

"Isn't that a fucking crime?" Foster said catching the others' attention. "God damn Simba has got financial aid up the wazoo – I don't think he pays $600 a semester – and he has all that money." Foster shook his head. "Every penny I make goes right here to old Beloit College."

One hour later, Foster and Doc hadn't unpacked anything but a couple of cans of Pepsi. Stubby was a little farther along, but he still had a long way to go. Although it was nice to be back talking about old times, they had to pull themselves from the comfortable couches back out into the heat to move their stuff into the house.

5

Stubby gave the entire set of house keys from the Residential Life office to Foster. Along with being co-captain of the football team, Foster was also president of the fraternity. He questioned whether he had taken on too much, but at this point he figured what was done, was done. He made his mind up that he was going to do the best that he could and not worry about it.

Stubby didn't need to get a key from Foster, but Doc did. He followed Foster to his room and went through all the necessary procedures for checking the key out. Rooms in the house were determined last Spring by a peculiar combination of chance and seniority. Starting with the oldest graduating, lots were drawn from a hat. The person with the lowest lot number got to have first pick of the rooms. The second lowest lot number had second pick and so forth until the entire class had selected rooms. Then the next oldest graduating class would draw lots and repeat the same process until all 26 rooms were taken.

The only exception to the room lottery involved the president of the fraternity. The hassles of being president were compensated for by not having to go through the lottery process. Instead, the president was given automatic first choice of all the rooms. Without exception, the president took one room down in the front part of the north wing. The special feature of this room was that it came with its own bathroom and two phones (one for outgoing calls and the other for on-campus calls). The phones usually turned out to be more trouble than they were worth, especially when the Dean called early on a Monday morning wanting to talk to the fraternity president. However, a private bathroom was always a plus. This luxury had passed to the Sigma Rho president ever since they decided that they no longer needed a house mother, the person who used to occupy the room. Rumors were that the first president to occupy the room had also made the suggestion that the house no longer needed a house mother.

Once Doc had his key, the trio began the long process of unloading their cars, the first and only project for the day. They wouldn't even be concerned with setting up the rooms the way they wanted them until they had a place to sleep. Priorities are priorities.

Doc and Foster unloaded their cars and lumped their belongings in one corner of their rooms. Only that which was absolutely necessary for the next 12 hours of living was set up or unpacked. What was in each of their cars only represented a small portion of what they had on campus. Most of their belongings were stored in the rooms they occupied the year before. For Foster, that meant coming downstairs. And for Doc, that meant going up.

It didn't take Stubby long to get all the belongings he had in the residence hall for the summer back to his new room -- he had drawn number two. Therefore, he had one of the more desirable rooms. Once he had his stuff lumped in some semblance of order, he began to re-assemble his waterbed.

Three-quarters of the Sig house had waterbeds. It was their trademark, and the tradition had been passed down for years. When someone graduated they would either sell the bed to someone else or the people would buy themselves a new bed. If you asked any of the guys with waterbeds why they had them, they would insist that it was because their bodies couldn't become accustomed to sleeping anywhere else. Both of these were reasons, but they weren't the deciding factor. It was simply the macho image that the waterbed carried with it: the mystique of someone who sleeps on a waterbed.

Stubby had his entire bed put together and filling with water in less than thirty minutes. He had taken apart and put together his bed numerous times. In fact, every time he went home for the summer or switched rooms or even just rearranged his room the waterbed had to be taken apart. In addition, he had also helped a lot of other guys in the house do the same. Like a Marine with an M-16, Stubby could probably take apart and put together a waterbed blindfolded. He was considered to be the expert in the house. Whenever someone had a problem with a waterbed, he was the one they turned to.

Shortly after Stubby had started filling his bed, he discovered that it was filling with cold water. He checked the sink where the hose was attached to see if the knob for the hot water was turned on all the way -- it was. The problem was that the hot water for the residence area of campus was still off for the summer. This was something that Stubby did not foresee when he asked to move in a day early.

A waterbed fills the same with hot or cold water. However, a waterbed has a heater that can only raise the temperature of the water at a rate of one degree per hour. So if the bed is filled with forty to fifty degree water, then it would take about two days until the waterbed would be at 90 degrees plus, a comfortable temperature. To sleep on a bed below 90 degrees would be unsafe because the cool water would drain the heat out of a person's body, like hypothermia, causing illness.

The lack of hot water irritated Stubby. He had worked hard most of the day to get all his stuff moved back over to the Sig house so he could set up his waterbed. He was desperate to get the bed set up so he could have a comfortable place to sleep for a change. Waterbeds weren't allowed in the residence halls so Stubby was forced to sleep on the standard college-issue super single. Bliss was going to have to wait. He had moved out of the room he had all summer earlier that day, so even the super single wasn't an option. Now Stubby would have to fight for one of the two couches.

Once Doc realized that he could only fill his bed with cold water, he was less anxious to put it together. He stopped arranging all the stuff in his room and grabbed another Pepsi. He decided to wait until warm, if not hot, water would be available. And it was worth not doing anything until his bed was set up.

Foster, on the other hand, decided to go ahead and fill his bed. At least then it would be done. He had plenty of other things to do. As soon as Stubby finished filling his bed, Foster borrowed the hose and the faucet attachment from him. Foster hooked up to the faucet in the bathroom in his room and turned both the cold and hot knobs on completely.

A water bed is filled with an ordinary garden hose, so the process doesn't take much more than a half hour. The garden hose attaches to the faucet and the bed by special attachments that usually come with the bed. Most people end up losing their attachments after the first time they fill the bed, so the guys in the house had to share the two or three sets of attachments that still existed.

Foster went out to the living room to sit with Doc while his bed filled. As the bed fills it doesn't require a whole lot of attention. Periodically, the mattress has to be shifted because of the way it lays in the frame. But once the water is turned on, it's just a matter of letting the bed fill.

When Foster's bed was filled, he carefully wound up the hose and placed it on the front porch so the water could drain. He walked through the front porch doors and took a seat in the chair between the couches.

Doc and Stubby were sprawled out on each couch. Stubby lay on his back with one leg resting on the floor and the other draped over the back of the couch. His eyes were closed, but he wasn't asleep. Doc lay on his stomach. His head was turned out towards Stubby with one side of his face pushing deep into the cushion. He stared down at the floor as he rolled the Pepsi can he had just emptied back and forth with his left hand. His right arm was tucked under his body.

Foster sat in the chair, tilted his head back and shut his eyes. It had been a long day starting with leaving from Houghton, Michigan, at 7 A.M. for the seven-and-a-half-hour trip to Beloit. The two hours spent getting the car unloaded and setting up the waterbed only added to the exhaustion. However, he knew that he had to find some reserve energy because, inevitably, they would be going out tonight.

"Where are we going to eat?" Doc asked as his eyes remained locked on the same point.

"I don't care," Stubby replied with a lethargic voice. He opened his eyes and rolled his head toward Doc and said, "Someplace quick and simple, though, because I'm starved."

"McDonald's it is then." Foster translated what Stubby meant by, 'I don't care.' "When are we going?"

"I want to shower first." Stubby avoided the question.

Foster thought about the cold water he had just put in his bed. "That ought to be fun -- cold showers. I think it might be better to smell." He pulled the neck of his shirt out and breathed deeply through his nose. Letting the shirt snap back, a cross look appeared on his face and he remarked, half under his breath, "Maybe not."

Stubby's face developed a perplexed look as he sat up quickly. The thought of a cold shower didn't interest him either. "Hey, we can shower in the fieldhouse; Coach Bonaventure let me have a key so I could lift weights on the weekends and in the evenings."

"Sounds good to me," Foster said. "I'd even settle for a lukewarm shower right now." Foster tried to bring some humor into the fold, but everyone was too tired to do more than smile.

Doc moved for the first time since Foster entered the room. He got up, put on his flip-flops and started around the couch toward the stairs. Foster and Stubby watched as he left without saying a word. Doc sensed that eyes were focused on him. When he got halfway to the stairs, he stopped and turned to face the two pairs of eyes.

"Hey Doc, I didn't mean that we have to go right now," Stubby said, speaking of going to shower at the fieldhouse. He sat up to hear Doc's response.

Doc paused for a moment to gather his thoughts. He turned his head away as if he weren't going to answer and then he turned back. "I've got to take a shit before we go if that's quite all right with you." Stubby smiled, knowing it was said in jest. Doc turned and walked up the stairs two at a time.

6

The water in the field house provided the trio with a nice, hot shower. Doc contemplated hooking up five or six hoses and then using the water to fill his bed. He let that idea pass when he realized that it would cost upwards of $125 to get all that hose. One night on the couch won't be that bad. Hell, he thought, if worse came to worst he could get a room at the Holiday Inn for that.

Stubby couldn't find the lights to the shower room, so except for the small amount of light that filtered in from the locker area, they had to shower in the dark. However, that didn't stop them from staying in the shower for half an hour. They justified the extended time by continually soaping back up or singing songs. Doc started to taunt Stubby about how he could no longer wash his hair like the good ole days. The taunting ended quickly when Stubby snapped Doc in the ass with a towel.

After they returned to the house they changed clothes and were ready to go get something to eat. The question again came up 'where do we go to eat?' By this time it was closing in on 8:00 and none of them had the patience to wait a whole lot longer. That meant fast food, as Foster had suggested earlier.

The selection of fast-food places in Beloit was about average -- basic McDonald's, Burger King, Taco Bell, and a few other local greasy spoons. Each choice provided about the same benefit and each choice was a repeat of their menus of the last two days. Needless to say, they weren't very excited about the prospects.

Finally, Stubby suggested that they go to the deli at the nearby grocery store. He had gotten to know the town well in the one summer he had spent in Beloit. The deli was a place that he and some members of his work crew frequented on their lunch break. For Stubby it was nice because the wide selection of home-cooked meals always ready made him feel more at home.

As it turned out, the decision was a good one. The guys could pick from just about anything that they wanted to eat. This wide selection posed a problem for Foster as he paced up and down the glass counter trying to decide what to get. The decision was easy for Stubby. He selected his usual 4-by-4 sandwich (four types of meat with four types of cheese) on an onion bun, a scoop of cole slaw, and an oatmeal cookie. Although there was a unique selection of meats and cheeses, Doc had the same. Foster's mouth began to water as he watched the woman prepare Doc's and Stubby's. He still hadn't decided on what he wanted so he told them to go on ahead. Doc and Stubby walked out of the grocery. They stopped at a pop machine to get a Diet Coke each and then they sat on a bench near the door.

Foster finally forced himself to make a decision. If he hadn't, he would have starved to death standing there. His order matched that of Stubby and Doc combined. He had always had a big appetite. He used to say that his brother got the brains in the family, his sister got the looks, and he got the appetite. He was a little embarrassed giving the woman the order, but she understood as she had sons of her own. Filling his order, she slipped a couple of extra cookies in the bag at no charge as she remarked how much Foster reminded her of her son who was in the Navy. Foster, flattered, paid the woman and thanked her politely as he turned to leave. Walking toward the door he put his wallet and all the change, except enough for a soda, in the bag.

After he got a Mountain Dew, a change from too many Diet Cokes for one day, he sat down on a wall adjacent to the bench where Stubby and Doc were sitting. He spread out the contents of his bag on the wall and arranged them according to the order he was going to eat them. He then took his wallet and the remaining change and put it in his pocket. As he turned to put the wallet away, Doc tapped Stubby on the shoulder to have him take note of everything that Foster had gotten. Stubby, chewing on his sandwich, indicated he had noticed. Foster opened his pop and took a long drink to wash down the saliva that had accumulated in his throat.

When Stubby and Doc were about halfway done with their meal, Foster had already downed one sandwich and torn through a double order of coleslaw. He took another drink of Mountain Dew to wash down the last swallow of sandwich. When he was certain that the large bite was going to make it down he paused before starting on the next sandwich and asked, "Where are we going next?"

Doc could no longer resist making a comment. He had only finished half his dinner and Foster was talking as if they were all done. "Christ, I swear you don't breathe when you eat," Doc said with a snicker. Stubby, who was in the midst of taking a long drink of Diet Coke, began to laugh. He quickly reached for napkins as soda came squirting out of his nose. Foster glanced at Doc, who was staring as if Foster were a caged animal, and then he looked over at Stubby, who was wiping his face, and then he examined the food he had remaining, a sandwich minus the bite he had just taken and was chewing. He shrugged his shoulders as if he didn't know what Doc had meant and then kept eating at the same rate. He forgot that he even asked a question.

Foster easily finished his meal minutes before the other two. He sat patiently and waited for them to finish, trying not to watch them eat because it would make him hungry again. When Stubby finished, he put his empty pop cans, napkins, Doc's bag, and the portion of food that they had not eaten in the bag the woman had given him. Stubby hadn't eaten a corner of bun which the meat and cheese had slipped away from. Doc left almost all of the cole slaw which he had vowed not to eat because it was too sweet. Leaving the bench, Stubby threw the bag like a basketball in a nearby garbage can. As they walked to the car, Doc yelled out, "GUN!" (short for shotgun) meaning he got to sit in the front by the window. Foster winked at Doc and countered by saying, "President," meaning he had the privilege of sitting in back.

When they got in the car, Stubby asked, in a fake Western drawl, "Whar to fellas?" He revved up the engine of his green Oldsmobile as he received an 'I don't care' and an 'I don't know' answer. Turning so he could at least see the outline of Foster in the back seat, Stubby posed another question: "Is it okay if we go to the Jungle?"

Doc turned to him as if he were crazy and asked, "What Jungle?"

Stubby turned his head to directly face Doc and looked at him as if what he had said was perfectly obvious. "The Jungle is a bar, dummy. Its full name is Jungle Safari."

"Okay baldy," Doc replied as he faced the windshield again. Stubby let this bald joke pass.

"Are there any women at this bar?" Foster's second hunger showed.

"Some," Stubby responded. "But they are all over 18," he qualified, making light of the fact that Foster's last girlfriend was still in high school.

Foster ignored the comment. He didn't want to think about it. "I bet the women are really animals at this bar. I'm game." Both Doc and Stubby moaned at Foster's pun as they drove off.

About half the businesses in Beloit were bars. It seemed as if you couldn't drive a block without seeing at least two or three. There were a couple of reasons for this. First, Beloit was close to the Beer Capitol of the World – Milwaukee. Second, the area was mainly comprised of heavy industry, whose workers are notorious for spending their spare time in their favorite tavern talking about the glory days. Finally, Beloit is in Wisconsin, where the drinking age is 18, but it borders on Illinois, where the drinking age is 21. At night, the population of this Midwestern city seemed to almost double as 18, 19, and 20 year olds came in force from a 50-mile radius in Illinois. The Beloit bars thrived on this business. So did the Illinois Highway Patrol which easily filled its quota of drunken drivers every night.

As Foster and Stubby got out of the car in the parking lot adjacent to the Jungle Safari, Doc wondered why he had never noticed this place before. On the wall outside the bar was a huge mural of a monkey swinging from a tree with a mug of beer in its hand. Once inside it was just another bar. It was barely wide enough to play a game of darts and some of the shots on the pool table were impossible due to limited space. Foster and Doc grabbed one of the two booths while Stubby went to get the first pitcher. They looked around and noticed that they were the only people, besides the bartender, in the bar.

As Stubby sat down and began filling glasses, Foster looked around and said sarcastically, "Boy, Stubby, you must have had a kick-ass summer -- this place is really rocking."

Knowing what Foster meant, Stubby tried to save face. "Yeah, I wonder where everyone is. This place is usually packed." He looked around, too. "I guess it's still early," he said, pouring the second beer.

"Bullshit," Doc jumped in. "Why don't you just admit you didn't have any friends this summer." Doc tried to look serious.

"Fuck you, dick," Stubby replied. "You can pour your own beer." Stubby pushed the partially empty pitcher and the remaining empty glass across the table to Doc. Doc smiled as he poured the beer.

When Doc was finished pouring his beer, he raised his glass. "A toast to our last year -- may it be a good one." The head from the beer slid down the side of the glass and on to the table as Stubby and Foster raised theirs, too.

Doc and Stubby immediately downed about half their beers, licking the foam off their upper lips. The beer, combined with the atmosphere of Beloit and the empty bar, sort of made them feel at home. Foster slowly nurtured the first few sips. He wasn't much of a drinker and really didn't like the taste of beer. He didn't drink all through high school and hardly drank now. However, this beer tonight was justified, just like a kid gets wine on Christmas -- Foster felt this was a special occasion and he considered these two family. But he still was careful in his drinking so he could keep his wits about himself.

Before they got too far along in their beers, Stubby suggested that they go out back on the patio, which was known as the 'beer garden.' He had done well with his suggestions so far. There was no reason to second guess him now. Stubby grabbed the pitcher and each man grabbed his glass and they walked towards the back of the bar, past the pool table, and out the back door.

The beer garden was simply a slab of concrete about the same size as the bar enclosed by an eight-foot cedar wood fence. Lined up and down were picnic tables. They chose one in the middle about three back. As they sat down, three women also walked into the beer garden. They looked around and then waved at Stubby addressing him as 'Mark' and then they went back into the bar.

Doc lightly elbowed Stubby and said, "You stud." Stubby explained that they were from Rockford, Illinois, and that he had met them at the very beginning of the summer. A few minutes passed and the women emerged again with their own pitcher of beer. They sat on another picnic table just far enough away so the parties couldn't hear each other's conversations.

Foster, Doc, and Stubby picked up their conversation where it left off in the living room earlier that day. They laughed about events of the past and wondered about their futures in school, football, and their careers. The tone of the conversation went from serious to joking around and back with no particular pattern. At one time or another, Foster made eye contact with each of the women. He thought to himself, 'I knew I should have taken a cold shower.'

Of the three, Foster was the only one who had a reason to be interested. Doc was confident of his relationship with Carli, and while Stubby's relationship with Sue was questionable at this point, he was very optimistic. Foster, on the other hand, knew that his relationship with Marianne was over. He had taken his lumps and now he had to start over. This was as good a time as any as the new school year was approaching.

About the time that the guys were finishing their second pitcher and were deciding whether or not to get a third, the women finished their beers and came over. Foster was a little embarrassed at first because he had been caught by each of them looking her way. However, they made no issue of it. They introduced themselves to Doc and Foster. Their names were Lori, Sue, and Andy (short for Andrea). After they got acquainted for a couple minutes, the women invited the group to go to a party on the east side of Rockford. Inside, Foster was screaming, 'yes,' but he politely accepted like the others. The women explained that they were going to go to the bathroom and then they would be leaving. Stubby, still unfamiliar with Rockford, asked if they would wait so he could follow their car.

As the women went inside, the guys quickly tied up any loose ends of their conversations. Foster tried to give Doc and Stubby a dollar each because he wasn't going to be able to buy a pitcher. They flatly refused, reasoning that Foster's beer and a half didn't warrant his having to buy a pitcher. Foster felt cheap as he put the money back in his wallet.

The drive to the party was long and complex. Foster and Doc were confused after the first three turns once they got off the main highway. Stubby followed the lead of the women closely, running stop lights just to keep up. After twenty-five minutes, they were at a house about the size of a garage. They parked the car in the nearest space about a half a block away and walked.

As they approached the party, people stopped what they were doing to see who was coming. Everyone greeted Sue, Andy, and Lori warmly. One guy happened to know Stubby and came over to talk. After five minutes of feeling totally alien, Doc and Foster were introduced to the guy tapping the keg. He quickly took them under his wing and made sure that they had a beer. Foster took one just to hold on to. As time went on, everyone got introduced to Foster and Doc, but eventually they ended up in the back yard talking to the original three women they met at the Jungle Safari. Stubby entered into a game of darts against the garage door with the guy he knew.

Doc had a few beers by now and was starting to get wild. He talked with funny accents and cut down whatever anybody had to say in a humorous manner. Foster wasn't affected at all by the beer he had, but he, too, was getting wild. He seemed to get a buzz by just having people around to laugh at him, especially women. Doc and Foster tried to out-crazy one another. Their antics included wrestling with each other, carrying Andy over their shoulders, and drinking a large dish of water that had been left out for the dog.

The backyard craziness was broken up when a white and maroon Plymouth hatchback pulled up in a parking space directly in front of the house. Lori said, "That's Jandi," and Andy and Sue followed her out to the car. Doc and Foster had no one to show off to anymore and so they went to the street, too.

Out of the passenger side of the car popped a small guy who ran toward the beer and then disappeared in the party. Lori helped a strawberry blond haired girl out of the driver's seat. As she got out of the car, she swatted away Lori's hand as if she didn't need help. She then took two staggering steps forward and announced as she leaned against the car, "I know, I know...I'm drunk." Her slurred speech confirmed the fact: she was drunk.

Doc and Foster came around the car and were introduced. Lori introduced Doc as Todd. Jandi had no problem with that name. Then she tried to introduce Foster. Jandi had trouble pronouncing it. When Lori introduced Jandi, Foster continued the fun he was having in the back yard by mimicking Jandi. "Pleased to meet you, Sandy," he said, trying to be serious.

Jandi tried to correct him by enunciating more, but instead she just spoke louder. "It's JANDI."

"Oh, I'm sorry Mand..," Foster could not even finish.

"No, it's JANDI," she said even louder, "With a 'J'."

Foster felt he better not cause any more trouble. "It's Jandi, oh okay."

Reinforcing him, she said, "That's right."

Foster couldn't quite pin down exactly what it was that made Jandi so pretty. Her white cotton jumpsuit fit her very well. She had thick, strawberry blond hair that was curly and hung just below her shoulders. Her butt was tight and cute, and her breasts were round and well defined.

But it was her facial features that made Foster's heart skip a beat. For the first time he forgot about the heartache that Marianne had caused him.

Everyone standing around the car was anxious to get another beer. Seconds later, Foster found himself standing all alone with Jandi. She still leaned against the car and stared off into nowhere with her glossy blue eyes. Her body wavered slightly.

Foster wasn't sure what to say. He knew in his mind that he had to get started again, but his broken heart was reluctant. He felt uncomfortable being alone with her. He had no idea what to talk about. "Can I get you a beer?" That was a natural thing to ask. She shook her head 'no.' The motion of her head made her lose her balance and she stumbled away from the car. Foster caught her and leaned her back against the car. She was silent. "Are you sure I can't get you something to drink -- you look like you're thirsty." Foster teased.

"No," she slurred.

"Are you sure? There is plenty of beer and it would be no problem for me." He continued, this time motioning as if he were going to walk over to the keg.

"No," Jandi shouted as she lunged forward and grabbed Foster by the arm. Her eyes were still focused at a point off in the distance. Suddenly she pulled her head around and said, "Can't you see I'm drunk?" Foster laughed. She leaned against the car again and began staring off into nowhere.

Foster was starting to loosen up around her. For some reason he did not feel threatened by her anymore. He started to see how much he could get away with -- test the water so to speak. He had seen his fraternity brothers do it before and always wanted to try it. "So Jandi, where did you get that jumpsuit? That's really nice." He ran his finger along the collar down across her breast. She didn't react. "Hey, is anybody there?" Foster whispered in her ear.

Jandi's head slowly turned and she looked Foster straight in the eye. Giving him a cold stare, she said, "You really think you're something, don't you?" trying to put him in his place.

This comment caught Foster off guard. He had been asked this question a hundred times before. It was the ultimate in rhetorical questions, and his answer in the past was always a defensive 'no.' Not this time, though. He was going to answer her bold question with a bold answer. He let the surprised look leave his face and a confident one took its place. With that same confidence in his voice he said, "Yeah, I do." He shook his head up and down.

Her face was blank for about ten seconds. Then the answer registered. He was waiting to get slapped or at the least for her to walk away, but she was too drunk to do either. She lightly laughed, shook her head and smiled.

Foster thought that one bold move deserved another since his confidence was now at an all time high. The next time their eyes met he leaned down to her and attempted to kiss her. She was reluctant for about a split second, then her instincts told her not to resist. She moved her face forward to meet his. It was a light kiss. He rested his hand on top of the car behind her. She still leaned on the car and put one hand on his shoulder.

When their lips lost contact she looked him in the eye and said she had to go to the bathroom. Of course it was not a romantic comment like Foster would have liked to hear, but he understood. He offered to walk her there, but she declined and insisted that he stay there. As she started to stagger toward the house, Foster made her promise that she would return. Foster leaned back against the car and crossed his arms. He patted himself on the back and wished that someone could have been there to witness his boldness. No one will ever believe it, he thought.

Almost ten minutes had passed and Foster was still waiting alone by the car. Doc came within earshot once to ask where Jandi was. Foster said, "In the bathroom," but at that point was beginning to feel as if he got stood up. Doc gave the thumbs-up sign and walked away. Time for bold move number three, Foster thought. He'd go looking for her. If he was going to get 'shit on' she was going to have to do it to his face, he thought.

He saw Andy by the keg and asked her where the bathroom was. She pointed him in the right direction. He walked in the house fully expecting to see Jandi in the arms of some other guy. There was no one in the house. He walked up to the door which Andy had said was the bathroom. Just as he was about to knock, it opened. Jandi started to step out. She saw Foster and darted back in, locking the door. Another rejection -- just like Marianne. So much for bold moves.

Just as he was about to turn and walk away, Lori walked in with an armload of towels. "What's the matter?" Foster inquired. Lori leaned close to Foster and explained very quietly that Jandi had gotten sick from being drunk. Foster felt bad because she probably was embarrassed that he saw her. He stepped aside and Lori proceeded to knock on the bathroom door. Reassured that Lori was alone, Jandi let her in. Foster sat on the couch on the other side of the room.

Another five minutes and the bathroom door opened. Lori emerged, carefully carrying a load of dirty towels. As Lori left the room, Jandi stood at the door and looked across the room at Foster. Her hair was wet along the edges. Before Foster could say anything she said, "Shut up." It was evident that she was embarrassed.

Foster tried to reassure her that it was all right. "It's no big deal, Jandi. It happens to all of us." He patted the couch in a manner that would invite her to come sit next to him.

"SHUT UP," she said louder as she walked across the room and sat down.

Once Jandi was on the couch Foster began looking at her. Kissing her was no longer of interest, but he was still intrigued by how good looking she was. She sensed that she was being observed and turned to face Foster. She felt uncomfortable with him watching. "Stop looking at me." She pushed his face away.

Foster didn't fight it, but just turned back and asked, "Why?"

"Just because." She pushed his face away again. "Get out of here."

Foster felt rejected again. "If you really want me to go, I'll go." He moved to the edge of the couch and started to stand.

As Foster got just about three-quarters of the way out of a squatted position, Jandi lunged forward and grabbed him by the arm. She seemed to have sobered up some. "No, you can stay," she said, pulling him back down on the couch. Caught totally off guard, he fell back to the couch like a rag doll. Instinctively he put his arm around her and let her bury her head in his chest. Slowly Foster felt her body relax as she fell asleep. Foster tilted his head back on the couch and started to let himself relax, too.

About a half an hour later, Doc found Foster on the couch asleep arm-in-arm with Jandi. He gently woke him and asked him if he wanted to go home. At first, Foster didn't know where he was, but then, slowly, he regained his bearings. He figured he better go because he really had no other way home. The party was quieting down and he really didn't want to spend the night in this strange little house even though he would be keeping good company.

Doc left to go find Stubby while Foster gently lay Jandi down on the couch. He watched her for a long minute, marveling at her looks. He wondered if he would ever see her again. He was unsure. He wanted to have her phone number, but he didn't want to wake her and ask for it. And he didn't think it would be proper to ask Lori for it. The only solution was for Foster to leave her his phone number.

He walked into the kitchen and searched for a piece of paper to write on. Failing to find a normal sheet of paper, Foster ripped off a dollar-bill sized piece of paper and scribbled on it in pencil:

Foster Addison
Box 381 Beloit College, Beloit WI 53511
608/ 555-0748
If you want you can give me a call!!!!

Foster went back to Jandi on the couch and slipped the note in her right-front pocket. Grabbing a blanket, he covered her up and tucked her in. He looked at her again until he heard Doc calling him from outside. He knew he had to go. He leaned over and whispered in her ear, "Please check your pocket." Foster then kissed her as gently as possible on the cheek before he left.

Lori borrowed Sue's car and led Stubby back to where he could find his way. Before driving away, Stubby pulled up alongside of Lori. Doc, who was riding shotgun again, rolled down the window so Stubby could thank her. As Doc began rolling up the window, Foster, who sat in the middle up front because he refused to sit in back on the way home, yelled to Lori to have Jandi check her pockets. Lori heard the message, but looked back as if the message didn't make any sense. Stubby pulled away. The radio was the only sound in the car as they drove home.

As they approached the Beloit College campus, Doc brought up the issue of which two would get the couches and which one would get the floor. "The way I see it, Stubby," Doc said with his drunken voice, "the football captains should get the couches." Doc nudged Foster with his elbow.

"Nahhh...Sorry, Doc." Stubby wasn't about to follow that logic. "I think it should be survival of the fittest." He flexed the muscles in his left forearm and nudged Foster with his right elbow. He took his eyes off the road long enough to get Doc's reaction. Doc's eyes widened at Stubby's suggestion. As much as the logic seemed barbaric, Doc realized that Stubby's rule would prevail unless another alternative could be suggested that was fair. Doc was quiet as he looked out the side window and thought.

Foster sat quietly. He was still thinking about Jandi and whether or not she would find the note he had slipped in her pocket. Besides, at this point he had a couch using either Doc's or Stubby's logic.

"How about this," Doc said as he quickly changed his focus from out the window back to Stubby. "Let's flip for it." Doc straightened his body and became rigid long enough to pull a quarter out of his pocket. "Odd man gets the floor." He flashed the coin at Stubby.

Stubby was caught off guard because he thought the issue was settled. He looked out of the corner of his eye. There was a pause as Stubby thought over the proposition to make sure he wasn't being had. He seemed reluctant, but finally agreed, nodding his head, "Okay."

When Stubby stopped at the next light, he also produced a quarter. The street lights were bright enough that he didn't have to turn on the dome light. As Stubby and Doc were about to flip, they both turned to Foster who was between them.

"You're in this, too," Doc said.

"Ya, you're not official President until school starts," Stubby added.

Foster was off in another world. It had been a long day and he wasn't used to these late evenings. All of the energies he had left were focused on Jandi. He went over the events of the evening, analyzed her every word and reaction, and imagined a potential relationship with her. As he refocused his energies, he was aware enough of what was going on to realize, "I don't have any change."

"You're not getting out of this that easy," Doc said. He again reached into his pocket and produced another quarter. Handing it over to Foster he said, "Okay...on the count of three."

Each man loaded the coins on their thumbs. Doc looked at Foster and Stubby to see if they were ready. Then he looked back to check his quarter again. Rhythmically he began to count: "One,...two,...three." The three coins each went up about a foot. The flip was limited by the car ceiling. As the coins came back down they were caught in one hand and then flipped over on to the back of the other hand.

Each man kept his coin covered waiting for someone else to reveal his first -- as if the outcome would be changed. Foster finally revealed his coin first -- a head. Stubby quickly followed -- another head. Doc's heart rate increased slightly. A tail would mean he would have the floor. He held his hand in a beam of light that came through the windshield. Slowly he pulled his hand away -- a head. There was no odd man.

"Now what?" Foster asked, still half in a daze.

"Flip again," Doc answered.

"Not now," Stubby insisted.

"Why not?" Doc called back.

"Because the light is about to turn green." Stubby pointed up at the light controlling the lane that was perpendicular to them. It had just changed from green to yellow.

"Come on, let's do it quickly." Doc spoke fast, trying to coax the other two: "One, two, three." Stubby and Foster caught up to Doc on about count two and were just able to get their coins in the air at the last second.

Doc quickly revealed another head. Foster followed shortly thereafter with a tail. Stubby made the swing decision as he revealed a head. As soon as Stubby revealed the head, the light changed colors. He dropped the quarter on the floor and punched the accelerator. The car headed down the street.

"Well, Foster, it looks like you're on the floor tonight. Tough break." Doc snickered.

Foster wasn't particularly happy. He went from a shoo-in on the couch to having to sleep on the floor. "Great," he said unenthusiastically. "Here's your quarter." He held the coin out to Doc.

"No, you can keep it." Doc pushed his hand back. "See, you didn't lose totally." Foster slipped the quarter into his pocket and resumed his trance.

When they got back to the Sig house, Doc and Stubby raced upstairs to grab pillows and blankets. The 'strong survived' as Stubby powered his way onto the better of the two couches. When Foster got to his room he took a look at his waterbed. It was warmer now, but still not warm enough. He was tired, but the floor wasn't an enticing thought. It was time to be innovative.

Foster quickly put a set of sheets on the waterbed. Then on top of this he put a blanket and a comforter. He laid his hand on top of the comforter. He could still feel the cool bed. Quickly he looked around. A down sleeping bag caught his eye. He unzipped the sleeping bag all the way and spread it over the entire bed. He felt the bed again. Perfect.

Out in the living room, Stubby and Doc were all settled on their couches. A couple of minutes passed and they began to wonder why Foster hadn't come back out. "Do you think he's mad?" Stubby asked.

"I don't know," Doc replied. "That's not like him." Their curiosity got the best of them. They decided to see where Foster was.

Foster left his door unlocked, so Stubby and Doc walked in slowly. "Foster? Where are you?" Doc called out almost in a whisper. He strained to see in the dark room. The room was quiet. All he could hear was the water from the back of the toilet. "You aren't mad, are you?" Doc called out again. Stubby was close behind.

Answering the questions in reverse, Foster replied, "No. I'm right here." He had almost been asleep. He wasn't exactly sure where he was. Doc moved toward where he thought the voice was coming from.

Stubby, who was a little way behind Doc, found the light switch and clicked it on. The light stung all their eyes, but once they were able to adjust they saw Foster sprawled out on the heavily insulated waterbed. "You son-of-a-bitch," Stubby said under his breath. "You rigged your bed and you weren't even going to let us know." Stubby inched towards the bed. "We're on those couches getting backaches and you're in here all cozy on the bed. Nice brotherhood." Stubby referred to their fraternal bonds, as they all did, when convenient.

Foster was at a loss for words. The first thing that came to his mind was a favorite saying of a guy he worked with in the summer: "Hey, when the mind is weak, the body suffers." Foster sat up to prepare himself for their reaction. Doc left the room like a flash. You could hear his bare feet slap the tile floor. Stubby stopped approaching the bed and looked at Foster puzzled. Then the slapping feet were on their way back.

Doc came through the door with his arms loaded down with both his and Stubby's blankets and pillows. Looking at Foster he said, "You mean when your mind isn't weak, our bodies won't suffer." He jumped on the bed. The wave he created almost knocked Foster off the other side. Foster moved over to make room for Stubby who was turning out the light. He was too tired to fight it. The waves created by Stubby helped to rock them to sleep.

After five minutes, both Doc and Stubby were fast asleep. Their breathing lacked any synchronization. Foster wasn't far behind as his body began to float. Just as he was about to go under, the phone rang. It was the outside line. He could tell by the ring. "Hello," Foster said with a groggy voice. Stubby and Doc even became restless.

The female voice on the other end was faint as if it were long distance. "Foster Addison please," the voice struggled to get out.

Foster couldn't place the voice. "Speaking. Who is this?"

"JANDI," the voice called out over the phone as if Foster should have known. "Where did you go?"

"I came home," Foster spoke as if the answer was obvious.

"How did I get home?" Jandi said.

Foster laughed. She was even more out of it than he was. "I don't know. When I left, you were still asleep on the couch. Maybe Lori took you home."

"Oh," Jandi responded. "Were you asleep?"

"Close," Foster responded.

"I'm sorry," she said in a sweet voice. "I just wanted to let you know that I got your note."

"Good," Foster continued his one-syllable answers. The conversation was fading as neither had the energy to continue. "Hey listen, I'm falling asleep," his voice started to fade. "I'll talk to you later, okay?"

"Okay," she answered. "Good night."

"Night," Foster said just before he hung up. After he put the receiver down he realized that he forgot to get her number. That disturbed him, but only for a second as he fell asleep, knowing that she had found his number, and wasn't afraid to call.

7

Foster woke naturally at about 7:30 a.m. His body-clock, which was still on Michigan's Eastern time instead of Wisconsin's Central time, thought it was 8:30 a.m. Either way, Foster considered it sleeping in. He had gotten used to getting up early during the summer when he had to get up at 5:30 a.m. just so he could get to work on his bicycle by 7:00 a.m.

Despite the longest sleep of his entire summer, Foster was still tired. He tried to get back to sleep, but gave up after fifteen minutes of lying there with his eyes closed. He was in that range when the body is too rested to fall asleep, but too tired to get up. Had it been nighttime, some would have considered this to be insomnia, but it was the morning and Foster considered it to be unfair. He glanced over at Doc and Stubby, sound asleep. Foster realized that he had a lot to do, so he didn't want to stay in bed.

Gently, he rolled over to the edge of the waterbed. He tried to disturb the water as little as possible, but as hard as he tried a small wave rippled back and forth across the bladder of the waterbed. Doc became restless as his body moved up and down with the passing wave. The wave, however, quickly dissipated and Doc's breathing returned to a normal rhythm.

Foster walked over to the corner where he had laid everything the day before and grabbed a red gym bag with his workout gear. It was almost ritual for Foster to start the day with some type of exercise. All summer he rode four-and-a-half miles to work on his bicycle. Today he was going running.

As he turned to tip-toe out of the room, he noticed that Stubby had wound up sleeping on the floor anyway. Stubby, who was sleeping in between Doc and Foster, got tired of being elbowed by the other two and so he took a pillow and his blanket and lay down on the floor. At the time he had gotten up he didn't have the energy to make it to the couches in the living room. Foster tried to tip-toe by unnoticed, but the floor creaked right by Stubby's head. Stubby sat up quickly and looked at Foster. He then looked all around the room as if he didn't know where he was. Realizing where he was, he put his head back down and went immediately back to sleep. Chances are he wouldn't even remember this incident.

Foster went into the dining room, which was just off of the living room, and took a seat on one of the metal folding chairs. Yawning, he unzipped the bag. The smell of his sweat filtered up to his nose. To him, that was the smell of accomplishment, although others probably wouldn't have agreed. Foster reached into the bag and pulled out a pair of socks and a pair of yellow running shorts. He stood up quickly, taking off the underwear he had on and then put on the yellow running shorts. He sat back down and put the underwear in the gym bag. Carefully he put on his socks so the toes and heels sat just in the right place. If they weren't he would end up with blisters. He reached in the gym bag again and this time produced a pair of gray Nike running shoes. They were already untied so he slipped them on his feet. As he tied the first one, he yawned. His eyes clouded over, but he made the bows without being able to see. When he re-opened his eyes to tie the next shoe, they were watering. As he tied the other shoe, all he could see was a gray blur. He rubbed his eyes to clear them and reached into the gym bag one more time and this time produced a navy-blue tank top. Whenever possible, he tried to wear the maize and blue of Beloit when he worked out. He flung the shirt over his shoulder, got up and went to the front porch doors.

Foster opened the doors as far as they would go and walked out onto the porch. He took a deep breath and could tell that it was going to be another hot day. It was a good thing he was getting his running out of the way early, he thought. He leaned against one of the big white pillars on the porch and stretched his calves. He stood back and walked between the two middle pillars and spread his legs about three to four feet apart. He watched a car drive by on College Street and then leaned straight backwards to stretch his stomach muscles. He held this position for about ten seconds and then bent over forward, trying to touch his elbows to the ground. He then rotated to each side, trying to loosen up his hamstrings. As he tried to touch his nose to each knee, he double knotted each shoe just to make sure that the laces wouldn't come loose while he was running.

Slipping on his shirt, he slowly jogged across the front yard to the sidewalk that ran along College Street. He took a couple of deep breaths to try and get his body going. Yesterday's long day was going to take its toll today. He shook his arms at his side to loosen the joints. As he crossed Emerson Street, he began to pick up the pace. He cleared the dozen or so stairs leading to the Morse-Ingersol Building in two strides.

At the top of the stairs, pain shot through his right ankle, causing him to favor his left leg. All his joints hurt, he started to breathe heavily, and he could feel his heart pound against his chest. Foster's body was telling him to quit this silly morning ritual. However, experience told him that as soon as his body got warmed up that these feelings would go away and, as the sports physiologist put it, he would reach his steady-state, the point where oxygen consumption equals oxygen intake.

As Foster ran across the campus, he tried to take the sidewalk blocks one at a time, setting his foot in about the same place each time. This stride established a smooth pattern in his breathing, an even flowing stride, and a rhythm for his entire body. As he stared ahead he concentrated on a point in the distance. This wasn't a jog, it was a workout. And to Foster, working out was more than just a process of toning the body. It was also readying the mind. After all, football, his coach said, is only ten percent physical and the rest mental.

This was by no means his first workout of the summer. The day he got home in May, training began. Sacrifice was the word that described his whole summer. In the morning he would bike to work. At lunch he would run about a mile each day. After work he would lift weights and jump rope for about two hours. Then he would go on another run, this time about three to four miles. Once he was done with all this he would rode his bike the four and one-half miles back home.

Foster began to pick up the pace again. It was time to test himself, to take his body to the limit and whenever the urge to quit was overwhelming, Foster would push himself a little harder. He had to do this because he was sure, or at least he had himself convinced, that someone else out there was doing the same. And to be the best, he had to do more than that other person was doing. But what this fictitious other person did had no limits, no bounds and so that's what Foster had to achieve, too. This was all part of the psyche.

Stubby slept for about a half an hour after Foster had gone running.

He was used to getting up early too. His summer job on campus required him to be at work at 7:00 a.m. In addition, Stubby's father would never let his boys sleep in. No matter how late they were out on the weekends, he would get them out of bed at the crack of dawn to start on the many projects he had going around the house. As much as Stubby hated it, he thanked his father for developing that attribute in him.

Stubby checked the water in the bathroom in Foster's room. He turned the hot water knob on full and let it run. After two minutes of rusty water, clear, steamy hot water began to pour out. The hot water was again on. No more fieldhouse. Stubby walked out into the main part of Foster's room and yelled to Doc, "We got hot water."

Doc put his head up long enough to say, "Great," in a voice indicating that he would have preferred not being wakened until the matter was more pressing. Doc rolled over and put a pillow over his head. He fell back asleep and began snoring. Stubby went up to the bathroom by his room and took a long shower to wake up.

Stubby's morning ritual was less rigorous than Foster's. His usually consisted of going to the bathroom, cleaning his contacts, and then taking a shower -- not necessarily in that order. During the school year he would usually make himself a large breakfast, like his mother always had for him, and then study an hour or so until his first class.

Since the school year hadn't started yet, there was no food in the house. Stubby, however, had some food left from his summer cooking. Two hardboiled eggs, a can of V-8 vegetable drink, and strawberry jam on two pieces of stale bread wasn't anything like his mother's home cooking, but at least it would curb his hunger until he had a chance to get something to eat. As he finished his jam sandwich, Foster came through the front porch doors.

Foster had run close to six miles. He hadn't planned to run that far, but once he got going he actually felt pretty good and decided to continue. As he explained exactly where he had gone, Stubby almost started sweating thinking about it. As hard as Stubby had worked out this summer, he wasn't ready to match his legs with Foster's running.

Foster was soaked with sweat. He took off his shirt and squeezed it until it dripped sweat. He then used the shirt to mop up the sweat that was running down his face. Once Stubby explained that there was hot water, Foster was off to his room to shower. He had been planning to just let it dry on his body, thinking that he would either have to go back to the fieldhouse or else suffer a cold shower in the house. He grabbed his gym bag that he left on the couch and went into his room. Trying to be quiet, he grabbed the clothes he planned to wear that day, a towel, and some shampoo and went in the bathroom. With the door shut, the sound of the shower running was no louder than cars driving by outside, so Doc didn't even become restless.

As Foster showered, Stubby sat quietly enjoying the cool breeze which was passing through the living room. He slowly sipped the remainder of his V-8 and thought about the end of the summer. Not only that, but it was the end of his carefree summers forever. Next year he would, in all likelihood, be working somewhere as the first step in his career, whatever that might be. Where had all the time gone, he thought. It seemed just like yesterday when he was spending his first few days on campus. He could still remember how scared he was then, and how excited he was to be able to start against Coe College his freshman year, and how his whole mood changed to disappointment when he broke his ankle that same game. He seemed so young then. Coming to Beloit had been the right decision for him. It was kind of funny how getting hurt his senior year in high school and therefore not being scouted by large schools made things work out. A sort of irony. Where was it all leading, he wondered. He constructed a dozen scenarios in his mind.

Despite having hot water, Foster took a five-minute lukewarm shower to try and cool himself off. However, when he finished showering, he began to sweat again. He put on shorts and a pair of flip-flops. In one hand he held the shirt he intended to wear and in the other a damp towel to wipe off the sweat that continued to accumulate on his body.

When Foster came out to the living room, he caught Stubby smiling and staring at a blank wall. Sneaking up on him, he blew in his ear. "Hey loverboy, who are you daydreaming about? Me?" Foster winked to emphasize the parody.

The question was just one of those that don't get answered because the answer is obvious. However, it served to bring Stubby out of his daydreaming trance. "Want to go check our mail?" Stubby asked as he stood up. Waiting for an answer, he quickly downed his V-8 and threw the can in the empty fireplace down at the other end of the couches.

"Sure, I'll go. I don't think I'll have any mail, but I'll go for a walk." Foster answered. Stubby started to move toward the porch doors. "Hang on," Foster yelled. He took the damp towel, ran it over his torso one more time and then put it over the back of the couch. As he moved to catch up with Stubby, he pulled on a white tank top.

At Beloit College mail comes to one central mailroom where it is distributed to mailboxes. Students are issued a mailbox with a combination their freshman year and they keep that same box for the entire time they are at Beloit. The Mailroom, as it is known, is about four-hundred yards across campus and generally serves as the social gathering place after class.

As they approached the stairs at the Morse-Ingersol Building where Foster had run, Foster ran ahead of Stubby and again took all the stairs in two strides. The energy from his run was still charging through his veins. He stood at the top of the stairs and waited for Stubby, who took each stair individually. When Stubby got to the top, he looked Foster in the eye, asking: "What do you think this is, a race?" Foster smiled.

When they cleared Morse-Ingersol, one of their economics professors was approaching from the vicinity of the Mailroom. It was Professor Jeff Ames, an associate professor who taught their Econometrics course the previous spring. They both did relatively well in his class, but he made them work for the results. The class had only about ten students in it so Professor Ames got to know everyone well. Stubby and Foster had worked together on a tough project dealing with time series analysis of housing starts in the United States over a fifty-year period. Because of the project's difficulty and their desire to get a good grade out of the course, Stubby and Foster met with Professor Ames frequently. He was a young professor and they both got along with him very well, mainly because Professor Ames was so personable. Ames was intrigued by the two of them because they were, in his opinion, the classical definition of scholar-athletes.

"Hi, Professor Ames." Stubby was short with his greetings because he had seen Professor Ames around all summer.

"Hi, Mark." Professor Ames nodded.

"How are you doing? Did you have a good summer?" Foster asked.

"I had a good summer; I stayed awfully busy." Professor Ames concentrated on the second question. "Although I'm not sure that the two of those can go hand in hand," he qualified his answer. "How was your summer?"

"I can't say I'm ready for school yet, so I guess that means it was good." Everyone chuckled. Foster always tried to get a laugh out of his answers.

"Foster, I understand that President Hardesty is trying to persuade you to apply for a Rhodes Scholarship." Foster nodded yes. This was the first Stubby had heard of this. Professor Ames continued, "If you're interested, stop off at my office." Ames pointed to the old North College building. "I think if we got you working on an extensive project, similar to the one you two did last year, it would look very impressive on your application." Ames looked for a response. "When do you have to decide whether you are going to apply?"

"By October 1st, I have to write a 1000-word essay on basically where I've been, where I am, and where I want to be." Foster talked as if it would be a long, drawn-out process.

"Well, I'm just throwing an idea out for a suggestion. Stop up if you are interested." Professor Ames didn't want to seem hard-sell, although he believed the Rhodes to be a fantastic opportunity.

"Okay, thanks," Foster said as he continued to walk toward the Mailroom. Professor Ames went on his way, too.

"Rhodes Scholar, huh? Tell me how this came up," Stubby inquired as he walked along beside Foster.

"Can we keep this under wraps?" Foster didn't want to reveal anything until he was sure that no one else would find out. He was a little disturbed that Stubby caught wind of it. Foster liked to be an achiever, but he liked to keep things to himself. He was doing well academically at Beloit, but he didn't particularly care to broadcast how well. He just felt he was better off if he kept other people guessing.

Stubby, who was overly curious, said, "No, I won't tell anyone."

Foster went ahead and explained how the president of the college had seen him on campus and asked if he might be interested in applying for a Rhodes Scholarship. Stubby continued to ask questions about the scholarship. Foster gave him what limited information he had and soon the inquisition ended.

Stubby emptied his mailbox first. He received a credit card bill, two pieces of junk mail, and a letter from Sue, which he slipped in his back pocket without opening or letting Foster know he had received it. He wanted to take any kind of good or bad news alone.

Foster was right. He didn't have any mail.

8

As soon as Stubby got back to the house, he went up to his room to read the letter from Sue. He told Foster that he had to go to the bathroom, but instead went to his room and shut the door. He took a letter opener and sat down on his bed. The water in the bed was still cool, but it felt nice compared to the hot day that was developing.

He knew this was the letter that was going to clear up a lot of the uncertainty -- for better or for worse -- that the relationship was experiencing as the school year ended last spring. He hesitated for about five seconds and questioned whether or not he should open it now, later, or never. Then he realized that no matter when he opened it, the message would still be the same and what would be, would be.

He held the letter up and saw his name on the front. As he slowly turned it around, sweat accumulated on his forehead. He wiped it off with his forearm as he brought the letter opener up to the letter. With a single pass, the letter was open. He stuck his tongue out part way as he concentrated on getting the letter out unmarred. His heart raced as he began to read:

Dear Mark,
How are you? I enjoyed reading your last letter. It sounds as if you are really getting in shape. I know, with the way you've told me you are working, that this year Beloit should do well in football.
The main reason I wrote was to talk about us. I know that right now our relationship is filled with question marks. Most of this is my fault, because I was uncertain whether or not I would be returning this fall. Well, Mark, I know now that I will be returning to school and I'd like to see you when I get there (that is if you still want to see me).
Sorry this is so short, but I've got a ton to do before I come

back. Good Luck with football, and say hello to the guys for me. In the meantime, Take Care. XXO

Love,
Sue
P.S. Go Bucs!!!!!

Stubby read the letter twice. He couldn't keep from smiling as he lay back on the bed and closed his eyes. He could envision her now. He quickly sat up and carefully put the letter back in the envelope. He put the envelope on his desk under his contact case to remind him to read it again before he went to bed. He jumped off the bed, danced around a little bit and then headed downstairs.

Foster was sitting on the couch paging through an old fraternity magazine he found in the house's library. He heard Stubby scamper down the first flight of stairs from the second floor and then, as he jumped down from the first landing, he saw Stubby smiling from ear to ear.

"What's up, Stubby?" Foster knew him well enough to see that he had had a major mood shift.

"Nothing." Stubby didn't want to let Foster in on his secret.

"Well, that must have been one hell of a shit," Foster spoke sarcastically as he lifted the magazine back up to his face.

Stubby had to tell someone, but he didn't know how to do it. In his excitement he ran around the back of the couch where Foster was sitting and used both arms to put him in a headlock. Foster sensed he was going around behind him, but he had no idea that he would be put in a headlock. Caught off guard, he dropped the magazine and fought to free himself. Just as he pulled the mammoth arms from around his neck, Stubby grabbed hold of his waist and lifted Foster onto his shoulders. Foster was stronger than Stubby when it came to regular weightlifting, but when it came to wrestling, five-foot-ten, 185-pound Foster Addison was no match for six-foot-five, 255-pound Mark Stubner.

"What the hell are you doing, Stubby?" Foster demanded. His face was still red from the headlock, and the bouncing around on his shoulders was making him lose his breath.

"She's coming back to school," Stubby shouted as he jumped up and down. "She's coming back to school and she wants to see me." He dropped Foster on the couch. As Foster hit, he crushed the magazine he had been reading.

Foster knew exactly what Stubby was talking about, but he didn't know or care how Stubby had found out the news. He quickly got up from the couch and grabbed his side, which was burning with pain, and said, "Great. I'm happy for you, but couldn't you have told me in a less violent way?" Foster had a look of concern on his face. Although it was nowhere near it, he thought he had just about been killed.

Stubby realized that he had gone a little overboard. He shrugged his shoulders and said in a boyish voice, "I'm sorry. I guess I was a little bit excited."

"I gathered that." Foster was still rubbing his side.

In the next room, Doc was wakened by the commotion. Checking the clock, he moaned. He wanted to stay in bed for another half hour. He quickly put on the same clothes he wore the day before, grabbed his wallet and car keys and walked out to the living room. His eyes were blood-shot and the usually well-groomed hair was going in every direction. Foster and Stubby heard his steps make their unique flip-flop noise as he rounded the corner.

"Guess what, Doc." Stubby took a step towards Doc.

Doc had his arm up motioning for Stubby to stay back and then said, "I know, I just heard the whole thing." He pointed to the wall that separated the the living room and Foster's room. He squinted and shielded his eyes as the sunlight reflected off the window on his face.

"Sorry," Stubby said again softly. It seemed he was pissing off everyone this morning.

Foster's morning ritual was to work out. Stubby's was to attend to his personal hygiene. Doc's was to stay in bed as long as he could. His classes were scheduled, if at all possible, between 11:00 a.m. and 3:00 p.m. When he had to get up before 10:30 a.m., he was impossible to live with until about the time he liked to get up. Once 10:30 a.m. rolled around, it didn't matter to him when he was awakened because he would have been out of bed at that time anyway.

"Well, I'm going to get something to eat. Does anyone want to go with me?" Doc changed the subject. He put his wallet in his back pocket and slipped on his sunglasses.

Doc liked to sleep in, but when he did get out of bed, the first thing he did was eat. Usually this involved downing a dry piece of toast on the way to class. However, on days like today when he didn't have anywhere to be, he would either cook himself a big breakfast or else go out.

Foster never could eat right after a workout. However, after some time had passed, his appetite would return to normal. "I'll go," he said calmly, trying not to draw attention to his hunger. "Just let me go get my wallet." He trotted out of the living room to his room.

Doc turned to Stubby, looking for a response. "I'd like to, but I've got to go pick up Simba at the Holiday Inn in ...," Stubby checked his watch, "about fifteen minutes."

"Okay." Doc understood, but would have been indifferent either way.

"Thanks anyway, though." Stubby tried to get back on his good side.

Foster took the side door, by his room, and met Doc out in the front yard. He yelled 'Gun' not realizing that Stubby wasn't going out with them. Doc made a sarcastic remark that it was a good thing that he called 'Gun' because if he didn't, he was going to have to sit in the back anyway. They got in the car and Doc revved up the tiny VW engine. As they pulled off, Doc beeped to Stubby. Stubby took a step out on the porch and waved.

Later, Stubby parked his car in the Holiday Inn parking lot and walked into the lobby area where the bus passengers entered once they got off the bus. The bus line which serviced O'Hare airport was the same bus line that the Beloit College football team used to go to away games, so Stubby recognized the gold and black Van Galder bus as it came off the service road that led to I-90. This bus made several trips daily from O'Hare to Beloit and then on to Madison and back. It was a convenient means of travel for Beloit students who not only wished to fly out of O'Hare airport, but also for those who wanted to go up to Madison to use the state library or any other resource the University of Wisconsin had to offer.

As the bus pulled in at the Holiday Inn, Stubby went out to watch the bus unload. He looked in the bus through the window to see if he could spot Simba. It was hard to see any definition of the people inside through the tinted glass windows. All he could really make out were shapes. Despite the difficulties, he had no problem discerning Simba from the rest of the people. Simba was about twice the size of most of the little old ladies who were riding the bus today. School wasn't in session at either UW or Beloit, so no students were traveling between O'Hare and Madison.

As Simba got off the bus, he and Stubby exchanged the fraternal handshake and before Stubby could let go, Simba gave him a big hug and a wet kiss that made about as much noise as a warm bottle of pop opening. Everyone there, either riding the bus or greeting someone who had ridden the bus, looked over, but no one knew what to make of Simba's stunt. Stubby quickly pushed Simba away and cursed at him for being an embarrassment. Simba laughed. Stubby's scolding didn't have the slightest effect.

Simba's real name was Dan Simpson. He was from Tampa, Florida, but usually spent his summers in Alaska working on fishing boats. He was everyone's friend, but no one really knew why. His language was gross at best, his jokes tasteless, and generally his actions were even worse. But these were probably some of the reasons why everyone loved to have him around, because no matter what anybody said or did, everyone knew that sooner or later (and it was usually sooner) Simba was going to do something that would grab all the attention.

But everything about him was misleading. He appeared to be the typical dumb-jock college football player. But he wasn't. Simba was very intelligent and was actually one of the smarter people on the football team. And nothing about him was self-centered. Simba was probably the best friend that anyone ever had, because he was always there when needed. When someone was down, he made a point of cheering them up. Simba hid his true qualities underneath a gross exterior. They weren't available for all -- only real friends.

Simba never claimed to be fashionable. In fact, he wasn't fashionable at all. He owned a T-shirt for every day of the week, all displaying obscene messages, and did one load of laundry a month. Because of the shape of his body, his pants always seemed to be falling down his hips. Every couple of minutes he would have to pull them back up. His hair was coarse enough that it always remained in one place. He always wore tennis shoes without socks. For the big event every year, the football banquet, Simba got dressed up. Once, he even wore a tie.

The bus driver checked the baggage claim tickets of everyone who waited to get their luggage from underneath the bus. When Simba stepped forward and pointed out the green Army-issue duffel bag that carried all but a few of his belongings, the bus driver took one look at the way he was dressed and handed him the bag without question. As Simba bent over to pick the bag up, his 'FUCK EM BUCKY' T-shirt pulled above the back of his pants and the crack of his ass showed. Stubby tried to act as if he wasn't with him.

"Is this all the stuff you have?" Stubby said as he opened his trunk to put the single duffel bag in.

"This is all my clothes. I had some other stuff shipped. Do you mind if we stop and pick it up before we get back? I sent it by Greyhound Package Express, so all we have to do is stop off at the Greyhound station on the way home." Simba loaded the bag in the trunk and got in the passenger side of the car. Stubby didn't answer, but nodded yes.

He got in the car and looked over at Simba before he started up the car. "Boy, you sure lost some weight," he said as he turned the key.

"Fifty pounds," Simba replied as he patted himself on the stomach. Simba's weight was seasonal. Every year when he came back for football he weighed an almost trim 230 pounds, but after football, that figure would creep toward 280 to 290 pounds. He was the champion of Twinkies, Ho-Ho's and Ding-Dongs. During the off-season, intramural basketball was the extent of his activity, and although he couldn't beat Foster on speed, he could out-eat him on volume. Simba's philosophy was that everything he ate at the fraternity was paid for before the semester started, so he was obligated to get his share. He usually ended up with about two other people's shares too. But when summer came along, Simba was off to Alaska, where he got more than his share of exercise working 16-hour days hauling in salmon nets. And his diet consisted mainly of low-fat seafood. Subsequently, he always returned to Beloit in great shape.

Riding the short distance from the Holiday Inn to the Greyhound station downtown where Simba had his stuff sent, the two went through 'how was your summer', 'what's new', etc., quickly. After that, neither had much to say. Simba was tired from the flight and his body was experiencing jet lag as he went from the Alaska time zone back to Central. Stubby was off in another world, reviewing in his mind the letter he just received from Sue.

OUT OF THE COMFORT ZONE

Stubby parked the car and Simba got out and put money in the meter. They had to walk about a half a block to get to the entrance of the Greyhound station. He sent the items almost a week ago from Seward, Alaska. He was pretty sure that the stuff had arrived, because when he shipped it out, the man told him it would take about ten days to cover the distance.

Stubby held the door open for Simba and then followed him into the station. Immediately, Stubby noticed the overpowering smell of fish. "Whew, smells like fish," he said with a scowl on his face. Simba turned to him as if he didn't know what he was talking about. Because he had worked so many hours in the summer knee-deep in salmon, the smell didn't register in his nose.

Simba waited in the Greyhound Package Express line behind two people who had things they were sending out. Stubby waited off to the side looking at a map on the wall which indicated exactly where Greyhound buses traveled. When Simba's turn came, he reached in his back pocket and pulled out his wallet.

As he began to dig for the claim check, the clerk asked, "Can I help you?"

"Yes," Simba replied, "I'm here to pick up a couple of packages I had sent, but I've got to find my claim check first." He sifted through mounds of A&W Root Beer coupons and video game tokens which he had accumulated over the summer.

"By any chance were these packages sent from Alaska?" The clerk said, merely guessing.

"Yes," Simba answered as he pulled three claim checks from his wallet. With a surprised look on his face, he said, "How did you know?" Stubby heard the conversation and came walking over to the counter.

The clerk looked at Simba with amazement as he took the claim checks. He quickly looked over the claim checks and shouted to the men loading boxes in the back area, "He's here."

Stubby was confused by the conversation, but Simba put two and two together. Simba had sent two boxes of smoked fish with the rest of his belongings. Apparently, the fish had been smelling up the entire bus station. One man came forward from the loading area, bringing a handcart with three boxes on it. Two of the boxes had 'smoked fish' stamped across them; they all were marked 'Dan Simpson.'

59

The man loaded the boxes up on the counter and said to Simba, "Boy, are we glad to see you." Simba laughed out loud. The boxes had arrived a day and a half ago, and the aroma had filtered through the bus station ever since.

As the first box was set on the counter, Stubby caught a strong smell of fish. At that point, he was able to figure out what was going on. "No way. You're not putting fish in my car." Stubby was serious. Simba just laughed harder.

"Well, he can't leave it here," the man with the handcart said as he loaded another box on the counter. Simba continued to laugh.

Stubby realized he was stuck. He shook his head as if he were pissed off. This didn't bother Simba in the least. As soon as the last box was loaded on the counter, Stubby grabbed the one that wasn't marked 'smoked fish.' Holding the box in his arms, he pointed at Simba and said, "Okay, but they go in the trunk and you have to buy air freshener for it when we're through." Simba continued to laugh as he picked up the two boxes of fish.

Stubby and Simba walked toward the door with people watching them the whole way. Just as they were about to open the door, the clerk who first waited on Simba shouted to catch their attention and stop them. Simba, who had finally stopped laughing, turned to face him. "Next time you send fish, call UPS, okay?" Simba began laughing again.

When Doc and Foster got back from breakfast, they noticed that Bert Lindsey's car was parked just ahead of Foster's car. Nothing from the car had been unloaded and there was also a trailer attached. The engine knocked as it cooled from the drive from the South side of Chicago. Bert had arrived an hour earlier than the twelve o'clock noon estimate, which was surprising for someone who never seemed to be on time.

As Doc and Foster walked up to the house through the front yard, Bert came out on the front porch, raised his hand and waved saying, "Hello," in a fake Swedish accent. Doc replied in the same manner. This was just one of the many ways in which the guys in the house talked to one another for whatever reason.

Bert walked out halfway to greet them with a firm fraternal handshake. Just as they turned to head toward the house, Bill Barton stepped out on the front porch.

They all said hello and went in the house and sat down on the couch and began to go over, again for Doc and Foster, their experiences for the summer. Doc began to tell the story about giving Carli pierced earrings again. He told Stubby the story last night at dinner and so now Foster was hearing it for the third time. He didn't find it extremely funny the other two times, so he figured it would be a good time to leave.

When he returned, Stubby's car pulled up in front of the house. He parked it on the side where parking was prohibited, got out and opened his trunk and stepped back as the blast from the fish hit him in the face. Simba started to grab his duffel bag, but Stubby made him put it down and grab the boxes of fish first.

Simba walked through the porch doors and stopped. Without even saying hello, he began to sing: "I don't know, but I've been told, Eskimo pussy is mighty cold." Everyone laughed and was glad to see that the summer hadn't changed old Dan Simpson. He sat down the boxes on the piano and went to shake everyone's hands. By about the time he was through everyone in the room, the smell from the fish permeated the entire area.

"Good God, Simba. What's in the box?" Bert yelled out in an almost obnoxious tone.

"Smells real nice, Simba," Bill added in a sarcastic tone.

Doc turned to Bill and said, "Now Bill, that's where we differ, because I don't think that's a real nice smell at all." Only his tone was serious, but he understood what Bill meant.

"It's smoked salmon." Simba ran a key along the packaging tape which sealed the box.

"Oh really, I thought it was bananas." Bill had a way with sarcasm.

As Simba opened the box, Stubby walked through the door with the rest of Simba's belongings. He put them down and was about to go park his car when he yelled at Simba. "You aren't going to open that shit up in here." He tried to keep a straight face, but it was hard because everyone else was laughing.

"What do you mean, 'shit?' Don't you know that fish is brain food?" Just then, Simba opened a can and pulled out a piece of fish about six inches long and lowered it into his mouth as if he were being fed grapes in a harem. Simba then offered some to everyone, but no one accepted. He then grabbed the boxes and walked toward his room and said, "Okay, more for me then." He took three steps and then raised his right leg and let out a deafening fart, continuing on to his room and ending the conversation.

Everyone lent a hand to help get Bert and Bill unloaded and moved in. They, by far, had the most stuff of anyone in the house. Each had a king-size water bed and a sophisticated stereo system. Bill had a thirty-gallon fish tank and Bert had a bar he bought from a fraternity brother who graduated two years before. Even with help, it took over two hours to get everything in the house.

Most of the rest of the afternoon, everyone worked on getting their own rooms in the condition they wanted them for at least the first semester. It seemed that between each semester and during each semester midterm break someone in the house was altering the way their room looked.

Doc finally got his waterbed filled and now he could no longer put off getting the rest of his room ready. Stubby and Foster put away clothes and hung stuff on their walls.

Only a few other guys came that day, mostly those who lived a long way from Beloit and had to fly. The majority of the guys lived in either Chicago or Milwaukee, so they didn't show up until just before they had to -- the first football meeting at noon the next day.

It was almost 7:00 p.m. by the time Bert and Bill were ready to fill their waterbeds. But then they had it planned like this. Their first priority was to get their stereos hooked up. And then while they tested them out, by playing them as loud as they could, they would sit and watch the waterbeds fill as they tried to carry on a conversation above the music. Doc went out to get pizza and beer for them to have while the beds filled. The sounds of the stereos carried for blocks. As Doc, Bill, and Bert drank beer and ate pizza, Simba came in and ate smoked salmon.

Foster enjoyed spending time alone. He went down to his room and turned his radio on WZOK, his favorite top-forty radio station out of Rockford. When he got tired of getting his room organized, he sat on his bed and started to compose a letter to Marianne. He had hoped to get a chance to see her before she went off to school, but she never replied to his letter asking to come down and see her. After he wrote three paragraphs, he ripped the letter up. He took all the letters she had ever sent him and threw them away. As of that point, it was officially over. He returned to his room, turned off the light and lay down on his bed. Just as he was about to doze off, the phone rang. It startled him at first. He thought it might be Jandi.

"Hello," he answered the phone.

"Is Danny there?" A woman's voice was on the other end.

"I'm sorry, you must have the wrong number," Foster said as he hung up the phone. He lay back down and wondered if he would ever see Jandi again.

Stubby closed the door to his wing and his room door. That combination just about drowned out the music from Bill's stereo. The only music he could still hear came from outside the house through his windows. He didn't dare shut the windows because that was the only thing keeping his room cool. Instead, he put a Charlie Daniels Band CD on his stereo, turned it down and put on headphones. He went into his closet and took out a shoebox full of letters. These were all the letters and notes Sue had ever given him. Carefully, he took them out and sorted them chronologically. He re-read the one he received earlier that day for the fifth time and then put it in its proper place in the box. He left his headphones on as he went to sleep.

9

The next day started like the day before for Foster and Stubby. Foster got up and ran. However, he didn't go as far because he knew he had to save some energy for pre-season testing. He mainly ran to loosen up. Stubby got up, showered, and then cleaned his contacts. In lieu of all the studying he would be doing soon, he started to look at the playbook that Coach Bonaventure had given him. He really didn't try to memorize anything because he knew that between the time he had gotten the playbook and the time practice started, the coaching staff would have made dozens of modifications. Instead, he just tried to get a flavor for what they proposed to do with the offense this year.

After Foster had showered up, he and Stubby walked over to the Mailroom again. Today was going to be a pleasant day. The temperature was about 76 degrees, low humidity, and there was a slight breeze that made the clouds race across the sky. Today neither of them got any mail. Instead of going straight back to the house, they went into the campus bookstore, in the same building, to see what their books were going to cost for the school year. Stubby's totaled about $220, close to the average. Foster's was $250, far above what he had ever paid. One-hundred-twenty dollars in books was from one class alone -- a history class. He started to think about alternative classes. One option was to take Professor Ames up on his offer to do a special research project. The idea had a lot of benefits, but the decision didn't have to be made for about two or three days, so he didn't dwell on it.

When they returned to the house, everyone was still asleep, which was expected. They had no intentions of making any noise to wake anyone because for once in about twelve hours, the house was peaceful. Foster recalled waking up as late as three o'clock in the morning and still hearing music playing. Stubby couldn't hear anything, even if he wanted to, because it wasn't until about 5:30 that he took his headphones off. Foster and Stubby opened up the front porch doors as wide as they could and then pulled one of the couches right up to it, facing out. It was almost two hours until someone else was awake in the house.

During those two hours, they talked football and nothing but football. Most of that topic was devoted to who, if there were to be one, would be the third captain for the team. The way Captain elections usually worked was that the team would elect one captain for the team right after the season ended, and then, just before the next season began, another captain would be elected. After last season, both Doc and Foster were elected co-captains, so no one was sure whether or not Coach Bonaventure would have another captain elected just prior to the beginning of the season. Stubby, who felt he was a strong candidate for the position, hoped that a third captain would be elected, but thought that it would be just his luck that Coach Bonaventure would decide against it. Foster tried to get him to stop worrying. He reasoned that there would be another election because Coach Bonaventure would want the incoming freshmen to have some say as to who led them.

Foster was confident that Stubby would be the third captain, and he told him so. But, as Foster explained, even if Stubby were not elected, it wouldn't matter because he already was a leader on the team. Some people use a title to lead and don't consider themselves a leader unless they have that title. Other people just lead. Stubby was the latter. Whether it said in the program or not that he was a captain, he was going to try and lead the team in the right direction. More importantly, people were going to follow him.

As the morning wore on, everyone on the team began to show up. Most of these people were on the team last year and so time was spent going over old times. But many of them weren't on the team before -- freshmen. Freshman football at Beloit College was different from being a freshman at most other schools. There was never any hazing or initiating of freshmen. Coach Bonaventure would not stand for it. So the upperclassmen came to view freshmen, not as someone coming in to take their position, but as someone who was there to help the team. And if an upperclassman was pushed by a freshman or even lost his position -- and it happened -- then that was best for the team.

Stubby and Foster did their best to get to know these people. They could see the doubts and fears in these people which they saw in themselves only three years ago. There weren't many players on the team who couldn't remember how they felt when they came to football camp as a freshman. 'Do I have what it takes to be a college football player?' 'What do I have to do to fit in here?' 'Have I made the right decision?' The freshman year as a football player is tough. Most of the guys who played college football had either been all-conference or all-state in high school, the most valuable player on their teams, team captain, or played on a team that won a significant championship. At Beloit, none of that mattered. You go from being a big fish in a small pond to just another small fish in a much bigger pond. For many, that is a tough pill to swallow, and sometimes causes a short college career.

Along with football, the freshmen have the pressures of college and the heartache of being away from home for the first time. Foster remembered that feeling all too well as he stood on the sidewalk with tears in his eyes as his father dropped him off here at Beloit for pre-season camp three years ago. For most, this is a shattering experience, requiring either learning to grow up or giving up in a hurry. Doc, Foster, Stubby, and the others had learned to grow. Those who didn't were no longer on the team.

Noontime came fast. Even for the seniors, there was a certain amount of anxiety mixed with excitement as the entire team would meet for the first time this season. As long as the seniors had been at Beloit, this first meeting took place in the cafeteria, known as the Commons. This was the only dining hall on campus. It was located at the extreme north end of campus, downstairs from Chapin residence hall. Coach Bonaventure arranged to have lunch served and then he would address the team.

The Commons didn't open until exactly noon, but players started lining up at a quarter-to. Heading the line were the eager, but nervous, freshmen. Stubby and Foster managed to get in line just behind this first wave.

The smell of food made their mouths water. They didn't bother to go out for breakfast, figuring that they could hold out until now. Experience told them that this lunch would be a good one. The Commons always had great meals for about the first week. During this period, it seemed as if they had elaborate spreads to impress the parents of the incoming students. Once the first week was over, it was back to 'a thousand and one uses for chipped beef.' That didn't matter to Foster or Stubby. In a week, they would be eating meals at Sigma Rho, which had its own cook. In the meantime, they would enjoy this first week of dining.

Eventually, the Commons opened. The four abreast mass reduced to a single queue as names were checked off and they moved down the service line. Freshmen only took moderate amounts. A combination of nerves and a desire to avoid appearing too greedy kept their hunger in check. Upperclassmen were less inhibited and knew that they had to begin stockpiling calories for the grueling pre-season practices.

Freshmen tried to group themselves together at a couple of tables. Their uncertainty about the upperclassmen was the one and only thing they had in common with each other. Stubby and Foster managed to squeeze in at one of these tables. They sat almost facing one another across the table. For Stubby, it wasn't so much a campaign for captain, but more of making these new players aware of his concern. Foster, on the other hand, was more interested in getting in good with the freshmen to provide a link with freshman women. He was trying to make every effort to recover from Marianne, and so far he didn't consider Jandi for sure -- not by a long shot.

Doc and Bert were at about the middle of the line. Bill and Simba weren't too far behind. Those four grabbed a small round table for themselves. They laughed loudly about the events of the previous evening. It wasn't long until Simba became the main attraction as Doc tossed whole pieces of cake in the air and Simba caught them in his mouth as if he were a seal. As Simba chewed each piece of cake, he laughed with his mouth open, dropping crumbs in his lap. Everyone watched in amazement. The freshmen enjoyed the entertainment, but they were not quite sure what to think. The show came to an end as the coaching staff entered the Commons.

Leading was Nick Bonaventure, the head coach. He was the one person who had recruited everyone in the room. For all the freshmen, his personality was a mystery. They had spoken with the man, some had even met him, but they hadn't been on his team. This was their biggest cause for uncertainty.

Bonaventure was born and raised in Butte, Montana. He played football at Colorado College and then later took a position there as defensive coordinator. This was his sixth season as head coach at Beloit College. Although football was his main interest, his family was his first love. He and his wife, Nancy, had three children, Joe, Dave, and Mike. His master's degree in history gave him a scholarly nature. He was a perfect coach -- the kind of coach most players dream about playing for -- tough and demanding, but also fair and concerned. Some of the upperclassmen could attest that during the football season Coach Bonaventure was the one person that they could both hate and love at the same time.

Not only was Coach Bonaventure a quality person, but he also surrounded himself with quality people. "Committed" was the single best word that could describe his coaching staff. Bonaventure was able to maintain a staff of six assistant coaches, which was unusual and impressive for a college of Beloit's size.

However, the unique thing about his staff was that only one of the coaches had a full-time position at the College. In addition to the rigors of coaching at Beloit (requiring over forty hours per week), one coach held a full-time position as a business loan officer in a bank, two taught junior high physical education at schools almost thirty miles away, and the other two were also head football coaches at local high schools. The last coach, Bob Nicodemus (known as "Coach Nic"), was a thirty-year veteran coach at Beloit College. Over the years, Coach Nic had his hands in almost every sport at the college, including intramurals. He was a wealth of information, jokes and stories. His kind-hearted personality dated back to before he coached Foster's father at Beloit.

After about twenty minutes, Coach Bonaventure pushed his lunch aside and began preparing for his address. As the other coaches continued to talk and Bonaventure walked to the front of the room, Simba started the room clapping. The coach was flattered. He blushed a bit, smiled and waved. His smile wasn't that of the traditional 'blood-n-guts' football coach, but that was part of his Jekyll/Hyde image.

Several players were bouncing from table to table exchanging greetings with other players and coaches. However, when Coach Bonaventure took his stance in the front of the room, they quickly took a seat. The only players still eating were those with appetites like Foster, but they too focused their attention on the front of the room as they pushed what remained of their food aside. Although Coach Bonaventure never explicitly asked for it, his presence commanded respect.

His address was a traditional one. He introduced himself, welcomed back the upperclassmen, and welcomed the freshmen. Then, he went into an elaborate introduction of his coaching staff. This included telling some background information about them and then perhaps a joke or a funny story about them. Bonaventure, at times, was an entertainer, too. After each coach had his opportunity to be roasted, he asked two of them to bring forward two boxes he had brought with him to the Commons. One box had gold-colored folders; the others were navy blue, the maize and blue of Beloit. Holding up a gold folder, he quickly explained that each folder contained a playbook in one pocket and an agenda for the coming week in the other. The gold folders were for the defense and the navy blue ones for the offense. He set the gold folder down and moved over to the blue ones. One of the coaches remained up front to help pass them out as Coach Bonaventure started down a list of offensive players. He introduced each player individually with the name of his high school and hometown. As various players stood up, shouts came from the crowd. Although mainly wisecracks, Doc managed to slip in a few that made even Coach Bonaventure laugh. When the coach finished with the offense, he started on the defense. While the defense was being called, Stubby took a quick glance through his playbook to see what changes had been made with respect to the one he received earlier. There were some, but nothing major. Coach wrapped up the first meeting by quickly going over the agenda. He dismissed the team and then went back to eat the lunch that was now stone cold.

Bonaventure's agenda made for a busy day. Between one o'clock and dinner they were involved with strength, speed testing, and equipment issue. After dinner, until about nine o'clock, they had physicals and then a meeting with Coach Bonaventure in the Morse-Ingersol Auditorium.

In the afternoon, the team was divided into seniors, juniors, sophomores, and freshmen for testing and equipment issue. In the past, Coach Bonaventure had never been too keen on the idea of strength and speed testing. In his experience, he felt that testing did more harm than good as usually a couple players would end up being injured with pulled muscles. However, in recent years, he decided to give it another chance.

The team was tested in four areas: the forty-yard dash, bench press, military press, and the squat. Doc was one of four people to have a forty-time below 4.6 seconds. Stubby led the team with a 500-pound squat and Bert and Foster finished one-two in both the bench press and military press. In addition to the top players' performances, Coach Bonaventure was pleased with the testing. He was confident that the team he had this year, although the youngest, was in better shape than any he had ever had.

It really didn't matter that the team was separated according to graduating class for testing. No one cared if he got to run the forty-yard dash after or before. However, it mattered when it came to issuing equipment. As a rule, equipment was issued to the seniors first, juniors second, and so forth. The seniors had been waiting three years for this privilege: the chance to have first pick of the new equipment.

All the equipment was placed at various stations across the fieldhouse floor, except for helmets and shoulder pads, which were issued at the Stadium. At the first station, each player received a bag which was to be used for equipment to 'away' games. This was convenient because, as they passed from station to station, pants, girdles, hip pads, thigh pads, jocks, socks, and anything else that was issued, was easily stored and carried in the bag.

Coach Nic shuttled a van back and forth between the fieldhouse and the Stadium to help people get equipment down to their lockers. Doc, who was the first to have all his equipment, boarded the van and sat up front next to Coach Nic in the passenger seat. It was almost five minutes until Foster, Stubby, and the rest of the seniors were ready to go down to the Stadium. In that time, Doc and Coach Nic discussed how the NFL draft was going to affect the Green Bay Packers' season.

Strong Stadium was located about a half-mile east of the campus. At the Stadium, as it was known, there was the game field, which was also used for men's and women's soccer. West of the game field, behind the Stadium, was the football practice field with an area for shot putting and throwing the discus. Around the game field was a 400-meter cinder track which, over the years, was becoming engulfed by weeds. Farther east of the game field was an area for soccer practice as well as a driving range for golf.

As the van came to the end of Chapin Street, it passed through a set of iron gates that had been painted a blue similar to Doc's car. Once past the gates, the Stadium itself was visible. The Stadium was nothing to marvel at. It was just a slab of concrete that went up in the air about 30 feet and extended the entire length of the football field. At the top of the Stadium was a makeshift press box, which was mainly used by team statisticians as opposed to media covering the game. On the east side were bleachers that tapered toward the center. To the west side was just a concrete wall that bore the Stadium's name. Inside were a home and a visitors' locker room, plus additional space for public restrooms and concessions. It was no Ohio Stadium or Camp Randall, but in its day, it more than served its purpose despite the fact that the rusting concrete reinforcing rods were causing streaks of rust to stain the outside of the structure.

As they entered the locker room, the damp air reminded them of football. It was the smell they had associated with the game since they started playing at Beloit. The walls of the locker room were wet with condensation. Simba ran his fingers along the wall and flicked the water on the back of Foster's neck. They walked carefully as their flip-flops slipped easily on the newly painted floor.

When they got through the short, winding hallways, they were in the locker area. All the lockers were open and nothing on them indicated which locker belonged to anyone. Before they could go ask Coach Nic what to do, two women appeared from the training room. They were Kathy and Heidi, the team managers.

As long as the guys had played at Beloit, they had female managers. It seemed natural. The locker room had been modified so the shower and dressing areas weren't visible from the area where the managers worked. Kathy, who was the veteran of the two, had always had an interest in the sport of football. Managing the team was just a way to get near the sport. Her plan after graduating from Beloit was to enroll in a graduate sport psychology program somewhere in the country. Heidi, on the other hand, was dating one of the guys on the team, so now she could spend more time with him.

Kathy carried a clipboard and Heidi a list of the players on the team. There was a warm exchange of greetings and then Kathy started reciting instructions to them. When they found their lockers, they were supposed to check to see if the helmet and shoulder pads fit and then check to see if the practice jersey was the right number and color. Each locker had a lock inside it, and the combination was taped on the back of the locker. If they had any problems, they were supposed to come into the training room. Heidi then directed each senior to his locker.

Stubby got his locker first. Everything was fine except he wanted a new face mask for his helmet. Simba was satisfied and made a remark that 'good guys wear white' when he realized that the offense would have the white practice jerseys this year and not the navy blue ones. Foster was irritated about this because he felt that the dark jerseys created more heat, especially in the late hot days of August. But he didn't say anything because he realized that someone had to wear them. Doc didn't try on either his helmet or his shoulder pads. He had them specially ordered last year and he could see that this year he was issued the same ones, so there was no sense in even checking. Besides, he was more concerned with memorizing his locker combination as he stuck the combination in his wallet.

By the time they were finished, Coach Nic still hadn't returned. Simba and Bert decided to wait for him. The others started the half-mile march back. They wanted to get back in time to either shower or nap before dinner time. The walk, to them, wasn't so bad. Even though most people drove to the Stadium, they had walked before. Doc remembered the adage Coach gave them as freshmen for finding their way back to campus through the streets of Beloit -- Church to Chapin/Chapin to Church, he recited the street names.

As luck would have it, though, when they had walked about halfway, Coach Nic approached them in the van. Bert and Simba were aboard. Bert explained that they had wanted to walk back and persuaded him not to stop. Simba had the cheeks of his bare ass pressed firmly against the van's rear window as the van passed by.

That evening, seniors led the line into the Commons. Most of the freshmen still hadn't returned from getting their equipment as the food line began to serve. To the upperclassmen's surprise dinner was made up of completely different entrees than lunch, except, of course, for the ice cream. Everyone had plenty to eat, including the freshmen who were starting to loosen up. Coach Bonaventure again stood and got everyone's attention. This time, however, he only spoke long enough to explain that a pot of hot water was being provided up front so everyone could form fit their mouth pieces, and then went over the agenda for the rest of the day quickly. He did not want his dinner to get cold like his lunch.

Right after dinner, everyone raced back to the fieldhouse for physicals. Like cattle at the stockyard, they were put in one line and then walked through each phase. This physical wasn't a very in-depth probe. Each person carried a card which was filled with information on height, weight, blood pressure, urine analysis, hernia and a few others. Coach Bonaventure had arranged to have several doctors there so the entire team was pushed through in a little over an hour and a half. After the last stragglers made it through the final station of the physical, Coach Bonaventure walked with them over to the auditorium for the meeting.

Only Coach Bonaventure and Coach Nic were around during the afternoon to direct people through testing and equipment issue. Despite the fact that the other coaches were at lunch, most of them had to go back to their other jobs for the afternoon. However, the entire coaching staff was back for this meeting, joking and laughing, like the players, in the back of the auditorium. The stragglers entered just ahead of Coach Bonaventure and quickly found seats. As Bonaventure walked down the slightly sloped stairs in the aisle to the front of the room, the room began to settle. Simba, sitting in the second row, tried to get the room clapping again. This time he wanted to go one step further by getting the entire team to stand, too. It didn't work. He was the only one standing. As the room quieted again, Coach Bonaventure looked over toward Simba, who was now seated.

"You must really be worried about getting a starting position, Dan." Coach Bonaventure grinned as he spoke. The team broke out laughing. Simba's ears began to burn.

When the room quieted for a third time Bonaventure began his address. He had to go over, as he put it, some 'nuts and bolts' first. These were mainly a review of questions or problems that had occurred during the day which he was now in the position to answer or solve for the team collectively. The majority of the team moaned in protest as he went over the agenda for the next week and explained that he expected everyone to show up for breakfast at 7:30 a.m. This meant an hour less sleep for most. Foster and Stubby shrugged their shoulders as they looked at one another. They had no problem with this. Doc put his face down in his hand and shook his head. He could already sense how he was going to feel in the morning.

Once the 'nuts and bolts' were cleared up and he had reviewed the week's agenda, Coach Bonaventure let the athletic trainer have the floor so he could address the team. The most fortunate event to happen to the

Beloit College football team was when the Athletic Department hired Jack Benson, the College's first full-time trainer. As he walked up to the front of the room Simba started the upperclassmen chanting softly 'Jack, Jack, Jack.' As Coach Bonaventure walked to the rear of the auditorium to sit with the rest of the coaches, he rubbed the hair on Simba's head in a friendly manner. Like Bonaventure, Jack also addressed Simba.

"BBBeeee asss nnn..nnice to me as you want, bbbbbbuttt ttthat's not ggggoinnng to make yyyyouu immmune to injury," Jack stuttered. The upperclassmen immediately started laughing again. The freshmen started to when they felt it was acceptable to do so. They weren't sure whether Jack's stuttering was an act, and if it wasn't, they didn't want to be rude and laugh at someone who stutters. But the upperclassmen weren't laughing at the stuttering. They had heard Jack talk so many times that they had grown accustomed to his stuttering. The upperclassmen laughed because Jack, despite how serious he was about his work, was a funny guy.

Not only was Jack a funny guy, he was also a quality trainer. He had a degree from the University of Wisconsin. He was also working on his master's degree there. Among his credentials was being selected to be a trainer to the U.S. Olympic hockey team. He used the team as his 'guinea pig' in trying to identify whether or not a person's mental state had anything to do with injuries. For two years, he gathered data by having the team fill out questionnaires on what their moods were. Most players didn't give a damn about what he was up to, but that never stopped his enthusiasm. But more importantly, he was well liked and well respected as a trainer by the entire team.

As the room quieted again, Jack began his address. "Innn caasse yyyouuu ffffreshmmen ddddidddnnnn't nnn...nnnotice, I sttttutterr." Everyone laughed again. This time the freshmen didn't hesitate. "Okay," was about the only word he could say normally. He directed the team to turn to the last page in their agenda booklet. On that page were five items that Jack wanted to go over. "I'll tttalk ffffforrr ffff..fivvve mmmiinuutees or fffive hundddreddd wordddds -- wwwhichhh evvver cccomess ffffirst." Once again the team started laughing, but this time not as long because they wanted to get on with the meeting.

Jack talked about rules and proper conduct for the training room. He was very protective of the atmosphere he provided for the female managers and trainers he had. He also explained the 36-80's system to the freshmen. This system simply meant that if a player were injured, he would have to run 36 eighty-yard dashes, ranging from half to seven-eighths speed, before he was allowed to practice again. This system was a good one, because it not only provided a benchmark to determine whether or not someone was completely healed, but it also deterred the faking of a slight injury to get out of practice.

Jack's speaking became much smoother as he became more comfortable in front of the new players on the team. He finished in the time he said he would and then handed the floor back to Coach Bonaventure. As Bonaventure approached the front of the room, this time he didn't have the playful look he had the two other times he spoke to the team. As he thanked Jack and continued to the front, the players sensed his seriousness.

"Men," he always started this way when it was serious, "We've had a good time today, but now I've got some important things to go over." As he paced back and forth, he began. He stopped and faced the dozens of pairs of eyes that were locked on his. "Before I get started, I want certain things when I'm speaking. Both your feet on the ground, you sitting up straight, and no hats." He began pacing again, but paused in his speech long enough to allow a dozen people to comply.

"I don't have many rules, but the ones I do have I expect you to follow." He waited for the attention to be glued on him. "I have two simple rules to follow. Never do anything that will, one, hurt you or your reputation, or, two, will hurt the team or the team's reputation." He pointed angrily at the team. Although he had heard it before, sweat rolled down Foster's back and he had to swallow hard to regain his breathing. "That's it." Bonaventure motioned that he was done with his rules. "If you can comply with those, then that's all I ask." Bonaventure began to pace again. Although his rules were few in number, like the Constitution, the scope they covered was broad.

In addition to his two main rules, he also recited a dozen or so ancillary guidelines. He expected the team to be on time. He expected that they weren't supposed to be involved in any sort of alcohol or drugs. He expected that players address the coaching staff by either 'mister' or 'coach.' He expected that individuals treat one another with respect, and that any sort of racial bias or other prejudice be kept to oneself. He continued with other guidelines that helped frame the two rules he had laid down.

"Men, I know a lot of you have heard this before, but it's important enough to hear again." Most of the team was uncertain as to what he was driving at. Simba was the only one to perceive that it was time for his pre-season fire-up talk. He turned toward the back of the room and rolled his eyes and gave the 'here we go again' look.

"We've all set goals for this season, both for ourselves and for the team. Some of us have even set goals as to what we want to achieve in school, or with the career some of you plan to start in less than a year." Bonaventure spoke calmly. Everyone began to relax a little bit. "And goals are good. They give us something to work for, right?" he softly reasoned to the team. "To achieve these goals, discipline is needed, because striving to achieve a goal without discipline is like going on a long trip without a map." Although he wasn't looking for it, a few chuckles came from his audience. He continued, "Discipline concentrates our efforts." He spoke loudly, pulling everyone's attention back. "Discipline keeps us on course and it gets us where we want to go." He lowered his voice again, but only for a brief period as it began to rise again. "Discipline is the means by which we achieve our goals." He shouted as he pointed at Stubby.

"But discipline is no stranger to a few in here. Some of you freshmen should take a lesson from some of these older guys. Guys like ...," he searched for a name, "guys like Mark Stubner who worked full eight-hour days so he could afford to come back to school, and still had the discipline to lift weights every night." Then he raced to the other side of the room and pointed at Foster. "Or guys like Foster Addison. He only weighed 175 pounds when he came here as a freshman, but look at him now, look what miles and miles of running and hours and hours of weight lifting have done for him. He's captain of the team, playing defensive tackle at 190 pounds, and he is one of the strongest on the team." Both Foster and Stubby turned red. "I could go on and on," and he did. "Todd Wallace," Doc perked up, "has developed one of the strongest arms in the league. Bill Barton. Bill may not be the greatest athlete in this room, but he sure has made a name for himself in the classroom. And that's important, too." He paused. "You know why? Because he's going to law school next year. He's going to be somebody." Coach Bonaventure raced over and grabbed Bill by the shirt and tried to hold him up as if he were an exhibit.

Bert and Simba felt left out, but Coach moved on. Bonaventure began talking softly again. "These guys have paid the price -- paid their dues, just like a lot of other people in the room." Raising his voice quickly, he said, "And your dues aren't going to get paid without discipline." He paused and gave himself a rest, but only for a moment. Then he began talking in a normal tone again. "Despite how essential discipline may be to achieving goals, some people seem to skimp on this important quality. They set a goal and then only allot about half of the discipline necessary to achieve that goal." He became quiet and paused. "Why?" he asked, not really looking for an answer. "It leaves them with a way out, an excuse in case they happen not to be able to achieve that goal they have set for themselves. The old 'if I had only tried a little harder.'" Coach Bonaventure was a great orator. The hearts of everyone in the room pounded as adrenalin raced through their bodies. Stubby used his forearm to wipe off the beads of sweat that had formed on his long forehead.

But then Bonaventure sounded as if he were going back on what he had said. "But that's not so unusual. We are brought up to always have an out." He began to elaborate. "We live in a zone of comfort. When we're cold, we turn up the heat. When we're hot, we go into an air-conditioned car or room. When we're tired, we rest. If we feel threatened by a challenging situation, we avoid that situation, or else only approach it at half speed." He slammed his hand on the desk. "Well, damn," he shouted. Veins protruded from his neck. "Let's not be afraid to give something all we've got. Let's attack life so hard that there are no excuses. Let's not be afraid to do whatever it takes to achieve our goals. When it's hot and you are tired tomorrow or any day at practice, don't ease up. Christ, it's hot for everyone and everyone is tired. When you think that school is just too tough, then it's time to give it an extra effort." He lowered his voice to almost a whisper, but it was still loud enough so the people in back could hear. "Let's take ourselves out of that Comfort Zone."

He paced across the front of the auditorium once, being very quiet and not looking up. He wanted what he had said to sink in and have meaning. When enough time had passed, he spoke again in the quiet tone. "But suppose ... just maybe ... that after giving it all we've got, we still haven't achieved our goals? We aren't conference champions? You aren't all-conference? You don't rush for a thousand yards or make a hundred tackles?" Before anyone could answer, he continued.

"So what!" he shouted. He continued at that tone as saliva began to foam at the corners of his mouth. "We won't be the first people not to achieve a goal. And just because our goals have been unachieved without an excuse, that doesn't mean that we are failures." The volume to his voice began to taper. "All that has really happened is that we've discovered an end to our abilities or a limit for ourselves. And there is nothing wrong with that." His voice became very soft again. "Because unless we discover this end to our abilities," he paused and watched the eyes that were focused on him. "Unless we try to determine our limits, how can we possibly realize our potential?" Again, he let the words sink in. Once it had occurred and knowing he had their attention, he said softly, "I'll see you all tomorrow morning at 7:30 a.m. for breakfast."

Everyone on the team felt moved, even Simba who knew that it was coming. If they hadn't been ready to play football before, they were now. When they returned to the house, a few people engaged in light conversation, which was mainly focused on football. The freshmen were motivated most by Bonaventure's address. It was the first time they had heard the 'Comfort Zone' lecture and so it still had its full impact.

Doc went to his room and closed the door. He polished his football cleats and then carefully laced them up. He tried to fall asleep, but his heart was still racing too fast to let him. He turned the light back on and paged through the scrapbook he had accumulated in high school. Re-reading the article that was written about him when they won the state semi-finals, he slowly became tired enough to fall asleep.

10

Doc was enjoying the end of a dream about Carli at 7:00 a.m. when Foster came pounding on his door. Foster had been up for a half hour already and wanted to make sure that Doc wouldn't be late. "Who is it?" Doc yelled just before pulling a pillow over his head to block out the light that was coming in his window.

"It's me," Foster said, hoping he would recognize his voice.

"Me, who?" Doc asked back. He sounded angry.

Foster shook his head as if Doc should have known. "Foster, you dummy, now get out of bed." Foster pushed against the wall to try and stretch his calves. He decided not to go running this morning because he knew he was going to be getting enough exercise before the day was over.

Doc pulled the pillow away and lifted the small digital clock off the head of his waterbed. First he checked to make sure he had set his alarm by feeling what position the knob was in. It was set. Then he pulled the clock up near his face. At first, the numbers were a blur, but he moved the clock in and out until they came in focus. It read 7:03 a.m. Doc had set his alarm for 7:15 a.m. "What are you waking me for? I've still got ten minutes to sleep." For someone like Doc, ten minutes at that time of the morning was a treasure.

"I figured that you might want to shower before breakfast." Foster now leaned against the edge of the door. As he stood there, Stubby and Simba walked up and listened to the conversation.

Doc got out of bed and was attempting to open the door as he spoke. "What the hell do I want to shower for? We've got practice in a little over two hours." As the guys on the outside heard the tumbler of the lock opening, they pushed against the door and forced their way in. Doc stepped backwards and fell on his bed. Simba fell on top of him and rested his big armpit on his face. This wasn't the way Doc wanted to get out of bed, but he had no choice in the matter.

Doc pushed his way out from under Simba and then got off the bed to get dressed. As he stood in his closet, putting on a pair of shorts, a grimace crossed Simba's face and he forced out a fart.

"Simba!" Doc shouted, as Stubby and Foster rolled away from him on the bed. Doc stopped zipping up his shorts and stared him down.

"What?" Simba shouted back, as if he had no idea what Doc was talking about.

Doc explained, "Don't fart on my bed."

"Hey, it's a natural bodily function." Simba tried to debate the issue.

"Not when you push it out like that and not when you're on my bed." Doc quickly zipped his pants and then shooed everyone off the bed so he could make it. "You're liable to shit all over the place," Doc remarked as he made the bed. Simba just laughed.

"Don't worry, he already shit down in the bathroom by my room," Stubby explained. "That's why we're here."

After Doc had made his bed, everyone climbed back on. However, it was only a matter of a couple of minutes until he had brushed his teeth and then they were off to breakfast.

Coach Bonaventure must have been there for a while before the rest of the team showed up. He had eaten and was checking off names as they entered. He gave everyone a hearty 'Good Morning,' shaking hands and patting backs. The man that they all had seen the night before certainly wasn't around this morning. Still, everyone proceeded with caution. Remarkably, he remembered every freshman's name and could even make comments about where they lived. For instance, he greeted Ed Conrad, a freshman from Foster's hometown, with, 'It's a little hotter than Houghton weather, isn't it?' or Kevin Digiacomo, a freshman from Chicago, with, 'What kind of breakfasts do they serve you guys from Chicago to make you so tough?'

Breakfast was on par with all the other meals of the day before, but no one really could enjoy a lot of it because they had to be at what was called the 'Captain's Practice' in less than two hours.

Beloit College was a member of the Midwest Athletic Conference. The Midwest Conference, as it was known, had a rule that football teams were only allowed twenty practices before the first game. A practice constituted any time a coach was present to lead drills on the field. This limited conference teams' ability to cover the necessary material before the first game. Coach Bonaventure tried to make up for this constricting rule any way he could. He had a lot of film sessions and 'chalk-talks' to go over plays so each man would know what he had to do on each play. This saved time on the field. He encouraged the team to come to camp already in shape, so less practice time would have to be spent on conditioning.

When the twenty-practice rule came into effect a few years back, the captain of the team stepped forward and asked if it would be all right if the team members went down to the Stadium and did some conditioning on their own. Bonaventure saw no problem. There was no rule limiting the number of workouts that a player could give himself. At first, only a handful of players went down for the 'Captain's Practice,' but as time went on and competition for positions and the peer pressure to work hard increased, the entire team took it as a given that they would have to participate in a practice that was run by the captains.

By 9:30 a.m., the entire team was on the practice field in shorts, shoes and a T-shirt and lined up for stretching. Jack explained the stretching routine to Doc and Foster the day before, so the only staff members present were a trainer, and Kathy and Heidi. The first three 'Captain's Practices,' Doc and Foster announced between stretching exercises, were going to be at the Stadium and they would be doing wind sprints. After that, the morning practices were going to be at the field house. Arrangements had been made for the school nurse, Patty, to lead the team in dance aerobics. The team cheered as they felt they were going to be getting off easy with aerobics.

As the 'Captain's Practice' began, it was evident who had trained hard in the summer. They were the ones who had little problem keeping up with the moderately paced sprints. Foster led the defensive players on one half of the field. Doc, with the help of Stubby, led the offense on the other side. Everyone was in high spirits, excited that practice had finally begun. After each sprint, players would exchange high-five slaps or words of encouragement to one another.

As the practice ended, both the offense and the defense huddled together in the center of the field. Doc and Foster gave some words of encouragement to the team and then each senior said something. As they broke for the first time this year, upperclassmen welcomed one another back and also congratulated the freshmen on the completion of their first practice and welcomed them to the team.

The cool air in the locker room felt nice compared to the hot day they left outside. Each man took off his jock, shorts, T-shirt and socks, grabbed a towel and headed for the showers. Before they entered the shower, they all lined up behind a single scale and weighed themselves. Jack required this to monitor who was losing (or gaining) weight too fast. The weight of each person was recorded on a wall chart and then compared to his weight after practice.

As they stood in line, Bill Barton told some younger players how he lost thirty-five pounds in a little over a week. He claimed that he was so out of shape coming into camp that he burned off thousands of calories each practice, but never replenished them because when it was time to eat he just slept because he was so tired from practice. Bert verified his story as the group headed off to the shower.

Simba, tilting the scale at an even 230, was the first one in the shower. He set the water on lukewarm and let it splash against the top of his head, trying to cool off. When he decided that he was cool enough, he reached for a bar of soap to lather up with. None was there. Normally the shower was stocked with little hotel bars of Ivory soap, but with everything else on their minds, the managers forgot to get the soap out.

"Hey, where's the soap?" Simba shouted. He had very little tolerance at a time like this. "Where's the soap?" He shouted again because there was no response the first time.

Kathy heard Simba's plea for soap, but wasn't quite sure how to solve the problem. She wasn't about to hand bars of soap out to sixty-five naked men. It just wasn't in the job description. As she searched for the box with the soap bars in it, she mulled the problem over in her head. While she continued her search, Simba had gotten the entire shower room chanting, 'Soap ... soap ... soap." Kathy was becoming flustered. The only solution appeared to be to slide the box of soap bars under the curtain that separated the training area from the shower room. As she approached the curtain the chants became louder and soon everyone was stamping their feet. She was about to slide the box when Heidi walked through the door carrying an orange water jug. From the chants, Heidi surmised what the problem was. She stopped Kathy.

"If they want soap, well then I'll give them soap." Heidi handed the water jug to Kathy and picked up the box of soap bars. She turned her shoulder and pushed her body through the slit in the curtain. "Who wants soap?' she shouted.

Some of the guys had given up on the soap and were already busily drying themselves off. They quickly wrapped themselves up in their towels as Heidi walked by. She caught most everyone in the shower by surprise as they turned away from her when they realized that she had brought the soap. Heidi wasn't fazed in the least by the multitude of manhood. She was a manager back when there wasn't a curtain in the locker room and so what she saw now was nothing new.

Simba, taken by surprise, turned away for a moment. He then figured that he had gotten what he deserved. He turned and faced Heidi. He calmly walked up to her and grabbed a bar of soap. He'd been seen naked in public before. Saying thanks, he turned and began lathering. Taking Simba's lead a dozen other players walked up to Heidi and grabbed enough soap for themselves and their shy teammates who still faced the walls.

By the time everyone made it back from practice, it was time for lunch. Most of the team was starved since they didn't get a chance to eat a good breakfast, or lost a good breakfast on the side of the field after wind sprints. Now the freshmen were starting to sit with their own circles of friends, which even included upperclassmen. With each passing day, they had more and more in common with each other and the upperclassmen. But wherever these circles sat, they didn't sit too far from the table where Simba was, because he was the life of the party.

The regular practice wasn't until 4:30 p.m. that afternoon, but Coach Bonaventure made sure that their time was occupied. From one to two o'clock, the offense had a 'chalk-talk,' and from two to three o'clock, the defense had one. While the offense was in its 'chalk-talk,' the defensive players either took naps or else engaged in conversation in the living room of the Sigma Rho house.

About three-quarters of the football team were Sigma Rho's, and about three-quarters of the Sigma Rho's played football. It just happened that most of the players on the team had similar interests and decided to join Sigma Rho together. However, anyone was welcome to come lounge in the living room. Although some players felt uncomfortable being there if they weren't Sigma Rho's, the football players who were Sigma Rho's looked upon teammates as being similar to fraternity brothers.

When the offense was finished with its 'chalk-talk,' it was time for the defense. They waited outside the fieldhouse lecture room while Coach Bonaventure finished going over the last couple of plays for the offense. As the offense marched out of the room, the defense caught a good smell of the stench the sweaty offensive team had created. Foster tried to remedy the situation by turning on a small vent fan in the wall of the windowless room. However, the little nine-inch fan couldn't work fast enough as now-sweaty defensive bodies filled the room.

Bonaventure could hold his own as an offensive coordinator, but his heart was in defense. Although he wasn't as motivating as the night before, he made the defense get excited about the new strategy he had instituted. As Bonaventure explained it on the board and the team followed in their playbooks, it seemed flawless. In his excitement, he grabbed two players and used them as dummies as he demonstrated the correct technique for shedding a blocker and making a tackle. Foster chuckled behind his hand, because Bonaventure used him as a dummy last year. He felt it was the hardest hit he had taken all season.

The defense got out of the meeting at about ten minutes past three. By the time they made it back to their rooms, it was time to start down to practice. Each man with a car loaded as many as he could into it and drove toward the Stadium. Those who didn't have a full car drove the traditional Church Street to Chapin Street route to see if anyone was walking the distance.

It didn't take any longer than fifteen minutes for most of the guys to get dressed, so they had gotten down there by 3:30 p.m. For the forty-five minutes or so until practice started, they either stood along the sidelines listening to the stories or jokes that were being told, or else they were engaged in contests devised by the offensive linemen that were similar to Ford Motor Company's 'Punt, Pass, & Kick.' At about 4:00 p.m., the coaching staff pulled up in their cars and dashed into the locker room to change from their business or teaching attire into what they coached in. As they changed Coach Bonaventure gave them a last-minute briefing on the practice schedule.

At exactly 4:30 p.m., Coach Bonaventure emerged from the hollows of Strong Stadium and blew his whistle to indicate it was practice time. Without instruction, the team took a warm-up lap around the field and then formed lines for stretching. Even to the freshmen, this was natural, as almost every football team in America starts practice this way. As the team formed their lines, Doc and Foster, who would lead the stretching up front, started the team in a rhythmic clapping. At first, the clapping was slow, but as it progressed, it became faster and faster until someone would start it over again at the slow rhythm. This continued until Bonaventure gave them the signal to begin stretching. He would have loved to have them clap all day, because he knew that the electricity their spirit was creating was good, but he had a schedule to keep, and they were already falling behind.

Beloit College was affiliated with the NCAA, and therefore was bound by that organization's rules. One of the rules the NCAA had with respect to football at all levels was that the team had to go through three days of light practice (helmets and shorts) before it could have contact practice. Coach Bonaventure, although reluctant, complied with this rule. The team wished he hadn't, because all the light practice held for them was close to two hours of running drills and sprints.

The practice schedule did provide for a five-minute water break to allow the players to replenish the liquids they had lost. Kathy and Heidi were waiting with five gallons of water and five gallons of Gatorade. But the five minutes seemed short in their exhaustion. Their hearts hadn't recovered when Coach Bonaventure blew his whistle to start the second half of practice.

The second half of practice seemed to go a little faster than the first as this half was mainly devoted to going over the plays they reviewed in the 'chalk-talk.' Before long, the team was lined up for the last conditioning exercise of the day, the infamous 'Pittsburgh.'

During the '70s, when the Pittsburgh Steelers were, without doubt, the best team in professional football, Coach Bonaventure caught wind of a conditioning exercise they did. They split the team up into four groups and put them at four points on the field. When the whistle was blown, they had sixty seconds to get around the field. At the end of sixty seconds, the whistle would blow again and they would have sixty seconds to rest. If a player finished the lap in less than sixty seconds, he had more time to rest. If it took longer than sixty seconds to round the field, then he still had to complete the lap, but just got less resting time. They had to do this four times. Coach figured that if it was good enough for the world champion Pittsburgh Steelers, then it was good enough for his team.

To the freshmen, it appeared easy. The perimeter of the football field is quite a bit less than once around a quarter-mile track, so sixty seconds should be no problem. But they didn't consider that they were wearing football helmets and that it was at the end of an exhausting day. They soon learned the truth. The sixty-second rest didn't seem nearly as long as the time they spent running. And with each lap, they did not seem to recover as much as the one before.

The running backs, linebackers, receivers, and defensive backs had the least trouble of all completing Pittsburgh. Only a few failed to make it around the field in sixty seconds. However, for the linemen, the story was just the opposite. Only a few could make it around the field in sixty seconds with any consistency. Foster was not surprised that he could run like that. He put himself in his 'psych' mode and pretended that he was taking sidewalk blocks one at a time. Stubby, however, turned some heads as he stuck right behind Foster every step of the way. In the past, he could barely keep up with the pack that was yards behind him. This summer sure paid off, he thought.

When Pittsburgh was over, Coach huddled the team, most of whom were bent at the waist gasping for air, and told them how pleased he was with the first day. He then dismissed them to shower up and go to dinner. As the coaching staff met in the middle of the field to discuss how things had gone at each position, the players lined up for Gatorade.

Simba slumped at his locker. He pulled his sweat-drenched clothes off and opened his locker. A fan was pointed in his direction. He enjoyed the breeze. A freshman came up to him and tried to get him to make a sexist or crude remark. He gave the freshman a look as if he were too tired for 'fun and games.' He was one of the last to make it over to the shower. There was no soap left, but now he didn't care about soap because he was too tired to lather up. After he had dried off, he stepped on the scale and tilted it at 224 pounds.

11

The next morning, Foster had trouble getting out of bed at the usual time. The radio on his alarm clock turned on at 6:30 a.m. just like he had set it, but now it was 7:00 and he still was in bed. He felt as if he had not gotten any sleep at all. The truth was that last night he went to bed earlier than any other night this summer. Right after dinner, he came back to the house. He straightened some things out in his room, talked for a while in the living room and then went to bed. He remembered that the last time he saw the clock it read 9:10 p.m. and it was still light out. Now, he knew he had to get to breakfast in less than a half hour, so he forced himself to get out of bed.

As he stood up, pain immediately shot up his legs. All his joints were sore and the front of his thighs felt bruised, as if someone had beaten him repeatedly with a two-by-four. As he walked into the bathroom, he could barely bend his leg. Stiff-legged, he marched in front of the mirror. His eyes were barely open. He tried to stand in front of the toilet to go to the bathroom, but his legs were starting to shake from the strain, so he sat down to urinate. As he relieved himself, he tilted his head back and closed his eyes. He thought to himself, all that running, all that time in the weight room. You'd think that after all that I'd feel better than this. But the fact of the matter was that the better the shape he came to camp in, the more he pushed himself, and so he wound up being this sore whether he trained or not. The benefit of training, though, is that the soreness might go away faster.

When Foster was finished urinating, he didn't bother putting his shorts back on. As he flushed the toilet, he kicked them off and turned on the shower. He let the water run over his face for about two minutes, then he slowly turned off the cold water and turned on the hot water. When the water was as hot as he could stand it, he sat down in the tub and let the blast of water hit the fronts of his thighs. With his hands he slowly massaged them. The blood was beginning to move in his legs again and soon the stiffness was gone.

He let the steam that had accumulated in the bathroom roll out into his room. Quickly, he put on some clothes, combed his hair and then went out to the living room. Although he was still sore, at least he could move. From the living room, he met up with Doc, who was suffering from the same symptoms. Even though they were a little late, they continued the slow walk to breakfast.

Coach Bonaventure wasn't checking names off this morning. He trusted that the team would be there as he had requested. He was watching football practice at Beloit Catholic High School, where two of his sons played. He had earlier made all the necessary arrangements so Doc and Foster could run the 'Captain's Practice.'

The next two days were similar to the first: breakfast, Captain's practice, lunch, chalk-talk, regular practice, dinner, a little free time, and then to bed. The only real difference in these days was what was served at meals, what was talked about at 'chalk-talk', and a new conditioning exercise other than Pittsburgh was introduced each day.

These first couple of days were trying for everyone, both physically and mentally. More than once everyone, especially the freshmen, asked themselves, 'Why the hell am I doing this to myself? What am I doing here?' But quitting was never considered because quitting was something that few of them knew.

One of the most difficult things for everyone, except, of course, Coach Bonaventure, was trying to learn all the new names and associating them with faces. Coach Bonaventure used to be as bad as everyone else until he got extremely embarrassed one year when he called out to put Steve Riley in the last game of the season. The only problem was that the kid's name was Steve Ryan and not Riley. Henceforth, Steve Ryan was known as Riley and Coach Bonaventure made a point of learning everyone's name.

Again, freshmen had the hardest time. Coaches and upperclassmen only had twenty to fifty new names to learn. The freshmen had to learn everyone's. In addition to names of people on the team, they had to become familiar with an equal amount of street names, buildings, and later, their professors. Not making their tasks any easier was when someone on the team just happened to look like someone else they knew. Some names were similar to another name they knew. For example, it took Foster over a year to stop calling Paul Waterman, Pete. Foster knew someone from high school named Pete Watertown. Fighting the urge to call out the more familiar name made learning the new ones more difficult.

To help solve the problem, the coaches suggested that each player write his name on a piece of tape and then stick it on the front of their helmets. They believed that this would help them to associate names with faces. There was only one problem. The way someone's face looks in a football helmet is almost completely different than without one. So what happened is that people could only remember one another's names as long as the football helmets were on. Even Doc did not have his all-American looks with his head smashed in a football helmet.

During these first few days, nicknames were born as the coaches and upperclassmen tried to make distinctions between the various Mikes, Marks, Pauls or any other name that seemed to be popular that year. How the team decided on nicknames wasn't something that could be predicted. Stubby's, Mark Stubner, and Simba's, Dan Simpson, nicknames were obvious, but what about someone like Doc?

Doc had no association whatsoever with the name Todd David Wallace. And, Doc wasn't in pre-med. In fact, he got a D in freshman biology. The name came from something he had done. The winter of Doc's sophomore year, he was on an all-Sigma Rho intramural basketball team. The team was playing for the championship against the TKE house. The Sigs were down with about five minutes left, when Todd started shooting. He couldn't miss. As a consequence, the team won the championship and the name 'The Doctor' was borrowed from Julius Erving of the Philadelphia 76ers for Todd. Eventually, the name evolved to just Doc for simplicity.

With each passing day, the freshmen got to know one another and the upperclassmen a little better. Likewise, the upperclassmen were now getting to know the freshmen. At first, all the freshmen seemed the same, quiet and reserved. They all sat back and were trying to get a feel for the situation. But time was breaking them out of their shells and soon it was evident what type of people they were going to be. Some still were quiet and reserved, and others loud and full of jokes, like Simba.

Finally, the light practices were over. It was a definite milestone. The hardest conditioning they would have for the season was over. Being in shape was good, but everyone knew that what the coaches were looking for were people who could hit and be hit. Everyone was hungry for live contact, and tomorrow they would get the chance. The team that was lethargic the two previous nights was alive with energy at dinner as they planned how they would celebrate the end of this drudgery. In addition, tomorrow was the day that all the freshmen were supposed to show up on campus for orientation. Things were starting to look up.

After dinner, Doc called Carli at home to find out when she was going to get back to Beloit. She told him she'd be there in two days. He was excited about her coming back, but it also was a reminder that school would be starting in little over a week. That was about the extent of Doc's conversation because Stubby was in line to call Sue in Boston. There was only one phone in the house on which outgoing long distance phone calls could be made without using a credit card or making a collect call. Foster didn't mind that it was in his room.

As Stubby tried to talk to Sue, Doc and Foster both hovered over him and talked as if they were sexy women kissing on his neck trying to coax him back to bed. Sue knew the guys too well to fall for this. Stubby was able to push them off long enough to find out that her flight was coming in the night after next.

Foster quickly checked the agenda and reported to Stubby that they had free time for the whole evening. Stubby told her that he would leave right after practice to pick her up. She explained that he might be waiting at the Holiday Inn for a while because her flight didn't come in until 9:35. However, he then made it clear that he wasn't going to wait for her to take a bus up from the airport and that he planned to drive to Chicago and meet her at O'Hare. She was flattered. As they said goodbye, she said she missed him. His heart skipped a beat. He said, 'I missed you, too.'

To amuse themselves that evening, Foster and Doc decided to give the Jungle another chance. Doc figured that since the rest of the team was going, it really didn't matter where they were going. Foster thought that, just maybe, Jandi might show up. After all, that's where her friends went. Everyone, including the freshmen who were interested, met in the Sigma Rho living room. Just like going to practice, they all piled into cars and drove down to the Jungle Safari, which was in the opposite direction from the Stadium.

Again, the place was empty as Stubby led the way into the bar, but this didn't last long as soon all the cars arrived. Stubby was greeted warmly by the bartender. He ordered a pitcher of beer, but didn't get the chance to pay. It was on the house for bringing in all the business. Stubby didn't argue. He grabbed his pitcher of beer and put it down by the pool table and began putting quarters in the coin slots to retrieve the balls.

The bar was wild from the onset: Fifty guys with a lot of steam to blow off. For the upperclassmen, it was the macho test of trying to be perceived as somebody who could drink. Freshmen wanted to give the impression that they could hold their own, too. Bert led the antics, as he made every freshman stand on his head and chug a beer, known as a 'head beer'. Bert neither chugged beer nor did head beers, but he didn't have to, because, in his self-proclaimed role as the king-drinker, it was a do-as-I-say, not-what-I-do dictatorship.

Simba loved the bar. Now he had an excuse to do his animal imitations. Using one arm as a trunk, he made the sound of an elephant and picked up a beer with his man-made trunk and drank it. Again, he was the center of attention.

Doc sat on a bar stool at the end of the pool table. As Stubby gave a younger player a lesson in pool, Doc made comments to Stubby as if he were his mentor. Stubby was in a good mood since he knew that Sue would be back soon. He just ignored Doc's comment, until he inadvertently sank the eight ball and had to give his cue up to another player in line. He jokingly went over to Doc and grabbed him by the neck and pulled him towards the bar. "Come on, let's go do a shot."

As Foster walked up to the bar and asked for a Coke, the bartender gave him a look as if he were kidding. He pulled a dollar out of his wallet and set it on the bar. The bartender then realized he was serious and started to chuckle as he went to get the Coke. This didn't bother Foster. He had seen this reaction before. The bartender returned and refused to take the money. He thought the reason why Foster wasn't drinking was that he was driving one of the cars down to the bar. He hadn't. He had come with Doc, leaving his car at home. Foster was in season now, so he didn't even engage in the moderate drinking he did before.

As long as no one tried to push a beer on him, he had no problem with everyone else living it up around him. He didn't try to impress his values on others. Doc and Stubby came over and made him chug the last part of his Coke with them as they did a shot. They not only accepted that he didn't drink, but they respected it. As Foster finished his Coke, Doc paid to have it refilled.

As Doc and Stubby moved to the other end of the bar, Foster stayed down where he was, at the other end of the bar, away from the craziness. He couldn't get into the evening. He had steam to blow off, too, but he wasn't in the mood to do it. He sat and stared in his glass at the ice cubes. He was happy for Doc and Stubby that their relationships were going well. But that also reminded him of what he didn't have. As hard as he tried, he couldn't help but break his promise to himself not to think about Marianne. He missed the days of being with her.

As he tilted the glass up to get an ice cube out to chew on, the bar door opened and Lori and Sue came in. Immediately, they called out to Stubby, of course addressing him as Mark. They ran down to his end of the bar and gave him a hug. Then, Doc stepped forward and got a hug, too. Doc and Stubby started introducing Lori and Sue to everyone who was in their circle of people.

Foster noticed Lori, but stayed where he was. There was too much commotion down there anyway as everyone fussed over the only two women in the bar. After a while, Lori noticed Foster sitting by himself and came over to talk to him.

"Pretty unsociable aren't we, Foster?" Lori said as she sat down to his right on the bar stool.

"I'm just really tired," Foster answered. It was a good excuse to cover up what was really on his mind. Foster retrieved another ice cube from his glass and twisted his stool toward Lori.

"Have you heard from Jandi?" Lori asked.

Foster tried to appear as if it didn't matter one way or another whether he had heard. "Yeah, she called that night, right after we got home." He looked down at his pants and wiped some lint off his leg. "But I haven't heard from her since."

"I told her to check her pockets." Lori put her hand on his shoulder. "I thought it was pretty sneaky how you slipped her your number." She removed her hand as Foster blushed. When she caught his eye, she got right to the point. "So tell me, are you interested in her?"

Foster didn't really want to spill his guts on how good looking she was or that he spent a lot of time waiting for the phone to ring. He acted as if he had to give it some thought. Seconds later, "Yeah," he said calmly, as he slowly shook his head up and down.

Lori started to play matchmaker. "Well, why don't you give her a call sometime, then? I know she would be excited if you called. And I know she would like to go out." Lori continued, not giving Foster a chance to say anything. "She doesn't get many dates. I don't think she has gone out since she had..." Lori stopped for a split second. "Since she graduated from high school."

Foster's heart came back to life. All this time he thought she wasn't calling because she was occupied with a lot of other guys. It surprised him that she didn't have that many dates, but he didn't inquire why. "I don't have her phone number," Foster calmly explained, as if this were the reason why he hadn't made contact with her.

"Oh," Lori said, as she fumbled through her purse. Pulling out an ink pen and a piece of paper, she scribbled Jandi's number and handed it back to Foster. She put it in his hand and forced his hand to make a fist. "Now, give her a call. She's dying to hear from you." Lori zipped her purse shut and got off the bar stool and walked around to the left side of Foster. Foster was still facing right and looking at the piece of paper that she had scribbled on, as if he were trying to memorize the number. He sensed Lori's presence to his left and slowly turned her way. As his eyes met hers, she said, almost ordering, "Call." She turned and walked over where Sue was, to share in the attention she was receiving.

"Thanks," Foster said under his breath. He slipped the number in his wallet.

12

By 8:30 a.m., freshmen were already starting to arrive on campus. It was estimated that this year's freshman class would be the largest in Beloit history -- close to 250 freshmen and transfer students.

Beloit College is a small liberal arts college, with a total enrollment of about a thousand. It has a community atmosphere in its small Ivy League-styled campus, and always gave the impression that there were more students than the actual count. The low student-to-teacher ratio meant that professors were easily accessible. Some even preferred students to address them by their first names. It was a great school to get a personalized education, kind of like ordering a car custom-made instead of buying it off the lot. Students had the option of what features they wanted their education to have. Nothing was prepackaged.

Foster sat in the living room and watched carloads of suitcases, trunks, and laundry baskets go by. This was the first morning he had gone running since before light practices had started. Although he was at the bar late and today was a practice with full pads, he felt full of energy this morning. Much of this enthusiasm came from Jandi's phone number. His whole body felt tingly with excitement since last night. Besides, he didn't run very hard. He just wanted to loosen up.

He got home too late to try to call Jandi. He carefully took the phone number, which better lighting revealed Lori had written on the back of a gum wrapper, and taped it to the wall next to the phone. He planned to try and make the call sometime after practice tonight.

Foster walked home from the bar before the others were ready to come home. He was asleep before they got in, but judging from the litter that was in the living room, they had gone to Taco Bell after the Jungle had closed. Foster was one of about three people who made it to breakfast. It was good that Coach Bonaventure allowed them a reprieve from team breakfast. Foster quickly ate his six eggs, three bowls of cereal and five glasses of orange juice with Ed Conrad, a freshman from his hometown who knew Foster's sister. The conversation was refreshing for both of them since it seemed to bring a little bit of Houghton, Michigan, to Beloit, Wisconsin.

After breakfast, he came back to the house and did a load of laundry. He never really learned how to wash clothes correctly. He didn't separate whites and colors. He just washed in loads according to what he was going to need the next week. As the clothes dried, he wrote two letters, one to his sister and the other to a girl named Nancy he had met that summer in Houghton. Foster was a morning person, and never could do just one thing at a time. Coach Bonaventure always told him that he thought that Foster did more in the morning before 10:00 a.m. than most people did in a week. Foster always thought that stretched reality a bit.

After his clothes were dry, he quickly folded them and went back out to the living room. He knew that everyone would be getting up soon because it was nearing 9:00. They had dance aerobics in the field house at 9:30 a.m., from which Coach Bonaventure granted no reprieve. Foster walked out on the porch to see how the day was shaping up. It was going to be warm, but not unpleasantly hot like the past three days. It was a good day to have the first practice with full gear. He leaned against the south pillar and looked north at all the mothers and fathers helping to unload their children.

As he leaned against the pillar, a mother and her daughter walked north on the sidewalk that ran along College Street. Foster thought the girl was cute, and judging by her mother, she had good years ahead of her, too. They were coming from the bookstore. As they passed the Sigma Rho house, Foster gave a charming smile and a light wave. He mainly focused his attention on the girl. Both the daughter and mother smiled back, but didn't return the wave. The daughter casually leaned to her mother, so Foster wouldn't notice, and said, "I think I'm going to like Beloit." Her mother replied by expressing a wish that she were twenty years younger. Both were obviously taken by Foster's charm. Foster continued to watch as they kept walking on towards the Phi Psi house.

About that time, Simba had come downstairs from his room and watched as Foster tried to flirt with the girl and her mother. As the woman and her daughter walked beyond the point where they could see him, but not far enough so that Foster was out of sight, Simba yelled as loud as he could, 'HEY, How about a blow job?' The woman and the daughter turned immediately to see only Foster standing there, still looking at them.

It took Foster a second to realize what was happening -- that he was being framed. He didn't have time to deny it as the mother turned the daughter back in the direction they were heading and this time said loud enough so Foster could hear, "I want you to stay away from that house."

Right after they turned back away from him, Foster ran in the house, looking for Simba. Although he didn't see him actually do it, he knew only one person who would think of something like that. Foster was right. He found Simba on the floor behind the couch laughing hysterically. Foster hit Simba as hard as he could in the shoulder. Simba said, "Ouch," and grabbed his arm in pain, but he couldn't stop laughing. At first, Foster wanted to be mad. He had given Foster a poor first impression with that girl. But seeing Simba there splitting his side laughing, Foster only started laughing, too.

It really didn't matter. Football players and Sigma Rho's had always had bad reputations because a lot of people considered them to be one and the same. Since Foster was both, he never really stood a chance dating someone on campus. As hard as the guys tried to come across as nice guys, it never seemed to work out. A single incident would occur and then the whole story was blown out of proportion. The R.A.'s always managed to brief the freshmen women on how the guys in the 'football player' fraternity were. After a while, it got sort of amusing, especially the rumors. For example, women on campus swore that they knew for a fact that in order to get in the 'football player' fraternity you had to gang-rape a girl. Those same women could never really explain how it could be that men in their, quote, 'football players' fraternity were virgins.

Simba thought the whole problem stemmed from the time they rated the campus girls from the roof with rating cards the spring of his freshman year. The ironic part about it was that the girl who complained got the highest mark of the day -- a four. Simba said he knew for a fact that this was the highest rating because in making up the cards he didn't think they would need a card over a four, so they didn't make one up.

But neither the Sigs nor those non-Sig football players actually declared war against the entire female population at Beloit. Some of the women were sweethearts, and they gave the guys a chance despite any past reputations. For example, Sue, Stubby's girlfriend, Carli, Doc's latest,

Peg, Bill Buckley's girlfriend; and many others, knew that things were not always what they appeared or what others claimed them to be.

By 9:30 a.m., the entire team was lined up in the fieldhouse. However, they weren't exactly ready for aerobics. Most of them lay on the gym floor with arms shielding their eyes from the bright ceiling lights. Lying across the floor in almost perfect lines, they looked liked war casualties. They felt like it, too.

Patty, the school nurse, was bubbling over with energy. She slowly made everyone stretch and then she put her aerobic dance routine tape in the tape player she had brought. She started out with a couple of slow songs and then moved on to more upbeat music. Between trying to keep rhythm and trying to keep their breath, the entire team was hurting. Even Foster, who was in good shape and didn't have anywhere near as rough a night as the rest, was wishing that they were doing wind sprints instead. Kathy and Heidi stood off to the side pointing and laughing at selected individuals. The only thing that made the morning bearable was the music and Patty's good nature. The workout couldn't have ended soon enough, although once they got going, they had a good time.

After Patty was finished honing the football Buccaneers in her own special way, Coach Bonaventure took an opportunity to address the team. He quickly asked the players to give Patty a round of applause and then he revised his agenda for the team. Because today was the start of freshman orientation, many of the players on the team were going to be occupied with school activities. Coach felt that it might have been an oversight on his part to schedule a 'chalk-talk' for the afternoon, since so many were going to have to miss it anyway. Before he could finish saying the 'chalk-talk' was canceled, all the upperclassmen began cheering. An entire afternoon was theirs. The freshmen were indifferent, as they were going to be tied up anyway. Instantly, life was put into the team and they raced for the shower as soon as Coach Bonaventure dismissed them.

After lunch, some guys took the opportunity to regain some of the tan they had lost from the summer since football practice started. Others went shopping for knickknacks for their rooms. The guys who were stationed in front of the Sig house laughed at their freshmen teammates as they walked by toward main campus, rubbing it in that they didn't have any free time. The freshmen countered by pointing out the multitude of freshmen women they were going to be meeting.

Doc was also happy that the afternoon 'chalk-talk' was canceled, but not for the same reason that everyone else was. Doc still had several questions about the offense that were almost impossible to be answered in the 'chalk-talk.' He took the opportunity to stop in at Coach Bonaventure's office and meet with him on a one-to-one basis.

Doc wasn't the most ambitious student ever to attend Beloit, but he was one of the most eager students of the Beloit offense. If he could have memorized political theories the way he memorized his playbook, he would have been bordering on Phi Beta Kappa. Much of his spare time was spent studying past game films, trying to determine clues that would indicate when another team would blitz, drop into a zone, or go man-to-man. On Sundays during the NFL season, he could be seen studying each team's defense, trying to decide, given Beloit's offense, what play should be called. School was important to him, but it didn't interest him as much as football did.

It wasn't easy for Doc to step forward and voice his opinion about the offensive philosophy or a particular play. With every utterance, he feared reprisals from Coach Bonaventure. With most coaches, a player would be unable to utter so much as a doubt about what the coaching staff had devised. Coach Bonaventure was more than willing to spend the time with Doc. He was excited that someone shared his enthusiasm about what he and the coaching staff had put together.

Through this continual questioning and answering, and thorough analysis of every situation, Doc and Coach Bonaventure detected flaws in the present offense. They didn't always agree on what the solution should be for correcting the flaw, but when they finally arrived at an acceptable solution, it was sound football. After two hours of this session, both Coach Bonaventure and Doc felt that the team was farther ahead than after the 'chalk-talk.' When Doc left Coach Bonaventure's office, Bonaventure offered his hand and a thanks. As they shook hands, Coach Bonaventure said, with a sincere voice, "You are doing a great job out there. Keep it up."

Foster had everything he needed for his room, and felt he had too much to do to just bask in the sun. This free time was as good a time as any for deciding whether or not he was going to complete an application for a Rhodes Scholarship. He could hear his father saying, "Foster, it's an invaluable honor which would benefit you the rest of your life." Foster lay on his bed and paged through all the materials the college president, Edmund Hardesty, had sent him regarding the prestigious award. With Professor Ames' offer to provide him with a research project to supplement his credentials, it seemed to Foster that everyone was trying to get him to apply.

A thousand-word essay had to be handed in to the Beloit College Department of Scholarships and Fellowships for review no later than October 1st. Foster checked his calendar. He had a little over a month at this point. His mind weighed both the benefits and the drawbacks. What the hell, he thought. He realized he would never know unless he tried. The first step was to set up the special project Professor Ames talked about. He got out of his bed and put on something a little more respectable than shorts and a tank top.

Foster had no problem finding Professor Ames' office. It was on the second floor of the newly renovated North College building, where the Economics department was located, just like Ames had said. The door to his office was open, but he wasn't inside. Foster heard him down the hall talking to Professor Munson, the senior economics professor. As they laughed about an article that appeared in the *Wall Street Journal*, Foster figured that he would be returning to his office shortly. Foster sat on the window ledge outside the office, waiting patiently.

A short while later, Ames left Munson's office and was on his way back to his own. He was looking down at the floor, smiling about what he and Munson had discussed. He didn't notice Foster until he raised his head to take a drink of coffee from the mug he had.

"Foster, how are you doing? Have you been waiting here long?" Ames was somewhat caught off guard.

"No, I just got here." Foster stood up from the ledge and followed Ames into his office. "I hope you're not busy, because I've come to talk more about the special project you mentioned the other day." Ames was in the midst of another sip of coffee and Foster thought he'd better clarify himself, "The one concerning the Rhodes Scholarship."

Ames shook his head to indicate that he understood and that Foster didn't have to clarify any more. He pulled the coffee mug away from his mouth and sat it on his desk. "Sure, I've got time. Why don't you have a seat." Ames pointed to a metal folding chair that was directly across the desk from where he was sitting.

Foster took a seat. "Well, I guess I decided to apply for a Rhodes Scholarship, and like you were saying, a special research project might look good on my application." Foster had thought about what he was going to say, but it wasn't coming out like he had planned.

"You don't sound so sure of your decision." Ames peered over his glasses with a concerned look.

"I guess I'm not," Foster sighed. "It's a big decision, but then I guess it's time for me to start making them." Foster chuckled as he alluded to the fact that it was his senior year. Ames smiled and shook his head to agree. He reached for his coffee as Foster continued, "I guess I'm afraid of making the wrong decision and wasting a lot of time."

"Wasting time? How would you be wasting time?" Ames was polite in his tone, but didn't give Foster a chance to answer. "I mean, think about it." A perplexed look crossed Foster's face as he listened to Ames elaborate. "Just applying for the Rhodes will be an experience, even if you don't get it. And the project I would propose wouldn't be focused at the Rhodes. It would be an experience that would look good on your resume or a grad school application. So, how would you be wasting time?" Ames took a long drink from his coffee, waiting for a reaction from Foster. He winced as he tasted some of the bitters from the bottom of the pot.

"I suppose you're right." Foster smiled. Ames' logic was overwhelming.

Over the next forty-five minutes, Professor Ames and Foster discussed various alternatives for the project Foster could do. They finally agreed upon one that could be done through the assistance of the Admissions Office. It involved determining the differences between people who decided to go to Beloit College and those who decided not to, using regression analysis. Ames talked fast and Foster didn't understand everything he said, but he knew he would eventually.

Professor Ames had to cut his meeting with Foster short because he had to go to a reception for the freshmen over at the Union. Foster walked with him to the doors of North College and then went to the library to start work on his thousand-word essay for the Rhodes Scholarship.

Foster only lasted a half an hour over at the library. He could think of a half dozen ways to start the essay, a half dozen to end it, and about two dozen things to put in the middle, but none of them went together. He concluded that he was tired from football and since school hadn't started yet, his mind was not ready to be in a thinking mode. Without much wrestling with his conscience, he went back to the house to take a nap before practice.

Today was the first practice with full equipment. Team spirits were high like the first day. The three light practices they had had, plus the 'Captain's Practices,' gave them a solid conditioning base. And so the added weight from equipment did not make much difference.

After stretching, but before any drills were started, Coach Bonaventure gave his annual speech on the difference between pain and injury. He explained that pain was something one could play with -- it was only a discomfort to a player's mind. Being able to play with pain was a measure of toughness, and playing with pain was another way of existing out of the comfort zone.

But injury was something that was potentially damaging, not only to the individual, but also to the team. If a player continued to play with an injury, he could potentially be lost for a game, or even the rest of the season, because the injury may be aggravated beyond healing in the available time. Losing that player, for even a short time, would be detrimental to the team. This was a distinction he expected the team to know, another guideline to comply with his "only two rules."

Even though it was full contact for everyone else, the quarterbacks were only supposed to be tagged and not tackled by the defense. As a reminder to the defense of this exception to the full contact rule, Doc and the rest of the quarterbacks were given bright orange half-shirts to wear over their regular white practice jerseys. Coach Bonaventure considered the quarterback to be an indispensable commodity. Doc jokingly explained to the defense that the rule was meant to protect them from him and not the other way around.

The first day with full gear contact was held to a minimum. There was no live tackling or bumping of receivers by defensive backs. Bonaventure wanted to ease the team into full contact. First, they were to gain a feel for their equipment and then they could start knocking heads. The only scheduled live contact for this first day was between the 'trench men' -- the offensive and defensive linemen.

OUT OF THE COMFORT ZONE

The coaches set up a drill to work on pass rushing and pass blocking techniques. An offensive lineman squared off against a defensive lineman. When the whistle blew the defensive player had to get through to tag a coach standing ten yards back. The offensive player had to prevent this.

Stubby stood first in the offensive line and Foster took the lead for the defense. To each other they were the ultimate challenge this team could offer. Each felt he was being tested by the best the team's counter position could offer. As they squared off, it was evident that Stubby towered over Foster, but Foster's speed and agility made up for the difference in size. When the whistle blew, Foster faked with his head one way and then quickly darted the other. Stubby barely brushed him as he ran back to touch the coach. Foster felt elation. Stubby felt humiliation.

The next time through the line, Stubby and Foster didn't match up with one another. Instead, they were pitted against younger players. Neither had any problem in defeating his opponent. The third time through, Stubby and Foster were matched up again. As the whistle blew, Foster tried his head fake again. This time Stubby did not fall for the fake and knocked Foster on his back. Stubby hovered over Foster for a split second, enjoying his redemption and then helped Foster to his feet. They patted one another on the back as they went back to their respective lines. Matching these two against one another repeatedly was like observing the outcome of a coin toss. Sooner or later, the score between the two would be even.

Coach Bonaventure and the rest of the coaches allowed only limited contact. There were two reasons for this. First, with every tackle or block, the team risked losing someone to injury. And, second, there was a fine line between making certain that the team had enough hitting in practice to be confident that they could do it in the game, and making certain that they hadn't had enough hitting so that when the game came along, they were still hungry for it. The process was mainly trial and error. However, Bonaventure and his staff had the experience to know precisely when that point was reached. The trick was to end the hitting drills with the team wanting more.

Coach Bonaventure had scheduled Pittsburgh as the final conditioning drill. He lined the team up and let them run one lap. Their spirit and hard work all week had to be rewarded, he thought, as they rounded the three-quarter point of the field better than he expected. As they rested, the players fully expected to have to run three more laps. However, as the sixty-second rest time expired, Bonaventure called out to them, "Great practice, men. Keep it up. Now go hit the showers. You're done for today."

The whole team was slow to react. Everyone was too busy waiting for the whistle to blow as they were doubled over trying to catch their breath. Once what Coach Bonaventure had said registered and they realized that he was serious, even the freshmen had reason to celebrate. Simba led the dash to the locker room.

13

Even though Foster had promised himself that he would call Jandi after practice, he was slow showering and eating dinner. It wasn't that he didn't want to make the call, because he did. It was a simple case of nerves. He was never real good at asking women out, especially over the phone. He always preferred to end up on a date because it was part of a bet or else someone had asked him to go out. For whatever reason, he hated the feeling of having to take his heart into his hands and ask someone if they would like to do something with him. A rejection, he knew, would be crushing. He only asked women who really interested him, and he hoped that the relationship would continue for more than one date. He needed the reassurance of knowing two things: the answer would be yes, and there wasn't another guy involved. The fear of rejection always seemed to outweigh the benefits. Even though he had never really been turned down when he asked, and even though he was gaining more confidence, he knew that he probably would always have a little bit of anxiety when asking women out.

His hands shook as he tried to dial. Twice he had to start over as his shaking hand pushed the wrong numbers. As he pushed the last digit, he took a deep breath and felt his heart pound against the inside of his ribs. Finally, the phone began to ring. After it rang once, he quickly cleared his throat, expecting to have someone answer. As it continued to ring, he thought of what he might say. A joke to start out the conversation, or maybe he should just get right to the point. He swallowed hard. After five rings, his heart began to slow and his breathing became more normal. He realized no one was there to answer. After ring number seven, he hung up. He had wished, even though he was probably so nervous that he would have stumbled on his words, that someone would answer. Not necessarily Jandi, just anyone who could have let her know that he tried to call. Each time he called again, he was just as nervous. Each time he got no answer. After the fifth time he tried, he went to bed.

The next day was generally similar to the one before, but in a few respects, it was different. Today Coach Bonaventure didn't give any reprieves from breakfast. He had Kathy and Heidi there checking off names. No one minded, however, because all the guys wanted to get maximum exposure to the freshmen women. It was actually the first morning that everyone on the team showed up to breakfast showered, shaved and dressed at least semi-respectably.

Dance aerobics had a much better acceptance than the day before. It was amazing what a good night's sleep did for the team. Everyone seemed excited to be there, and most of the guys jumped at Patty's offer to have them do aerobics at the faculty talent show which was performed in front of the freshmen. Patty felt much more welcome among the team, and was delighted when a couple of players stepped forward to suggest songs for her to work into a routine.

Like the day before, Coach Bonaventure had to cancel the chalk-talk because the freshmen were involved in orientation activities. The team didn't seem as excited as the day before. By now, they were taking these little surprises for granted. In the afternoon, Doc didn't stop in to see Coach Bonaventure. He felt he had bothered him too much for one week. Instead, he spent the afternoon straightening up his room. He didn't know if or when Carli would stop by to see him, but he wanted to be ready.

For Bert and Simba, just lying in the sun wasn't enough. They went to K-Mart and bought an inflatable kiddie pool, set it up in the front yard and filled it with water. Then, they got in -- all four-hundred and fifty pounds plus of them. Bill added to the scene by playing lifeguard. He took a three-foot bar stool out of his room and set it up on milk crates. He climbed up in it, put dark sunglasses on, a whistle around his neck, and zinc-oxide on his nose. As freshmen walked by, they were amused by the two lugs in the pool and the third acting as a lifeguard.

Foster went to the library again to try to work on his essay, but found the same mental block as the day before. He still wasn't discouraged. He knew his ideas needed a chance to incubate. After he left the library, he went to the registrar and added the special project he and Professor Ames had talked about. He then went to try to drop the history class. He explained to the history professor that he was going to apply for a

Rhodes Scholarship and that the special project was a unique approach to supplementing his application. The history professor quickly agreed and signed his drop card. Foster didn't mention that he could have dropped any of his classes, but the history class was the one with $120 worth of books. Instantly, Foster only had to pay $130 for books.

Stubby spent his afternoon napping. It was going to be a long drive to O'Hare to get Sue. Once her flight came in at 9:30 p.m., he still was going to have to drive back to Beloit. Since he and Sue hadn't seen one another for about three months, he knew it was going to be a long night.

The spare time the team had this afternoon seemed to go by much faster than the day before. In no time, they were back out on the practice field. Before practice started, several members of the team entered into a debate on which team position had the toughest practices. No one could really support their own case, but everyone involved was busy trying to establish why other positions couldn't be considered to have the toughest practice. The defensive linemen were criticized for being allowed to have 'story time' each day when someone would get to tell a story, or to play leap frog. The quarterbacks were scoffed at because all they did all day was throw passes. Linebackers and defensive backs stood around and talked about the other teams' offense. Kickers never did conditioning. The offensive linemen did everything half speed, and running backs and receivers got to handle the ball the entire practice, which was more fun than everyone else's drills. Before anything could get resolved or before anyone conceded any points, Coach Bonaventure blew the whistle to start practice.

The practice went like the day before. There was more hitting but still not enough. Spirits were still high, but Coach Bonaventure didn't let them out of conditioning. As they ran eight 80-yard sprints, Coach Cain, the defensive line coach who was also a banker in town, made the sprints more interesting by telling jokes as the team ran. He kept track of the exact percentage of conditioning they had completed to the second decimal, and dedicated each sprint to anyone from Jerry Lewis' kids to the Red Cross. Coach Henderson, the defensive back coach, paced the players as he ran alongside them, encouraging them to give it just a little bit more.

Coach Bonaventure huddled the team up right after the final sprint. It was the end of their fifth practice, and Coach Bonaventure had to start making some decisions as to who would be starting. Bonaventure, along with the coaching staff, regretted having to make this decision. He felt that everyone had been working hard so far and wished that everyone could be a starter, but rules permitted that, at the very most, there be only twenty-two starters. Sixty-five players on the team waited for his decision.

Bonaventure explained that in his experience the best way to find out who 'really wanted to play' was to have an intra-squad scrimmage. Since they had been practicing for a week and had gotten through most of the playbook, he thought that tomorrow would be an ideal time to have a scrimmage. He was trying to keep the scrimmage atmosphere as close to that of practice as he could. Even though this was only going to be the first of two scrimmages and even though no final decisions were going to be made until after the second scrimmage, everyone's nerves tightened.

When Doc returned to the Sig Rho house, he found a note on his door from Carli. She explained that she had gotten on campus while he was at practice and that he was to call or stop by later that night. Energy surged through his body as he folded the note and put it in his pocket. He raced down to the living room like Stubby did when he had received the letter from Sue.

When Stubby got back to the house, he ran up to the bathroom next to his room and gave himself a quick shave with an electric razor. He put on some aftershave and then the same brand of cologne. He put on a pair of dressy jeans, a button-up shirt and a pair of cowboy boots. When he got out to his car, he quickly checked his wallet for money. He was going to have to stop at the automatic teller machine. He had enough money for tolls there and back, or he had enough money to get something to eat at McDonald's, but not enough for both.

As soon as Foster got back to the house, he made himself sit down and call Jandi. He tried not to think about what he was doing so he wouldn't get nervous. I'm calling to see what time it is, he thought, trying to trick himself. It worked. It worked until someone answered the phone at Jandi's.

"Hello," a woman's voice said on the other end.

"Is Jandi there?" The words stuck in Foster's mouth. He was so used to no answer that he was taken by surprise.

"No, I'm sorry she's at work. May I take a message?" the woman politely responded. Foster figured that it was Jandi's mother because he heard a young child crying in the background.

"Yes. Could you tell her Foster called?" Foster wondered if that would be enough information.

"Foster." The woman verified what he had said. She spoke as if she recognized the name.

Could it be possible that Jandi knew more than one Foster? he thought. "From Beloit College," he quickly qualified.

"Okay, I'll give her that message," the woman said in a hurry as if she needed to hang up quickly to attend to the child.

As Foster hung up the phone, he breathed a sigh of relief. The call was made. She would get the message. The ball was now in her court, he thought.

After Doc got down to the living room, he and Simba went to dinner together. Although they walked down to the Commons alone, they met several other teammates inside. He thought he might see Carli while he was there, but he didn't. However, on the way back to the Sig house, he spotted her crossing Emerson Street down by the intersection with College Street.

He stood in front of the Sigma Rho house, waiting for her as she came up the walk. He quickly finished the portion of waffle cone that remained from his ice cream cone and then wiped the crumbs from his face. She was walking with a couple of the women she hung around with. She was so deeply involved in catching up on what had happened to everyone during the summer that she didn't notice him until he was right there. As she looked up to see him, she smiled warmly. He had been smiling the whole time.

"Hi," she said with her head slightly tilted as she looked at him through her long, flowing brown hair. She stopped right in front of Doc and let her friends continue walking.

"Hi. I got your note." Doc spoke in a very low-key voice. He slowly produced the note she had written which he stuck in his pocket.

"Good. So does that mean you are going to call me or stop by tonight?" She kidded with Doc.

"Actually, I was going to try to avoid you this whole term," Doc kidded back.

"Oh, you were?" she said with a sly look. They still hadn't made physical contact. Neither of them was into the practice of affectionate greetings. Both of them were as nervous as if they had first met, and each searched for something to say.

There was a moment of silence between the two. They moved towards one another as if to kiss or hug. In this split-second, Simba, and his bad timing, came on the front porch. "Hey Doc, that dumb blonde you have up in your room wants to talk to you," he yelled. He started to laugh and then walked back in the house.

Doc didn't know what to say. He appeared shocked. Carli started to laugh. She knew Doc, and Simba, for that matter, well enough to know the truth. "Come on, you can help me unpack." She was still laughing as she motioned toward her room. Doc followed. As they walked along the sidewalk, their swinging arms hit one another. They took the opportunity to hold one another's hand.

Stubby was fortunate that he was traveling southeast on the Northwest tollway. The cars headed in the other direction were bumper to bumper as they made up the later portion of the Chicago rush hour traffic. As he waited to get his change from the last toll booth attendant, he finished off the ice that remained in the bottom of his McDonald's cup.

O'Hare International Airport was a little over ninety miles from the Beloit College campus. When Stubby saw the first sign directing him to the airport, it was 8:30 p.m. Perfect, he thought. He would need every minute of that hour until Sue's flight was supposed to arrive to find a place to park, get into the airport, figure out what gate she would be arriving at, and get there.

Sue's plane landed right on time -- 9:30 p.m. exactly. However, it was another ten minutes until it could taxi over to the gate where Stubby was waiting. Minutes passed like hours for both of them. As the plane started to unload passengers, Stubby swallowed hard to get rid of the lump in his throat. He couldn't believe he was nervous. He quickly checked to see if everything looked all right. He found the time to buy her a rose at one of the shops in the airport and hid it behind his back.

Sue was near the middle of everyone getting off the plane. As she rounded the corner in the boarding chute, she was busy talking to her female seat companion from the two-hour flight from Boston. She looked up the chute and saw Stubby. What the other woman had to say no longer mattered. She started to walk faster. Before she could get to him, he produced the fresh red rose.

"You shouldn't have," she said, taking the rose from him and smelling it. Stubby shrugged his shoulders as if he didn't have a reply. She quickly dropped her carry-on luggage and gave him a big hug and a kiss. He hugged her back, being careful not to squeeze too tight. When he released her, she quickly picked her luggage back up. He promptly took it from her and carried it in his right hand. With both her arms, she latched on to his massive left arm.

By the time they had gotten the rest of her luggage and found the car it was 10:15 p.m. They exchanged stories about what had happened since they talked two days ago. She sat as close to him as she could. Stubby told her about the scrimmage the next day. She said she was interested in seeing it. Right after they passed the first toll booth, Sue buried her head in Stubby's shoulder, watching the road out of one eye. It had been a long day of packing, fighting traffic to get to the airport in Boston, and then the flight to Chicago. After a mile or so as she slipped off to sleep, he put his arm around her and massaged her shoulder. Stubby relaxed in his seat and listened to his heart beat strongly.

Foster, a senior captain, started the year before and was everybody's pick to start again this year. To most, this would be a reason to relax. For Foster, this was all the more reason he had to have a good showing in the scrimmage the next day. All the years when he played behind Bob Loomis and Craig Vetter, two of Beloit's all-conference defensive linemen, he felt he had nothing to lose so he gave it all he had in the preseason scrimmages. Now he had everything to lose, which gave him the same motivation.

He sat on his bed polishing the white shoes he wore in games. Then he carefully laced them so they were tight enough to feel secure, but loose enough not to cut off his circulation. His door was locked and he quietly listened to a CD of movie theme songs he had made one summer. He tried to relax. The themes from the movies *Patton*, *Star Wars*, *Rocky*, and *Chariots of Fire* helped a little. At about 10 o'clock, he turned out the light and drifted off to sleep even though other members of the team were talking to freshmen women in the front yard.

At 12:30 a.m., the phone rang. Foster woke from a dream about football. He debated whether or not he should answer it. He thought it might be that same woman who had the wrong number the other night. After the third ring, he slowly rolled over in his waterbed and picked up the phone. The water swished back and forth as he tried to put the phone to his ear.

"Hello," he said with a groggy voice.

"Is Foster there?" A faint female voice was on the other end.

"This is," he responded without thinking. He was sure it was Jandi. Foster recognized the same voice from the last time she called. But he had to be positive. "Who is this?" Foster sat up in bed.

"Jandi," she said again as if Foster should have known.

"How are you? I've been trying to get a hold of you for a couple days." Foster tried to talk as if he hadn't been asleep.

"I know. That's what my mom told me when I got home." Her voice was still real faint.

"You should come up to the Jungle Safari tomorrow night. A bunch of us are going to be there." Foster thought that would be a non-threatening way to ask her out.

"I can't. I work second shift at Ingersoll Manufacturing down in Rockford." She tried to explain her schedule.

"Well, what time do you get off?" Foster quickly asked.

"Midnight," she responded without hesitation.

"Why don't you come up after you get off work. We don't have practice the next day so I'm sure we are going to be there late." Foster tried to work around her first excuse. "Lori will probably be there."

She paused for a moment to think about it. "Okay, but I want to come home and change first."

"Fine. I'll expect you a little after midnight. I'll sit right by the door so you can see me right away when you come in." He talked fast. "You do remember what I look like, don't you?"

"Uh huh," she said, sounding very sure of herself.

They talked for a little while longer and then they hung up. Foster was happy with the way things were turning out. As he put his head back down, he quickly fell back to sleep. In no time, he was dreaming about football again.

14

Stubby, as usual, woke up early. He let Sue sleep in as he took care of his daily routine and then looked over his playbook. Every couple of minutes he would take the playbook away from his face and watch her. After she woke up, he helped her move all her luggage from the trunk of his car to the Zeta Kappa Zeta house, where she was going to be staying for the year. He single-handedly carried both large suitcases, and she held on to the carry-on bag. As he bent down to put the luggage inside the door of the Zeta Kappa Zeta house, she gave him a kiss on the cheek. He blushed as her sorority sisters watched.

She was hungry. She hadn't eaten since noon yesterday. Stubby wanted to take her out for an early lunch, but it was too close to the scrimmage, which was scheduled for 1:30 p.m., for him to eat. So Sue borrowed Stubby's car and took three other Zeta Kappa Zeta's with her to get something to eat. Stubby went back to his room to go over his plays once more. But each time he tried to stuff the pages of circles and X's, his mind snapped back to the night he had just spent with the woman he loved.

The evening was a little less passionate for Doc. Upon returning to Carli's room to unpack, a half-dozen women from her floor stopped over to see her. As Doc unpacked boxes and handed the items to Carli to shelve, the other women sat around and giggled at nonsense that Doc didn't try to understand. It wasn't coincidental that these women happened to stop over when Doc was there. Doc was the most sought-after male on campus. He was the one interest that most women at Beloit had in common. Because of this, Carli was not only the envy of her friends, but also of women she didn't even know. As flattered as she was, it still bothered her that she was referred to as Doc's girlfriend. Although they never discussed the point, she felt that this made her lose her individuality.

It wasn't until about 1:30 in the morning that everything was unpacked. When it was done, Doc was walked back to the Sig house by Carli and three of the original women who were in the room. As Doc turned to walk in the house, he gently waved and said goodbye to the entire party.

He awoke about 10:30 the next morning still feeling irritated that her friends had stuck around all night. The least they could have given him was a couple of minutes to say goodnight to her alone. He didn't expect anything physical to occur that night -- or any night. That wasn't her way and Doc respected that. But somehow or another a kiss good night didn't seem like asking for too much. Patience, he thought, patience. Sooner or later he'd have a chance to talk with her alone, but for now the scrimmage, only a short time away, was what he had to concentrate on. Doc started to redraw each play in the playbook on scrap paper from memory. Since he was the quarterback, he not only had to know what he did, but also what everyone else did.

Foster lay on his bed and shut his eyes. It was almost 11 o'clock. He had been up for hours, and most of the morning, after his two-mile light jog, had been spent like this. He wasn't tired, just trying to relax. The radio was turned to WZOK and the top-forty tunes could barely be heard over the sounds of people talking as they passed by. He tried to block out his excitement about Jandi meeting him at the bar later that night. Every time he thought of her, he'd open his eyes and try to regain his concentration.

Foster didn't have to do much learning of a playbook. The only things a defensive tackle had to know were left, right, and straight. It was kind of ironic that one of the smartest players on the team (or so grades indicated) was the one who was least bothered by having to learn plays. Instead, he focused on the many situations he would encounter while playing on the line. With each situation, he envisioned what move or technique he would use to overcome it. Although a defensive player is taught the proper technique for avoiding a blocker or making a tackle, in the end, instinct would have to take over to get the job done. Continually going over each move that was taught him, in his mind, was Foster's way of making what he had to do 'second nature.' When Foster felt he had had enough, he got up off the bed, grabbed his shoes, and started the half-mile walk to the Stadium, all alone.

OUT OF THE COMFORT ZONE

At 1:30 p.m., Coach Bonaventure blew the whistle and practice started like any other day. Normally the practice field ran parallel to the Stadium. However, today Coach Bonaventure arranged to have the grounds crew put another set of lines on that were perpendicular to the Stadium. This way the offense would always have its back to the Stadium and would be trying to move away from it. Coach Nic set the film camera on top of the Stadium and now could get a back view of the action. This gave the coaches a better view of all positions than if the field ran the other way. In addition, they had the opportunity to see if each play developed – both offense and defense -- the way they had planned.

After the players did ten jumping jacks to end the stretching session, Coach Bonaventure huddled the team at the center of the field. He explained that the first-team offense would line up against the second-team defense and they would scrimmage for 20 plays. There was no punting. The offense had four plays to get a first down. If they didn't, the ball would be moved back to the starting point, which was close to the sidelines of the field running in the other direction. If the offense scored, or there was a turnover, either a fumble or interception, then the ball would also be moved back to the starting point. When 20 plays were up, the same rules would apply, as the second-team offense would be against the first-team defense.

This was the fairest way to give everyone a chance to show what they could do. Bonaventure felt he knew what the first-teamers could do, so this way he could see what the younger players could do against the veterans. This was the closest to simulating a real game. Besides, he knew the rivalry the offense and the defense had against one another. Scrimmaging the first-team offense against the first-team defense would only result in the injury of valuable players and perhaps even bitter feelings on the team.

Foster was on the first-team defense, while Doc, Stubby, Simba, and Bert made up a portion of the first-team offense. Although Bill came into the pre-season in better shape than he had before, and although his performance in the defensive-line/offensive-line drill had turned some coaches' heads, it wasn't enough to get him a position on the first-team. He was the anchor of the second-team offensive line, leading the freshmen and the sophomores.

Bill had been bounced around from several positions before finally becoming somewhat stable on the offensive line. He came to Beloit as a linebacker from Bloom Trail High School near Chicago (graduating with Stubby). However, he lacked the foot quickness to make it as a college linebacker, so the coaching staff decided to move him to defensive tackle. He was a sound defensive tackle. The only problem was that several sound players were already there. In fact, at that time Foster was only a back-up to two potential All-Americans.

Finally, Coach Bonaventure felt that the best way to utilize Bill's talents was to put him at the offensive line. The offensive line was solid, but it lacked good back-up people. If someone were hurt, the team would be forced to use inexperienced players, a situation which Bonaventure wanted to avoid. So Bill made the switch. He took it upon himself to learn the plays for all five positions so he could back up anyone. Bonaventure now felt confident with this versatile offensive line back-up.

Bill, at first, was content with this role. Anything to help the team was his thinking. Eventually, though, Bill's ambition was a starting position and he continued to work for that. However, none of the starters on the offensive line was graduating ahead of him. To get a starting position, Bill was going to have to beat out one of the regular starters. This wouldn't be easy, and he knew that. To him, scrimmaging against the first-team defense would be his chance to prove himself to all the coaches.

As the first-team offense huddled up for the first time of the day, Sue drove Stubby's car through the gates of the Stadium. She didn't go back to the campus after going out to lunch but instead came right to the scrimmage with three other Zeta Kappa Zeta's. Her interest in football was limited, but she did have an interest in Stubby and that's all the reason she needed to be there.

Her sorority sisters, although not as heavily involved, were interested in guys on the team. They moved within about twenty-five yards of the field and spread out a blanket to sit on while they watched. Stubby noticed her presence, but tried to put it out of his mind so he could concentrate on making sure he did his job on the field.

Carli also came to the scrimmage. She had walked down with some of her friends and they didn't get there until after about ten plays were finished. She walked right up to the field to look on. Doc waved to her discreetly, so the coaches wouldn't see, before he called a huddle. She blushed as the entire first-team offense looked her way.

Sue and Carli didn't know one another very well. To Sue, Carli was Doc's girlfriend, and to Carli, Sue was Stubby's girlfriend. As close as Doc and Stubby were, there was never any kind of double-dating or even an introduction. On occasion they would say hello as mutual acquaintances do when they passed one another on campus.

Part of this was due to Sue's wanting Doc to date some of her sorority sisters. So Sue didn't view Carli as direct competition, but more as competition to other Zeta Kappa Zetas, which was a natural reaction among sorority sisters.

Carli didn't dislike Sue, but just didn't feel an urge to go out of her way to be friends with her. Carli didn't agree with the concept behind sororities. She believed that they were a way for people to pay to be one another's friend. They noticed one another at the scrimmage and each said hello. Then they did their best to politely ignore the other's presence.

It was easy to tell whether the first-team offense or the first-team defense was on the field just by how the ball was moving. When the first-team offense was on the field not only did they get a first down within four plays, but they usually scored, too. The only trouble they had was running behind one particular offensive lineman, Charles Ellis. Big El, as he was known, was a starter from the previous year, but had returned this season in poor shape. Big El was the guy that Bill was hoping to beat out -- the weak link in the offensive line. Bill felt a sense of optimism as the second-team defense would stop the first-team offense for little or no gain each time a play ran where it depended on Big El's blocking.

When the first-team defense was on the field, the second-team offense only got four plays before the ball was moved back to the original starting point. Many times, when the ball was moved back to the original starting point, it would have to be moved forward because the defense had caused a loss of yardage.

The only time the second-team offense managed to get any kind of gain was when they ran behind Bill. Despite Bill's excellent blocking, however, they couldn't run behind him too many times because then the defense started keying on what he was doing.

No one really stood out on the defense. It was a combined effort as they all swarmed to wherever the ball was. Bonaventure was pleased to see this. This was the youngest defense he had ever coached, and so he knew that more than just Foster and a couple other veterans on the defense would have to come through for the defense to be effective.

Doc didn't have a chance to be tested. The weather was overcast and misty. It wasn't a good day for throwing, so the coaches stuck to the running game. Doc became frustrated when he realized that all he would have the chance to do was hand the ball off. He even knew that he would not have the chance to run the ball. Coach Bonaventure made him wear the orange half-shirt so he wouldn't be tackled, so it wouldn't be fair if he were allowed to run the ball.

After an hour and a half, Coach Nic yelled down that he was out of film. Coach Bonaventure gave both offenses ten more plays each and then he huddled the team in the center of the field. Separately, both Carli and Sue and their respective circles of friends went back up to the campus.

Bonaventure asked the players to crouch down on one knee. This signaled that he had a number of things to go over. In addition, it gave the coaching staff a sense of dominance as they had to look down to talk to even the tallest players to go over the points they needed to make. With Coach Bonaventure, one knee was the only resting position that could be taken. He felt that on two knees or sitting, the players' minds would start to wander. It also gave the team a lazy appearance as compared to the uniformity one knee gave the team.

Before Coach Bonaventure took over, he gave each coach an opportunity to say something. Most of the coaches kept it brief, but one started to ramble and began to talk about things that Coach Bonaventure had planned to speak on. This coach, Coach Gibson, was also head football coach at a local high school, so fire-up speeches were part of his nature, too. It was evident by the way Bonaventure reviewed the list of things he had to talk about that this made him restless. He started to look back and forth rapidly from his clipboard, to the players, his watch and then Coach Gibson. However, Bonaventure still politely let him finish what he had to say while searching for a new way to restate Gibson's points.

Bonaventure started by emphasizing the good things he had seen. He indicated that he thought that both first teams had done well, but he also mentioned areas they would have to work on. But the purpose of the scrimmage was to get more of a look at what the less-experienced players could do. He singled out about a half a dozen younger players and praised them for their play. As outstanding as his performance was, Bill received no mention. At first this made him angry as if he were deliberately overlooked, but then he rationalized that it probably was a simple oversight. He concluded that Coach Bonaventure might figure that the younger players needed the positive feedback more. Besides, the offensive line coach, Coach Terry, had called him aside and told him how impressed he was with the way Bill was playing. That, in itself, meant a lot, because Coach Terry had as much say in who was going to start as Coach Bonaventure.

Then Coach Bonaventure switched to the topic of whether or not a third captain would be elected. A lump immediately formed in Stubby's throat. He could feel his ears start to ring as Coach Bonaventure spoke. The coach reviewed the usual situation for the freshmen on how the team normally only elected one captain at the end of the season and the other was elected at about this time. Then he explained that both Foster and Doc were elected at the end of last season and everyone was wondering whether another captain was going to be elected. Stubby started to feel his heart sink as he thought that Bonaventure was going to tell them that there would be no election of a third captain. He started to waver on his one knee as Bonaventure began telling a story.

"When I was a senior at Colorado College, back when they had leather helmets, right Danny Simpson?" He pointed to Simba, expecting him to make that comment anyway. The team laughed as they directed their attention towards Simba. Simba smiled. That comment had crossed his mind. When the joking stopped, Bonaventure began talking again. "Anyway, however long ago it was, when I was a senior, the same situation occurred. Our team had already elected two captains in the fall after the last season when it normally elected one. I was sure that when it came time to elect another one in the preseason that I would be a shoo-in. So I worked real hard. I was first in line for every drill and hustled to demonstrate my leadership, just like a lot of you are doing. But when it came time to elect another captain, our coach decided we didn't need it. And so the election wasn't held."

Coach started to stare off in the distance as if he were having a flashback. "I'll never forget the betrayed feeling I had when I found out there would be no third captain." Then he snapped his attention back to his team. "So men, unless there are any real objections, next Friday we are going to elect a third captain. It doesn't have to be a senior, or a starter. You're supposed to vote for the person who you feel would help Foster and Doc lead this team. So, between now and next Friday, each of you think about that. We'll vote on Friday and then I'll announce the results before the scrimmage next week."

Foster, who was kneeling about three yards from Stubby, moved over far enough to nudge Stubby and say, "What did I tell you?" Stubby couldn't help but smile.

The first week had been a long one. So much had happened. Everyone felt as if they had been there a month. Coach Bonaventure knew he had demanded a lot of time and effort in the first week and he felt that the team, on the whole, had responded well. Everyone's schedules soon would be overloaded with school work and so he wanted to give them all one more opportunity to have a vacation before classes started. So Bonaventure, along with the rest of his staff and the two captains, decided that it would be best if the team had the next day off. He told the team to enjoy themselves, but to also keep in mind the two rules he had given them. Before he let them go for the next two days, he had them each do ten 40-yard sprints. The offense did its sprints as one big group with Doc calling out signals to start them. The defense broke up into three groups -- linemen, linebackers, and backs -- and had their respective coaches start each sprint.

With no practice the next day, everyone on the team was getting ready for a wild evening. Although dinner was over at 6:30 and no one planned to go anywhere until about 9 o'clock, everyone managed to start winding up. At first, they were all in the living room of the Sig house, joking about events of the week. Simba kept recapping the reaction everyone had when Heidi came into the shower room. Then the upperclassmen made each freshman tell a story about a girl they had been with in high school. The story had to be just right or else the freshman would never get a chance to finish it. If it was too good, no one would believe it. If it wasn't good at all, the upperclassmen got bored.

Again, Doc hit Stubby with an ill-placed bald joke and Stubby started to chase Doc around the living room. However, this time as Stubby started to take Doc to the floor, he slipped and Doc managed to roll over on top of him. With Stubby's great strength, Doc wouldn't have been able to stay there long, but Doc managed to call out 'Stubbypile.' This meant that everyone in the room was supposed to pile on top of Stubby, and they did, all fifteen or so bodies jumped and lay on top of Stubby. When everyone cleared, both Doc and Stubby were red in the face. It was hard to say who took the worst abuse, but when Stubby recovered before Doc, he put him in a headlock and rubbed his fist against Doc's hair.

After an hour or so, Bert returned from the liquor store with a bottle of Seagram's 7 and a bottle of 7-Up. When it came to drinking, 7&7's were Bert's trademark. He announced that he was having a pre-bar party in his room and that it would be BYOB, but he would provide the ice. Doc ran up to his room to get his car keys while Stubby took orders from the younger guys on what they wanted bought for them. Although the drinking age in Wisconsin was 18, it was cheaper to buy alcohol across the border in Illinois, and the older guys always had to buy for the guys who weren't 21 yet.

Bert, who lived just off the kitchen, had Jim Morrison and the Doors CDs playing on his stereo. The music played so loud that everyone in the room had to shout to hear what was said. Four people crammed onto each of the two couches he had in his room -- three lay on his bed, and several others stood in various spots around the room. Bert was out in the kitchen singing to the song while he mixed a strong drink for one of the freshmen.

Foster was able to put the noise in the living room out of his mind as he tried to work on his Rhodes essay, but when the party started down in Bert's room he threw up his hands and put it away. He didn't plan on doing any work on the essay tonight, but a couple thoughts came to him and so he figured he had better jot them down. He went downstairs and Bert offered to give him all the 7-Up on the rocks he could drink with the stipulation that he chug the first one with him. Foster agreed.

Unlike the first night they were there, the Jungle Safari was packed. And unlike the summertime, the bar was filled with students from campus. By now most everyone was back for the school year, even though classes had not yet started. The bartender was now a little miffed at Stubby. He raced up and down the bar trying to fill orders for drinks. Sweat streamed down his face. In desperation, he gave one of the local players on the team a part-time job, starting that night.

Bill was occupied at the bar, talking to his girlfriend Peg. She was a sorority sister of Sue's, only she was a senior. She was extremely well liked among the Sigs for a lot of reasons. Some were that she was very friendly, she gave the guys advice on women, and she was always game to go out for a beer. But more important was that most everyone in the house was in debt to her for typing their papers. She could type about eight pages an hour and did it while she proofread. Most guys sincerely believed that when she typed a paper the grade would automatically go up a half a grade because she did such a good job. She got Doc and Bert out of a jam more than once by agreeing to type a paper on the morning it was due. But as secretary-ish as her skills appeared, she was one of the top students in the class. She and Bill were the perfect couple.

Simba didn't join the party down in Bert's room, but instead sat up in his room and chewed tobacco while he read *National Lampoon*. When he showed up at the Jungle, he was rather dressed up, for Simba that is. He had on a nice pair of corduroy slacks and a polo shirt that actually matched. It was his new image. He always had the reputation of being sort of a foul-mouthed slob, but now he wanted to overcome that. He knew he could never become the heartthrob that Doc was, but he felt he had other qualities to offer. With the new school year, he was going to try to put his best foot forward and make a good impression on all the women. He felt he was long overdue to have a girlfriend, and tonight he was going to make some advances toward a couple of women he had had his eye on since his sophomore year.

Stubby played one game of pool when he got inside the Jungle. He won, but then gave the table up and went over to stand next to Sue, who was seated at a bar stool. Sue was talking with Peg when he came up from behind and wrapped his long arms around her and gave her a kiss on the forehead. She reached around and grabbed a hold of his thighs and leaned back against his body while finishing her conversation with Peg. In the meantime, Stubby exchanged some joking with Bill, who was sitting on the far side of Peg.

When the two women were finished with their conversation, they turned to their respective boyfriends. Sue grabbed Stubby around the waist and squeezed him as hard as she could. He then backed up against the bar and put his arm around her. Still sitting, she also leaned back against the bar and put her arm around him, except her arm was only long enough to reach into his far pocket.

One of the women that Simba had his eye on was sitting all alone at the bar. It was his big chance. He walked up to her and addressed her by her first name and then offered his hand to shake. At first she was uneasy. This wasn't what she expected. She expected him to start in with his foolish compliments, like 'a thousand bees couldn't make honey as sweet as your ear wax.' But that was the old Dan Simpson.

He sat down next to her and began asking her questions about her classes. He bought her a drink and they continued to talk. He wasn't being himself. He was being a true gentleman. It was easy for her to figure out that he had a crush on her. A couple of her friends looked on and laughed as they saw her speaking with Simba. She giggled back at them, but Simba was too love-blind to figure out what was going on. He just figured she was laughing at something he had said or else she was flattered that he was being so sweet. After about fifteen minutes, she told him that she had to go to the bathroom. As she stood up to leave, she made a motion to her friends that she wanted to stick her finger down her throat and throw up. Simba didn't see this. He ordered two more drinks, one for himself and one for her when she returned. He was feeling good. He felt that his new image was paying off.

Doc and Foster stood together at the jukebox, looking through the songs and making jests about the various artists and titles. There were at least a dozen other women at the bar who were interested in these two and it probably would have been worth their while to return that interest had they both not been waiting for someone else. Occasionally they would wander around the bar and talk to these women, but neither wanted to give any wrong impressions or get something started that they weren't going to be able to finish. However, they were as polite as they could be so as not to 'burn any bridges' just in case things didn't work out.

Carli walked into the Jungle looking as if she felt uncomfortable. Even though she was with her friends, it was her first time in this bar. She stood at the doorstep and searched for Doc. Her friends glanced across her shoulders as if looking too. However, they were more concerned with the numerous other women they didn't know (mainly Zeta's). This made them uncomfortable, too.

Doc saw Carli and called out to her. She couldn't hear over the sound of the jukebox and everyone talking. He started to move in her direction, but then stopped. He saw all her friends standing with her. Immediately, he had a bad feeling about the evening.

"Oh fuck," Doc said with a smile.

"What's the matter, Doc?" Foster started to laugh when he realized it wasn't critical.

"Carli's friends are here. They hang by her like bodyguards." Doc looked over at them and then back at Foster. "I don't think I've had a moment alone with her since she's returned. Fuck."

"Oh relax, I'll take care of the situation." Foster led the way over to Carli.

When Foster got over to Carli, he greeted her. She could tell he was up to something when he pushed her towards Doc. Doc grabbed her in his arms as she was forced his way. Doc still was curious as to what Foster was up to.

Foster proceeded to walk up to Carli's friends and greet them. "I know you all don't know me, but my name is Foster. Doc has told me an awful lot about you guys." The women looked at one another and giggled. They weren't used to the attention. He shook all their hands and took the time to make sure he had each of their names correct.

By then Doc had caught on to what Foster was doing and used his stall to get two drinks and then sneak Carli outside. Foster continued the act by introducing the group to various freshmen he had come to know. Although these women weren't the best looking at the bar, the freshmen immediately took to them. To a freshman who has dated younger high school girls for the last four years, the thought of someone older was an ego booster.

After Foster had distributed all of Carli's friends among the circles of freshmen football players, he took a seat at the bar. He was close to where he was the time before. He ordered Coke and sat there watching over everyone. He looked at the bar clock and saw that it was 12:10 a.m. -- bar time. He thought to himself, that means it's actually midnight; Jandi just got off work. Time seemed to slow as he continued to wait.

Simba was patient for about twenty minutes. He knew that a crowded bar always meant a long line at the bathroom, especially the women's bathroom. However, twenty minutes was more than ample time. The ice cubes in her drink were nearly melted. He turned on his bar stool away from the bar as if he were going to get up to go look for her. He saw her immediately. She was in one of the only booths at the bar, making out with another guy. The few seconds he watched seemed like hours. He turned back to the bar in shock. He could still see them in the bar mirror. He looked down. He didn't know what to feel: hurt or anger. First was anger.

Foster had seen Simba with the woman earlier, and he also saw Simba's reaction. He immediately went over to him. "Simba. Are you okay, buddy?" He rested his hand on Simba's shoulder.

By that time, Simba was breathing heavily, trying to control his anger. "Yeah," wheezed out of his mouth. He shook his head, too. He grabbed the drink he had bought for her with a tight fist.

"You aren't going to do anything crazy, are you?" Foster was worried. Simba didn't know how to control his rage. "She's not worth it. Whatever you're thinking, she's not worth it. Okay?" Foster pleaded.

Simba quickly downed the drink. The ice cubes had melted down enough so he could swallow them whole. "I just need to get out of here." He stood up from the bar.

Foster started to follow him. Unsure, he said, "Yeah, let's go for a walk." Foster was no longer concerned about meeting with Jandi. Simba's well-being was his first priority.

Simba turned back to Foster and lifted his drooping head. He looked Foster in the eye and said, "I just need to be alone, okay?" Since Simba couldn't be angry, the only alternative was being hurt.

Foster could see the hurt in his eyes. It reminded him of how he felt when he and Marianne had broken up. He stopped in his tracks. "Okay." He stood and watched Simba leave the Jungle.

Doc and Carli weren't alone outside in the 'Beer Garden,' but at least everybody else out there was keeping to themselves. Doc finally had a chance to be alone with Carli. What they talked about wasn't really any different than when her friends were around, but now he felt more comfortable saying it. Together they shared a pitcher of beer, as they discussed topics like football, the best professors on campus, and the various gossip each of them accumulated since they had gotten back to school.

After the pitcher was empty, she said she was tired and wanted to go home. Doc offered to help her find her friends, but she was happy to be rid of them, too. She explained they were good friends, but even too much of a good thing was bad. She asked if he would walk her home. He agreed and they walked out of the back gate, hand in hand, without saying goodbye to anyone.

Foster thought he had been waiting forever when Jandi finally came through the door. After the door had closed behind her, she was reluctant to go any farther. She felt as if the music stopped playing and everyone stopped what they were doing to look at her. It was intimidating for her. She was in a bar where she knew no one else. Foster called to her and offered her a bar stool right next to him. She was still uneasy, but came over and sat down. Although she hardly knew him, she knew him better than anyone else in the bar.

"Can I get you a drink?" Foster asked. She shook her head yes. "Beer?" Before he could name anything else, she shook her head again. "What kind?" She shrugged her shoulders to indicate that she didn't care. Foster caught the attention of the bartender and ordered two Bud Lites. The bartender was so surprised to see him order a drink that he tried to give them on the house. Foster declined, though. He would have felt cheap offering her a drink that he didn't have to pay for.

She took her drink and poured about half of it in the glass. Foster thought to himself that this wasn't the same woman he had seen drunk a little over a week ago. He continued to watch her as she sat there quietly drinking the beer slowly. Some time passed without either of them saying anything. Foster thought that he had better break the ice before the evening turned into a disaster.

"How was work?" Foster took a drink of beer. He noticed that she was occupied with looking around the bar at all the people she didn't know.

"Okay." She continued to sip her beer slowly. Several people turned to stare at her. Everyone knew she was there to see Foster, so they were curious. He rarely had a date. She began to feel self-conscious.

"Where did you say you work again?" Foster asked.

"Ingersoll Manufacturing." She had answered almost immediately after the question was asked. This time she didn't even move her head to look at Foster. She stared back.

Foster continued to try and break her out of her shell. "What do you do there?"

"I clean offices." She again quickly explained as she continued to look away.

At that point, Foster realized how out of place she must be feeling. Although she dressed as nicely as everyone else in the bar, she worked as a janitor, whereas the other people in the bar were college educated. Not that it made a damn bit of difference to him, but she was probably worried as to how she would be accepted by college women. Foster quickly drank the rest of his beer and got up off the bar stool.

"Come on, let's go for a walk." He wasn't so much commanding her, but just finally agreeing with what was on her mind. He knew that this would be the only way to really get to know her. She didn't even finish her drink before she sat it down. She got off the stool and quickly walked out the door Foster held open for her.

Foster didn't know about Jandi at this point. He knew she was nineteen and had graduated the year before from Harlem High School in Loves Park, Illinois. He knew that her last name was Parks, and that everyone in the Parks family had a first name that began with a 'J.' And, he also found out that her cousin, Matt, whose real first name was Joe, was his roommate freshman year. But he had gotten all this information from Lori and her friends. Jandi told him nothing.

As they walked along the sidewalk, she was still quiet. Foster reached over and grabbed her hand to try to hold it. She didn't take her hand away, but then she didn't hold on to Foster's hand very tightly either. When they had almost gone completely around the block, Foster suggested that they have a seat on a set of stairs that came down from an apartment building. She was still quiet and avoided even looking at Foster. He rubbed his thumb all over the back of her hand, massaging it. He was all out of things to say to try and get her to communicate, so he sat there quietly too and watched cars drive by.

"Can I tell you something?" Jandi spoke. It was the first full sentence Foster had heard her say all night. He was in such disbelief that she had said something that he was unable to talk. He nodded his head yes. "You're probably going to have nothing to do with me when I tell you this, but I have to tell you because you'll find out sooner or later."

Foster couldn't imagine what could be so bad. His heart started to pound. The only thing that came to his mind was that she used to be a man and had a sex change. Boy, if that were the case, he'd never hear the end of it from the guys. Well, at least he hadn't slept with her or him. "What?" He could barely enunciate.

"I've got a kid." Jandi came right out and said it. Foster looked at her as if he didn't understand. She elaborated. "The child you said you heard my mother taking care of...well, that's mine."

She went on to explain that two years ago she had gotten pregnant by her boyfriend. She didn't agree with abortion and before she could marry her boyfriend, she caught him in bed with another girl. So a little over a year ago she had a baby girl named Jennifer. Her mother took care of Jennifer while Jandi was at work.

Foster didn't know what to say, but he knew that he still wanted to see her. He wondered how he would explain to his parents that he was dating a woman with a child. But then he figured the only difference between an unwed mother and a woman who had an abortion was a sense of responsibility and commitment. He wasn't going to fault Jandi because she had those qualities. Foster leaned over and kissed her on the cheek in a passionate enough manner to indicate that he was still interested in her. He looked her in the eyes and smiled. She was unsure at first, but she also smiled back. He got up on his feet and took her by the hand. As they started walking back toward the Jungle, she held his hand firmly.

Doc took Carli home and they kissed on the stairs outside her building before she went inside. They had taken the long way home, so it took an hour for them to get from the Jungle to where she lived in Chapin Hall, which was just above the Commons. He didn't want to go back to the Jungle at this point. By the time he got back there, it would be about time for the bars to close.

When he got back to the Sig house, immediately upon entering the door by Foster's room, he came upon Simba, who was drunk. After Simba left the Jungle, he stopped off at the Coffee Haus, which was a bar that was located right on campus. He continued to drink like he did just before he left the Jungle. At the Coffee Haus, after he had six or seven drinks, he threw his glass against the wall. When some of the regular patrons tried to get him to leave, he punched a guy and then walked out with a full pitcher of beer. No one pursued him or the pitcher of beer. They were all happy that he was gone.

Doc found him leaning up against the wall, drinking beer out of the pitcher he had taken. He swayed back and forth. His eyes were bloodshot and glassy. He was very drunk. The nice shirt he was wearing was torn and it was wet all down the front from the beer he didn't manage to get in his mouth.

Foster had told everyone about the incident with Simba, so Doc knew what the problem was. However, he couldn't get a word in before Simba started.

"Fuckin' bitches. All the women on this campus are fuckin' bitches." He swayed, taking another drink of beer. Most of the beer spilled out the side of the pitcher and down his chest. He could only focus enough to discern that he was talking to Doc.

"Simba, they aren't all like that." Doc tried to be sympathetic. "Just think of it as her loss. There are plenty of girls out there who would like to go out with you. It's just a matter of finding the right one."

Simba wasn't listening to Doc's reasoning. Even if he did listen, the chances are that in his state he wouldn't have been able to understand. "You know what all women are?" He didn't wait for an answer. "They're all Mollusk Crustaceans." Simba referred to a term he learned in biology describing a snail. It didn't make any sense, but to him it sounded good.

Doc realized that he wasn't listening. "Come on, Simba, let me help you up to bed." Doc grabbed his arm gently. He figured that Simba would be all right if he could get him to sleep it off.

Simba moved away from Doc's grip. "No, I'm going down to watch some T.V. You can go to bed." He staggered.

"Okay, will you be all right?" Doc was concerned about the depression Simba was feeling, but he was too tired to try and reason with Simba in his intoxicated state.

Simba swayed as he shook his head "yes." Doc moved around Simba slowly. As Doc started to go up the stairs to his room, he heard Simba fall down the stairs leading to the basement television room. The sound of the glass pitcher shattering as Simba hit the landing echoed through the stairwell. All Doc could envision was the cut he had seen once on a man's face from being hit with a beer mug. Doc's heart began to pound.

"SIMBA!" Doc cried out, as he raced down the stairs.

When he got down to the bottom, he breathed a sign of relief as

Simba didn't have a single cut on him even though he was surrounded by silver dollar-sized pieces of jagged glass. Simba sat there, still tightly gripping the handle of the pitcher, which still had the bottom attached to it. The tumble hadn't sobered Simba at all. Doc positioned himself in front of the beer-soaked Simba and placed his hands on the wet shoulders.

"Are you all right?" Doc said reflexively. His voice was panic stricken.

Simba looked Doc in the eyes. His drunken eyes started to well up with tears. As the first tear rushed down his face, he tried to speak. He had trouble enunciating. Then all at once it came out. "How come they don't like me?" Those were the only words he could get out before he started to bawl.

Like reaching for his mother, Simba grabbed around Doc's body and held him tight. The broken pitcher fell out of his hands onto the floor. Doc held Simba's head on his shoulder to comfort him. "I guess they just don't know you like we know you." Doc was very gentle.

15

The next day Simba didn't remember much about the previous evening. When he finally got up about noon, he understood why he was hung over, but could not understand why his body was so sore. By the time Doc got around to telling Simba what happened, he had already heard bits and pieces of the incident from a number of people. He laughed to hide his true feelings. He was hurt, but he wasn't going to let it change his good nature. Doc was right. She wasn't worth it and sooner or later someone would come along who understood his personality and appreciated him for it. He resolved himself to the fact that he might not find that person at Beloit College, but then he only had one more year there.

Simba wasn't the only one who couldn't remember much about last night. In fact, there were several people who wished that Coach Bonaventure had made them practice that day so they would have been a little more moderate in their actions. Bert was one of them. Between his pre-bar party, the bar, and the post-bar party to finish off any booze from the pre-bar party, he spent most of the day either in bed or hugging the toilet bowl. By now he was quickly becoming a legend among the freshmen.

No one had much planned for the day off. Most people didn't know the free day was coming, and those who did didn't have a lot of time to plan something to do. With all the running around the team had done during the week, it was nice to just sit and relax. People called home to check in with their parents, ask for money, and let them know how football was going. The guys who had family nearby went home for a day of home-cooked meals and to have their mothers tend to the dirty laundry they had accumulated over the past week. These were the guys who always had a fresh supply of clean underwear and socks.

Coach Bonaventure had picked a good day to give the team free time because it was the start of the NFL regular season. For a better part of the afternoon, all the seats in the TV room were lined with hungover bodies dressed in bathrobes cheering for their favorite team.

Because of Beloit's location, there was a constant debate between Chicago Bear fans and Green Bay Packer fans on the team as to not only why one team was better than the other, but exactly how poor the other team was, using any criterion including this week's games, the NFL preseason, or even season records dating back ten years.

Despite the team's day off, classes would begin in just a few short days, and everyone had quite a bit to do. Once again, it was time to stock up on pencils and paper for the semester. Everyone began the semesterly bargain, borrow and trade of textbooks for the various classes. There weren't many classes that someone on the team hadn't taken. With the team's built-in network, it was easy to find used books for classes to either borrow, buy cheap or trade for books someone else needed.

For a person majoring in economics or philosophy, it hardly made sense to pay $75 for a freshman-level biology course, only taken because they needed a lab science. Because of the size of Beloit College, there was only one bookstore. Books were sold at a premium and then bought back at heavily depressed rates. A true monopoly. However, the almost underground exchange on the football team made for considerable savings each semester.

Just as everyone on the team was beginning to be comfortable with the routine of football by day/Jungle Safari by night, classes began. By the time one figured in practices (including getting there and back, getting suited up and showering), film sessions, and games, football took about 30 hours a week. On the whole, this affected how the team members performed in school. However, there were the exceptions, who seemed to do better during the season because it required them to be more disciplined. They knew that when they weren't on the field they had better be studying, but without football they didn't know when to stop playing around and when to start studying.

With Coach Bonaventure, school always came before football. No exceptions. As classes began, he took the time to emphasize this more than once. There were no breaks for the athletes, nor were there any easy courses to pad the schedules. The players on the team had to 'sink or swim' just like everyone else at Beloit. Bonaventure had scheduled practice around any class conflicts. The last class each afternoon ended at 4 o'clock and there weren't any evening classes until 7 o'clock. Any player could easily get from class to football and back to class with little problem. And if ever someone on the team was having problems with school, either falling behind or studying a subject that was particularly difficult, then Coach Bonaventure would do one of two things. He would allow the player to miss practice, without jeopardizing their possible starting status on the team until they got caught up. Or, sometimes, in extreme cases, he would pull whatever strings he could to get that player the appropriate tutor or special instruction.

To Bonaventure, school was more than important, it was the main reason everyone was at Beloit. Bonaventure had Beloit College football in perspective. It was only an NCAA Division III football program. That meant that no one on the team had any sort of athletic scholarship. Unlike many larger institutions, it was college that gave these guys a chance to play football, not football giving them a chance to go to college.

Bonaventure thought that athletics were great. He wouldn't have traded his days as an athlete for anything. However, he knew that he had to put athletics in perspective, too. It's not a career; only a fortunate few can have a professional football career. At some point, it all ends and all that is left are memories, and even fewer people could make a career out of those. Sooner or later, a person was going to have to rely on his mind. He advocated making the most of the education Beloit College offered. He didn't feel this meant being on the Dean's List or any other academic standard, even though those are nice goals to set. To him, getting the most out of one's education wasn't so much being concerned with grades; that's a short-run measure. Getting the most out of the education was being concerned that the players learned something, that they enjoyed what they were learning, and that they were able to use what they had learned.

This philosophy must have been correct because only those players who held to it in some respect survived the academic rigors of Beloit College. Most players on the team came to Beloit with this philosophy already ingrained in their minds. Most players were good students in high school. However, like most college students, they had to learn that the days of studying one hour for a high school test were over and that the effort to get A's and B's in high school probably translated to C's and D's in college. Despite all that was said on campus about the football players, Bonaventure felt that his team's average was equal to the campus academic average. Some players on the team, like Bill Barton, Foster Addison, and several others, excelled so much in academics that the average was, in fact, quite respectable.

The first day of class was overwhelming, leaving everyone feeling behind. This was a situation that couldn't be avoided, not even by the best students. The team helped the freshmen by explaining that the professors always expected the class to have read a chapter or two from the textbook before they came into class. However, there never was any way to determine what this assigned reading was until they got to the first class because it wasn't until then that the professor got around to handing out a syllabus or class assignments. But to add to that, professors usually front-loaded the class. All the tough assignments and much of the work were placed at the beginning of the semester. By hitting the ground running, students could have the opportunity to gauge whether they were capable of handling the course requirements before it was too late to drop that class and add another.

For the football players, especially, this contradiction became a real conflict. The sense of being overwhelmed usually won out. There were only so many hours in a day, many of which were already committed to football. Soon the sense of a new beginning turned into a sense of just let me get through the semester.

With the start of classes came the second week of football practice. The team didn't look anything like it had just one week ago. Instead of the stretching being marked by loud counting and clapping, now it was marked by signs of disinterest, personal conversations, and yawns. The spirit and energy displayed in drills became going through the motions. The coaches did their best to motivate the team, but experience told them that its lethargic state was inevitable.

Instead of having afternoons and evenings to rest, now everyone had to be at class or plowing through the mountain of homework they received each day. However, the major cause of disinterest was the schedule. Despite the day off, the team still had one week of practice in, but it still had two weeks to go until the first game of the season. The incentive to be spirited wasn't there.

To each of the players, football was about games, not practices. At this point, everything seemed needlessly repetitive to the team. They were ready to put to the test all their hard work. Each day seemed to trickle by. But eventually Monday, Tuesday, Wednesday, and Thursday passed.

Not only was the week over, but the last hard week of football practice was over. Friday, Coach Bonaventure intended to institute the team's special teams (kicking, punting, kick receiving, and punt receiving). That was not so much a light practice, as opposed to just a change of pace. Then Saturday, another intrasquad scrimmage, Sunday the day off again, and then it was game week. From here on, everyone thought they could make it.

Foster learned quickly as a freshman at Beloit that to do well, one had to be disciplined. Although he felt overwhelmed like everyone else, he discovered how to use this to his advantage. Instead of looking ahead at what studying he still had to do, he would look back at all he had completed. Every night after dinner he would go to the library as quickly as he could and start, piece by piece, to get through the work. He kept a log of what he had to work on, indicating its priority with respect to joint value of the course and due date. He always stayed ahead in his coursework. Others on the team, who marveled at his ability to keep up with school, termed him a 'machine.'

By Friday of the first week, Foster felt comfortable with his studies. He decided to utilize the spare time in the afternoon before practice to work on his Rhodes essay. But again, he ran into the same mental block. It was all there, but it wasn't going together. He put the notebook he was using to draft the essay aside and sat back in his chair as he gazed out the library window. Then he remembered that when President Hardesty first approached him about the Rhodes Scholarship, he had mentioned various professors on campus who had a connection with the Rhodes. They weren't necessarily Rhodes Scholars, but just people who knew something about what the selection committees might be looking for.

Foster went to each professor with hopes of getting help sorting out the many ideas he had. But instead he seemed to get advice that either messed up the ideas he already had or else added to the number. One professor provided him with a pamphlet on the Rhodes which did nothing but reiterate what he already knew. Another provided Foster with a list of six or seven books to read on Social Darwinism, which were 'must' readings before he wrote any more on the essay. The final professor listed questions that Foster should think of answers to because these questions might come up in the Rhodes interview.

Foster politely thanked each of them. By now his frustration had turned to a headache. He went back to his room and thought about what each professor had offered. Back to square one, he thought. He again started to look over the notes he had taken on the various introductions and conclusions he had. Nothing came to his mind to fill in between. "Fuck it. Go to practice," he said to himself. He put the pamphlet and the list of books he received in the notebook and threw it on his desk. As he locked his door he tried to relax the muscles in his neck to get rid of his headache.

The spirit at practice was much improved over the rest of the week. Coach Bonaventure was relieved that the depression period had passed. Although he knew that the team would experience highs and lows throughout the season, he hoped to try to minimize their effects. Usually the low periods occurred when the team lost a player to either an injury or attrition. This season they had been lucky -- only one person quit and the injuries were minor.

Bonaventure huddled the team right after practice to talk about the scrimmage they were having the next day. Because the first game against North Central College was going to be under the lights, it had been arranged that the scrimmage would be under the lights so quarterbacks and receivers could get used to the circumstances. Just before the scrimmage, the team would be getting pictures taken for the program and for media use. Finally, he reminded them to vote for the third captain when they got to the locker room.

Before Coach Bonaventure could finish and dismiss the team to shower up, Simba quickly stepped forward to speak. "Hey, I'm not proud." Coach Bonaventure, who had been interrupted, turned to hear what he had to say -- along with the rest of the team. "I'd like to take this opportunity to announce my candidacy for captain. I'd appreciate votes from anyone." Everyone laughed.

Bonaventure found this to be a great note to end practice on.

During the football season, not only was there a strain on bodies and minds, but also on relationships. Coach Bonaventure never spent the time he wanted to with his family during the season. Once practices began, he arrived at the college earlier to plan practices and then would stay late for coaches' meetings. On Saturdays, the games occupied him until at least six for home games, and much later for away games. Sunday, he would meet with both the offensive and defensive coaches separately to go over the game film. These sessions lasted from noon until usually the late hours of that evening.

During the season, the family learned to enjoy the limited time Coach Bonaventure could spend with them. It had been taken for granted that during the fall he was the adoptive father to sixty-five physically grown men.

Although it never seemed to bother his wife and children, it did bother Bonaventure. He did the best he could to arrange that his wife could be at every game. Every time he could, he brought his sons to practice or to film sessions. The team understood the priority his family took. No one ever questioned for a moment Bonaventure's decisions not to ride back from an away game with the team, just so he could see his sons, Joe or Dave, play high school football. Even considering all the time he had to spend away, Bonaventure was still the model family man. The team, players and coaches, knew that someday, if they had a family and if they could be half the family man Bonaventure was, their home lives would be a success.

Although on a much smaller scale, the relationships team members had were also strained by the demands of the season. Boyfriend/girlfriend combinations hardly got to spend any time with one another. This caused the demise of many relationships through the years, especially among the freshmen. High school sweethearts almost always broke off their relationships because the demands of football severely cut into the attention they had grown to expect. The relationships that lasted were those in which there was an understanding of the need to have one's macho image fulfilled on the football field. Concessions had to be made by both sides.

Peg and Sue were those understanding types. Peg didn't demand a lot of time from Bill, but she wanted the time they did spend together to be quality time. Aside from the weekend, they would usually plan to go out to eat or to a movie one night during the week.

Sue didn't demand a great quantity of time either, but Stubby enjoyed having her over to study every night. While he worked problems from his business classes on his desk, she kept herself occupied by reading her psychology on the couch.

Doc managed to see Carli a few hours each evening at the library. By the time Doc got to the library each evening after practice, Carli had already been there for a couple hours. He would usually sit at or near her table so they could talk to one another. Of the one or two hours they spent at the library together, about half was spent in conversation

During the first week, Foster didn't see Jandi at all. She called the morning of the team's first day off and Foster sent her a card, but other than that there was no communication. While Foster was busy during the day, she was home with Jennifer. When Foster had any spare time in the evenings after studying, she was at work. The relationship wasn't developed enough to make this a strain, but chances of further development on the weekend were limited, too.

Because the scrimmage wasn't until the next night, Coach Bonaventure didn't impose a curfew or even prohibit the drinking of alcohol. He felt that the team was responsible enough to watch out for one another. Moderate drinking wasn't going to hurt the team's ability the next evening in the scrimmage. He wanted them to be able to relax after a long week. Besides, this would be their last Friday night out for nine weeks.

Most everyone appreciated Coach Bonaventure's thoughtfulness. This was the first weekend that the entire student body was back on campus. They needed the opportunity to go out. Some players, like Bill, passed up the opportunity, so they could get in the proper frame of mind for the next day's scrimmage. Others, like Foster, delayed the opportunity so they could get a couple of hours of studying in before everything had a chance to get started.

At this time the year before, the Jungle Safari hadn't been discovered by the campus community of Beloit College. However, now it was becoming the standard place to socialize on Friday and Saturday nights. The bar was filled with more than just football players. In fact, the bar was so overrun with Beloit College students and other campus people that the customers who frequented it in the summer no longer stopped by.

Foster's usual Coke became the standard drink for most of the team. Everyone was serious about the scrimmage the next evening and this was a sign of their commitment to the program for the rest of the campus to see. Heavy drinkers, like Bert, did not go as far as just having a Coke, but instead limited their consumption of beer. They drank, having high-priced beer in bottles, rather than cheap beer by the pitcher.

After a week of practices, meals, and 'chalk-talks,' the upperclassmen had a pretty good idea of what each freshman player was like. Most players were tolerable, and some would become good friends. Most types of people were accepted by the upperclassmen. Bonaventure did a good job of recruiting players who could not only get the job done on the field, but also fit in with the rest of the team.

A few players were annoying, but keeping within Coach's guidelines that individuals on the team had to respect one another, the upperclassmen did their best to accept these players anyway. It was possible, but many times it really required biting one's tongue. Usually all that was required for these freshmen to overcome their annoying behavior was just the feeling that they had been accepted. All they needed was a reason to be themselves, and acceptance gave them this chance.

The only type of person no one could tolerate was the person with the cocky attitude. This was the guy who thought he was a real world-beater, and who was going to take every occasion to announce not only how good he was, but also exactly how much better than everyone else. Coach Bonaventure tried to get the team to give them a chance to become accepted, but acceptance wasn't the problem. The problem was that these players just needed to be brought down a notch or two. Every year there seemed to be one player like that. This year it was a guy by the name of Joe Whitman.

Whitman was a cocky linebacker from Moline, Illinois. When Joe did his best to impress everyone with his stories of glory, the more naive freshmen believed him. They had no reason to doubt him. However, the upperclassmen knew that his stories were nothing more that just that. Through the years, the upperclassmen, especially the seniors, had seen two types of football players at Beloit: good ones and ones who talked about being good. The team never had to do anything about overconfident people like Joe, because somehow or other their overconfidence always took care of them. The team just tried to ignore these people. But Joe's overconfidence seemed to be growing at an exponential rate and by this time he was becoming extremely irritating, too much to ignore.

Joe was confident that he was going to be a premier player for Beloit, and he probably was, but everyone was getting sick of hearing it. He -- only a freshman -- was going to get a starting position as a linebacker. The scrimmage the next evening to him was just another day between him and his starting debut as a college football player, unlike many others who needed the scrimmage to earn a debut.

With this confidence, he felt that it wouldn't matter if he drank moderately or not the night before the scrimmage. So he began to drink heavily. Besides, being able to perform in the scrimmage after being drunk would only further substantiate his superiority.

Despite the reputation that Bert cultivated as a fun-loving partier, he was concerned about the football team just as much as anyone else. Because he normally drank so much, he felt that he had good reason to approach Joe on the issue of his alcohol consumption. After all, if Bert were able to give up drinking heavily, then so could everyone else. Bert tried to explain this reason to Joe, but Joe just laughed.

"The rumor has it that I was elected as the third captain for the team, Bert. What do you think about that? A freshman captain." Joe downed another shot and then blew Jack Daniels breath on Bert's face. Bert knew he wasn't getting through and he could feel his temper start to heat up. It wasn't worth getting angry over, he thought as he walked away. "Hey, Bert, it's a good thing we don't have to play against one another tomorrow night." Joe sipped part of another shot. "I'd hate to have to hurt you." Bert turned and scowled, but just kept walking away.

Bert explained the situation to Doc because he was the only captain there at the time. They decided to just ignore him, and hopefully he would get what he deserved. Bert kept his distance because he knew that just the sight of Joe made his blood boil. Doc was bothered, too, but he had good control of his temper. He walked about the bar just trying to ignore Joe's comments.

Doc went up to the bar to get another Coke. As he stood there waiting for his drink, Joe moved down next to him. Doc still tried to ignore his presence, but it soon became impossible.

"Hey, Doc, did you know that I wanted number twelve this year, too?" Joe leaned against the bar as he referred to Doc's jersey number.

Doc gave an honest reply. "Well, that's probably because I'm a senior and I've had that number ever since I got here, and you are only a freshman." Doc tried to seem calm. He paid for his Coke and quickly took a sip.

"You're probably right." Joe agreed. "But I bet I get that number next year after you're gone."

Doc couldn't hide his irritation any longer. "Joe, you're a linebacker. Number twelve is a quarterback's number."

"No, number twelve is a bad ass linebacker number." Joe patted his chest with his hand and spoke in a cocky tone of voice that everyone had grown to loathe.

Doc felt his blood boil, but hid it under a cool look. "Well, Joe, when this team gets a bad ass linebacker, then they can have number twelve," Doc said calmly as he walked away without giving Joe another comment.

A short time later, Foster entered the Jungle. Every once in a while, he would study on Friday and Saturday night to get some work out of the way. During that time, the library was the quietest and he could get more accomplished. Then he would not have to worry about getting right to the books the next morning. Besides, nothing ever got started those evenings until nine or ten o'clock.

Bert greeted him at the door to explain the situation concerning Joe before Foster found out on his own. He let Foster know that he had tried to deal with the situation, and that Joe's attitude only caused him to become more irritated. Foster thought he had better talk to Joe.

Joe's first mistake was greeting Foster as if he were an old buddy. Joe erroneously assumed this friendship because they were both on the first-team defense. Immediately Foster's blood started to boil. Foster was probably one of the hardest people to get respect from. His respect was something that had to be earned, and the only way to earn it was to show some sign of commitment to something. What Joe was doing, to Foster, was a sign of noncommitment. Foster never had any problems with people drinking as long as it didn't affect him. He felt other's drinking affected him when they woke him up unnecessarily, tried to force alcohol on him, or when it stood to hurt something he was working for.

"What the hell do you think you're doing? We've got a scrimmage tomorrow." Foster demanded. Bert stood behind him. He knew Foster's temper and was there to protect both Foster and Joe from it.

"Don't worry, I'll be ready to play. We're going to kick ass," he yelled, not sensing Foster's anger.

Foster could feel the anger mounting in his body, but he couldn't control it enough to walk away like Bert or Doc. Stubby and Simba heard Joe yell, saw Foster and quickly surmised the situation that was unfolding. They moved in to help Bert. Doc was the only one who could control Foster's temper, but he was playing pool and didn't know what was happening.

"We don't do that shit here, at least not the day before a scrimmage." Foster's tone became angrier.

Joe finally realized how angry Foster was. He still felt that he could calm Foster down. He put his hand on Foster's chest and said in a reassuring voice, "Don't worry. I used to drink like this all the time when I played in high school. I used to have my best games the day after a good drunk." He smiled as if those words would serve to calm Foster. He began to raise another shot to his mouth, in defiance of what Foster was asking.

"I don't give a damn what you did in high school," Foster said through his teeth as he grabbed Joe by the shirt and pulled him in so their noses met. Joe spilled the shot all over the bar. Bert put his hand on Foster's shoulder. Foster felt it and knew he couldn't let himself get any more out of control. Stubby and Simba were ready to help. "You're at Beloit College now and that means you're going to play by our rules." Joe's body began trembling in fear. Foster shook with anger. "You got that?" Foster said, clenching his teeth tighter and pulling Joe closer. Stubby put a hand in to make sure Foster would go no farther.

Joe was too shocked to answer. Besides, there was only one answer. When Foster perceived that he had scared Joe enough, he let him go, pushing down on the barstool he stood next to. Foster turned to walk away. Bert and Stubby took their hands off him. Foster turned back to face Joe's terror-ridden eyes. "You better be ready to play tomorrow or else I'm going to kick your ass." Foster left the bar. He knew, with his anger like it was, he couldn't relax at the bar.

Joe started to explain himself. "You guys don't understand." Joe's fear turned to tears. "I love football." He cried out. "Someday I want to make a living playing football." As tears streamed down his face, he put his head down on the bar and whimpered.

Bert, Simba and Stubby still stood around Joe. They agreed with Foster's words, but didn't necessarily agree with his methods. However, consoling Joe wouldn't reinforce the point Foster tried to make. They slowly moved away from Joe and let him alone.

The fear and crying had not only helped Joe to sober up. It also made him realize a few things. He realized how much this season meant to the seniors and everyone else. This wasn't high school football where glory was being someone in the hallways. At Beloit College it wasn't being someone to others that mattered. It was being someone to yourself. A self-realization. A simple measure of this self-realization Coach Bonaventure said was the ability to put your head down on your pillow each night and say to yourself, with all honesty and sincerity, "I'm good." Achieving that meant leaving the comfort zone, because being something to one's self was always more difficult than being something to someone else. One can fool others, but not one's own self. Although only each person could know if he had taken himeself to the limit, everyone turned to others on the team to help push them to achieve. Joe realized that the way he had been acting wasn't helping anyone. When he recovered a bit, he stood up from the stool and left the bar, thinking about how he could redeem himself.

16

"Can I come in?" Joe Whitman stood at the entrance to Foster's room the next day and knocked on the open door.

After Foster left the Jungle the night before, he came home and went right to bed. Instead of the late evening he had planned, he had a very short one. He got a lot of sleep and still managed to get up early. After a short run and then a breakfast of Cap'n Crunch, Foster went to the library to study. The library wasn't open when he got there, so he had to wait outside the doors patiently until it did. By noon, he had done all the studying he had intended to do for the day. He had a mid-term paper that he wanted to get started on, but he didn't plan to work on it until the next day. So he came back to the house, had some lunch, and then went to his room to polish his game shoes for the scrimmage that evening.

As he put white polish on his shoes, Doc came in his room with just a bathrobe on and lay down on the bed. By that time, most of the house had heard what Foster had done to Joe and approved. Doc caught wind of it, too, but wasn't in total agreement with the way he handled the situation. Doc also had been rubbed the wrong way by Joe, but he was interested in keeping good relations among the team members. He was the team diplomat or mediator. There was seldom an argument where Doc wasn't trying to get each side to see their fault or to find a middle ground.

This time, Doc had trouble convincing Foster that he may have been a little in the wrong the night before. His blood was still warm from the incident. He tried to avoid thinking about the situation, because it made him feel mad all over again. He wondered how he would react when he saw Joe later that day. He couldn't say for sure to himself that he'd ever be able to look Joe in the eye. But with skills of reason, persuasion, and luck, Doc got Foster to concede a little guilt.

"Sure, come on in," Doc said. He was still lying on Foster's bed, hugging a pillow under his chest. The bottom part of his buttock stuck out from beneath his maroon bathrobe. Foster was in shock that Joe was at his door. He felt that everything was happening a little prematurely. Through his conversation with Doc, he had pictured himself being the one who would go in search of Joe to apologize, not the other way around. The whole thing seemed like it was set up. Had Foster not known Doc better, that's what he would have concluded.

Joe walked in and motioned, asking if he could shut the door. Foster nodded his head yes. Joe took a couple of small steps forward and scratched his head before he began to speak. "I guess I came here to apologize for a few things." He searched hard to find the words, but the ones he had planned weren't there.

Doc had about a half a word out when Foster interrupted. "Well, I've got to apologize, too. I was out of line last night."

Foster swallowed some pride to say it, but it had to be said. Foster was in the wrong to a certain extent, and unless that was cleared up, there would always be bad feelings between them. It wasn't like other people with disputes on campus. These two had to see each other every day for the next ten weeks in trying to prepare to fight a common opponent. It hardly made sense to be at odds any longer than necessary.

If nothing else, Foster and Doc were impressed by Joe's courage in trying to resolve the matter. Foster invited Joe to have a seat. Although the apologies were over, Joe was still concerned about his behavior. In so many words he said he wanted to be accepted, but that it was really hard to determine what had to be done to achieve that. Doc and Foster agreed that it was hard to be accepted, but they had no answers for what it took. It just happens. However, Doc and Foster tried to give him some guidelines that experience had taught them.

Stubby knocked on Foster's door and walked in. He perceived that the captains were meeting with Joe, so he excused himself. Although the forum was informal, he didn't want to be accused of acting as captain until it was actually so.

Joe stayed for about a half hour. By the time he left, the three were laughing about events of the first two weeks of practice. It was evident that the conference brought them a little closer, especially Foster and Joe. Conflict breeds companionship. On several occasions, Doc, Foster,

Simba, Bill, Stubby, or Bert had stood toe-to-toe, yelling and screaming at the top of their lungs, only a short way from violence. But each time, no matter what, eventually they shook hands and the bonds between them were stronger than before. Joe was in the early stages of this sort of relationship.

After Joe and Doc left, Foster tried to relax a little before the scrimmage. But his time was cut short because the team had pictures the later part of that afternoon. Picture day was always something the team looked forward to. Each man had a shoulder picture taken by the Sports Information Director for the program and then a professional photographer would come in to take the team picture.

Ever since the seniors were freshmen, Coach Bonaventure arranged with a company from Milwaukee to take the pictures. The pictures they took were similar to those of the NFL -- high quality twenty-inch by sixteen-inch glossy prints. Each player had the opportunity to purchase a copy of the team picture.

In addition, for a small charge, the photographer would take individual shots of anyone who wanted them. Some players had the traditional picture taken for Mom and Dad (down on one knee, football in one hand, helmet in the other). Others used this as an opportunity to be creative. Stubby and Bert stood side by side holding rifles with Doc in the background, as if that was the way they protected their quarterback. The defensive backs stood together with footballs spread all over the ground at their feet. In the background they had erected a 'No Passing Zone' sign. Bill Barton, who was known for talking about winning the Heisman trophy while he was standing on the sidelines, had his picture taken in the stance of the man on the Heisman trophy.

Soon the evening came and the team took the field for the scrimmage. The team took a warm-up lap, but before they lined up, Coach Bonaventure had them huddle in the middle of the field so he could announce the third captain.

Stubby's heart had been pounding all afternoon. He had been both waiting for and dreading this moment since last fall. As Coach Bonaventure announced that Mark Stubner had run away with the election, Stubby breathed a sigh of relief and broke out in a huge smile.

Everyone congratulated him as the team broke into lines for stretching. Foster offered Stubby his hand and said, "What did I tell you?" Stubby kept smiling.

All in all, the second scrimmage was similar to the first. The first-team offense squared off against a now-improved second-team defense. The first-team defense had to contend with the same improvements from the second-team offense. Bonaventure had instituted a kicking game, so each team wasn't on the field for twenty plays. Both first teams made up the gold team, while the second teams made up a blue team.

In the first series, Foster caught a helmet in the thigh and got a charliehorse. After Jack Benson took a couple seconds out of the scrimmage to check the knotted muscle, Foster continued to play. "Itttttt's onnnly ppppainnnn," Jack said, referring to Bonaventure's distinction between pain and injury.

As far as Doc was concerned, the weather had cooperated. The evening sky was clear and the ground was dry. He was finally able to show what he could do. It was easy for him to pick up on what the inexperienced second-team defense was doing, as he threw for three touchdowns and ran for another.

Bill remained frustrated. He was certain that after his performance the week before, he would easily have stepped into a starting position. That wasn't the case. What did he have to do, he thought. As he watched the mistakes that Big El continued to make, he became frustrated and angry. This anger helped him make another good showing against the first-team defense. He knew he wasn't good enough to take away any of the other starting jobs, but he felt that he proved himself worthy of Big El's.

By the time the scrimmage was over and everyone was showered up, it was closing in on ten o'clock. Everyone came home to get ready to go out. Tomorrow was another day off, so the only thing they had to worry about was homework and whether or not the Packers beat the Bears. It was too late to have a pre-bar party, so they raced down to the Jungle with their hair still wet. Foster started to walk down to the Jungle, but his leg hurt too much.

During the scrimmage it hurt, but his muscles were warmed up so the thigh wasn't stiff. But now the muscle had a chance to cool off.

Because if was stiff, Foster had to force it to move which made it hurt more. He grabbed a bag of ice out of the freezer in the kitchen and wrapped it around the thigh. Applying heat to the area would loosen it up and help heal it. However, by applying cold to the injured area, the blood would move there to try and warm it and the increased blood flow would speed the healing even faster.

He sat on the couch in his room with his leg propped up and began catching up on the many letters that he owed to people who had written him since he had gotten back to school. When he was halfway through the third letter, there was a knock on his door.

"Come in!" he shouted. No one came in. Apparently the radio was playing so loud that whoever it was didn't hear. "Come in!" he shouted louder. This time they heard and the door opened.

"They told me I'd find you here." Jandi walked through the door. "How come you aren't at the Jungle?" She stood just inside the doorway, reluctant to come in any farther until invited.

Foster was wearing his reading glasses while he wrote letters. The prescription was for his myopia, so when he looked up all he could see was a blur at the door. He quickly took off his glasses when he determined that they were hindering him. "Oh, hi Jandi. I couldn't see you there for a moment. Come on in." He put the glasses back in their case and was about to set them down when she coaxed him into letting her see him with them on.

"How come you didn't come to the Jungle?" Jandi asked again since he didn't answer the first time.

Foster shrugged his shoulders, started to mumble and then said as if embarrassed, "I got a charliehorse." As he stood up from the chair a rush of melted ice came out of the plastic bag and rolled down his leg. The cool water made him cringe. Jandi laughed as he proceeded to take the bag off and let the ice melt in his sink.

At the Jungle, Doc and Bert got up on the bar and, arm in arm, sang 'New York, New York.' Carli didn't show up at the bar, so Doc decided to get drunk with Bert, probably a mistake. Doc wouldn't realize that until the next day.

Stubby and Bill teamed up on the pool table and were able to control it for close to three hours. Finally, Bill accidentally sank the eight ball and control of the table passed to the team they lost to. During this time, Peg and Sue sat at barstools on the edge of the pool area talking Zeta Kappa Zeta gossip and watching the pitcher of beer. When it wasn't their shot, Bill and Stubby would stand next to them and keep them company.

Simba wandered around the bar carrying a glass and a pitcher of beer. The woman who had blown him off a little over a week ago was with that same guy again. He carried on, trying to ignore her to show that she wasn't anything special. Simba would find a freshman woman whose glass was low on beer. He'd fill her glass and then tell her that 'a thousand spinsters couldn't weave cloth as fine as the lint in her belly-button.'

Jandi had been at the Jungle with Lori and Andy. Like Foster the week before, she waited for him to show up. When Doc told her that Foster was back at the house and probably wasn't coming down to the Jungle because his leg hurt too badly, she decided she would go up to see him.

Foster bought Jandi a Diet Coke from the pop machine and they sat on the couch catching up on the events of the week. She talked about Jennifer and work. He talked about school and football. Each pretended to be interested in what the other had to say, but the plain truth was that they were just interested in one another and not what was being said.

After she had been there an hour and a half, Foster leaned over and kissed her. She responded warmly and thought to herself, "It's about time." He took the can of pop from her hands and sat it, along with his own, on the desk before he clicked out the lights. Although his eyes still hadn't adjusted to the dark he was able to make it back to the couch without hitting the corner of his bed.

They sat on the couch for close to fifteen minutes. Foster slowly rubbed her back, then her arms and then her breasts. She started to bite on his ear lobe. He then took his hands off her and stood up. She was slow to respond in standing up, too. As he led her towards the waterbed, she said that she had to go back to the Jungle before it closed to get her friends. He said he knew and told her not to worry. The warmth of the waterbed came up through the comforter.

Carli was at another bar on the other side of campus with some girls on her floor when she first went out. She didn't plan on staying as long as she did. She had every intention of going over to the Jungle to see Doc and find out how the scrimmage had gone. However, it was impossible for her to get over to the Jungle because no one else was interested in going and it wasn't safe to walk alone. She tried to have a good time despite what she wanted to do, and she hoped that Doc would understand.

However, after some time had passed a woman she knew showed up at the bar, and Carli was able to get a ride over to the Jungle. She knew it was a chance she was taking. If no one was at the bar that she knew, she might be forced to walk home alone. She asked her ride to wait in front of the bar before she took off, so Carli could be certain that she would have a safe way home. As she stepped out of the car, Simba walked out of the bar. He had worn out his welcome with that crowd for the evening and it was time to get home before he got in trouble.

"Is Todd in there?" Carli yelled to Simba. She only had one foot out of the car.

"Yeah," Simba responded. "Hey, are you going back to campus?" He yelled to the woman Carli had gotten a ride with.

"Yes, would you like a ride?" The woman yelled back as Carli ran towards the doors of the Jungle. She recognized Simba from one of her classes as Simba jumped in the car and shut the door.

As soon as she walked through the Jungle Safari's door, Carli and Doc spotted one another. Doc had just gotten up from wrestling with Bert on the floor. His eyes were glossy and red. Not one hair was in place. As he recognized her, he said under his breath, "Oh fuck." Then, he hiccupped.

She was shocked at first. She had never seen him in this condition. But as she watched him sway back and forth, trying to straighten himself up, she began to laugh.

Foster carefully unbuttoned Jandi's blouse as he kissed her on the neck. When Foster was rubbing Jandi's back, he took note that her bra unsnapped in front. As she lay on her back, he ran his hand down her smooth chest and quickly undid the hook on the bra. The two cups pulled aside exposing her breasts. Her breathing was heavy but controlled. Now the warmth of the bed couldn't be felt over the heat their bodies were giving off. Foster quickly pulled off his shirt and then lay back down on her. He slowly moved his hand down to her pants.

The belt and snap on her pants were easy to undo, but as he worked on pulling down the steel zipper, someone started pounding on the door. "Hey Foster. It's me, Simba. Open up. I locked myself out of my room."

Foster thought how Simba never had good timing as he handed Jandi her blouse and bra. As they hurried to get dressed, Simba continued to pound relentlessly. "Come on, Foster. I know you're in there. Don't pretend like you're asleep now, I need to get into my room." He started to pound again.

When Jandi was ready, he opened the door and let Simba in. Before Foster could turn on the light, Simba had walked in the room and sat down on the bed. Jandi didn't know what to think as this hulk sat down next to her on the bed. When the light was clicked on, Simba turned to discover Jandi who was flushed with embarrassment.

"Oh, hi. I'm Simba." He extended his hand as if this were just a casual meeting. "You must be, a ..." He didn't dare make the wrong guess for fear of not getting the spare key to his room.

"Jandi." She completed his sentence. At this time, Foster was digging in his closet for the box which contained the spare keys.

"Hey, you're the one with the kid." Simba sounded delighted. Foster poked his head out of the closet and gave Simba a dirty look. Simba realized that he had said the wrong thing. "Hey, I wasn't interrupting anything, was I?"

Foster walked out of the closet and handed the key to Simba and said, "No," as if he really didn't mean it. Simba looked to Jandi for reassurance. She shook her head no. She was blushing again. "Good night, Simba." Foster gently tried to inform him that he had worn out his welcome.

Simba got up and walked to the door. He was almost out of the room, when he turned back in to address Jandi. "Hey, if you two ever want to go out and you can't find a babysitter, I'll be happy to do it. I'm great with kids."

"Good night, Simba," Foster said again.

When the door closed, Foster told Jandi he was sorry for the intrusion. Jandi got up off the bed and started to tuck her blouse in her pants and fix her hair. "You aren't mad, are you?" Foster had a concerned voice. "I'm really sorry."

"No, I'm not mad. And don't be sorry, I'm kind of glad it happened this way." She pushed the back part of her blouse in her pants.

Foster gave her a puzzled look and said, "Glad?"

She sat down next to him on the bed and pulled her brush through her long curly strawberry blonde hair. Some time passed as if she were searching for words. Then Jandi put the brush down and looked Foster in the eyes. "Foster, you really turn me on, and if he hadn't come to the door then, something probably would have happened. But I've already got one kid from one guy. I don't need one from another. Okay?" She looked away, waiting for a response. None came. "Look, I like you, but I'm just not ready for that yet with you."

"Okay," Foster said reluctantly. "But you won't be mad if I take cold showers while you're over?"

He smiled to let her know he was kidding. She laughed as she started to brush her hair again. When she was finished, she gave Foster a big kiss on the cheek. Then she left to go pick up her friends at the Jungle.

17

Carli ended up getting more than she expected. Not only did she have to walk Doc home, but she also had to look after Bert. When she finally made it back to the Sig house she had to bring them both up to Doc's room because she didn't know where Bert's was and he was too drunk to remember. She only went as far as taking their shoes off and making sure they got on the bed. She figured they couldn't have done that for themselves. Before she left, she had the foresight to empty the trash out of the plastic wastepaper basket in the bathroom and sit it next to the bed.

Doc slept for about an hour before the alcohol and the motion Bert created on the waterbed made him sick. He woke up and caught his bearings in time to make it over to the wastepaper basket. However, he slept on the inside of the bed and had to crawl over Bert to get there. After his first set of heaves, the ones where everything comes up, Bert woke up.

Bert was a heavy sleeper, but not heavy enough to sleep through someone sprawled across him going into convulsions. As soon as he realized what was happening and that he wasn't in any danger of being hit, he started to laugh. The shaking from his laughter did not help Doc -- who was still sprawled across Bert's chest -- at all. In between heaves, Doc mumbled under his breath, "Fuck you, Bert, fuck you." After all, it was he who got him in this mess.

Doc got up and emptied the wastepaper basket in the toilet and then cleaned it out in the shower. When he came back into the room, Bert was still chuckling. Doc ignored him and grabbed some change off his desk and went downstairs to get a Coke. By the time his stomach was settled and he had gotten back to sleep, it was close to four in the morning.

It wasn't until noon when they both finally awakened. They lay in bed trying to remember the night before and then laughed when they finally did. When Stubby heard them laughing, he came in the room and sat on the bed. Immediately, he noticed the smell of vomit in the room. Doc and Bert reviewed the entire story for him, laughing just as hard as the first time they had told it. After a while, they decided to get out of bed and go to the living room.

Every Sunday morning, the living room was alive with stories of the night before. Who went home with whom? What happened? What was said? The stories of one week were never the same as any other week. And there were always one or two surprise stories that would keep the guys amused for the rest of the week.

Simba was the overlord of the living room on Sunday morning. He made it a practice to get up early on Sundays, quickly grab the Sunday Milwaukee paper and sit in the living room keeping an eye out for what women would be leaving from whose room. Most of the time, it would be just one of the guy's girlfriends who always slept over. That was no big deal, but every once in a while someone would come creeping down the stairs, hoping she wouldn't be noticed. But Simba was always ready to greet them. His parting remarks only added to their embarrassment at being seen. Remarks like: "How were the mattresses?" "Did you have a nice stay?" or "Come again."

When Doc, Stubby and Bert came down the stairs, Simba was seated in his usual chair and a half dozen people sat around him on the couch. Simba began laughing at them and making comments, but they hadn't the faintest idea what he was talking about. The people on the couches laughed, not at what he was saying, but just at the way he was laughing.

Doc lay across the laps of two people on one couch and Bert and Stubby squeezed in between two others on the next couch. As Simba started to recap what he had seen that morning and what he knew from the night before, Bill came in through the front doors. He and Peg had gone out for brunch and were just returning. Doc sat up and made room for them to sit.

The library opened at noon on Sundays and Foster still wasn't there at one. By his schedule, he was an hour late. Every night before he went to bed or every morning, usually when he ran, he would map out a schedule in his mind. He made a mental note on half-hour intervals of exactly where he was supposed to be and what he was supposed to be doing. Twelve o'clock noon: At the library reading the Management assignment and doing research for the Econ paper. Five o'clock: Back to the house for dinner. At 5:30: Back to the library until ten o'clock: review problems for Statistics. At ten o'clock: Go to the informal team meeting. Whenever that ended, to bed. Each day was mapped like this. And whenever something would disturb this schedule, he would either panic or readjust the schedule accordingly, depending on how important the things were that he planned to get done. It was early in the semester, so most weren't that critical, and the schedule was readjusted.

When Jandi called him at a quarter of twelve, another readjustment was required. She called just to make sure that he wasn't mad about the night before. However, the call evolved into a long talk about anything and everything they could think of to stay on the phone. They knew that the next time they would have a chance to see one another would be the next weekend. And that wasn't even certain because he had a game on Saturday night which was away. He didn't expect to get back to Beloit until after midnight. But they kept the option open and remained optimistic. As they hung up, each promised to write the other sometime that week. Foster adjusted his schedule for the day, before grabbing his backpack full of everything he needed for the afternoon study session. He walked out of his room, locking the door behind him.

"There's a bad guy right there," Simba said as he pointed to Foster who was cutting through the living room to get to the door. Everyone in the room started cackling at Foster.

Foster gave a puzzled look. "What are you talking about?"

"Okay. Go ahead, give us the dumb act. But remember, I caught you with that little blonde last night." Simba winked. He had told everyone what he had seen when he went to get his spare keys. Foster immediately knew what he was talking about and couldn't stop the smile that ran from ear to ear. Everyone picked up on his smile.

"Are you sleeping with Parks' cousin, Foster?" Doc didn't give him a chance to answer.

"I bet you had a Charliehorse," Bert added.

Denying anything would have only made them believe him less. It was best to let them believe what they wanted. If he hadn't let them believe what they wanted, then they would continually let him know what they did believe. In these circumstances, a man was guilty until proven innocent. But to try to prove innocence was to them admitting guilt. It was a Catch-22. Foster knew he couldn't win, so he didn't say anything, but started again for the library. When he was just about out the door, Bert called to him.

"What are you going to study?" Bert had almost identical classes as Foster so he knew what work there was to be done.

"I got to start to do some research for the paper in Econ." Foster talked very quietly. He knew he was working well ahead.

Bert started to laugh. Everyone waited for an explanation. Through his laughter, he said, "That's not due until the week before mid-term break. Don't you think you're working a little ahead?"

Foster just smiled as everyone laughed. He was always one to have things done ahead of time. Some people work well under pressure. Foster didn't work well unless he could relax, especially when he had to think about something like writing a paper. To relax, he had to work ahead. That was just his way.

"Oh Christ, Foster. You've got a bar exam to take four years from now. You had better start studying for it." Bert proceeded to tease him. Everyone laughed.

Foster came back at Bert, who was noted for being one of the worst procrastinators on the team. "Oh Christ, Bert. You had a high school biology final four years ago. You had better start studying." Everyone laughed again just as hard, giving Foster credit for a witty comeback. Foster left while he was ahead.

Every Sunday night during the season, the entire team would get together in the living room of the Sig house to have an informal team meeting. Attendance wasn't mandatory by the coaching staff. In fact, the coaches knew nothing about it. Like the 'Captain's Practices,' regular attendance was enforced by peer pressure. The captains oversaw the meeting, which was mainly just a discussion circle.

The team sat around the room in order of graduation. From left to right the circle went freshmen, sophomores, juniors, and then seniors. The captains sat at the front of the room. A football was passed to the freshman sitting farthest to the left. When a person had the ball, he had the floor and no one was allowed to interrupt him. He was permitted to say anything he pleased as long as it was constructive. When he had said all that he had to say, he passed the ball to the next person to his right, who then had the same opportunity. This continued around the room until the captains, who were last, spoke.

The purpose of this session was to get out in the open any problems that might be developing between particular personalities on the team, and to try to stop them before they affected the team. Seldom was anything brought up that was critical of individuals. Usually the ball passed hands and all that was exchanged were thank-you's between players for things they had done for one another like loaning cars, helping with calculus, or just listening, or wishing one another good luck. Sometimes the ball exchanged hands and some people had nothing to say. Other times, people were critical of an earlier situation when they didn't feel it was proper to express that belief at the time. It was a time for tears. It was a time for laughter. It was a time for apologies and for gratitude. It was the one time during the week when they could put their macho football images aside and be sincere.

This Sunday, the first session, had to be explained to the freshmen. Bert went ahead of the first freshman to demonstrate what was meant by the explanation. He thanked Doc for getting drunk with him and took the chance to get back at Foster for the comment he had made prior to leaving for the library. Most of the freshmen were still uncertain about the process, so they passed the ball on without saying anything. Joe Whitman stood and showed his courage by apologizing to the entire team for his behavior. A lot of upperclassmen used the time to sincerely welcome the freshmen to the team, and to wish everyone else good luck in the upcoming games. After an hour, each man had spoken and they all went their own way for the night.

By the second Monday, everyone on campus had pretty much accepted that school was back to stay, and that classes were part of their daily routine. However, for the football team, it was now game week. The cruel, hot practices of August with no game in sight were over. Spirits were again high as the team now began to focus on one game and not just a season in total.

Along with the single focus, the practice schedule also changed. On Mondays, the team divided into offense and defense for film sessions. For an hour in the afternoon, Coach Bonaventure reviewed films of the opponent. Beloit College had an agreement with the teams it played for a film exchange between the teams. Each team sent the other its most recent game film for preparation of the week's game. More often than not, Beloit would end up with the poorer quality film and the players would have to squint to see the plays develop on the screen. Coach Bonaventure would point out each player to watch and what tendencies to look for. The team gave him a flashlight pointer two years earlier, but Bonaventure still resorted to racing up to the screen to point things out.

Beloit's opponent for this week, North Central College, had already had a game that season and so Bonaventure received one of their films. However, in return, Beloit didn't have such a recent game film, so the coaches at North Central received a copy of the first scrimmage. As he explained this to the team, Bonaventure smirked as if he had just pulled off a great swindle.

In the evenings, the entire coaching staff would be present for the second film session, which was a review of the prior week's game. Bonaventure would go back and forth over each play in the game numerous times so each coach could have an opportunity to comment on the various positions. For those who played in the game, the session wasn't bad as long as they didn't make too many mistakes in the game. If they made several mistakes, they would be subject to harsh criticism from not only their position coach, but also Coach Bonaventure. When Coach Bonaventure started in on a player, it was best to have no feeling because it was no holds barred -- public ridicule, four-letter words, the Lord's name in vain, the works.

Those who didn't play wished they could have been so lucky as to get yelled at. Bonaventure told them to watch the position they played on the film because they might learn something. But after ten minutes of watching the same play over and over, it was time to invent new ways to take a nap without being detected.

This week, the freshmen were forced to be attentive. Since there was no game film to review from the previous week, the coaches used the scrimmage film from the previous Saturday. For at least half the scrimmage, the freshmen were on the field, and were fair game for the coaches' abuse. One of the freshmen, who was everyone's bet to be grilled by Coach Bonaventure for something he had done in the scrimmage, lucked out when Bonaventure had to go take a phone call just as the play was about to occur.

After an hour of reviewing the film, Bonaventure stood up and started to give his pre-game week motivational speech on the comfort zone and how this was the time that pain had to be separated from injury and that all excuses for not giving 110 percent had to be put aside. Part of this speech re-emphasized a few of the guidelines he had laid down for the team the first day. The most controversial of these guidelines was the one concerning drinking during the week.

When the seniors were freshmen, Bonaventure had no rule against drinking during the week of a game. He figured that the team was responsible enough not to be drinking toward the tail-end of the week. But he was mistaken, at least with respect to a few individuals. Some players were out until all hours the night before the game. When this was discovered, the Athletic Department determined that they had a crisis on their hands and brought in all sorts of psychologists to talk to not only the football team, but all of Beloit's athletic teams, on the psychology of alcohol dependency. Most people thought the college had gone a little overboard.

That next season the 'moderation rule' was invoked. During the weekend, after the game Saturday to Monday films, a person could drink as much as they wanted while still keeping within Bonaventure's two main rules. In the middle part of the week, Monday night through Wednesday night, the team was on moderation. Moderation meant that they could drink, but only in moderation. For the remainder of the week, there was absolutely no drinking until the game was over.

The middle part of the week caused great controversy. The problem was, what did moderation mean? Different players had different definitions. For a light drinker, one beer was moderation, and for a heavy drinker, a pitcher was moderation. Because the distinction was blurred, Bonaventure discarded the moderation rule after only one year, and instituted a new rule. Simply stated, there was absolutely no drinking from Monday through the end of the game on Saturday. There was little controversy about this rule. Most people figured if Bert could live by it, so could they. Bonaventure, who didn't drink, made his own sacrifice as a symbol of his commitment to the rule. During the entire season he would not eat any ice cream, which was his vice.

On Tuesday, they were back on the field. Dressed in full gear, there was limited conditioning at practice. In lieu of physical exertion, Bonaventure gave them plenty of mental exertion by reviewing the opponent's plays, strategies, and strengths. Bonaventure always had posterboard-sized cards with the opponents' plays drawn on them. The coaches would line up the second-team defense in an offense and make them walk through each and every play at least once. Likewise, the second-team offense would set up in the opponent's defense and show the various defensive looks they gave.

During the review, Bill discovered that he was still a second-stringer. He couldn't believe it. As the offensive line coach, Coach Terry, and Coach Bonaventure walked the second-team offense through the various defensive looks it was supposed to give the first-team offense, Bill couldn't even look them in the eye, he was so mad. He felt betrayed.

After practice, Bill stormed in the locker room ahead of the rest of the team and drop-kicked his helmet against the locker in disgust. Doc tried to find out what was troubling him, but he couldn't figure out what it was. When Bill got mad, he talked extremely fast and switched back and forth from saying what was on his mind to being ruthlessly sarcastic. Doc figured he'd wait until Bill cooled off to try to get any answers.

On Wednesdays, otherwise known as hump-day, the coaches inflicted as much conditioning on the team as they felt was necessary. Usually they felt a lot was necessary. This wasn't like high school where if you played well the week before the team didn't have to condition as hard, or if the team played poorly, the coaches loaded up on the wind sprints. In college, win, lose or draw, a team could count on doing a certain amount of conditioning. Conditioning wasn't punitive. Rather, it was a basic necessity to survival on the field.

Most of the conditioning was integrated in drills, like hitting the blocking sled or running through the tires. But a lot of it consisted of just running for the sake of running, with no other purpose but to get the team in shape. Only the quarterbacks, receivers, and running backs saw balls the whole practice. Even then, they were on the move -- dropping back to pass, running over blocking dummies, or working on pass patterns, both long and short.

Bill was still full of piss and vinegar even though a day had passed since he found out he was still on the second team. This anger motivated him to push himself to the lead of every drill. He was determined to show the coaches their mistake.

Thursday was taper-day. Like Tuesdays, the team was subject to limited conditioning. Instead of reviewing the other teams' plays by walking through plays that were drawn on posterboard-sized cards, most of the practice was devoted to dummy scrimmage. The second-team offense worked the first-team defense by running the opponent's plays against them at half speed. By the end of the week, the second-team offense knew the opponent's plays better than they did.

Bill was no longer feeling the bitterness that he had felt the previous two days. He lined up across from Foster and simulated the best he could what Foster suggested his opponent might do. When he could, he made comments to Foster on what might be some good tactics, based on what he had learned the past two years on the offensive line. He was back to being a team player.

The previous night Doc had the opportunity to sit Bill down and get at what was bothering him. Doc didn't disagree with his conclusions that he should be playing ahead of Big El. He merely suggested that perhaps Big El was still playing because he had three years of proven game experience. Despite the fact that El looked bad in practice and scrimmage, the coaches expected that his experience would help him in the pressures of the game. Doc compared Bill to the soldier who never had seen combat before -- no one could say for sure whether or not he could handle the pressures. With El, they knew. Bill was willing to accept that logic for now. He decided to let Saturday's game determine whether or not his conclusions were still correct.

On the other end of the field, the second-team defense lined up against the first-team offense and imitated what the opponent might do in the game. The offense didn't particularly like going half speed against the defensive second-stringers. There was always one who figured he could impress a coach by getting a good, hard tackle in this spar. The offensive line called these guys 'dummy All-Americans.' They were All-Americans only when everyone else was going half speed.

Even though the spirits were high the week before the game, it was a long week and everybody welcomed Friday. No one left for practice until four o'clock. No one had to. For Friday's practice, everyone just wore their game jersey and game pants. No pads or helmet.

At each player's locker, on a hanger, were his game jersey and a pair of game pants. Since tomorrow's game was an away game, the team would wear its white game jerseys. The budget was always a limiting factor at Beloit College. For that reason, Coach Bonaventure ordered the highest quality jerseys with the minimum amount of extras. The white jerseys had standard numbers on the front and back, the standard three stripes on the sleeves and numbers on the shoulders. In high school, players were usually allowed to keep their jerseys during the season, but Coach Bonaventure didn't want to risk their loss. They were issued before each game and afterwards collected again.

Doc inspected his number 12 jersey to see that all the holes he had worn in it the season before were neatly mended. Bill had worn number 66 since his first days of Pop Warner football. The number 55 was ideal for Stubby. At center, he added symmetry to the offensive line. Bert and Simba had traditional offensive line numbers, 64 and 76 respectively.

In the spring, Coach Bonaventure would allow each player to put down on a sheet of paper the three numbers they wanted to wear. He would then spend the better part of a month sifting through these requests, trying to give as many people as he could their first pick. His criteria were simple. First he looked at the position a person played, then the number they requested and finally what year they were in school. Seniors had priority. Despite all this planning, players were still concerned about what number everyone got when jerseys were first issued. They would talk back and forth about each other's number saying, "That's a good number." Bonaventure was always puzzled by this comment. What was a bad number, he wondered.

Coach Bonaventure always seemed to do a good job in issuing the right number to the right player. Backs wore number 49 and below; linemen numbers 50 to 79; and receivers numbers 80 and up. There was only one oddball, as Bonaventure put it, on the team. Foster Addison, who wore number 43 and played defensive tackle.

When Foster played at Houghton High School, in Houghton, Michigan, he was number 40 as a junior varsity player and then number 60 when he made varsity, because they moved him from fullback to the line. In the spring of his senior year at Houghton, Coach Bonaventure sent the letter requesting his preference for three numbers. His choices were number 60 because that's what he wore in high school; number 41 because he was a fan of a running back from the University of Michigan; and, number 40, his junior varsity number.

He explained this logic in selecting the numbers to his high school football coach. His coach, a graduate of Michigan State University, became irate because Foster had selected the number of someone who went to the University of Michigan over him. In an effort to be fair, for whatever reason, Foster replaced number 40 with number 43. Number 43 was his coach's number at Michigan State. Foster sent in his preferences and got number 81. This, he thought, was evidence of his value to the team his freshman year.

The spring before his sophomore year, Coach Bonaventure talked to Foster about switching him to linebacker. That is the position Bonaventure figured he'd be playing the next season when the numbers were issued, and so he issued Foster number 43. However, when Foster reported to pre-season camp his sophomore year, the switch to linebacker never materialized. He stayed at the defensive line position with the number 43.

Friday practices before a game were short and sweet. Usually, practice would begin with awards being handed out for the previous games. There was always an offensive player of the game, and a defensive player of the game. In addition, Bonaventure would hand out stars to worthy players to be pasted on their helmets. The criteria for who got stars was determined by the captains at the beginning of each season. Since there had been no game the week before, the awards ceremony was skipped.

Then, systematically, Bonaventure would review the special teams on the chalkboard by explaining who had what position, what their duties were, and then naming that person's back-up. Second-teamers usually made up the special teams, and first-teamers backed them up.

After the team took the field, a quick warm-up was followed by going through on the field what each person on various special teams had to do. He kept them on their toes. The special teams won the game, especially a close game. First-team punt team. Run four plays and then send in the back-ups to see that everyone knew what to do on the special teams. Then on to the kick-off team, the punt-receive team, the kick-receive team, and then the end with the field-goal team. After a kick from the center, the right and the left went through the uprights, the team divided into offense and defense again.

The offense ran through a couple of special plays added late in the week. The defense ran one sprint for each victory they had in a row. Out of optimism, they counted the game they were about to play as a victory, so the defense had one sprint. Then the first game week was over. The only thing separating them from North Central College now was a trip to Naperville, Illinois.

18

When the team came in from practice, they found that each player's helmet had a Buccaneer emblem on each side. It looked just like the one the Tampa Bay Buccaneers once had on their helmets -- a pirate with a large feather in his hat and a knife in his mouth. It was a surprise that Coach Bonaventure had been planning for the team since the last season. Heidi and Kathy worked quickly to get all the stickers on while the team was out on the field.

In the past, the team's navy-blue helmets were just plain. However, Bonaventure had been taking a lot of pressure from the team and alumni to liven up the image of the Buccaneers. There were several suggestions: new jerseys, swords painted on the pants instead of stripes, and sprucing up the helmets. However, the only one that was "in the budget," as Bonaventure put it, was the helmet suggestion. As each player loaded his equipment in the travel bag for the next day's trip, they were extra careful not to mar the new emblems.

Not many players showered after practice. No one did enough to feel that it was worth their while. The only players who showered were the ones who were going to a date straight from practice or the ones who were obnoxiously obsessed with their appearance. There weren't many of those. For most, it was off with one set of clothes and on with another. Once the bags were completely packed and closed, they were thrown in a pile in the center of the room. The managers would load the bus in the morning.

When the team got back to the Sig house, the members of the house who didn't play football pointed out an article about the team in the single *Beloit Daily News* that the house received. Realizing that the article would hardly endure the handling of at least half the team, Doc drove downtown to get another paper. Simba, who came along for the ride, put the required fifty cents in the machine and opened it for Doc. Doc grabbed and opened the paper to make sure that it had the page he wanted as Simba let the newspaper dispenser slam shut. It was there. He took all but that page and discarded the rest in a garbage can that was near where his car was parked. Doc had the most complete scrapbook on the team. This article, with his picture, would add to the collection.

He and Simba got in the car, but he didn't start the engine until he had completely skimmed the paper, looking for each instance in which his name was mentioned. As Doc closed the paper and proceeded to start the car, he turned to Simba. "You were mentioned in the article."

"Hang on," Simba said as he forced himself out of the passenger side of the car and back to the newspaper dispenser. He reached into his pocket and pulled out two quarters. He wrenched open the dispenser and grabbed all the remaining papers and let the machine shut again. He raced back to the car as Doc watched the whole thing.

"Come on Simba, you can't do that." Doc tried to be stern. He glared at him over the top of his sunglasses.

"Why?" Simba gave him an innocent look in return as he was trying to stuff himself and the papers back into the car.

"Because it's just not right." Doc used the old Catholic-school reasoning.

"Have you got fifty cents to get them back in?" Simba appeared to be giving in, but unfortunately he was out of change. He pulled the pockets out of his jeans to reveal nothing more than weeks of accumulated lint.

Doc searched his pockets too, but only found the pennies that remained from his lunchtime purchase at the bookstore. He then opened the ash tray of the car. There, among a half-dozen more pennies, were a quarter, two dimes and a nickel. He quickly sifted them out of the copper coins and handed them to Simba. "Here."

Simba got out of the car with all the papers. Doc, who was assured that Simba would be putting the rest of the papers back, focused his attention on adjusting the mirror outside the driver's side window. Simba looked back to see that Doc wasn't looking and proceeded to just take out the page where the article appeared from each paper. He quickly refolded the papers and put the loose sports pages into the single paper that he had originally paid for and put the other dozen, minus the one sports page, back into the machine. Doc turned just as the papers were once again sealed up. Doc smiled, thinking there was hope yet for Simba. Simba could barely keep from laughing. He knew that he had fooled

Doc, as he hurried back to the car with a bloated paper. Simba got in the car and they drove home.

Once Friday's practice was over, no one wanted to do anything but play the game. The team had been keying up all week for Saturday evening's contest, but now they found themselves with almost a full day until game time. Time moved slowly and there was really nothing to do. They needed their rest for the next day, so they couldn't go out. Their minds were too preoccupied with football to study. And there wasn't much on television. Some were inclined to go to bed, but they all knew that with their minds focused on the game, they would be restless. The good players learned early on that getting a good night's sleep two nights before the game was necessary to be rested for the game. However, that knowledge did nothing to pass the time now.

Foster sat quietly in his room. The one thing he had learned from his relationship with his old girlfriend, Marianne, was that letter writing was a way to relax and pass the time. Although he didn't write to her anymore, there were other people to whom he could write. He sat on his couch and reviewed the mail he had received the last week. Carefully, he took the time to draft a personal response that was not just a listing of what had transpired in his life, but a letter that was entertaining. He addressed and stamped each envelope and set them by the door so he wouldn't forget them.

Initially he was hoping to take advantage of this time to work on his Rhodes essay, but straining to try and make the bits and pieces of notes fit together only gave him a headache. This isn't relaxing, he thought, and put the essay away. With each passing day, the essay was getting harder to write. He sensed the deadline drawing closer and he felt the heavy demands that school was starting to place on his time. It was becoming impossible for him to focus on either of these individually. He tried to block one out and concentrate on the other. But the process of trying to block one out only created pressure that inhibited him from concentrating on the other. He felt himself losing on both ends. Foster resolved himself to the fact that the only solution to the dilemma would be to take one or two evenings out, put all his homework aside and work on the essay. But that wouldn't be for a week or so. After all, he had until the first of October. For tonight, it was only wasted energy to think about either, and he began to write more letters.

Before he retired for the evening, he re-read the cute cards Jandi had sent him. He smiled as he felt his heart pound out full strokes. He didn't write her a reply, because he had already written to her twice that week and he was certain he would see her the next night. He taped the cards to the wall above his desk and then turned out the light.

Stubby spent the long evening in his room helping Sue begin studying for a statistics exam that was only a week away. The reason there was so much uncertainty with her returning to Beloit in the first place was her grades. She was very bright in the classes that pertained to her major, psychology. However, Beloit was a liberal arts college and at least half of all the classes were outside of a student's chosen field of study. The rigors of quantitative theory like math and science were stumbling blocks for someone, like Sue, who was accustomed to the qualitative theory that the social sciences demanded. She was doing well enough to get by in these classes, but not well enough for her.

It didn't make sense to have her grade-point lowered, and thus mar her record, taking these classes when she could go to a state university back in Boston, where she wouldn't be required to take courses out of her field of study. The bottom line was that she wanted to avoid having her ego bruised. Stubby was the only reason she had endured this ego bruising this long. Stubby wanted her to have the best of both worlds. He felt by helping her study she would avoid the ego-bruise these classes once gave her and then she wouldn't feel reluctant to stay at a liberal arts institution.

Doc arranged with Coach Bonaventure to use the team projector to show some NFL highlight films. Each film helped those watching to envision themselves in the shoes of heroic professional football players past and present who were part of fantastic seasons and plays. The commentary and music only added to their enthusiasm. Most of the younger players used this as not only a means of passing the time but as a way of getting psyched for the game.

For most of the older players, the magic from these films was gone. The library only had about a half-dozen of these films and they had seen them all. Watching them would be like watching re-runs of *Star Trek* episodes. They knew that any psych they created would not only be gone the next day, but would cause them to expend valuable emotional energies.

However, as slowly as time moves sometimes, Foster recognized, it eventually passes. The time spent awake seems like an eternity, while the time asleep seems to pass in mere seconds. Each player receives the amount of sleep that his anxious body would allow, and each player dreams the maximum amount of football the mind could concentrate on during that time. However, regardless of how much sleep he got, his body seemed to be tapped into a new source of energy as it was game day.

The team wasn't scheduled to leave until the early afternoon, so the morning passed as slowly as the previous night. But right after the team went to the Commons for the pre-game meal that Coach had arranged, they boarded the bus and they were on the road to Naperville, Illinois, the home of the North Central College Cardinals.

The team traveled to each away game on Van Galder Bus Lines, a local charter bus service. Essentially, they were traveling on Greyhound buses, with limited seating. Usually it was impossible to take the entire 65-man squad to each game, but Bonaventure did all he could to take as many people as possible. Some players drove to the game with Coach's wife or in the WBEZ car, with the local radio station crew which broadcast each game.

The coaches sat in their traditional seats at the front of the bus. Unlike high school, the seating on the bus did not give the oldest players priority seating. Seats were taken on a "first come, first served" basis. But then no seat had a real advantage. The view from either side of the bus was essentially the same, and although the very last seat offered about a third more room, those people had to deal with the continual use of the bathroom on board.

Nevertheless, players lobbied for particular seating arrangements. For the most part, this lobbying was done to ensure that people could sit next to or near people they wanted to talk with. The larger players on the team, usually linemen, would try and coax the smallest players on the team, usually kickers and punters, to sit with them so they could have more than their share of the double seats.

For the first fifteen minutes of the trip, the bus was filled with chatter as the team was excited about finally being on the way. As players talked back and forth, they had to struggle to hear one another over the noise of the engine. Before long, though, all that was left was the bus engines as the excitement of being on the road quickly turned to boredom. The immediate surrounding area of Beloit had a lot to look at, but once past that, in every direction, there was nothing but corn. Players stopped talking to one another and started to listen to a variety of different types of music. Reading soon lost its appeal, too. After a while, most of the players and coaches took a nap.

The trip only lasted two and a half hours. Naperville is a western suburb of Chicago, so most of the trip was made on interstates and main highways. Coach Bonaventure had arranged with the Commons staff to provide each player with a sack lunch to serve as their dinner. This was passed out about halfway through the trip, and players began the barter and trade of the usual two sandwiches, apple, orange, can of pop, and two oatmeal cookies. Not much of this food went to waste as everyone knew that not until after the game would they have the chance to eat again.

Once the team got off the bus and unloaded their equipment into the visitors' locker room, they made their way in small groups to examine the field. Individually, or in groups, they marched to various points of the field as if examining it for peculiarities that should be avoided or used to give them an advantage. Players indicated to one another various dips in the field or remarked on how soft or hard the turf was. For the most part, only the kickers or punters knew what they were looking for or what they were talking about. These players had the time when they got into the game to make adjustments for soft turf or an irregular bump. For anyone else, the game moved too fast to utilize what was found in this pre-game field examination. It didn't matter if they were playing on broken glass or plush carpet. They were going to do whatever the situation required. This examination of the field was just a tradition passed on through the years, a sort of body language in which a team or a player could make it appear as if he were a little more sophisticated in his approach to the game.

Once the field had been examined, the team headed back to the locker room in the same manner as they had gone to the field. It was time to start getting ready for the game. As this zero hour approached, lumps began to form in the back of people's throats and nerves began to tense up. Every player has his own particular way of getting dressed for the game. It was a tradition that most had developed in high school and now it was second nature. Doc waited around until the last minute to get dressed, Foster slowly put everything on and was putting on his shoes just before it was time to take the field. Stubby made sure that their equipment was put on in the same order: girdle, socks, pants, shoulder pads, jersey. Bert had to wear his 'Harvey Wallbanger' shirt under his equipment for each game. He wore this same shirt for four years of high school football, and by now it was so beat up that his mother had to sew it into another shirt.

Periodically, one of the student trainers would come into the dressing area and call the name of the player who was scheduled to be taped next. Not everyone got taped -- only people who were required to by Jack Benson or individuals who requested it. Some of these people requesting to be taped got taped to prevent injury or add more support to an area. Some got taped to avoid further injury of an area, and some got taped just for show -- they would have felt left out if they didn't.

Everyone was usually dressed and ready to go at the same time. However, the specialists (kickers and punters) were sent to the field first to warm up. Then a short while later, the ballhandlers, backs, receivers and their defensive counterparts, followed. The wait was agonizing for those players who were left in the locker room while the rest of the team began its drills. They crashed shoulder pads together and slapped helmets to relieve the tension. It seemed as if all they had done since practice ended the day before was wait.

Like parachuters leaping from a plane, the remaining players left the locker room when the coach who stayed back with them gave the word. When they reached the field, the other players who were already there stopped their drills and the team formed lines just like those in practice every day. After stretching, the team broke into groups by position for more drills and then slowly they regrouped into an entire team for a last-minute check on the plays they had rehearsed for the day.

Midway through this rehearsal, the captains were called to the center of the field by the referee for the coin toss. Stubby, Doc and Foster introduced themselves to the referees and then to North Central's captains. The coin was tossed and Beloit won. They elected to receive the ball in the first half. North Central made its decision on the end of the field it wanted to defend. As the referee motioned to the fans what had just transpired in the coin toss, Bonaventure looked on. Once he knew that they were receiving, he directed the team back to the locker room. Foster, Stubby, and Doc shook the opposition's hands one more time, wishing them good luck, and then they followed the rest of the team to the locker room.

"Okay men, this is it." Bonaventure clenched his fist as he spoke to the team that was huddled around him. "The test of one hell of a lot of work. It doesn't matter what anyone predicts the score will be, because they won't be on the field." He became more intense, and his voice began to rise. "It doesn't matter that they have a hundred guys suited up on the sidelines, because they can only put eleven guys on the field just like us." Saliva began to form at the corners of Bonaventure's mouth. "And it doesn't even matter that they're ranked ninth in the nation, because they haven't proved anything to us yet." His eyes became demon-like as he stared at the players who were lined up directly in front of him. Then his body relaxed.

"Everyone take a knee." Bonaventure bent down and rested on his right knee. He looked at the players and spoke in a soft voice. "Men, this is a time when we all ask God in our own special way not that we win, but that no one get injured and that when it's all said and done that he make us better people for the experience." Bonaventure tilted his head down and became silent. The team, including coaches and managers, joined him.

All the players knew Bonaventure didn't want people to push their religious beliefs on others. He wanted respect for one another's beliefs. It wasn't so much praying to God that made this the most important part of the warm-up to Bonaventure. Wishing could do the same thing as praying, he felt. The important thing, whether they wished or prayed, was what he asked the team to focus on. Bonaventure hoped the team would realize that although winning in the traditional sense was important, it was more important to win in the ultimate sense.

An ultimate victory to Bonaventure wasn't having more points or a better record than any other team. His ultimate victory was knowing that the individuals on the team were better people because they were associated with one another. He knew his life was a little better because he had been associated with Foster Addison, Todd Wallace, or any of the other players on the team. He hoped the team benefited from him, too. If a game was over and the team didn't have as many points as the other team, or if the season's end left more tallies in the loss column than in the win column, everyone could still have the sense that he had accomplished or conquered something -- then it all wasn't for naught. Leaving the comfort zone was just a means to these ends. Ultimate victory was derived from taking one's body, mind and heart to their limits. To pray or wish for a win was senseless because the other team was doing the same. Traditional winning was only a positive reinforcer in the process by making the benefits of ultimate victory more prominent.

After about ten seconds of complete silence in the locker room, Bonaventure lifted his head and rose to his feet. Some players sensed his movement and followed his lead. Others waited for him to speak. "Okay, men, let's strap it on and get ready to give it sixty minutes of all we've got." He stepped aside and let the team funnel out the doors. He and the rest of the coaches followed close behind.

It was about a hundred yards from the visitors' locker room through the admission gate to the field. The attendants at the gate stopped taking tickets from the thousands of fans who were arriving close to game time and let the Beloit team thunder by. Just inside the gates was the assemblage of Beloit followers dressed in the traditional blue and gold. Although a small crowd in contrast to the home town fans, their cheers gave the team a sense of being at home as they entered the stadium.

Bonaventure was proud of his team's following. His wife would never be sitting alone in the stands when the team was on the road, and the team had much-needed support. Ever since they were freshmen Doc, Stubby, and Bert's parents made it to every game. This game was no exception. They were ready to cheer the team on with homemade pom-poms, bells and buttons. Each tailgate was a potluck lunch with several kinds of sandwiches and several kinds of desserts which always managed to last until after the game. The parents got to know one another almost as well as their kids. It was a weekend club for them. Membership was exclusive, requiring only acquaintance with someone on the team. Each week, they welcomed friends of families, families of girlfriends, and parents of players who weren't fortunate enought to make it to every game.

But the Beloit College following went well beyond parents of players on the team. The Vetters attended games on an almost regular basis even though their son, Craig, had graduated two years earlier. In fact, they were more famous among players on the team than their honorable mention All-American son, Craig, as they provided each player with a 'care package' full of sweets to take on the long road trips. The following also included academicians. History professor Bob Howard was a follower of the Buccaneers before Bonaventure arrived on campus and led other professors in cheering on the team, often from the sidelines. Although on the road as a part of his job, Jim Francia, sports editor for the *Beloit Daily News*, couldn't help but cheer for the Bucs from behind a notepad or a camera lens when the game was tight.

Immediately after the player introductions and the national anthem, Bonaventure huddled the team one last time before the game started. Nerves were tense as younger players tried to swallow the lump that was forming in the back of their throats. The veterans knew that it was useless to swallow the lump, but they also knew that it would disappear after the first play. The only cure for the pre-game jitters was the game itself.

The hot day had turned into a warm evening. Most of the team was sweating as Bonaventure gave them some last-minute words of encouragement. The eye-black the team wore to shield their eyes from the glare of the stadium lights was starting to smear, but no one cared as they stared toward Bonaventure.

"Go, go, go, go..," the team chanted until the huddle broke and the kick-receiving team took the field. The ball was kicked out of the end zone. Beloit had the ball on its own twenty. The Bucs came out in the first series looking flat. After three plays, they had to punt the ball back to North Central. The defense picked up where the offense left off -- flat. North Central marched down the field in ten plays and scored a touchdown. After the two-point conversion, Beloit was down 8-0 early in the first quarter.

North Central had the psychological edge. As much as Bonaventure tried to downplay the factors, the thousands of screaming North Central fans, their hundred players lining the sidelines, and their number-nine ranking in NCAA Division III seemed to be having an effect on Beloit, who had never been ranked in the conference, let alone nationally. Beloit was in awe of North Central's reputation.

North Central kicked off again. The Bucs' next series was almost a replay of the first. Three plays and the ball was punted back to North Central. A half-dozen or so more plays and North Central was back in the end zone. The only difference this time was that they kicked the extra point instead of going for a two-point conversion. North Central was up 15-0.

On the next kick, Beloit was able to field the ball. The kick-receive team returned it to their own thirty, where the offense took over. This time the offense managed to get a first down on a third-down run around end. By the next set of downs, however, Doc went deep. The ball was thrown right into the arms of his receiver, but the receiver allowed the defender to rip the ball away before the whistle blew. Again, the defense was on the field, and again, North Central was driving for another score.

On a critical third-down play within the twenty-yard line, two Beloit linebackers managed to break up a pass. The momentum of the game was switched over to Beloit in North Central's first fourth-down situation. They sent their field goal team on the field and salvaged three points out of the series, at the cost of giving up the psychological edge. However, North Central had an 18-0 advantage as the first quarter ended.

In the remaining three quarters, Beloit dominated the game. However, the 18-point deficit was too much for them to overcome against the tough North Central team. Beloit gave up one other hard-fought touchdown, but the Bucs had scored two touchdowns of their own, each with a two-point conversion plus a forty-yard field goal. The game ended with North Central winning 25-19.

On two occasions, Beloit had opportunities to go ahead. Both resulted in interceptions by North Central. One was clearly Doc's fault as he tried to force a pass up the middle of the field. The other was an end zone interception resulting from a pass late in the game that would have provided the Bucs with at least a tie. Doc threw a perfect pass to where his receiver was supposed to be, but at the last moment his receiver took it upon himself to cut across the field shallower than he was supposed to. The pass sailed over his head and into the arms of a defender. Doc swore under his breath. No matter who was to blame, an interception went down against his record.

Of the three he threw that day, he only deserved one. On paper, that made his spectacular last-three-quarter performance appear mediocre.

After both teams exchanged handshakes at the end of the game, the Bucs headed back toward the locker room. The jog back had little of the enthusiasm that it did on the way to the game, despite the fact that the team's loyal fans cheered them for a good game showing, and optimism for the future. It was a long, hard game, one they should have won had they begun believing they could. There were some critical mistakes made in the game, but the real difference was between believing and not believing.

The team still didn't have enough confidence to win purely as a matter of tradition. The tradition that had been passed down at Beloit was that if you played hard in the game then you might win or you might lose. The winning tradition was dependent on fate. In the past fourteen years, Beloit College hadn't had a winning football season.

Bonaventure knew that he had to get the team's confidence to a point where the winning tradition was 'will dependent.' This meant that the team won because that's what they willed themselves to do, while opposing teams would be made to lose, not as just a twist of fate, but actually because they were beaten. Traditions are, unfortunately, difficult to re-establish. It's not an overnight process. It takes patience.

When everyone was back in the locker room, Bonaventure had the team drop to a knee again and pray for the same things they had prayed for earlier. As he stood, some players were able to join him. Some were too tired to get off the floor.

"Men, we know we should have beat that team. They know we should have beat them." Bonaventure spoke very softly. He was as dejected and tired as the men who sat exhausted on two knees in front of him. "Christ, I bet you right now their coach has got them on one knee thanking dear God they got out with a victory." He changed his direction. "I saw some good things out there. I know we're going to have a helluva football season this year. We've come a long way from the first day of practice." He always tried to be positive in his post-game speech. "But we've got a long way to go, too. We all made some mistakes out there. I know now that I could have prepared you a little better for what they were going to do, and each of you knows that you made some mistakes, too. Those are the things we've got to concentrate on. And if you're willing to work with me, we'll take care of them together." He paused to let what he had said sink in. "Let's shower up and get home." As everyone went to get undressed, Coach Bonaventure walked from locker to locker, thanking each player, whether they had played or not, for giving it their all.

Around the bus were the loyal family, friends and fans of the team, eager to console and encourage the dejected players. Bert's parents and Doc's parents stood at the door of the bus, handing out tailgate leftovers to players as they boarded the bus. Eventually they sent the entire box of goodies on the bus to be enjoyed on the bus ride back. Stubby's mom greeted each of the seniors with a big hug and a kiss. After about a half an hour of socializing, the locker room was cleared and the bus loaded with equipment and players.

Before they left town, Coach Bonaventure had the bus driver stop at a McDonald's so the team could get something to eat. He apologized for not being able to provide them with a better post-game meal as he had Coach Nic give each player a single five-dollar bill. Everyone knew it wasn't in the budget, and besides, no one was all that hungry since they polished off the box of cookies that had been placed on the bus.

The stay at McDonald's was a brief one. It was now back to Beloit. The ride home seemed to be longer and more sober than the ride there. Aside from the fact that the loss made for a long trip, each of their football-battered bodies found it nearly impossible to get comfortable as the bus bounced down the highway. No one had reading lamps on and only a few people engaged in light conversation. Most players rolled their jackets into balls and used them to rest their heads. Others had the foresight to bring a pillow. Some had resorted to resting their heads on the shoulder of the player next to them, but no matter how they managed to get comfortable, they each tried to get as much sleep as the bumpy ride would allow.

Foster sat in the very back on the left-hand side of the bus next to the window. He was disappointed with the way he had played. During the entire game, he felt he was a half a step behind where the ball was going. He seemed to be watching instead of reacting. Because of this, he had been banged around for the better part of the game. His head pounded with pain. It wasn't a tension headache, so relaxing wasn't going to help. The roar of the engine under his seat made his head throb harder with every bump. He looked over and saw Doc fast asleep next to him. Foster was envious. Even though he shut his eyes, the light from the cars in the other lane shone right through his eyelids. He turned away from the window, but still wasn't comfortable. Finally, he decided he wasn't going to be able to get to sleep. He tilted his head back and tried to endure the ride as his head continued to throb.

For those who were able to sleep, the ride back didn't seem too long. However, as they awoke, they discovered that their bodies were stiff from the abuse they had taken during the game. Doc complained that he could hardly turn his neck. Foster was starting to get stiff, but it wasn't to the point that Doc was feeling. However, for him, the trip seemed to take days.

No one was real keen on the idea of going to the bars. In the first place they were all too tired. Secondly, they had lost and they didn't feel like answering the question, "What happened?" a dozen times. Finally, the bars were going to close in a half hour. Even Bert just sat on the couch, trying to recover from the game and the trip.

Foster immediately went to his room. He pulled back the sheets on his waterbed, stripped to his underwear, and lay down. The aspirin that Jack Benson gave him while the team was at the Stadium unloading equipment seemed to have no effect on the pain that was still in his head. He tried to relax, so he could get to sleep, but the headache wouldn't allow it.

After lying there for a half an hour, someone knocked on his door. The pounding made his head hurt worse. He tried to ignore it, hoping whoever it was would go away. They didn't. They pounded again.

"This better be good," he yelled. Foster got up out of bed and ripped open the door. Jandi stood on the outside. She was startled by the way Foster opened the door, and she stood there quietly with wide eyes. Foster quickly realized who it was and felt bad for yelling. "Oh, I'm sorry, Jandi. I thought it was someone in the house trying to get me to open up the kitchen." He tried to justify his actions. "Come in." He held the door open so she could walk through.

Jandi blushed as Foster realized that he only had on underwear, but his head hurt too much to make any quick reactions.

"How did you guys do?" she asked as Foster lay back down on the bed. The room was still dark.

"We lost," he replied. She could tell by his voice that his head was down by the foot of the bed. "You can come over to the bed. I promise I won't try anything." She sat down next to him on the corner of the bed.

"How did you do?" she asked.

"Terrible," he quickly responded. She was about to ask another question when he interrupted. "Please don't quiz me all night. I've got a headache that could kill a horse." He spoke with his eyes closed, trying to relax. "I missed you. I want you to stay, but just lie here and be with me."

Jandi didn't say anything more. She gently kissed him on the forehead and then she lay down on her side next to him and felt the warmth of his body. Jandi reached her hands up along Foster's body until she felt the muscles that protruded from his back to his neck. He was tense. She moved her hands up to his temples and began massaging them.

Slowly, Foster felt his body relax. His breathing took on a deep rhythmic pattern. It was nice to have her there, he thought, before he drifted off to sleep.

19

When Foster awoke the next day, Jandi was gone, and so was his headache. He wasn't sure she had really been there. In fact, he couldn't say for certain that any of it happened. To him, the whole thing could have been a dream. He wondered if it was. Although he was still in this underwear with his head toward the foot of the bed, and even though the clothes that he thought he had worn to North Central were still in the same heap he thought he had left them, he wasn't convinced that he hadn't dreamed the whole thing.

If it were a dream, though, he thought, then today is the day we have to go to North Central to play. He glanced at the clock to see what time it was. It's 9:30 a.m. Christ, I'm late, he thought. As he jerked to get out of bed, pain shot through his body. This was his first sign that everything wasn't a dream. Every joint was stiff and every part of his body felt bruised. Slowly, he leaned over to the clock-radio and turned it on. Every motion could only be made at about half speed and even then pain screamed out of each muscle. Like Doc the night before on the bus, he could barely turn his neck. When he finally was able to turn the radio on, he fell back down in bed close to where he originally woke up. The church music that played on the radio convinced him that yesterday wasn't a dream. Today was Sunday.

He lay in bed until about eleven o'clock. No one appeared to be stirring in the house, and the library didn't open until noon anyway. Every half hour or so he faded in and out of sleep. Each time he awoke, he still didn't feel any more rested or any less sore than the previous time he woke up. Finally, he couldn't fall asleep anymore, so he got up.

The first few steps to the bathroom were painful. It was a given at this point that he wasn't going to go running. He could feel the pain in each spot where he remembered getting hit. He noticed some spots that he didn't remember. The hot water was again the cure for his stiffness, but he still felt sore as he toweled off. He cleared the steam from the mirror and studied the abrasions on his rib cage. Then he examined the inside of his mouth looking for any place from where the taste of blood might be emanating.

Getting dressed was a chore, so much so that he decided to leave his shoes untied. Foster loaded his book bag with what he planned to study. As he headed to the library, after grabbing two pieces of dry toast and an apple, he reconciled himself to the fact that following the schedule he had laid out for himself last night would be nearly impossible. Getting anything at all done would be a plus.

Walking down the sidewalk, he felt like an old man slowly shuffling his feet. As he crossed Emerson Street, Simba was crossing in the other direction farther on down the street. Judging by the way he walked, Foster concluded that he felt just as sore. He was coming back from getting his weekly Sunday paper. They saw one another, but neither had the energy to say anything. It took all each of them had to wave at one another. They continued in opposite directions.

Normally, Foster followed the method of studying for fifty minutes and then relaxing for ten. He found he was most efficient that way. However, today he could only keep his mind focused on the textbook he was reading for about thirty minutes at a time, with an equal amount of relaxation time in between. This relaxation time usually entailed walking around the library or paging through the magazine rack. Today he had neither the energy nor the endurance for pain. Foster sat and rubbed his sore muscles. He went over each play in his mind, trying to determine what he did wrong. Systematically, his mind had either a "could've, should've, or would've" answer for each scenario.

Almost immediately after Foster left for the library, others started to get up. Stubby led the second wave by going down to the kitchen and cooking himself a big ham and eggs breakfast. The house cook usually had the weekend off. As the aroma filtered through the house, one by one, everyone started to get up.

Foster had about average soreness. Doc, who had been sacked a half dozen times and made a tackle on one of his interceptions, was probably the sorest. As if it were his last request, he slowly hobbled down to the T.V. room in his bathrobe to watch the Packers' game. Other players weren't nearly as bad off. But then some of them only played on an occasional special team and didn't even get a single grass stain on their uniforms.

Most players spent the better part of the afternoon sprawled around the TV, room watching the football games and then the highlights which followed. They had the same attitude as Foster, that anything accomplished today would be something for the plus column. However, they weren't as anxious to get something in the plus column. It was nice to have the entire day off football, so why ruin it by doing school work. The semester was young and so nothing pressing had to be done.

After dinner, Bill and Simba led a group of a dozen or so players down to the fieldhouse to go swimming. Jack Benson told them that this would be the best way to cure a stiff and sore body. They were willing to try anything at this point. However, swimming turned into a combination waterpolo game and belly-flop contest, ruining the enjoyment of non-football players who were there for a recreational swim.

Sunday's informal team meeting was full of words of encouragement as everyone tried to revive each other's spirits. Individuals tried to focus on the strong points of the game and how the team should be optimistic about the conference opener that was fast approaching. Even freshmen, the majority of whom all talked, tried to take the lead in getting the team to 'lick its wounds' and get on with the rest of the season.

Although everyone was still ailing from the game, Monday brought anticipations of the week to come. A new team. A new approach. Time to look ahead. What changes would be made to the game plan? Who would these changes include or exclude? But Monday also brought the film sessions, which weren't very enjoyable, especially after a loss. Rumors started early of how Coach Bonaventure was going to really lay into the team. What actually happened was never as bad as the rumors made it out to be, but they were still bad enough.

In the afternoon, Coach Bonaventure reviewed the film that he had received from the other team. Bonaventure was optimistic about the week to come, but then he always was. He had no doubt in his mind that they could easily handle the inferior Northwestern College.

The goal this week was to try and break their will. To beat them so badly that they wanted to give up. Bonaventure spent the better part of Sunday examining every play Northwestern College made. He grinned a little deeper every time he found a flaw that he felt his team could exploit.

As the hour-long film session continued, Bonaventure's confidence began to rub off on the team. They could soon see the flaws that it took Bonaventure hours to uncover. The only thing that kept the North Central game from being history was the evening film session.

Players tried to glean from the tone of Bonaventure's voice the approach he was going to use in the evening film session. It was impossible. Looking ahead to Northwestern College, there was too much optimism in his voice. They knew Bonaventure too well to believe that he would use the same tone in the evening session.

The defense had its evening film session first. Foster was the "goat to be slaughtered." Not only did Foster not live up to Bonaventure's expectations for him, but he also was a senior. The defense was comprised mainly of younger players who had never seen the side of Ed Bonaventure that comes out in film sessions. Foster had not only seen it before, but had experienced it. And so Bonaventure could demonstrate his ruthlessness in film sessions without taking the chance of hurting a younger player's feelings. To Bonaventure, this was an ideal situation. To Foster, this hour-and-a-half session was longer than the bus trip home on Saturday night.

Bonaventure took almost every opportunity to find errors in Foster's play. Sweat continually poured down Foster's back and he jumped every time Bonaventure shouted his name. "Foster, what the hell were you thinking here?" "Addison, what are you doing?" "Foster, quit standing around in there. Get moving." "For 'criminy's' sake, what did we teach you in practice, Foster?" "Come on Addison, you're a damn senior. You should know better than that." The tips of Foster's ears burned. Bonaventure made law school's Socratic method look like a television game show.

As Foster walked toward the door of the film room, his whole body felt drained. Sweat continued to roll off his forehead. Bonaventure caught his eye before he walked through the door and he smiled and winked. Bonaventure knew he had lit a fire under Foster, one that would burn the whole season. And he knew that that fire would spread among the younger players.

Foster thought to himself, you bastard. On any other given day, Foster would have done nothing but praise Bonaventure. However, it was hard to like a man after he made someone endure something like the torture he made Foster endure, even though it was in his best interest. As the offensive players stood outside the film room waiting to enter, they asked how it was and what was Bonaventure's temperament.

Foster said to them in a long, drawn-out tone, "Have fun." He kept walking.

Bonaventure had more potential targets to choose from among the offensive players because they were mostly older players. Everyone seemed to get a chance to be the 'sacrificial lamb,' as the team termed it. Even players like Doc, who had fairly good games, weren't immune from Bonaventure's wrath. Bonaventure didn't want anyone to become complacent this early in the season. His view was that good could continue to get better until it was 'the best,' and at that point, it was time to redefine what 'the best' meant.

Although Bonaventure had a variety of offensive targets, much of his criticism was aimed toward Big El. El was slow off the ball, missed his blocks on several occasions and was responsible for four of the six quarterback sacks North Central recorded. His play wasn't what the team had seen in previous years.

Bill felt sorry for the thrashing El was taking, but he could not help but feel optimistic. He felt this would be his chance to step into a starting role. Even Doc agreed with this conclusion, since the only basis left for keeping El in the line-up was the coach's knowledge that he had proved himself in a game situation. Even that basis was gone now. Bill tried to hide his glee as he left the film session.

Another day of classes and it was Tuesday's practice. The team's emotions were in another slump. For three weeks, they worked hard and they still came up with a loss. Even though each of them knew that half the teams had to lose the first game, it didn't make the loss any easier to take. They searched for some sort of positive reinforcement, but there was none. Everyone felt that they had worked as hard as they could to win the last game. No one knew where that extra effort was going to come from to win the next one.

In addition to their emotional state, everyone was still feeling stiff and sore from Saturday. Everyone labored to get through the stretching routine. It was hard to be enthusiastic when every move sent pain rushing through their bodies. Unquestionably, to Bonaventure, they were playing with pain and not with injury. The team wasn't looking for any sympathy from him.

The final problem was that there didn't seem to be a weekend to separate the past two weeks. It seemed to go from Friday to Sunday night all in one leap. No one could go out Friday night and most of the waking hours on Saturday were spent either on the bus going to or from Naperville, or else playing the North Central game. It was too late to go out when they got back from the trip and by the time they woke up on Sunday, half the day was gone. It was going to be another whole week of practice before a real weekend would be coming along.

There was a little light at the end of the tunnel, however. The first home game was this weekend, and it was tradition for the non-football players at the Sig house to throw a party that night. But even that was too far off to affect them today.

Even Bonaventure's spirits were unusually low. In these circumstances, he would normally be trying to get the captains fired up so they would fire up the rest of the team. But today he seemed to be preoccupied and perplexed. He knew what the mistakes and problems were. Aside from the typical mental mistakes the team was expected to make from time to time, there was one other crucial problem. He knew that the big problem was that the team lacked a belief in themselves.

Knowing the mistake or problem was one thing. Trying to determine its cause was another. The mental mistakes did happen, so the team had to learn to deal with them instead of avoid them. The real question on his mind was: What is the cause of the team's lack of belief? Was it a lack of concentration? Was it something the coaches didn't get across because of a misunderstanding? Or maybe it didn't get across because no one attempted to put it across? Without the answers to these questions, the approach to solving the problem was difficult.

There were drills to teach the team how to block, tackle and carry the ball. Plays and various formations could be learned through a little bit of study. But how is someone supposed to teach someone else to believe in himself? Bonaventure equated it to teaching a blind person what was blue. Bonaventure continued to strain over the problem as the warmup continued.

It was a typical Tuesday practice, not much running and a lot of standing around listening to the coaches walk the team through everything they had seen Northwestern College do in films the day before. It was obvious to Bill that he wasn't going to be starting this week either, when Coach Bonaventure started directing his comments about the Northwestern College defense to Big El specifically. Bill's jaw dropped. He was shocked. He turned to Doc, hoping that perhaps Doc would have an explanation for this one. Doc had the same shocked look. All he could do was shrug his shoulders.

Bill had a hard time concentrating for the rest of practice. Maybe he was kidding himself when he thought he was better than El. Maybe he should wait one more week to see if El's play improved. "Shit no," he said to himself half under his breath. He knew he wasn't the only one who thought he should be playing over El. Even Doc thought so, and his opinion was as impartial as one could find. Waiting one more week wasn't going to change anything. Bill had been waiting one more week for too many weeks now. If he kept putting it off, there would be no more weeks to wait. It was his senior year. He'd wanted to start for over a year now.

What should I do? he wondered. He knew he had to confront the coaches. Particularly Coach Terry, the offensive line coach, and Coach Bonaventure. They were the two who made the decision. Should a hard approach be used? Should he corner the coaches, demanding an explanation? Or should a soft approach be used? Should he approach the coaches when it was convenient, inquiring if there had been an oversight, or even something that Bill had missed himself?

The soft approach would be the best, he decided. There had been no harsh feelings between him and the coaching staff to date. In fact, he felt they got along rather well. So there was no sense in starting any trouble at this point in his career at Beloit. The first step would be to call Coach Terry aside after practice, talk to him and see what he could learn from his position coach. Bill decided he would voice his concerns that he wasn't playing. Coach Terry seemed to be impressed with his play in the scrimmages. Maybe it was just an oversight that he wasn't starting. Maybe it could be all cleared up with Coach Terry. Then Bill wouldn't have to approach Coach Bonaventure, on the matter who was much more intimidating.

When conditioning started, Bill tried to keep an eye on Coach Terry to see where he went. Bill didn't want to take the chance that he might be called into an informal coaches' meeting before he had a chance to speak with him. Worse yet, he didn't want Coach Terry to take off for home before he had the chance to speak with him.

When the last sprint was run, most of the team went over to the water buckets. Bill went searching for Coach Terry. Terry was easy to find. He was the biggest of the coaches. He played offensive tackle for Eastern Illinois University, and every bit of his size indicated that he had been an outstanding player there.

Bill caught up with Coach Terry as he and Coach Cain, the defensive line coach, were taking the dummies off the blocking sled to store for the evening. Coach Cain removed all the pins holding the dummies on the sled, grabbed a dummy and started walking toward the Stadium. Terry was trying to wiggle one of the dummies loose when Bill finally caught his breath long enough to speak.

"Coach Terry, may I talk with you?" Bill leaned on the blocking sled to catch his breath.

"Sure." Coach Terry smiled, showing all his teeth. His smile was so pleasant, it was hard to believe that he had been a mean offensive lineman. The offensive players would joke about him because he would smile even when he yelled at them. This seemingly good nature made him easy to approach.

Bill started to remove a blocking dummy too. It was hard to look Coach Terry in the eye, despite his good nature. "Can I ask why I'm not starting?" There was a silence while Terry pulled his dummy free. "You seem to think that I've been doing well in all the drills, and I've had two good scrimmages." Bill paused for a moment to free his own dummy. "Let's face it, he's a great guy, but El isn't playing like he used to."

Terry put the dummy over his shoulder and faced Bill. He appeared reluctant to speak. "I don't know why you're not starting, either."

"What do you mean?" Bill looked puzzled. "Don't you choose who starts?"

"I requested that you start, but Coach Bonaventure put El in the line-up." Terry shrugged his shoulders. "I don't know what to tell you. You've got to ask Coach Bonaventure." Terry turned and started to follow Coach Cain toward the Stadium.

Bill stood in shock. Everyone thought he should be starting, but Bonaventure was keeping him out of the line-up. It didn't make any sense. He didn't remember ever getting on Bonaventure's bad side. Then his shock turned to anger. His eyes started to water as he could feel the anger make his face flush. Enough of the soft approach. It was time to get some answers. Bonaventure was keeping him down and he wanted to know why. He put the dummy over his shoulders and marched toward the locker room.

When he got inside the locker room, the coaches were in a meeting. That was good, Bill thought. He didn't know what he'd say when he was feeling so angry. Whatever it was, he knew he'd end up regretting it. He went to his locker and started to get undressed. As he slowly peeled off his equipment, he kept a close eye on the coaches' office. After fifteen minutes, Bonaventure walked out with his arm around his youngest son, Mike. As angry as Bill was, he realized that it was not a good situation to create a scene. He'd stop off to see Bonaventure in his office tomorrow afternoon. As Bonaventure turned the corner to exit the locker room, Bill muttered, "You asshole," under his breath.

That night, Peg came over to Bill's room. She ran her fingers through his hair. He stared off at the wall. He couldn't get any studying done that night. Every time he started to read his political science book, his mind drifted back to what had taken place that afternoon. Peg could see that his mind was elsewhere. Bill felt badly that she was around to see him in this condition. It wasn't giving their relationship the quality time it deserved. However, he was glad she was there. She was someone he could tell his problems to, someone who understood how much he wanted to start, someone who knew how much heart he had put into this football program, the only one who could possibly know how much he hurt.

"I had so much respect for that man. I trusted him." Bill started to speak. He was still staring off at the wall. Peg remained quiet, listening, as she combed his hair with her fingers. "He always told us that if we work hard and we pay our dues, things will come our way." Bill shook his head. "Is it all a big lie? How can I ever look him in the eye?" Bill was confused.

"I think that maybe you owe him a chance to explain." Peg spoke softly. She didn't want to make him angry or even cross him, but she believed that Coach Bonaventure had done enough for Bill, actually for all of them, to deserve at least that. "Think about it, Bill. You want to make your career the law. Well, isn't a man innocent until proven guilty?" She tried to reason with him

"A career in law?" He shook his head again. "I wonder if that will ever materialize, too. I was going to ask Bonaventure to write me letters of recommendation to the schools where I applied." He forced a fake chuckle. "I can't see that happening now, either."

Peg realized that he was still too angry to reason with. She just continued to pet his hair and listened to him vent his frustrations.

By Wednesday morning, most of the soreness from Saturday was gone. Most of the team entered into the practice of eating meals that were high in protein for three days after the game, and then meals that were high in carbohydrates the three days before the game. The high-protein diet that followed the game consisted of protein drink mixes, eggs and red meats. This was to help rebuild all the muscle tissue that was broken down during the game. The high-carbohydrate meals were made up of pastas and breads. This was to start storing energy for the game that was coming up. On the day of the game, the team ate mainly fruits and drank juices, anything that the body could quickly digest and turn into energy. No one knew for sure if this regime worked. One of the guys got the diet from a muscle magazine. But the team believed it did. Football and everything that surrounds it are 90 percent mental. Whatever was believed, was.

Bill took a small portion of spaghetti and a piece and a half of garlic bread. He really didn't feel like eating. His nerves were tense. He sat quietly and ate.

After lunch, he planned on going down to the fieldhouse to speak with Coach Bonaventure. He had classes for most of the morning and so this was his first real opportunity. Besides, Bonaventure usually worked late hours once the season began. He would either be in a coaches' meeting or examining game films until ten or eleven o'clock each night. This meant that Bonaventure didn't get to the campus until between ten or eleven o'clock the next morning. He liked to talk with his wife and kids in the morning, and perhaps even catch up on the events of the world by reading the paper.

Bill cleared his dishes from the table, disposed of any food he hadn't eaten, and put them in the dishwasher. He wiped his mouth on his forearm and then quietly went to the field house. Aside from Peg, no one knew what he was doing. He was afraid that someone might talk him out of it, or else the whole story would get twisted around. This way, whatever happened was between him and Bonaventure.

Bonaventure was in. His door was closed, but not tightly shut. Light shone through the half-inch crack that ran all the way up the door frame. Bill could feel his heart pound as he walked along the basketball court toward Bonaventure's office, trying to gather his thoughts. At least with the soft approach, he could take the time to think of what he was going to say. But Bill could still feel the remnants of yesterday's anger. He stuck to his guns. No more soft approach. He had to be ready to rifle off what he was going to say. He swallowed hard once to try to get rid of the lump that was forming in his throat, and then he knocked on the door.

"Come in," Bonaventure's voice clearly came through the door. Bill pushed the door open and stood in the doorway.

"Can I have a word with you, Coach?" Bill was firm, but not pushy.

"Sure." Bonaventure paused. "Shut the door and have a seat." Bonaventure motioned to a big yellow lounge chair he had in his office.

Bill shut the door and walked toward the chair. As he sat down, the phone rang. It always seemed to ring whenever one of his players would stop in to see him. The team used to joke that Bonaventure had a button under his desk to make the phone ring. He pushed it when someone was in his office and then pretended he was talking to someone important. This was his polite way of trying to get rid of someone. However, this wasn't the case, at least not today. It was only Jack Benson giving Coach Bonaventure some information he had requested. As Bonaventure quickly jotted down the information, Bill sat quietly and looked around the office.

Bonaventure's office was a monument to Beloit College football. On every wall was a picture of one of his teams over the past five years or an article about a particular game. On his desk was everything about the Northwestern College game that he needed to know. On the table in the corner were stacks of letters he was getting ready to send out for the next recruiting season. Pasted all over the bulletin board behind him were sayings and quotes that Bonaventure had acquired from other coaches or from his former players.

When Bonaventure hung up the phone, he quickly put the sheet of paper he was writing on in the folder where it belonged, and then looked up at Bill.

"What can I do for you, Bill?" Bonaventure said with a smile, in his normal tone of voice. He appeared to be in unusually good spirits.

"I want to know why I'm not starting." Bill spoke firmly and to the point. He was ready to continue with all the evidence he had gathered as to why he should be starting, but Bonaventure interrupted.

"Yeah, I know. Coach Terry talked to me yesterday after practice." Bonaventure spoke very calmly. Bill expected him to come back with the same tone Bill was using, so he was thrown. He remained silent as Bonaventure pulled his arms up over his head and grabbed the hair on the back of his head. He looked disturbed. "I don't know what to say."

"You mean I'm not starting and no one can tell me why?" Bill's anger started to show.

"No Bill, it's not like that. Not at all." Bonaventure continued to speak calmly.

Bill felt uncomfortable. This wasn't how he planned this session to go. He expected it to be a heated argument ending either in his starting or his quitting the team. He didn't plan for these reactions by Bonaventure so he didn't know how to react. It was hard for him to stay angry, but he tried once more.

"Then what the hell is it?" Bill shot back.

Bonaventure turned his head down and away and held it there for about five seconds. As he slowly turned it back, Bill could see tears starting to form in his eyes. Immediately, Bill's anger left his body. Bonaventure pulled his glasses off just far enough so he could wipe his eyes, and then he sniffled. There were actual tears in his eyes.

"I just can't bench El. I just don't have the heart to do it." Bill sat patiently and listened as Bonaventure continued. "I don't know how to explain this, and I don't expect you to ever understand it. I guess all I want you to do is to respect what I have to say and what I've decided." Bonaventure sniffled and cleared his throat and continued. "All things considered right now, you are a better player at that position. You should be playing. But I'm torn. Big El came here as the first one in his whole neighborhood to go to college. The big reason he's here is to play football. He started for three years for us. He was a big factor in the success that we had those years. Now that he may not be what he once was, I can't desert him. I just can't find it in my heart to take all that away from him." Bonaventure looked to Bill for sympathy or acceptance.

Bill was looking down at his feet. He felt ashamed that he had come to yell at Bonaventure. Bonaventure was only doing what he had done all along. He looked out for everyone's best interest. Sometimes, like this situation, there was a conflict. It hurt Bonaventure to make a decision of one player over another, but he tried to be fair. And what didn't seem fair now would even out in the end. Although nothing seemed perfectly fair, Bonaventure did his best to come close.

Bonaventure continued to reason for acceptance. "It's not that I don't have any respect for you, Bill. Because I do. Christ, I'll be the proudest man alive if any of my kids turn out to be like you. It's not easy to do this to you, but you've got to understand. El is from the inner city of Chicago. Chances are, that's where he's going when he's done here at Beloit. This isn't the Big Ten where he'll have a shot at the pros. But you, Bill, Christ, you're going to make something of yourself." Bonaventure was pleading. "Not starting as a college football player is going to seem so trivial to you ten years from now." Bonaventure lowered his head. That's all he could say. He wasn't ashamed of what he did. However, he felt that he had lost some respect. That hurt him. "I'm sorry. I'm really sorry."

Bill had nothing to counter what Bonaventure said, mainly because it was uncounterable. How could he blame a man who cared about the players on his team so much that he'd be willing to let it bring him to tears? Bill realized that Bonaventure didn't coach for himself. He didn't coach to be coach-of-the-year or coach of a conference championship team. These were only secondary goals. No, Bonaventure coached for the players on the team, to make their lives richer, even if it was at the expense of a little of his own. To Bonaventure, that was an acceptable sacrifice, one he was willing to make.

"I understand, Coach. Don't worry. It's okay." Bill's voice was softer than Bonaventure's. He was willing to respect the decision.

Bill got up out of his chair and started for the door. His throat had another lump in it. This one wasn't because of nerves, but because he was trying to hold back tears. Bill could feel what was in Bonaventure's heart. He blinked quickly to try to keep his eyes from welling up. He put his hand on the door knob and began to turn.

"Bill," Bonaventure uttered as he raised his head. "Don't give up on us. We need people like you." Bonaventure swallowed hard and sat up tall in his chair. "If you stick with me, Bill, I promise you that you'll be a factor in something big this season. I promise." Bonaventure clenched his fist at Bill, and looked over his glasses with teary eyes. "Please stick with me," Bonaventure firmly pleaded.

Bill slowly turned and looked him in the eye. He nodded his head, not a lot, just enough to let Bonaventure know that he would do exactly that. Stick with Bonaventure. Any lost respect had been more than replaced.

As he walked out of the office and closed the door behind him, he thought to himself about what he had said the night before about law school letters of recommendation. Bill knew after today, if he were only allowed to send one letter of recommendation to each school, it would be Bonaventure's.

Bill felt so proud to be a part of Coach Bonaventure's team and was so touched by what was said that he started to cry. He whimpered against a pillar in the field house for five minutes. As he did, he vowed not to let Coach Bonaventure down, to be everything that Bonaventure believed he was and could be.

When it was all out of his system and he had made all the resolutions he could, Bill cleared his eyes once with the back of his hands and left the field house.

20

Wednesday, Thursday, and Friday practices went quickly. Bonaventure managed to get a little excitement going on the team by having a half-an-hour live scrimmage on Wednesday instead of conditioning. It was an excellent tactic to vent frustrations. Egos were restored as the first-team offense and defense got to beat up on the second-teamers again. This made them forget the beating they had taken the previous Saturday. This spirit carried over into Thursday's and Friday's practices.

Bill stuck to his vows. He was resolved that he wasn't going to get Big El's position, because he knew the reasoning and the man behind it. His spirits were higher than they ever had been. He carried on like a 'gung ho' freshman during the first week of practice. He set an example for everyone. Bill was the first to line up for drills and the first to try to cheer the team out of its lethargic state at Wednesday's practice.

In all the offensive line drills, he made sure that he was paired with El. It used to be that Bill would pair up with Bert or Simba, and then they would 'pussyfoot around' through the drills, as Bonaventure termed it. El usually was paired up with a younger player, which never was any match for him. It was like having Muhammad Ali sparring with a featherweight. He was not being worked at all. Not the case anymore. Bill worked El hard. He figured if he wasn't going to have El's position, then El was going to be the best he could at that position. No more pushover practice partners for El.

Big El didn't quite know what to think when Bill came out there Wednesday and started to run him ragged. What did I do to deserve this? he thought. But by the time Thursday's practice was over, he pretty much resolved himself to the fact that he was going to have to work hard in practices from now on. Instead of Bill having to find El and then move freshmen down to pair up with someone else, El waited for Bill and reserved the place in line so the two of them could be paired up. This was the best thing to happen to El.

Coach Bonaventure was well aware of how Bill had been carrying on, and he was pleased. During one drill, he happened to be watching when Bill knocked El on his ass, a rare event. As Bill helped all 310 pounds of Big El to his feet, he looked Bonaventure in the eye and winked. This was sort of a confirmation of their unwritten contract: I stick with you; you let me be a factor in something big this season. Bonaventure smiled and clenched his fist, in the same manner as he had early Wednesday afternoon, to acknowledge Bill's efforts. He walked away wondering how he would ever be able to make good on his promise. Half under his breath he uttered, "Lord help me."

Saturday. Game day. What every football player dreams about and works for. Every ambition has its focus. This was football's. The difference between practice and the game was not too unlike other disciplines. For the hunter, it was the difference between the stalk and the kill. For the lawyer, it was the difference between the preparation and the trial. Football players lived for Saturdays.

And this Saturday was a home game. That meant that the number on the jersey was more than just a number. It corresponded in the program to a name and then perhaps onto an image -- the player's identity. For the big schools, like Ohio State or the University of Michigan, it meant 100,000 people cheering you on. For Beloit, this wasn't so.

Beloit College was a basketball school. It had been renowned since its basketball teams used to clean up on schools like DePaul and Loyola. In fact, during the early '50s, Beloit was kicked out of the Midwest Conference for unnecessarily running up the score on its inner-conference opponents. The fieldhouse was packed for every game.

However, the football team didn't really mind. The stands were full while the weather was nice, and at least the crowd didn't cheer for the other team like they did in the late '70s. It was a campus event to come down to Strong Stadium on a sunny afternoon and play frisbee on the field until the teams came out to warm up, or to eat underpriced brats and drink beer behind the Stadium.

For the Bucs, the routine was the same, whether the game was home or away. The day still started early with breakfast at about nine o'clock. For those who wanted, Coach Bonaventure showed NFL films in the classroom of the field house, the same NFL highlight films that were seen the week before. For most, it was just a time to get into themselves and think about what they had to do. There was no noisy bus ride, just the solitude of a room.

After the abuse Foster took in the film session, it was time for him to take some evasive action with respect to this humiliation. He had Doc put the *Rocky* soundtracks on a CD. When he returned to his room after breakfast, he put it in his player and turned it up as loud as it would go. As he lay on his bed, he shut his eyes and envisioned every situation he would be in and then envisioned every move he would have to make, just like he had done before the first scrimmage.

Soon it was time to go to Bonaventure's pre-game meeting in the Morse-Ingersol Auditorium. Bonaventure quickly took roll, and then started, as he put it, reviewing special teams again. At this point in the season, it was no longer review. It was boring, especially for those who weren't on a special team. He ended this meeting just like he ended the first one of the pre-season -- with fire and brimstone. If the team wasn't psyched before then, they were now.

There were still two hours to go until game time. Most players went back to their rooms to get some last minute things together before they headed down to the Stadium. Foster had been to his room for the last time until after the game. He had his shoes and his CD player and began to walk the half mile to the Stadium. It was time to get totally intense. He concentrated on football and stared straight ahead. Other players on the team offered him rides, but he stayed to himself and continued to envision everything that he might have to do.

Everyone had his own way of getting ready for the game. Stubby and Doc felt that light conversation helped them to prepare. Bert paced back and forth, trying to look and feel as mean as he possibly could. Simba walked around the locker room shaking hands and wishing people luck. If they got psyched, then that was the best possible way to do it. All this showed that football is 90 percent mental.

When Foster got to the Stadium, he quickly got dressed from the waist down and sat at his locker. He continued to stare straight ahead, focused on football. His intensity was relentless. People tried to communicate with him, but he continued to stare through them, almost in a trance. Soon he was in the frame of mind needed to play the game.

Bonaventure was right. Before an almost record Strong Stadium crowd, Beloit won 15-6. Although the score didn't necessarily indicate it, the Bucs handled Northwestern College quite easily. The win was not without problems, however. Although the defense held Northwestern College to under ten first downs and under 150 yards in total offense, the offense had problems moving the ball. Again, Doc was plagued with interceptions that weren't entirely his fault.

However, the main problem was penalties. Each time the Buccaneer offense tried to sustain a drive, they would get a penalty that would either force them to punt or cause them to lose momentum. But when the final gun sounded, it didn't matter, at least not for now. A win was a win.

Once the game ended, it was almost ten minutes until everyone was back in the locker room. The teams shook hands and then the Beloit players took their time talking to the family and friends who came to the game. Jandi came to the game, but stayed in the stands afterwards with Lori and Andy. She was intimidated by the crowd on the side of the field waiting to greet the victors. Sue stood with Stubby's parents while they talked to Bill, and Stubby talked with Bill's parents. Bert and Doc chased Doc's little brother around while Simba made the Wallaces and the Lindseys laugh with his silly stories about practice. Finally, Bonaventure sent out a manager to hurry everyone on into the locker room.

After Bonaventure quieted the team down, he had everyone take a knee. While he had their attention, he began to address them.

"Well, men, we didn't beat 'em bad, but we beat 'em." Bonaventure's voice had an excited tone to it. The team cheered even more wildly than when they first entered the locker room. One by one, they settled again to let Bonaventure finish what he had to say. "But then, we didn't have a particularly good week of practice. We were coming off a big emotional loss."

"Hey, some days the Pittsburgh Steelers win fifteen to six. Some days the Pittsburgh Steelers win seven to nothing. That's the sign of a good football team." Bonaventure had a fixation on the Steelers. "It was an unemotional, workmanlike win for us." Bonaventure paused. "We weren't discounting them, but we felt that we were the better team and we went out and won. In the past, we had to get all pumped up to beat people." He paused again. "Today we just won. That's the sign of a team coming of age."

OUT OF THE COMFORT ZONE

The locker room broke into cheers again. Before Bonaventure could get it totally quiet again, he finished what he had to say.

"Let's have fun tonight, but let's also be smart. I'll see you all on Monday in films. Offense at four, defense at five. Let's get ready for Knox." He clenched his fist like he did to Bill and tried to yell above the increasing commotion, "Good job, men."

Bonaventure then walked around the locker room shaking everyone's hand and congratulating them. The team moved around so much that Bonaventure congratulated some players more than once. With all the excitement, he had no desire to keep track of who got congratulated and who didn't. Hell, they deserved it, he thought.

Following closely behind Bonaventure was the President of the college, Edmund Hardesty. He was also handing out congratulations to the team. Although his pin-striped suit didn't exactly go with the now towel-wrapped, naked, dirty bodies, he was still welcome in the Bucs' locker room. Win or lose, he was there with words of encouragement. He wasn't a 'fair-weather fan.'

Hardesty had a demanding schedule. Most of the week he was on the road trying to raise money for the college. However, that didn't stop him from getting involved on campus. He taught classes when professors were ill. He made sure that every senior got to come over to his house for pizza. And, every fall, he set aside four or five Saturdays to attend the home football games. He wasn't a passive fan, either. He was the first to complain at a referee's bad call, and the first to stand when the team took the field.

Still in their game pants and sweat-stained undershirts, Doc and Stubby sat reminiscing about particular plays of the game when Foster approached them. Foster was undressed even less than they were. He had taken off his shoulder pads, but then had put back on the soiled number 43 jersey.

"Come on. Let's go take a victory lap." Foster motioned as if he would lead the way.

Stubby looked at Doc and smiled. He turned and said to Foster while laughing, "Fuck you." Doc laughed with him.

"Oh, come on. It's only a quarter-mile. You guys can set the pace." Foster tried to plead with them.

"That's a quarter-mile more than I'm willing to run right now," Doc added, still laughing.

This wasn't the first time Foster had approached them on the subject. Each time the response was about the same. Foster was into these sorts of 'corny' rituals. He was certain of Doc's and Stubby's reply, but he thought it wouldn't hurt to ask. For Foster, one lap around the track on his own was no big deal. For Doc or Stubby, it might be, at least in their own minds, catastrophic. However, they were good natured about Foster's request. It was sort of a reciprocal understanding: Foster didn't drink, and they didn't run any more than absolutely necessary.

Foster walked back out to the field. Only a few people remained on the game side of the Stadium. Family and friends of players started the second-half of their tailgate party on the practice Stadium. All that remained were the managers for both teams, who were picking up the remaining equipment, the grounds crew, who was busy trying to sweep all the torn paper into a single pile, and the members of the local radio station who were recapping the game.

Foster started out running slowly. He noticed how nice it was not to have to breathe through a mouthpiece, and how light he felt not wearing shoulder pads and a helmet. All in all, the victory felt good. It was amazing how all the little aches and pains aren't noticed as much after a win.

As he turned the final corner, he could feel a slight breeze ripple through his hair. It felt nice. He lengthened his stride and sprinted back to the locker room.

One good celebration deserved another. After everyone was finished showering and basking in the general glory, they went back to the Sig house to get ready for the annual 'Post-first game party.' Officially the Sigma Rho's put the party on for the rest of the campus, but actually the work to put the party on was done by the non-football player Sigs. The football players claimed that they never had enough time.

Cort Dieter Meister, or Dieter as he was known, was Foster's right-hand man in the fraternity. He was the Vice President. Foster and Dieter were roommates for the second part of their freshman year, so they had developed a good working relationship and strong friendship. Dieter didn't play football, which made things work out well.

He ordered all the beer, and assigned other non-football players to take care of all the other little tasks to be tended to before there could be a party. The dining room was set up into a dance floor complete with lights and a sound system. A tarp was laid down over the living room carpet once all the furniture was hauled down to the T.V. room. Aside from enjoying the party, this was the extent of the football players' involvement in getting the party ready.

By the time everyone was back to the house and had finished eating, it was only about 6:30. The party wasn't due to start until nine o'clock, at least for the rest of the campus. Again, Bert appointed himself as chairman of the pre-party bash. He got a blank check from the house treasurer and then left all alone in his car. Everyone joked that one of these days when he was given a blank check, he was just going to take off. However, they knew that Bert would never take off knowing that a Sig house party was waiting in the wings. The party itself was insurance that Bert would return.

An hour later, Bert came back. He had forty pounds of ice, a new plastic garbage can, a grocery bag filled with grapefruit, oranges, and pineapple, and an assortment of cheap gin, rum, and whiskey. He went to the kitchen and grabbed two knives and instructed two guys just standing around to slice the fruit up for him. He then grabbed twenty gallons worth of Kool-Aid mix out of the pantry. It was evident to everyone by now that he intended to make what he called 'Jimmy Jones' punch.

With all the ingredients for Jimmy Jones punch ready, he put the garbage can on the front porch and began filling it up to about the three-quarter point by hose. He then mixed in all the Kool-Aid and then added the sliced fruit.

Next came the tricky part, or so he had everyone believe. He started to add the alcohol. At this point he would allow no one to come near his concoction, let alone help out. No one could ever understand. Bert would add dashes and cupfuls of this and that, appearing careful about how it was being mixed. Each time he did it, however, it was never mixed the same. And no matter whether he started out with a dash of gin and a cup of whiskey or vice versa, he always ended up putting all the alcohol in the punch. Everyone humored him. But it didn't matter. The end result was the same. Good times.

By nine o'clock, about half the punch was gone and most the guys were pretty well 'lit.' The party began and slowly the campus arrived. Everyone took shifts serving beer to people as they arrived, and one member of the house was paid to spin records for the entire party. It was campus policy that students bring their I.D.'s to all campus parties for verification that they were students. So naturally someone had to check I.D.'s at the door. Simba loved that kind of power so he volunteered.

Simba took a tall stool from his room, put on mirrored sunglasses and sat by the front door checking I.D.'s. If a person wasn't a Beloit College student, then he would politely inform them that they weren't allowed to enter. If the person persisted or else tried to sneak in, Simba would forcibly throw them off the front porch.

Only a few non-Beloit College students were allowed in. Jandi and her friends were allowed to pass, but Simba made the condition only if she would allow him to watch Jandi's daughter, Jennifer, if she ever needed a babysitter. Knowing that her mother was always there to watch Jennifer, she saw no harm in agreeing.

Simba sat with a beer in one hand and a black El-Marko Magic Marker in the other. When a valid Beloit College I.D. was presented he indicated it on the back of their hand with one of two marks. For those people he liked or couldn't make a judgment on because he didn't know them, he would indicate that they had valid I.D.s by marking an 'X' on the back of their hand. For those he really disliked, the "bitches, fags, and assholes" of campus, as he put it, he would draw the outline of a penis on the back of their hand. When people inquired what it was, he told them it was the symbol for the 'W-bar' ranch. If the mark or penis outline was turned just the right way, it could be interpreted to be a 'W' with a bar across the top.

Doc didn't like to dance, but when he had as much to drink as he had before the party, Carli had no problem getting him on the dance floor. Once on the dance floor, he was the center-stage entertainment. Unlike his football, his moves seemed to have no rhythm at all.

After a while, Bert would find a dance partner, and together they would work their way over to Doc and Carli. The partners would then switch. Bert would go with Doc, and the two women were left standing. Bert would take the lead and the two of them would ballroom dance from one end of the room to the other. At the end of the song, Bert would dip Doc, and then they would go find their original partners.

Slow or fast song, Jandi and Foster would be over in the corner slow dancing. Intermittently, he would lean down and give her a kiss. It was the start of a good relationship. She didn't demand a lot of time, mainly because she didn't have a lot of time to be demanding. This was good because Foster didn't have a lot of time. Period.

Before Jandi met Foster, she got drunk a lot. Now she seldom drank, and when she did she only had one or two. She did not need to get drunk anymore. Foster was her new high -- her new addiction.

The relationship was built on quality of time during the weekend, and cute cards and sweet letters sent during the week. It was always exciting for Foster to check his mail to see what kind of card Jandi had found to send him. Jandi looked forward to laughing at Foster's letters. Although both admitted that they weren't falling in love, it was plain to everyone that deep affection was developing between the pair. If nothing else, the grounds for a life-long friendship had been laid.

Every party at the Sig house had some controversial incident occur. Usually it was between one of the guys and either a townie, another person on campus, or the campus security. Unfortunately, the incident at this party involved Stubby and Sue.

It was the same problem they had been having since the school year ended the previous year -- Sue's future at Beloit College. Sue was sure of her feelings about Stubby, and he was sure about his feelings toward her, too. But Sue wasn't sure that Beloit College was where she wanted to be. That presented a conflict, because for Stubby, Beloit College was the only place to be.

Things were happening for Stubby there. He was a starter on the football team along with being captain. He had lots of friends and was well respected on campus. He had even brought his lowly first-semester freshman year grade-point average up from a 2.3 to a respectable 3.0. He had made a name for himself there, and he was proud of the college.

For Sue, there wasn't really much of anything, except Stubby, binding her to Beloit. The sorority she belonged to wasn't a national one. There were no extra-curricular activities to keep her occupied. Her grades weren't a highlight either, and the prospect for their improvement wasn't entirely bright. She didn't feel very comfortable about the statistics test she took earlier in the week. She had studied hard the entire previous weekend for it and that didn't even seem to make a difference.

The only thing keeping her at Beloit was Stubby, and she knew that wasn't enough. She also knew that if she left, that the chances of their relationship surviving weren't very good.

That was unfortunate. Stubby had put a lot into the relationship, when he could have been putting it into other relationships. Sue knew that and appreciated it. But if her future at Beloit College was so uncertain, she didn't want him putting anything else into the relationship. She wanted him to be happy and she wanted to minimize the pain he would feel. She wanted him to start dating other people, or at least looking around in case she did decide to leave, so the ties could be slowly broken. She knew that a breaking of their relationship would hurt both of them, but she was less concerned with her feelings than his.

She had tried to suggest that he become interested in other women in private conversations before, but it never went over very well. He never took her seriously, or else became suspicious of other guys. Inevitably, she would drop the topic. However, tonight when the topic was brought up, it was only dropped temporarily. The combination of alcohol in both their systems and all the women at the party who had an eye for Stubby made Sue persist.

It started out as a joking suggestion by Sue, but when she realized that her point wasn't being taken seriously, it became heated. Stubby tried to walk her up to his room so they could talk in private. They never got beyond the center of the living room before they broke out into a heated argument.

"Either come up to my room and talk about it or else drop the subject. If I wanted to see someone else, don't you think that I would have indicated that a long time ago?" Stubby screamed.

"No. We never get anything resolved up there or anywhere about this." Sue stopped where she was. "I'm not asking you to go get married next week, but try and consider what's going to happen if I leave school."

She tried to look away. Sue knew if she stared at him she would start crying. By now they were the focal point in the room.

"I don't care what happens, if you leave." He put his hand on her shoulder, and moved closer. "Don't you understand?" He tried to talk softer. She ignored him. "Don't you understand?" he began shouting in frustration. "I love you."

"I hate you," she turned and screamed back in his face.

Sue swatted his arm off her shoulder. It hurt her to say what she did. She knew she couldn't keep from crying, so she turned and ran out of the house through the back door.

Stubby was in shock from what she said. When he got his first impulse to chase after her, she was already out the door. By that time, Bert and Doc had converged on him and were trying to hold him back. They didn't know if he was angry or just upset. However, they weren't going to take any chances on letting him do something he might regret.

They held on tight and weren't going to let him pass out the back door. Stubby knew that, but in his frustration, he didn't want to stay where he was.

"Let me go!" he shouted.

"Just settle down, Stubby." Bert's voice was strained as he struggled to hold on.

"Let go." He started to shake violently.

"Stubby, Stubby." Doc tried to get his attention, so he could reason with him.

But there was no reasoning with him now. He freed one hand and pushed Doc away by the face and he started to walk toward the front door with Bert hanging on around the waist. Stubby stopped long enough to pull Bert loose.

When Bert fell to the ground, Stubby took the opportunity to run. Doc and Bert were yards behind him by the time they got united again. Simba got up off his stool and inquired what was going on. Stubby got in his car, started the engine, and squealed his tires as he pulled away. Doc, Simba, and Bert watched as he sped down College Street and squealed his tires again as he turned the corner onto Clary Street.

"I'm going to get my keys. We'll follow him." Bert took a step toward the house. His mind was in panic.

"Hang on, Bert. He's long gone by now, and we don't know where he went." Doc had settled himself. He was covered with beer. Stubby made him spill his own beer, plus two other people's beer, all over his shirt.

Bert didn't understand Doc's coolness. "He can't be out there driving like that. He's drunk."

"And if we go out after him, that'll make three of us." Doc always weighed all the options.

"Good point." Simba agreed, but he still didn't have any idea what the whole commotion was about.

Simba went back to his post, and Doc and Bert went back into the party and searched for Sue. She needed help as much as Stubby did. They couldn't find her. All they could do was try to enjoy themselves and hope for the best.

21

Sunday morning the sun shone brightly. The birds sounded like Spring. Foster woke up naturally at nine o'clock. However, since the party, which was in the next room, didn't get over until 3 a.m., this could be considered early. He wasn't nearly as sore as the morning after the North Central game, but then he didn't have to spend two and a half hours on the bus.

He grabbed his running gear and walked out to the living room. Everywhere he looked there were plastic cups half filled with beer. Some had cigarette butts floating on the surface. There was a big soil mark on the carpet where the tarp had moved. At the Sig house this was general 'wear and tear.'

The furniture still was not back in the living room, so Foster went out to the front porch to put on his shoes. He sat on the very edge of the porch and draped his feet over the overhang. Bees hovered around the area where the beer was served. The ground was still soaked with spilled beer.

Foster sensed the presence of someone else on the porch with him. He turned and found Simba passed out on the concrete. After he had finished checking I.D.'s, Simba did the best he could to catch up with the other guys. He managed to make up a lot of ground by chugging two pitchers of beer in less than ten minutes. Again, he was the hit of the party. Foster grabbed a table cloth from the bureau in the dining room and covered Simba. He then started his slow trot down College Street toward the main part of campus.

Foster wasn't trying to break any personal time or distance records. He slowly moved along, weaving in and out of the street, looking at the houses, and enjoying the early part of the day. He tried to put everything pertaining to football and school out of his mind. He thought of Jandi and the wonderful time they had the night before.

He ran through town and then over to Milwaukee Avenue. As he headed north on Milwaukee Avenue past Chapin Street, he noticed

Stubby's car parked down by the blue iron gates that closed off the road to the Stadium. Foster was aware of what had happened. Doc filled him in before he went to bed. Foster chuckled at he ran down toward the car, probably the most obvious place to look for him.

Foster crept up to the light green car and peeked into the window. Stubby was curled up like a baby in the back seat. He was still sound asleep. Foster could hear his snores through the windows of the car.

Stubby was sober enough to know that he should lock all the car doors. However, Foster was still able to wake him by pounding hard once on the roof of the car. Stubby awoke immediately. He had a look of terror on his face. It was evident that he didn't quite know where he was. After about ten seconds, he caught his bearings and got out of the car.

"Are you that anxious about practice on Tuesday?" Foster kidded. Stubby still was too far out of it to have any response.

"What time is it?" Stubby rubbed the top of his head.

"I don't know. About 9:30." Foster reflexively looked at his wrist, even though he never wore a watch. "What the hell happened last night?" Foster chuckled.

"I don't know." Stubby did, but he really didn't want to talk about it.

Foster sensed that, and so didn't pursue it. "Come on." Foster motioned Stubby to follow.

Foster walked around the pillar that held the iron gate. The fencing right after this pillar was worn and bent. Foster stepped up with one foot and then over with the other. He had done this dozens of other times when he came down to the Stadium to run intervals on the track. Stubby carefully watched how Foster got over and mimicked his moves.

Once they were both inside, the pair walked across the practice field to the Stadium. As they walked through the area where the locker rooms exited, two pigeons swooped down from their roost and scared them. They laughed once they realized what they were frightened by. They continued to walk through to the the game side of the Stadium. Each took a seat on the concrete railing that separated the stands from the field.

"You gonna miss football?" Foster asked in a perky fashion as he waved his arm down the edge of the field.

At first, Stubby didn't acknowledge what Foster had asked, mainly because he wasn't sure if he was awake or still asleep. But after a few moments had passed, Foster's question registered.

"Yeah," Stubby responded in a trance-like fashion. "Yeah, I will." He responded again as if he now had given the inquiry some thought. "It's hard to believe that football is almost all over." Stubby shook his head and looked out at the field. "Shit, I can't remember a fall when I didn't play football." He looked back at Foster. "It's kind of scary to think it's all going to end."

Foster slowly nodded his head in agreement. And then added: "We must be idiots to play this game."

Stubby gave Foster a perplexed look.

"We bust our asses, for what?" Foster said as he looked back out to the field. "None of us gets any kind of scholarship. We've got to work all summer so we can have the money to go back to school. We play in a league where no one has heard of you, let alone give you any respect."

Foster paused and looked off as if daydreaming. He grabbed some pebbles that were sitting on the cement railing and threw them as far as he could. Then he broke out of his trance, bringing his dreams.

"Can you imagine how easy it would be to go to practice each day knowing that tens of thousands of people were going to be there every Saturday to cheer you on? Or when you know that you have a good chance of winning a major conference title? But win or lose, when college is over someone will be waiting there with a healthy check to entice you to play for the Washington Redskins or the Dallas Cowboys, so you can be a winner all over again." He shook his head. "That's a lot of incentive. It would be nice to go out to practice knowing all that. Christ, all we know for sure is that when it's all over and we've played that last down, all we'll have are memories."

He started to fade off. Stubby seemed to fade with him. "Memories that remind us of our hunger to play the game some more and to feel that rush of energy through our bodies."

Foster shivered, as if feeling that rush. "Knowing all this, for some reason we still play."

Foster quickly snapped back to reality. "Yeah, we must be idiots."

"Have any other great insights, Plato?" Stubby chuckled, even though he knew Foster was right.

"Okay, I'll get off my soapbox." Foster was a little embarrassed. He reached over and grabbed Stubby by the ear. "Besides, we've got to get back home. I'm hungry and you've got company." Stubby was in tow as Foster started to walk back towards the fence.

"Ouch, that hurts." Stubby knocked Foster's hand from his ears. "Company?"

Foster didn't elaborate, but kept walking.

Foster cut his run short. He got in Stubby's car and they drove back to the Sig house. Simba was on the front porch starting to clean up from the party. He had a garbage bag and was filling it with beer cups after he emptied the beer on the front lawn. He was wearing the same clothes as the night before and his hair was standing on end in the back. He probably still was a little bit drunk.

When Stubby pulled up, he left his bag where he was and walked out to the beer-drenched lawn. "Where the hell did you take off to so fast? Did the CIA send you out on a mission?" Simba ribbed Stubby for his actions of the previous night. This was just the beginning of the teasing Stubby was going to take. "Aren't you a bit old to be running away from home?" Simba laughed, thinking that was one of the funniest things he had ever said.

Stubby was a little embarrassed, and he had nothing to counter with. He took the teasing well. He pretended like he was mad and chased Simba around the front yard. Simba knew the chase was in jest and so he was laughing as he tried to elude Stubby.

Simba was able to avoid Stubby until he was laughing so hard he couldn't run any more. Stubby slipped behind Simba as he grabbed hold around his waist. Foster stepped back as the two giants started to tussle. He squeezed Simba as hard as he could, lifting him off the ground. When he couldn't hold Simba up anymore, Stubby let him fall back on his butt on the ground. The beer-soaked ground made a funny noise as Simba hit. Beer immediately soaked through Simba's clothes to his bare skin. Now Stubby was laughing hysterically. Simba got up and looked at his wet behind and started laughing, too. Simba figured that they were even so he left well enough alone.

Simba continued to pick up the mess that the party had left, and Foster went to his room to shower. Stubby hadn't had a real sound night of sleep in his car. The fresh air had cleared the alcohol out of his system, but his back was sore from tossing and turning all night trying to get comfortable on the back seat. The thought of his waterbed was attractive. A couple-hour nap would do wonders.

As he put his keys in the door, he could sense that it was already unlocked. He knew he didn't leave it open before he went to the party, so he opened it slowly. He expected to see that his room had been robbed or ransacked, but instead he found Sue on his bed.

After Sue left the party, she went to the bleachers by the tennis courts and cried for a while. Then she just sat thinking. She wanted to talk to Stubby, but she didn't want to be seen at the party. She went up to his room after the party had quieted down, but he wasn't there. She carefully sneaked around the house and woke Foster to get the spare key for the room. She stayed awake for a while waiting, but eventually she drifted off to sleep. Being associated with Stubby, she had also acquired the habit of waking up early. She had been up for a little over an hour and was busy reading for one of her classes.

She removed her reading glasses and set the psychology book she was reading down as the door squeaked open. She had an uncertain look on her face, and her heart started to pound.

"Hi," she said in a very soft voice as if she were afraid that Stubby might still be mad and was going to ask her to leave.

"How are you doing?" Stubby's voice was soft also. He was surprised to see her there, but he didn't want her to know this by the sound of his voice.

"I'm okay, I guess." She continued in her soft voice. "I'm a little tired. I waited up pretty late for you." She patted the bed next to her, motioning for him to sit down. As he moved toward the bed, she pointed to the desk. "We have to return the spare key to Foster later. I borrowed it last night."

"Why don't you hang on to it. I'm sure he'll understand." He pushed down on the bed, making the water ripple in all directions. "How was my bed last night?"

"Nice." She pulled her body over to his and rested her head on his chest. "A little lonely, but nice."

He kissed her on top of the head and then rested his cheek on her forehead. "I'm really sorry about last night."

"Don't be. It just happened." She stroked his arm for a second and then pulled back and looked deeply in his eyes. "I want you to know that I really care about you. I don't want you to be hurt if I decide to leave. There are so many people out there who would love to have you, people you can be sure will be around for you." Her motives were well intended. She was looking out for him.

"What about you? What about your feelings?" Stubby waited for an answer.

"I know if you find someone else that I'll be hurt, but at least I'll know that you'll be happy." It was hard to say what was in her heart, but she did her best to sound sincere.

Stubby smiled. "I appreciate that." He grabbed her with both his arms and hugged her. "But you don't seem to understand. I'm a big boy now." She laughed. "I can make decisions for myself. I'm willing to take the chance of sticking with you. And if you decide not to stay, and it does work out then we'll at least have the time we had together. It's perverse logic to end it because something might happen. The chance I take of getting hurt is well worth it."

He pushed her back and looked into her eyes. As he cleared the hair that had fallen in front of her eyes, he carefully enunciated the words, "I love you."

She paused for a moment to take in what he said. "I love you, too," she said with as sincere a voice as she could.

She put her arms around his neck and he grabbed her around the waist. They kissed deeply for over a minute and then they embraced as hard as they could. She pulled away and tears began to form in her eyes. Seeing her tears, Stubby started to develop some, too. Before they could start to really whimper, they started to laugh out of embarrassment. They hugged again.

When they released again, they both fell back to the bed and lay in one another's arms. No more words were said. They both faded off to sleep.

22

Shortly before noon, other people in the house started to get out of bed. By then Simba had the entire living room cleaned and he was ready to get help rolling up the tarp. Normally no one would have been willing to help. However, without the tarp up, they couldn't bring the furniture up from downstairs. And without the furniture, there would be no place to tell stories about the night before.

Their mood was completely different from the previous week. Everything was said with excitement and laughter. Simba started the round of stories going by explaining how Bert was trying to pick up one of the women from town that Simba illegally allowed in the party. Bert tried to make this seem insignificant by drawing attention to Doc's pissing out the back door, where several women were having a cigarette. Everyone else was amused as the two debated back and forth, trying to make the other's actions seem more foul. Even though each was a little embarrassed by what he had done, they also felt a certain amount of pride, pride in knowing that for years to come, what they had done would be remembered as one of the highlights of the party. On occasion, someone would add something that would supplement the story or else bring up another incident that had occurred. Then the guys would be off on another tangent.

Most of the pain people felt was from their hangovers. Aside from the pre-party punch, the party had gone through fourteen kegs of beer, half of which seemed to be used to water the front yard. Where the tarp had moved back, the carpet was soaked with beer, giving the living room a moldy smell. Bert found one keg of beer which hadn't been tapped and he fought frantically to keep it cold by wrapping it in ice so they could have beer later that day. A post-party he called it.

Everyone seemed to be considerably less sore than after North Central. The initial shock of the actual football game was gone. Now the body was used to the roller-coaster ride it would take each week by being beat up on Saturday and then fighting to recover, but only in time to get beat up again. Any pain that was caused by the football game was ignored. It was the price of victory.

There was no shortage of pride in the team. Either they talked about the game, or wore Beloit football paraphernalia. There was just cause for this overabundance of pride. This was the best record Beloit had ever had in the past fifteen years at this point in the season. In years past, the team was already 0 and two. Everyone carried on as if the team were a Big Ten contender.

Last Sunday, the disappointment of the first loss and the physical pain that went along with it was the reason for not studying. This Sunday, the excitement of their first victory was the motivation to stay away from the books. Actually, no one really needed a reason not to study since not studying was built into Sunday, but it was always nice to have an excuse. It was even nicer to have an excuse which the team could celebrate, instead of mope about.

People who had rooms that faced the front of the house pointed their speakers out the front window and all played the same radio station. Bert and Simba brought out the kiddie pool again. Others drank from the left-over keg. The people who played wiffle baseball in the front yard added more damage to the soggy grass. As people passed to go to the library, they were invited to help finish the last keg of beer. Some responsible types declined, but some were enticed by the lawn party and decided to join.

The celebration carried on throughout the day and into the evening. There was a short break for the informal team meeting, and then it started up again and continued until very early Monday morning. Like Foster, who sometimes got a second wind while running, the guys usually got a second hangover after Sunday. This occurred Monday morning. The people who had eight or nine o'clock classes didn't go and used the extra time to sleep off the weekend. But even when they made it to their ten, eleven, and twelve o'clock classes, they could only concentrate on the throbbing pain in their heads. But this pain was worth it. They were able to get out of their systems all the frustration that had been building up over the past two weeks.

The Northwestern College game had improved Coach Bonaventure's ability to scout the other team by watching their film. Although the team was not able to take advantage of all of their weaknesses, the ones Bonaventure pointed out were definitely there. This made it easier for him to scout Knox College's football team. His confidence in his skills was evident to the team on Monday afternoon when they had to review Knox's game film with Bonaventure. Instead of saying, "I think this might happen," he was saying, "This will happen."

In addition to his confidence in what Knox College would do, Bonaventure was also confident of what his own players could do. Talk would no longer be of just winning, but of dominating the game against Knox College.

Reviewing the Northwestern College game films on Monday night was relaxing. Although the coaches still found poor playing to criticize, they didn't hesitate to praise outstanding play. Bonaventure would review a bad play about four or five times and move on, but he would spend considerably more time on play where people had done well. And as much as he could bring players down when they made a mistake, he could bring them up twice as far with his compliments.

"Some of you younger guys take a look at this block Danny Simpson throws. Look at it," he'd shout. "That's what we're talking about in practice. That block is right from the hips. That's a textbook block. Where is Danny Simpson?" Coach Bonaventure would turn around, as if Simba would even consider blowing off films, and search him out. Once he found him: "Excellent job, Danny Simpson. Excellent. Now that's football," he'd say as he turned back around.

It was a toss-up as to whether someone was more embarrassed when Bonaventure singled them out for something bad or something good. It was a no-win situation. Nearly everyone played to the best of their abilities in the game, one-hundred-and-ten percent all the time, always looking for the big play. However, if the team had to play with film sessions in mind, they hoped to play in such a manner that they got the job done. They didn't do it to draw attention to themselves.

Bonaventure seemed to use the film of the Northwestern College game as a moment to show his humorous side. He would show the film backwards when unusual plays would occur, or else point out something that might have come out on the film which happened in the stands or on the sidelines. Even when a player would screw up in this game, the criticism they received from Coach Bonaventure wouldn't compare to that which they took the week before. Bonaventure found ways to use humor to get the team to correct their mistakes.

"Foster Addison. Where is Foster?" He would search the room again. "What are you doing with their offensive tackle? The two of you look like a couple of Russian dancers out there. Don't dance with the guy, get rid of him." The team would break out laughing hysterically and Bonaventure would sit up in his chair and smile.

For the most part, this light attitude carried over into each practice the week of the Knox College game. The coaches would reach into their bag of tricks for drills that not only got the team in shape and taught them what to do, but also let them have fun. Coach Cain, defensive line coach, would have the defense line up according to 'mother's maiden name' and then have them leap-frog up and down the field for conditioning.

The only exception to the fun the team had during the week was when Bonaventure really wanted to concentrate on the offense. That was the weak spot against Northwestern College, and so by putting a little bit of extra effort into this aspect of the team, he felt that they could be a real contender for the Midwestern Conference title. The offensive coaches added a couple of plays that they thought might complement the type of players they had.

The practices were the same length, but they seemed to go a lot faster as the team's spirit lasted from the beginning to the end of each practice. Tuesday, Wednesday, Thursday, and Friday all seemed to merge together. The week was gone. There seemed to be no time between when Tuesday's practice had started and the defense was able to run two sprints at the end of Friday's practice -- one for Northwestern College the week before, and one for Knox College the next day.

Knox College was an away game. Knox was located in the western-central portion of Illinois, in the city of Galesburg. Bonaventure liked to arrive at least three hours in advance of the game. This left them some time to regain their legs after the long bus ride. Since it was a three-hour trip and the game started at one o'clock, the team had to leave at seven o'clock in the morning.

Bonaventure arranged to have breakfast served at 6:30 and the team was on the road by seven sharp. Along with the usual magazines and CD players, almost everyone packed a pillow. Aside from Stubby and Foster, very few other people ever saw this side of eight o'clock. These people were determined to get straight back to sleep once the bus got rolling.

Even for Foster, it was hard to stay awake. Everyone around him was fast asleep and the only thing to look at out the bus windows between Beloit and Galesburg, Illinois was the nearly complete fall corn harvest. He started to nod off to sleep, but then would slowly jerk his mind back to consciousness. A phrase he had heard in high school kept playing through his mind: 'If you snooze, ya lose.' Although he never found any validity to this phrase, he avoided sleeping on the bus ride before a game.

Foster wondered if he should have tried to get in touch with his old girlfriend, Marianne, and invite her to the game. At that time she was going to Western Illinois University in Macomb, Illinois, only an hour south of Galesburg. He concluded that there was no sense in trying to restart any romances. He began thinking how Jandi had more than filled Marianne's place in his heart.

Thoughts of Jandi continued to occupy Foster's mind and keep him awake. He wondered where the relationship would end, if at all. And if it wasn't going to end, then what would happen. He closed his eyes from time to time to try and imagine exactly what she looked like or the expressions on her face when they had particular conversations. These flashbacks and ponderings entertained him until it was time to start getting ready for the game. He popped in the *Rocky* CD and started to get psyched.

Thirty miles out of Beloit, Stubby's head was tilted back against the seat. It had been a long week for him. Sue had decided to give Beloit one more chance. This time she was really going to apply herself to the classes that gave her problems. Stubby offered to help. In between doing his own school work, Stubby stayed up late explaining various statistical formulas to Sue.

The bus arrived in Galesburg almost on time. People got off, trying to stretch and get awake for the second time that day. After checking the field again, the pre-game ritual of getting dressed and then work-up went as usual. Before long, it was game time.

The hard work the offense put in all week paid off. The Bucs received the opening kick-off and drove it the length of the field for the score. After a quick extra point, they were ahead seven to nothing. However, it didn't take long for Knox College to bounce right back. Three minutes later the score was tied.

Bonaventure was disappointed not only that the shutout was gone, but also that the defense looked like 'shit,' as he told them when they came off the field. The whole day it didn't seem like they could stop much of anything. Any time Knox College wanted to pass the ball, they did. Any time Knox College wanted to run the ball, they did. Knox didn't make big plays, but even their little plays of three or four yards retained possession of the ball for them. Although the defense was able to stop Knox in a couple of key situations, they had allowed themselves to be on the field for too long. Bonaventure's rule or goal for the defense was three plays and then the other team should have to punt. Keeping the defense on the field for so long tired them and denied the field to the offense.

The only saving grace for the Bucs was the offense. Although they had limited time on the field, they made good use of it. The only difference between Beloit's offense and Knox's offense was that Beloit came up with the big plays and Knox had to work for every yard. Doc had a great game by completing 20 of 28 passes for 213 yards and running for another 50 yards. One was a ten-yard touchdown run.

Bonaventure had spoken of the Pittsburgh Steelers the week before: good teams win. Sometimes by a lot; sometimes by not much at all. The Bucs won, too. Only by a six-point margin (35 to 29), but they won. After Bonaventure had them take a knee, he made them believe there was a cause for celebration. Even though it was a hard-fought win and the game was closer than they had planned, they won,

Now they had two wins and one loss, the best record Bonaventure had ever had at Beloit, the best the college had seen in years.

An offense operates by executing its play with precision while a defense exists on pride in being able to disrupt the opponent's precision. Over the previous two weeks, the Beloit defense had established some pride for itself. Knox College shattered that pride.

The defense rested on its self-proclaimed reputation and got burned. It was tough to have any great celebration even though the offense was enthusiastic about its own play. They all knew what mistakes they made and they weren't looking forward to hearing about them in films. Even the defensive coaches were a little stunned by how flat they played. Immediately after the game, they tried to assess where the problems were and how they could be solved.

On the bus ride home, the defensive players sat and stared, trying to determine where they went wrong. What was so different between this week and last week? It was hard to feel any pride after giving up 29 points. They were happy that whatever went wrong didn't cost them the game. Whatever it was, they knew they had a week to correct it, a week to regain their pride.

Foster sulked the most of all the defensive players. He knew he hadn't been playing real bad. He knew he had had a couple of fair games, decent games without any really critical mistakes. However, they weren't the kinds of games he dreamed about playing, or the kinds of games he was capable of playing. Most importantly, they weren't even the kinds of games he had worked so hard to play. He just wasn't really into what he was doing. He continued to go over each play in his mind, looking for the key to unlock the game he was capable of playing.

By films on Monday, the defense was sick of hearing from the offensive players that they was the backbone of the team. The offense seemed to forget a week ago when the defense was the big factor in the win over Northwestern College. Also by that time the coaches had determined what had caused the defensive unit to let down against Knox. It was simply that the week before they had concentrated too much on the offense and neglected the defense. The coaches were relying on what the defense had shown them against Northwestern College.

This neglect wasn't a psychological neglect. The coaches didn't take the time to hone the defensive skills and get them prepared to play against Knox. But they weren't going to make the same mistake twice. This week they planned on working both the offense and the defense.

They couldn't afford to leave anything to chance any more. This week they played Grinnell College -- a team which Bonaventure never lost to in his five years at Beloit. He didn't plan on making this year the first. Besides, a win against Grinnell would give them a three and one record. That would be only two games away from a winning season, with over half the season still to play.

By the fourth week of the season, classes had been going for six weeks and were now well established. Looking back, it was hard to remember what not being in class was like. It was the time of year when everyone was so used to being in this place at this time on this day that the routine was taken for granted. It was also the time of year when the majority of mid-term examinations were scheduled and term papers were due.

Usually the lower-level courses gave two exams during the course and then a final. Sometimes in lieu of one of the exams, the professor would assign a paper to be written. For the higher-level courses, the professor usually had only one exam and a final, and sometimes a paper. For the lower-level courses this was the time of year in which those first 'mid-terms', as they were known, were scheduled to begin. They would continue for about two or three weeks until the midterm break and then the second round would start up again a couple of weeks after the break.

For the upperclassmen, this was part of the routine, but for the freshmen, it was the cause of great anxiety. This wasn't like high school, where there would be a couple of chapters on each exam, with mainly multiple-choice and short answers. This was Beloit College, a school that prided itself on Ivy-League academic standards. Each exam consisted of hundreds of pages of reading where, instead of marking A, B, C, or D on the computerized score card, a student had to be able to discuss the similarities and differences between *Beowulf*'s Grendel and *King Kong*. People who were 'A' students in high school welcomed with open arms grades of B and below.

The upperclassmen are called upon to coach the younger students through these weeks. Mostly, the younger students looked for any insight on their professors: Do they grade hard or easy, on-a-curve, or straight-scale? Do they accept knowledge-of-the-material or bullshit? What kind of questions do they ask -- do they come straight from the reading or does it take ten minutes to figure out what the hell they're asking for?

Although they looked for these insights, they welcomed any kind of support material. The value of old exams and papers, formula sheets, Cliff's-notes, or answer keys increased like the value of water in a drought. Soon it was evident who had been studying and who had just been talking about it.

Although all of the critical dates for Foster weren't coming until the week right before the mid-term break, October 1st was closing fast. That day, the Rhodes essay was due at the Beloit College's Graduate Scholarship Committee. The rigors of school had prevented him from doing much more than manipulate the notes he had taken down the first time he went to the library to work on it. He knew he could put the notes into a good essay if he would just take a couple days to set everything else aside and work on it.

However, Foster knew himself well enough to know that he wouldn't be able to concentrate on the essay until he was secure with the other work he had to do. Ahead, before the mid-term break, were two exams and an Economics paper. The exams were far enough ahead in time so that he could not even worry about them. But the Econ paper was a substantial project which he knew he had to get out of the way before he could really concentrate on the Rhodes.

His plan was simple. For the rest of the week, he would work on finishing the Econ paper. That would give him two weeks to get it to Peg to type. Then, for the first two days of the next week, he would work on nothing but the Rhodes essay in hopes of finishing it. This way he could concentrate and be able to get everything done.

The coaches were concentrating, too. The offense got just as much attention as the week before, but the defense got that much, also. It was hard for them to tell if they were right. Football isn't like track or golf. It's a hindsight sport. In track or golf, training methods are tested by having a time trial or by playing a round of golf. If things seem to be improving, then the training methods are sound.

But with football, no one can be certain if the training philosophy is right until after the game. By then, the philosophy was either adequate or else it's too late. All a coach can do is develop a philosophy, implement it, stick with it, and hope for the best. And even if it does work out, the philosophy has to be changed for the next week, because then everything has changed: The opponent, the team's record, how the team feels about its last game, and how they feel about themselves. The Beloit coaches' philosophy only had to wait one week before it got tested. They were well aware of that on Friday afternoon when the Grinnell football team took the field at Strong Stadium for its day-before-the-game practice.

Grinnell College was one of the elite academic schools in the Midwest Conference. The only one more prestigious was University of Chicago, whose endowment was substantially larger than Grinnell's. Actually, Grinnell had only one shortcoming. It was located in Grinnell, Iowa, not just inside the border of Iowa, but almost in the center of Iowa. A desert of corn for miles on every side surrounded the small liberal arts college.

When the seniors were freshmen, the Beloit College football team made the trip to Grinnell, Iowa. The trip was seven hours long. On the way there, the team stayed overnight about two hours from Grinnell before driving the rest of the trip the next morning. After the game, they made the entire trip back without a stop. All Bonaventure could think of the whole way back was, "Thank God we won."

Since then, Bonaventure had managed to keep Grinnell as a home game. For three years straight, Grinnell made the trip to Beloit. They would drive the entire distance on Friday, have practice at Beloit, and then stay overnight in Beloit, which at a population of 37,000, must have seemed like a bustling metropolis.

As part of the deal to keep Grinnell traveling to Beloit, Grinnell had its Friday practice on the game field while, simultaneously, Beloit went through its own on the practice field. It was an unspoken agreement that neither side would look at what the other team did for its final-day preparations. Only Jack Benson, who was making sure that the Grinnell trainers had the proper training facilities, saw anything of what the Grinnell Pioneers were doing.

Before the Bucs went out to start practice, Bonaventure handed out the team awards for the previous week. He gave two sets of awards each week. One was yellow, star-shaped stickers that he awarded to individuals for certain achievements. Everyone got a star for the victory. Whether they played or not, Bonaventure felt that they had a hand in the victory. To him, a second-teamer who ran the other team's plays well helped by preparing the first-teamers. Multiple star awards, however, mostly went to offensive players. Doc and Stubby each got five; Bert, Simba and Big El had four apiece. Very few of the defensive players managed to get awards. Joe Whitman led the defense with three stars. Foster and three other players received two.

After all the stars had been awarded, Bonaventure announced the player-of-the-week award. He usually gave one for the offensive player-of-the-week, called Buc-of-the-Week, and one for the defensive player-of-the-week, called Pirate-of-the-Week. This week, he felt that no one on the defense was deserving of being named Pirate-of-the-Week, so he gave out two Bucs-of-the-Week. One went to Doc and the other to Stubby. Everyone congratulated the two as Coach sent the team out on the field

Bonaventure quickly ran the team through the special drills, and then divided them into their respective offense and defense. The offense walked through the new plays they had put in during the week, and the defense lined up to run its three ten-yard sprints -- one for Northwestern College, one for Knox, and one for Grinnell.

Friday evening passed and Saturday morning came as it had in the previous weeks. The team's nerves seemed to be tighter than they were for the North Central game. As much as they appeared confident in their ability to play football, deep down inside they wondered whether or not it was their football ability or luck that had won the last two games. They weren't used to having the record that they did. If it were their football ability, then there would be no problem. But if it were luck, they wondered when it was going to run out.

Another reason why their nerves were tight was because the stands at Strong Stadium were packed. The guys weren't used to playing before a large home crowd. They joked that when they were away, they were away, and when they were home, they were often away, too.

This crowd was unusual for the fourth game of the season, and the second home game. In years past, the football team had grown accustomed to having a big crowd for the opening game and watching it diminish game by game for the rest of the season. Generally, at the last game, the only people left would be the loyal parents and friends of the players, and a handful of professors, diehards when it came to following Beloit College football.

This year, the crowd had increased between the first and the second game. The reason was obvious. The Beloit College football team, two and one, was picked to be three and one by the end of the day. Everyone likes to back a winner.

As the Bucs took the field after Bonaventure had them in the locker room for final instructions and the pre-game prayer, the crowd stood and roared. It was like they had always backed the team. The team began to huddle around Coach Bonaventure for the last-minute cheer before kick-off.

"Fucking fair weather fans," Simba said as he looked up into the stands.

His words summed up the resentment that most of the older players felt. The empty stands of the last home game of the previous season and the heckles for not finishing with a winning record were still vivid in their minds. For the younger players, it made their adrenaline flow. This is what they had dreamed college football was all about.

Beloit received the ball and drove the length of the field for the score. A conversion and they were winning seven to nothing. On Grinnell's first possession, they made three first downs and had racked up nearly forty yards. It appeared to be a repeat of the Knox game, where it would be a high-scoring offensive battle. However, on the very next play, the Grinnell quarterback dropped back and threw the ball directly into the hands of Beloit's middle linebacker, who returned the ball twenty yards before he was out of bounds on the Grinnell sidelines.

The defensive unit ran over to greet him and escort him back to their own sidelines. As they trotted toward the bench, the crowd was cheering and the team was hugging one another. The offense told the defense 'good job' as they passed each other on the field. The defense was feeling pretty good about itself. The players felt they had done the job.

Coach Bonaventure pushed his way through the mob of players and coaches who were waiting to greet the defensive unit.

"What the hell is going on out there?" Bonaventure didn't expect an answer. "You guys look like shit." He barked at the shocked defensive players. "I don't want to see them get another first down for the rest of the game." Bonaventure's other side was coming through loud and clear. "If you guys don't want to play football, I'll find someone else on the sidelines who does. Christ, I could find people from the stands to do better than you guys look out there."

The fans looked down at Bonaventure in amazement. He was known to have yelled at the band when it played so loud during a time-out that he couldn't hear. He had yelled at the timekeeper for not starting the clock on time, and he'd yelled at the cheerleaders for doing inappropriate cheers. He would have yelled at anyone who was doing something to prevent football from being played the way it should be.

Bonaventure followed the defense back to the Gatorade. Nothing was more alarming than to be chewed out when players are trying to give themselves a pat on the back. He didn't care; he was right. And although he had pissed off most of the defensive starters, they knew he was right, too. The interception was just a silver lining in a dark cloud of defensive play.

The interception left the ball where the offense had no problem scoring another touchdown. After another successful extra point, the Bucs were up 14 to nothing. The defense came on the field after the kick-off. They still had fire in their eyes from Bonaventure's "ass-chewing." His threat to replace them with second-teamers really stuck in their craw. Everyone had "I'll show that son-of-a-bitch" on their mind.

And they did. After three plays, Grinnell was forced to punt the ball. The defense ran to the sidelines, trying to contain their excitement to show that they were still pissed off. It wasn't easy. Most the team came halfway on the field to greet them.

"That's what I want to see. That's football." Bonaventure led the wave of people on the field to greet them.

He reached for Foster's hand. Foster was reluctant to shake. He was still burning with anger. However, he raised his hand out of respect. As he squeezed Bonaventure's hand tightly, he gave a look as if to say 'that'll show you.'

The offense only managed to score one more touchdown in the first half, and the defense continued to slow down Grinnell's offense. In the second half, the Bucs only scored one more touchdown. Bonaventure had the second-team offense in the game for most of the second half. Because they had spent the majority of the week executing Grinnell's plays against the first-team defense, the timing on their plays was off. However, they still managed to hold their own against Grinnell's first-team defense.

The second-team defense was in the game for just as long as the second-team offense. The fire of the first-teamers carried over, and they were able to hang on to the shut-out. At game's end, the Bucs went to a record of three and one by the score of 28 to zero.

There was no doubt now in the team's mind about whether it was ability or luck. Luck wins games by a touchdown, maybe two. However, only ability can support beating a team by close to thirty points. Learning that, in itself, was cause for celebration.

Bonaventure and the rest of the coaches had other reasons to celebrate. They knew all along that the team had the ability. They were finally happy because the team was able to put together a solid showing on both sides of the ball: offense and defense. Their approach to the previous week's practice was successful.

After the game, excitement was high in the locker room. They were three and one. For the first time, the Beloit College football team was a factor. But the celebration wasn't focused on beating Grinnell or any of the other teams it had beaten. The three games they had won were victories to be sure. However, they weren't victories that a true athlete dreams about. A true athlete dreams of being the underdog who conquers the champion.

Next week, they would be the underdogs. And next week, they played the champion. In fact, they played the Midwest Conference champion of the last five years. And they were already looking ahead. The coaches didn't have to worry how they ran practice the next week, or even if they had practice at all.

"Lawrence, Lawrence, Lawrence," the team simultaneously started to chant. The team was not only ready to play Lawrence University. They were ready to live their dream.

23

Although the post-game celebration was different from what it usually was, Saturday night, for the most part, was like every other. Bert warmed the guys up with a pre-party again. However, this time he and Stubby each chipped in to get the fixings for strawberry daiquiris.

The party wasn't held at the Sig house this week. Usually the party rotated among the fraternities, sororities, and other special interest houses on campus. Only one thing changed. Instead of trying to preserve the the Sig house as the guys did for their own party, they now tried to inflict as much abuse as they could on the other houses.

Sunday was uneventful. Uneventful, at least, if you didn't root for either the Chicago Bears or the Green Bay Packers. This was the first of the two meetings between these NFL Central Division rivals. Every available space to either sit or stand in the T.V. room was taken. Although they didn't go as far as segregating the room according to Packer fans and Bear fans, it was evident by the shirts and hats that everyone wore.

All differences outside of Bears vs. Packers were set aside. Doc was the unofficial leader of the Packer constituents, and Bill was the counterpart for the Bears. Although no formal cheers were led, these two instigated most of the verbal abuse that was passed about the room.

Both teams were, at best, mediocre, so usually each set of fans would end up cussing out the mistakes their own team made as opposed to cheering for the good ones. In the long run, however, it didn't matter. The Packers happened to come out on top, giving the Packer fans bragging rights until the teams played one another again. Bears fans were forced to dig for some other fact or figure which would serve as evidence of their team's superiority despite the outcome of the game.

The fun-filled controversy of this game made Sunday go quickly, and Monday brought the same routine of classes. But the football films made the day seem worthwhile. Coach Bonaventure revealed flaws he was able to discover in the Lawrence team. The way Bonaventure explained the game plan on the board and its design to exploit their weaknesses, it was hard to see how it could go wrong. His optimism gave even more hope of having dreams become reality.

The evening film sessions were even more fun than the week before. All the coaches tried to get in their one-liners about plays in the game to make the team laugh. Bonaventure even managed a joke or two out of the defense's first series on the field, especially when his ranting-and-raving showed up on camera. "Who is that crazy man running up and down the sidelines? I guess they let anybody in the game nowadays."

Everyone played well. It was amazing the improvements the team had made since the beginning of the season, both individually and as a whole. Bonaventure was especially pleased with the showing of his second-teamers. He knew that his recruiting had paid off and that he had good football teams to look forward to in the future.

Although Foster still didn't have the type of game he hoped to have, it was closer than any of the other games he had played so far. Doc and Stubby weren't as good as the week before, but they still did very well. Stubby was well on his way to becoming an all-conference center, and although Doc was still being plagued by interceptions, he had become a threat in the league as a quarterback who could run with the football. The surprise was Big El. He had made vast improvements since the first game of the year. Even Bill would not go so far as to say that he should be playing over El anymore.

The defense had the first film session so they were done by about 8:30. Some of them went to the library to catch up on what they should have done during the Packers/Bears game, and others went back to the Sig house to watch the rest of Monday Night Football.

Foster stuck to the plan he set for himself. He worked hard the entire previous week and on Sunday to get his Econ paper finished. Although it wasn't completely done by Monday night, he was able to finish up the last page of footnotes within an hour. He raced it over to Peg's room so she could start typing whenever she found the time. She laughed at him as he dropped it off. He apologized for getting it to her later than he said he would, but he was still a week ahead of everyone else.

Now he was no longer panicked. He felt comfortable that he could finish the Rhodes essay and deliver it to the Scholarship Committee almost a week or so ahead of schedule. This would allow him to put this behind him and focus on the remainder of the semester. He went back to his room and got out all the notes he had jotted down about what he wanted his essay to encompass. It had been over two weeks since he had looked at them, so he spent the first hour reviewing them.

Although he still wasn't entirely sure what direction he was going to go in the essay, he had narrowed his ideas down from about a dozen to three. Each of these three was a good idea, but which was the true Rhodes material? It was hard to say. The only material he had about the Rhodes, other than the list of unread books various professors told him to read, was just an information packet on the Rhodes Scholarship Program. That was as good as any way to find some clue on what exactly the selection committee would be looking for.

He carefully read each section and made notes on how the information fit with his ideas. The information was helpful. He was able to eliminate one idea and was on the verge of eliminating a second. Finally, it appeared as if he was making some headway. However, when he started to read the last section, that panicky feeling returned.

According to the information packet, the essay wasn't the only thing due by October 1st. The essay had to be accompanied by eight letters of recommendation, a physical, an official transcript from the college, and a list of college activities and awards. No one mentioned anything about this to him before. "Why did I ever agree to do this?" he thought. He dropped the pencil he was using to take notes and went over to the couch to sit down.

He could feel a tension headache start to come on. The scholarship essay had caused more than one such headache since he decided that he would apply. Then he got a grip on himself. He relaxed and tried to look at things one step at a time. It really wouldn't be too hard to get everything that had to be done by the time it was due. It would take a lot of running around and take most of his spare time, but it could be done. He figured that he had gone this far, he might as well continue.

Foster sat back down at his desk and started jotting down a schedule of how he would complete everything he had to do. The tension headache was still there, but fading. He could get a physical from the school nurse, and there were eight people on campus from whom he would want to get recommendation letters. The official college transcript and the list of awards and activities would be easy. However, the big thing that had been looming over his head from the start was the essay. Although he had finally narrowed it down to the idea he wanted to write about, all he had was a bunch of notes that had to be somehow linked together and edited into prose that would impress the Rhodes selection committee.

Just as it seemed that Foster was getting the revised Rhodes situation organized, someone knocked on the door.

"Come in," Foster responded out of reflex.

Stubby, Simba, and Doc came through the door. The offense just got out of films and those three needed to talk to Foster. Simba ran and jumped on Foster's bed and then Doc jumped on Simba. Their horseplay made Foster forget about his problems for a second. He laughed. When the fun ended, they began explaining the reasons they came to see Foster.

"Hey, Foster, Coach Bonaventure wants to meet with the captains tomorrow afternoon." Doc's voice sounded funny as the ripples of the bed caused him to bob up and down.

Foster put his head down and shook it. "How long is this meeting supposed to last? I've got a million things to do." He grabbed his temples as the pressure from the tension returned.

"I don't know. It's a Bonaventure meeting. Anywhere from a half hour to ten years." Doc laughed.

Simba raised his head from a pillow to speak. "Hey, did you see the assignment we have to do in Accounting?"

"Where?" Foster closed his eyes and tried to ward off the headache pain.

Simba chuckled. "It's on the syllabus, but it's almost hidden at the top of the next page. I talked to Peg. She says it's supposed to take about ten hours to do, and it's worth ten percent of our grade."

Foster grabbed his folder for Accounting and verified what Simba was saying. "Shit," he said angrily. He ground his teeth together, making his head hurt more.

"Whew," Simba said. "If you didn't catch it, then I don't feel so bad." He put his head back down on the bed.

Stubby sat one of his legs down on the desk as he started to add to Foster's agenda. "We have got to put together the semi-annual reports for the national fraternity by two weeks from Friday. When do you want to meet to do them?" Stubby spoke softly. He sensed that Foster was under a strain.

Foster didn't answer. He didn't even hear what Stubby had said. All he knew was that what Stubby asked required more time, time which he was going to spend completing not only the Rhodes essay, but now the whole packet of requirements. He searched for a way to fit everything in.

"Foster?" Stubby waited for an answer.

"Please leave," Foster said as he raised his head. "We'll do it. I just don't know when right now." His speech was labored because of the strain.

"Try to fit it into your busy schedule." Simba joked. He didn't think Foster was serious. Stubby knew he was serious and started toward the door.

Foster turned to Simba. "Just leave."

Simba chuckled, still not knowing if Foster was serious. "Nah, nah, bet you can't make me." Simba whined like a little kid.

Foster slammed his hand down on the desk. "Leave, God damn it," he spoke through clenched teeth. His head was now inflamed with pain.

Simba knew he was serious now and carefully got off the bed. He didn't want to move too fast as if he were scared, but he didn't want to move too slowly and appear as if he did not take Foster seriously. Stubby opened the door and walked out.

"Sorry," Simba said sincerely as he followed Stubby. Foster scowled back at him.

Foster put his face lightly into one hand. His head hurt, and he felt bad about yelling at Simba. He knew there would be no hard feeling between them as these little spats happened all the time, but he still felt bad.

Doc, who was on the bed, slowly got up and moved toward the door. He knew that there was something wrong, but he also knew that there was no sense in speaking to Foster then.

"If you need to talk, you know where I'll be." Doc paused momentarily.

Foster slowly lifted his head. "Thanks." His voice was soft.

After Doc closed the door behind himself, Foster swept his hand across his desk knocking all the notes he had taken about the Rhodes on the floor. "Damn," he said as he went back over to the couch to sit down.

He tried to prioritize everything he had to do. There was no way school could take a back seat to anything, at least not at this point. Football and the fraternity were things he had made prior commitments to. In both of those, people were relying on him. Putting everything in perspective, the Rhodes had low priority.

The Rhodes had been nothing but a pain from the moment he had decided to undertake it. It was hurting his concentration not only in school, but in football too. He didn't know why the hell he was doing it anyway. Maybe he was doing it to please his father, or maybe it was just because he didn't have the nerve to say "no" to President Hardesty when he first asked. He had no desire to go overseas. It just wasn't in his plans. It seemed so much like putting his entire life on hold for two years. That meant by the time he was done with law school, he would be close to thirty years old. He couldn't see not working until then. Could one award be worth that much?

But if he backed out of the Rhodes, so many people would be disappointed. President Hardesty, Professor Ames, his father, and so many others who felt that this would be such an opportunity for both Foster and the college. Nonetheless, it was evident that the Rhodes, as great an honor as it is, was a great burden for Foster. He had to make a decision, one way or the other, on continuing this pursuit.

He got up from the couch, picked up the papers that were spread out around his room, and neatly stacked them on his desk. He knew it was going to be a late night, so he grabbed some change and got a Coke from the pop machine. By now, news of Foster's mood had spread throughout the house. No one said anything to him as he passed through the dining room to the pop machine. When he returned to his room, he grabbed his pencil and began scribbling notes on a fresh piece of paper.

Morning came too quickly for Foster to even consider going running. He had stayed up until about 2:00 a.m., so he was content with just getting out of bed at 7:30. He took a quick shower, ate a bowl of Cap'n Crunch, and then went to the library to make copies of what he had written.

Foster had decided when he got off the couch and began picking up paper that he wasn't going to continue his pursuit of the Rhodes. He had to do what he felt was right for himself. He was doing the Rhodes application because everyone else thought it was right for him. His own heart wasn't in it. He figured, why do something if your heart's not in it?

Right now, all that was important to Foster was playing football. After that, he just wanted to get into law school, get his law degree, and then get on with his life. He never really could see the Rhodes fitting into his plans, at least not this year. He had other years to apply if his heart changed. Maybe a year of maturing and thinking of what he was all about would do that.

When he sat back down, he almost changed his mind, but one look at all the notes he had scribbled over the last seven weeks reconfirmed his decision. He began composing a letter to tell not only those who encouraged his pursuit of the Rhodes, but anybody who knew of it, that he no longer was a candidate.

The letter was almost as difficult to write as the essay, but the letter was where his heart was. Once he got the feel for what he wanted it to say, the letter began to flow.

To whom it might concern:

I am writing this letter to tell you of my decision not to pursue a Rhodes Scholarship. I appreciate all the help I have been given on this, and I am flattered that I was even asked to apply.

At this point in my life, a Rhodes Scholarship is not where my heart is. Therefore, I believe that I would not be a good candidate.

I realize that a Rhodes Scholarship could have opened many doors for me. However, I believe that those doors that are no longer open I can kick in through dedication and hard work.

Sincerely,

Foster Addison

After Foster made ten or twelve copies of the letter, he hustled back to his room and signed each one. Then, he carefully folded each and put them in envelopes, indicating on each who was to receive them. Now came the hard part. He had to distribute the letters.

He contemplated doing it the easy way, by going through the campus mail system. However, he felt that the letter deserved personal service. His heart pounded at the thought of facing some of the people, especially President Hardesty. But he had to do it, and the sooner he got started, the sooner he would be officially out from under the pressures he was feeling.

The first two were easy. Foster taped Stubby's copy to the outside of his door. He was the only one in the house who knew, so he was the only person to get a copy. This was one of the reasons why he decided not to advertise the fact that he was applying for a Rhodes Scholarship. It wasn't that he contemplated not finishing the application from the beginning. He just didn't want to have to explain his own progress a dozen and a half times a day.

The second letter was being sent to his father. He addressed the letter in his room and then found a stamp in the back of his desk drawer. He got in his car and drove about a mile to put the letter in a particular mail box. It wasn't the closest mailbox to campus. In fact, there were nearly a half dozen within two blocks of campus. However, Foster wanted to be sure that the letter went out with that day's mail. He made the ten o'clock pickup. He knew the departure times for almost all the mailboxes in a one-mile radius of campus. He learned them the previous year when he wrote his old girlfriend, Marianne, almost every day. He knew which boxes would get the letter to her in two days and which ones the next day. He knew it was a silly bit of information to possess, but today it was useful.

When Foster returned to campus, he delivered the letters, one by one, to everybody to whom he had talked about the Rhodes. The first few letters were difficult just because they were the first. With each letter, he seemed to get more comfortable with what he was doing.

Foster would go to the person's office and hand deliver the letter. He would stand there and wait for the person to read it and then allow them to make any comments or criticisms they wanted. Most had no criticisms, but were still confident that he would be successful even without a Rhodes Scholarship.

Professor Ames was the second to last person to whom Foster

delivered the letter. Foster wasn't sure how Ames would react. Ames had spent a considerable amount of time so far with Foster working on his special research project, either talking about how economic theory applied to the college admissions process or else reviewing what Foster had written.

Foster's heart pounded as Ames began to read the letter. However, he became more relaxed as Ames began to chuckle at the last paragraph of the letter where Foster spoke of kicking doors in.

"Okay, Foster. The Rhodes isn't the only honor or achievement there is." Ames smiled and gave his support to Foster. He took the letter and put it in the file he had started for Foster's special research project.

"This doesn't change anything about the research project. I still plan on continuing with it." Foster's voice had a questioning tone to it.

"That's right. The research project would have been a nice supplement for your Rhodes application, but it was never intended to be totally dependent on your applying for the scholarship." Ames was pleased. He took a sip from his coffee and then continued. "The project will be a tool you can use to kick in those doors." Ames laughed.

Foster and Ames talked for another fifteen minutes on what the next step in the project would be. Then they spent another ten minutes on how the football season was going, before Ames had to go downstairs to teach a class. Ames wasn't a real vocal football fan, but he was a fan nonetheless. Although a silent observer, he made it to all the games. That was appreciated by the players more than having someone who was loud and belligerent, but who had 'checkerboard attendance.'

The last person Foster had to deliver a letter to was Edmund Hardesty, the college president. It was Hardesty who first suggested the Rhodes Scholarship to Foster. Foster knew from Hardesty's Ivy-League background and the way he spoke of the Rhodes that Hardesty saw this scholarship as the ultimate in academic achievement -- an opportunity which one doesn't even think about passing up. His reaction to the letter was certain. Hardesty wouldn't be angry. He was too calm a person for that. Instead, Hardesty would do his best to try to talk Foster back into applying for the Rhodes. Foster knew this and he tried to psych himself up to counter it.

As Hardesty's secretary announced Foster's arrival and led him into the President's office, Hardesty got up from behind his large, neatly ordered desk and extended his hand. Foster had called ahead and was able to schedule an appointment. However, Hardesty had no idea what the subject matter of the visit was. They shook hands and then Hardesty offered Foster a seat in a chair on the far side of the room.

Hardesty's office had two halves to it. One half was office, where his desk was. This was the area for tending to business. On the other half of the room, there were three high-backed cushioned chairs surrounding a shiny brass coffee table. This area was designed for casual conversation and meetings.

Foster was quick to hand Hardesty his copy of the letter. Hardesty grabbed a letter opener off the coffee table and carefully opened the envelope and removed the letter. Hardesty sat back in the cushioned chair he was seated in, crossed his legs and began to read. His poker face made it impossible to determine what he was thinking. This made Foster uneasy. He tried to focus his attention on books, paintings, pictures, to avoid having to concentrate on Hardesty's blank face.

Hardesty read the letter three times slowly as if he wanted to inflict silent torture on Foster. After minutes of silence had passed, he put the letter in his lap, still holding it with one hand. He looked at Foster, cleared his throat and began to speak.

"I want to try and get you to change your mind, Foster." Hardesty's words were expected. "The Rhodes would be an excellent opportunity for you."

Foster swallowed the lump in his throat slowly so Hardesty wouldn't notice. "I really appreciate the support, but my heart isn't in it." His eyes started to water out of nervousness.

"I know that, but do you know what this could mean to you years from now?" Hardesty paused.

Foster nodded an affirmative response. "But it's just not there." Foster referred to his heart again as he shrugged his shoulders.

"Where is your heart then?" Hardesty's voice was curious.

"Football, I guess." Foster wasn't entirely sure. "I know that I'm not going to make a career out of it, but that's what makes this year so special." He sat up and spoke with confidence. "I know this is my last season. I've been dreaming about this season for four years now. I want to give it all I've got. There are no tomorrows anymore."

Foster had a peek at what this season meant his senior year in high school. His teammates, who were also seniors, cried before the last game in anticipation of the end of their short-lived football careers. The tears they cried weren't out of sorrow, but of emotional overload caused by being totally psyched to give the last game all their bodies had left. The last game is all anybody ever really remembers. That was the game when a player had to absolutely reach his potential, not only physically, but mentally and emotionally too. There was nothing to save for another game.

At that time, Foster couldn't muster any tears. He knew he would be going on to play college football somewhere, and that there would be other games. However, now his time of emotional overload was approaching. Everything had to be right to give the remainder of the season all he had. The Rhodes didn't fit into this.

"Okay." Hardesty nodded his head as he folded the letter up and put it back in the envelope. "I think you're making a mistake, but I understand what you're feeling."

Hardesty realized what he was up against. He had seen it before in other players, but he hoped that this desire to play that last football season with all its intensity would not reach Foster. However, it had. No reason could overcome this drive. Like most fevers, this football fever just had to run its course.

"Thanks," Foster said as he got up out of the chair and moved toward the door. He could feel sweat roll down his back. It was a long morning. He could feel that his stomach had digested the lone bowl of cereal he had for breakfast. Now it felt as if his stomach was digesting itself.

Hardesty stood up and walked to the door and opened it for Foster. He again extended his hand. He shook Foster's hand firmly to indicate his support.

"Give Lawrence some of your heart this weekend." Hardesty smiled
"All of it." Foster grinned back.

Foster kept his composure until he was well out of Hardesty's office. He then ran his fingers through his hair and breathed a sigh of relief. He had cleared the last obstacle. He didn't have to worry about the Rhodes anymore. His body felt so light. It was as if a ton of pressure had been lifted off him all at once. He tried to hide his smile, but he couldn't make it go away.

As he walked out of Middle College, the building where the President's office was, Stubby happened to be walking by on his way to class. Stubby saw Foster first but was afraid to approach him because of the night before. However, when Foster saw Stubby, the smile had increased in intensity. Stubby knew then that it was all right.

"Why are you smiling?" Stubby's face had a smile to match Foster's.

"I don't know." He didn't want to answer directly. "Didn't you get the letter I taped to your door?" Foster continued to smile.

"Yeah. I thought you were serious, but I wasn't sure." Stubby remembered the note after Foster mentioned it.

"Well, I am." Foster clarified. "It's a load off my mind." He ran his fingers through his hair again.

"So you're no longer going to apply for the Rhodes, huh? What made you change your mind? You seemed so sure before that Oxford, England, is where you wanted to be next year." Stubby checked his watch to see how much time he had to get to class.

Foster didn't want to go into details. It was over. The question was moot. He didn't even want to give a straight answer since he was in such a good mood. "Well, Stubby, I guess I've just got too many 'stars and stripes' flowing through these veins of mine." Foster looked at the veins that protruded on his forearm. Stubby chuckled, but before he could respond, Foster started up again. "Besides, if the good Lord had wanted me to be anywhere other than the old U. S. of A., he would have had my little ass born there." Foster winked.

Stubby checked his watch again. "Hey, I've got to get to class." Stubby started moving in the direction of his class. "I was wondering, and I know you're busy, but could you help me get started on my Econ paper sometime this week?" Stubby slowly moved backwards, waiting for an answer.

"Is Sunday too late? Remember, we've got those semi-annual reports to finish." This was Foster's way of apologizing for the night before.

Stubby smiled. He accepted the apology. "Sunday would be fine."

They both started moving in opposite directions.

24

At one o'clock on the same day, Foster, Doc and Stubby showed up together at Coach Bonaventure's office for a team meeting. Bonaventure invited them to have a seat. Before Bonaventure could re-take his own seat, the phone rang. Doc laughed, remarking that Bonaventure was already trying to get rid of them with his phone trick. Bonaventure didn't hear the comment, but ended his conversation quickly.

"The reason I called you here is because I want your input on what I should do to make this week of practice a spirited, productive one. We need to have a good practice this week to be ready to play Lawrence." Bonaventure paused for a moment and then continued. "Should I have the team divide up into smaller groups for stretching? Or should I offer an extra star for the players on the particular position who show the most spirit?" Bonaventure caught his breath while he interlocked his fingers behind his head. "I don't know. That's why I'm asking you. You've all played here for four years. You know what makes you have a good practice, and what are the things that don't." He leaned forward again. Foster tried to jump in, but he wasn't quick enough.

Bonaventure continued. "Your suggestions don't have to be elaborate ones. First of all, we don't have the time to implement them, and second, there isn't money in the budget for some of the things you'll dream up, even though they might work." Bonaventure continued to ramble.

This is how Bonaventure conducted meetings. He would ask someone in to talk and then he would do all the talking. He wasn't rude, and it wasn't that he wasn't interested in hearing what people had to say. It was simply that he had a lot to do during the season, and time just couldn't be allotted for the traditional brainstorming session. He would pose a question or problem and then he would also generate answers or solutions until he hit on one that seemed to suit everyone. It was a highly efficient process.

But he wasn't always like this, only during the season. During the off-season he would have players in his office for normal conversations on almost any topic. Bonaventure would listen to high school stories or stories of things that happened on campus. Bonaventure would listen patiently, and then when the time was right, supplement the conversation with similar stories that he had experienced or had heard. It was just that during the season Bonaventure had to be all business to get everything done.

After five minutes of listening to Coach Bonaventure talk, Doc interrupted. "Excuse me." Bonaventure stopped his sentence as if he had been waiting. "There is something that you haven't mentioned that I think would help us have a good week of practice." Doc shuffled in his chair and swallowed the lump in his throat. "I know it's going to sound as if this is just an excuse to be lazy, but I think this would help the team concentrate more." Doc started to heavily qualify what he had to say to soften the blow. Stubby and Foster leaned forward because they knew it was going to be good, but they wished he would just come right out and say it. The suspense was agonizing. "I think if you cut down on conditioning at the end of practice or cut it out all together, the team would concentrate more in practice."

Stubby and Foster chuckled as if he couldn't possibly be serious. Only Doc had the courage to say something like that. Surprisingly, Bonaventure seemed to give the idea some consideration. He sat with a perplexed look on his face and fiddled with a pencil on his desk.

"How are we going to keep from getting tired in the games?" Bonaventure voiced the obvious flaw in Doc's idea.

Doc felt pressured. He could feel the skin on his face warm up. He knew he was right, but he just had to be able to explain it. He was on his own. Stubby and Foster were waiting for a response just like Bonaventure.

"Coach, the team is in good enough shape at this point in the season. We do more than enough running in all the drills to keep us in shape." Doc stumbled over the first sentence, but then his thoughts started to roll. "In dummy scrimmages, everyone's mind is on what conditioning is going to be, and how they can conserve energy for it, instead of on what the plays are." He looked at the other captains for support. They affirmed what he had to say with an uncertain shake of their heads. "With conditioning always hanging over our heads, it's hard to concentrate." Doc summed up his point.

Bonaventure half bought the idea. He didn't want news of this potential alteration of practice to get out until he had a chance to talk with the other coaches about it. If the coaches agreed that it would make a difference in how the team performed at practice, then he would announce the change just before practice started that day.

Within forty-five minutes, the meeting with Bonaventure was over. Foster had to get to a class, so he excused himself from Bonaventure's office. He was so much more relaxed now that he did not have to be concerned with the Rhodes. After class he went over to check his mail. Jandi had sent him a card. It made his day even better. He went back to his room and lay down on his bed. Foster read the note Jandi had enclosed in the card three times. It made his heart beat strongly to think about the closing, 'Love and Friends Always.' It was unique to her.

Stubby and Doc stayed behind to discuss the Lawrence defense with Bonaventure. Bonaventure went over in detail exactly what he had planned to discuss with the rest of the offense in practice. He pointed out some key things that Doc should be aware of with the Lawrence defense. Then he gave them the projector and the game film Bonaventure had acquired in the film exchange and let them review it for the next hour in the fieldhouse classroom.

Foster fell asleep on his bed for about half an hour. He probably would have slept through practice, if Simba didn't come to the door looking for Foster to give him a ride. During Foster's nap, he happened to roll over onto the card Jandi had sent him. He made one futile attempt to straighten it out before he had to throw it down on his desk and rush to practice.

Practice started like any other, but after warm-ups, Bonaventure huddled the team around him on one knee. He had discussed Doc's suggestion with the other coaches and it received a positive response with only one minor alteration. The coaching staff would reserve the right to reinstate conditioning if they thought the team wasn't concentrating like they were supposed to. Bonaventure introduced the idea as coming from all the captains. Stubby and Foster gladly took partial credit even though it all belonged to Doc. The team didn't much care who was given credit for the idea. The only thing that mattered to them was that it had been suggested.

For whatever reason, the elimination of conditioning or Lawrence week, the team had an exceptional week of practice. Bonaventure felt it was the best one they had had all season, including the very first week of camp. There was a lot of spirit throughout the entire week. Drills were run with intensity. And instead of playing 'grab ass,' as Bonaventure termed it, everyone was attentive to what he was going over when he walked the team through the other team's formations.

However, the spirit the team exhibited didn't come only from those who felt they had a substantial role in the game. Players who weren't even going to be traveling with the team this week did all they could to keep the rest of the team fired up. Bonaventure made a mental note of what each one of these players did. He knew it hurt not be able to travel with the team. He admired a player who, when everyone was watching him, thought he was down and beaten for the last time, would stand tall and say, "I don't quit," and then keep on going. These players were not quitting.

For Thursday's practice, the second-team defense taped on their helmets the name of the Lawrence defensive player they would be imitating when they lined up against the first-team offense in the dummy scrimmage. Although the scrimmage was only at half speed, the second-teamers said that they wanted to make it as close to the actual game situation as possible.

On Friday, the offensive coaches kept the offense out on the field for a longer time than usual. Lawrence was a team notorious for being able to pick apart a team's offense, like Bonaventure did with film, while the team went through plays in warm-ups. Beloit hoped to circumvent this problem by having many formations they could use. So, during the course of the week, the offense had put in several new formations. The coaches wanted to make sure that everyone understood what they had to do.

The defensive coaches only kept the defense for a short while. The main things the defense had to know were hustle and hit. They made the defenses simple and concentrated on execution. They planned that their first down on the field was going to be, as Coach Cain put it, a 'straight-up, welcome-them-to-college-football' play. The defense wasn't supposed to worry about where the ball was. All anyone was to worry about was hitting the player across from them legally as hard as they could to let them know Beloit was there. The other team could even get a touchdown, as long as each man made the guy across from him think of how hard he was hit that first play each time he lined up on the ball.

After the defensive coaches explained the philosophy, the defensive unit lined up for ten-yard sprints. Everyone started on Coach Bonaventure's count as he ran with the team during the four ten-yard sprints: one for Northwestern College, one for Knox College, one for Grinnell College, and the one everyone cheered on, for Lawrence.

Foster untied his shoes and loosened the laces after the last sprint. The rest of the team hustled to the locker room to get changed. Coach Bonaventure waited about five yards ahead of Foster as the other defensive coaches walked down by where the offense was still going over plays.

"Hey Coach," Foster said. He was almost startled to see Bonaventure still standing there.

Bonaventure stuck out his hand. "You had a great week of practice, probably the best week you've had your entire four years here. Good job." He winked.

Foster blushed. "Well, I've got to get out of this slump. I haven't had a really good game yet this season." He shrugged his shoulders. "I'm just sort of there."

Bonaventure stopped to say something. Foster stopped, too, and faced Bonaventure. "You know what your problem is?" Bonaventure didn't give any time to answer. "You think too much. You're too damn smart. You bring all sorts of 'what ifs' from the classroom onto the field." Bonaventure was very frank, but not harsh in his words.

Foster lightly laughed as he smiled.

Bonaventure continued. "Before you do anything, you think, 'If I do this, what if this or that happens?' By the time you've done that, you're a step behind. Christ, don't think so much. That's my job." Bonaventure gently grasped Foster behind the neck and started him walking toward the locker room. "Play the game, Foster; just play football. Go out there and make things happen. If you screw up, big deal. One play doesn't make a game." Bonaventure shook Foster's head once or twice and then pushed him on toward the locker room, before he went to join the other coaches.

No one slept well that night. In fact, they hadn't even slept well the night before. They felt tired, but they couldn't sleep. Even on the bus ride to Lawrence, no one was able to sleep. They just sat quietly looking out the window thinking. The anticipation was too strong. Sleep didn't matter, however. They were going to be playing on pure emotion.

Lawrence University was located in Appleton, Wisconsin, about three and a half hours north of Beloit and a half hour south of Green Bay, in the Fox River Valley. In the Appleton area, the paper industry was the economic mainstay. In fact, Lawrence University had a College of Wood Product Sciences on its campus. When the air was still, the odors from the paper plants were almost unbearable.

Not only was this game special to the team because Lawrence was the team to beat, but because the game was being played in the heart of Wisconsin. Since at least half the players were from Wisconsin, a lot of Beloit families showed up for the game. In addition to the regular family, friends and professors, Foster's father and his brother, Mike, made it from Houghton, Michigan. And a special surprise was that Simba's mother had flown in from Tampa, Florida, to Green Bay and then driven down to the game with Doc's parents. Everyone finally got to see Simba act civil.

Lawrence's athletic facilities were about a half mile from the university's main campus. The team dressed in the field house and then had to walk another 200 yards across the practice field to the game field. At the game field, there was a cinder-block building equipped with toilet facilities, benches and chalkboards that the team could use as a meeting area so they didn't have to go back to where they dressed.

Lawrence had the best football stadium in the conference. The field was located at the bottom of a valley, with two sets on stands built right into the grassy valley walls on both sides of the field. The field had thick green grass like a plush carpet. The stadium was called the Banta Bowl. Lawrence had obviously named it after a distinguished coach or professor at the university. Players on other teams thought that the word 'Banta' was either an Indian word or slang meaning football superiority.

It was a cool, damp day. It didn't rain, but the mist was heavy. In the three times Bonaventure had been to Lawrence for games, he never remembered it being sunny. But then, each time he brought a team here, they were beaten miserably, which accented the particularly dismal weather.

Despite the weather, the Banta Bowl was filled with people, most dressed in the blue and white of the Lawrence Vikings. Of all their games, this was the one in which the Bucs felt most like they were playing in a big college atmosphere. No one was allowed on the field except for the grounds crew and the football teams. The press box was lighted and completely enclosed in glass. Movie cameras were at almost every angle in the stadium. And Lawrence had both a band and a set of cheerleaders that resembled a big-time program. All this did nothing to intimidate the Bucs. Instead, it seemed to add to the emotion of the game.

Lawrence took the field while Bonaventure was still giving a last-minute agenda to the team. The 100-and-some-odd players of Lawrence appeared to overwhelm the Bucs as Beloit only sent out their special-team players. Beloit's centers didn't know when to hike the ball to their punters or kickholder as the Lawrence players roared over the snap count. When Beloit's entire team took the field, forty-four players looked like a handful compared to Lawrence's army. But the Bucs didn't seem the least bit shaken. They went through their routine as if Knox College or Grinnell College were on the other side of the field.

Since Beloit had fewer players, it didn't take them as long to warm up. The Bucs were back in the tiny meeting room that the home team had provided while Lawrence finished up its pre-game. The whole team was deep in thought. Stubby sat on the floor, with his head between his scrunched-up knees. He coldly stared at a knot in the wooden bench in front of him. Bert and Foster paced up by the chalkboard. They tried to relax, but the adrenaline that ran through their systems was making them feel sick. Doc slowly rotated his neck and shoulders, trying to stay loose. The coaches were waiting outside, giving the players this time to collect themselves.

Just about when the coaches were going to go inside, the Lawrence team went into their meeting room. Bonaventure still hadn't seen any of their coaches, only players. It was as if the Lawrence team were guided by remote control. As the last man pushed into the Lawrence side of the building, Bonaventure wondered how they all could fit in the tiny locker room.

Inside the Beloit half, the silence was pierced by the noise created by the Lawrence players. It was evident that they intended to be heard. They intended to have the Bucs hear them laughing and carrying on as if they weren't even worried. Despite this, the Bucs' intensity remained intact. Foster swallowed hard to fight the sick feeling. Doc leaned his head against the wall and gently closed his eyes and went through each one of Lawrence's formations in his mind. Stubby shook Simba's hand without taking his eyes off the knot in the wood.

Bonaventure led the coaching staff into the room. Everyone turned their attention to them. They were anxious to leave. Lawrence's antics were getting to them. Bonaventure directed everyone to take a knee. When everyone was kneeling, he instructed them to gather around. The noise Lawrence was creating made it impossible to give any sort of fiery pre-game speech. Besides, nothing he could say would increase the intensity the team had. Something short and simple would do.

"Men, the hell with all this hype. Let's just go do it." Bonaventure led the team to the field.

Since it was a cool, damp day, Bonaventure instructed the captains to line the team up for a couple of sets of quick warm-up drills. The team formed its lines and then started doing an abbreviated series of stretches and warm-ups. They had gotten through four stretches and were ready to end the session on a spirited set of jumping-jacks when the Lawrence team exited their locker room and came onto the field.

Just before the captains got the team started doing the four-count jumping-jacks, the Lawrence team, either out of total disrespect or a lack of any sort of sportsmanlike conduct, cut through the lines the Beloit team had made. The Bucs patiently waited as the Lawrence players heckled and pointed fingers at them.

Bonaventure expected something like this to happen. Every year Lawrence did something to rub his team's face in its inferiority. Lawrence had taken cheap shots to injure players, or run up the score unnecessarily. Like everyone else, he remained calm.

Once the Lawrence team had passed, the captains did the jumping-jacks as if there were no Lawrence. Bonaventure then called the team over to the sidelines, as the captains went to the center of the field for the coin-toss. Lawrence won the toss, and was receiving the ball. Bonaventure was happy.

"Stuff them early, and make the rules," Bonaventure stormed, as the defense ran on to the field. The Bucs called no defensive play in the huddle. They all said 'Let's do it!' simultaneously and broke to line up on the ball.

As the man Foster was going to be lined up against approached the line, Foster stared coldly into his eyes. The man looked back at Foster and then tapped the shoulder of the man who was lining up next to him. They both looked at Foster and laughed. Foster continued to stare intensely.

Foster took his stance. He let the energy in his legs and arms gather so he could power into the cocky offensive guard. Rip through the man, he thought. His body started to shake as Lawrence took a long count. He still stared coldly.

At the snap of the ball, Foster exploded his entire body toward the player opposite him. He led with his right forearm, catching the man under the chin and knocking him back. Foster didn't even see where the ball went. In uppercutting the man, Foster's hand caught on a metal rivet and it ripped the skin off the second knuckle on his middle finger. Blood began pouring down his finger. The offensive guard looked at Foster with surprise and terror. He could see stars. Ignoring the pain in his finger, Foster brought his hand up into his face mask and smeared a streak of blood, like war-paint, on each cheek. He stared back just like he had when he first lined up and said under his breath, "Keep laughing, asshole."

Lawrence gained seven yards on the first down. That was a small price for the jolt the Bucs gave them. The Lawrence team was filled with nervous tension as they approached the line the second time. This time it wasn't a 'straight-up, welcome-them-to-college-football' play. Bonaventure signaled in a regular defensive formation. When the ball was snapped, the guy across from Foster flinched as if he expected to be hit again. This time Foster just threw him aside and went in looking for the ball.

Since Lawrence had second down and short yardage, they dropped back for a pass. Foster and the other defensive linemen honed in on the quarterback. The quarterback was the son of Lawrence's coach, which made the pursuit all the more exciting. Foster had a distaste for athletic nepotism ever since he had to sit the bench in Little League because the coach wanted to play his kids.

Foster didn't get to the quarterback in time to prevent the pass, but he was still there in time to hit the passer. He rammed his body into the quarterback as if he were trying to go through the man. As they both fell to the ground, Foster still had a hold of the Lawrence quarterback. He stuck his face mask tightly up against the quarterback's and squeezed his body to get his attention.

"I'm going to be in your face all day," Foster said through his clenched teeth just like Bonaventure. "It's just going to be me and you, mother fucker. Just me and you."

Foster got up without even lending the quarterback a hand. As he walked back to the huddle, Lawrence's quarterback screamed at his offensive linemen for protection.

Beloit broke up Lawrence's pass and then took them for a five-yard loss on the next play to bring up a punting situation. Lawrence managed to get off a good punt under a heavy rush by the punt-block team. Bonaventure gave Doc a play to run as he sent in the rest of the first-team offense.

Bonaventure wanted the offense to use the momentum that the defense had created. The offense was going immediately to the air. Doc dropped back for the pass. The offensive line held off the Lawrence defense, giving Doc plenty of time to find an open man twenty yards down the field.

On the sidelines, a student trainer came up to Foster and, without asking, began bandaging up Foster's finger.

"It's only a scrape. It'll be okay." Foster pulled his hand back.

"I'm not worried about your finger, but you're getting blood all over your pants. I've got to scrub that stuff out later," the trainer replied.

Foster looked at him, appalled. "Get away from me." Foster walked down the sidelines to get a better look at the offense and to move away from the badgering trainer.

The next play was brought in by a wide receiver who took the place of the tight end. Beloit was going to go with two wide receivers for the next play. Doc lined the team up, and was about to call the count when he noticed that the Lawrence team was lining up as if they were reading the play. It was obvious that they already had figured out the offense Beloit was using in warm-ups. Doc stopped the count and changed the play at the line. Instead of the pass Lawrence expected, Doc handed the ball off to his tailback, who scooted down the field behind Big El.

It was an eight-yard gain. Running behind Big El was a definite strength for Beloit if they needed it. Doc continued to move the ball for

Beloit. Every few plays he would change the offensive formation to keep the Lawrence team guessing. When they got within the thirty-yard line, Doc went back for another pass. It was right to the receiver. However, the referee called Simba for holding. Simba was irate. He swore that he wasn't holding. He cursed the referee under his breath for the controversial call. The loss of the yardage and the penalty yardage caused the offense to lose momentum. They had to punt the ball back to Lawrence.

On the next series, Beloit's defense again stopped the Lawrence offense without a yard. However, when the ball was punted, it was fumbled deep in the Beloit end, and five plays later, Lawrence was ahead by seven points.

Lawrence then kicked off to Beloit. The offense was content running the ball for three plays, but then found itself in a third and long situation. Doc dropped back for the pass and found a receiver open. The throw was perfect. The receiver caught the ball and began running, but a Lawrence defender caught up with the receiver and started to tackle him. When everyone thought the receiver was down, another Lawrence player tore the ball loose and recovered it. The referee awarded the ball to Lawrence.

Bonaventure stormed onto the field. He screamed that the play should have been called over. The other coaches herded him back to the sidelines as the defense stormed onto the field, vowing not to let Lawrence get another touchdown. The offense led the cheers for the defense on the sidelines.

The defense gave up two easy first downs and then held tough. Lawrence was forced to settle for a field goal. They now led ten to nothing, but the Beloit offense would have another chance. Other than the controversial plays, they were moving the football. They somehow had to avoid those controversial plays.

Two plays later, they did just that. Doc hit a receiver on a quick pass up the middle and the receiver was able to run the length of the field for the score. The play was so quick and clean that there was no room for any controversy. After the extra point, it was only ten to seven in favor of Lawrence. The momentum had switched back to Beloit.

The defense stopped the Lawrence offense in three plays and the offense was again marching down the field. Lawrence was doing an excellent job covering the receivers, and the Beloit offensive line could keep the rushers out all day. What Doc couldn't get by passing, he ran.

In four plays, he ran for close to forty-five yards. Although he didn't score, he made the pass defenders loosen up their coverage enough so he could throw another touchdown pass. Beloit was up by four points.

The whole game went back and forth like this. The Beloit defense would stop the Lawrence offense and force them to punt, and then the Beloit offense would march down the field. However, the Bucs couldn't manage another score, even though they made 34 first downs and gained over 500 yards against the Lawrence defense.

In the middle part of the fourth quarter, on one of the few times Beloit had to punt the ball, Lawrence ran the ball back for the score. The Beloit defense stopped Lawrence's attempt for a two-point conversion, but the touchdown still caused them to lose 16 to 14.

As the team shook the Lawrence players' hands, they realized that they had won their respect. That was a victory in itself. But it was still hard to believe they had lost. They hung their heads as they walked to the locker room. Their fans tried to cheer them up, but it was no use. They had played their hearts out and lost.

The team sat quietly in the locker room. Bert sat next to Stubby and put his arm around him, squeezing him tightly and trying to comfort him. He was on the verge of tears. For the seniors, the dream of beating the champion was gone. Like most dreams that people put all their hearts into, it died hard.

No one started to undress. The locker room was silent until Bonaventure stormed in as if they had won. Immediately, he caught everyone's attention.

"Boy, I hate to lose, but we didn't lose." Bonaventure had fire in his eyes. "Sure, they scored more points than we did, but I'll tell you something, you played them RIGHT OFF THEIR FEET!" He shouted: "That's supposed to be the championship team. That's the number one team in the Midwest conference." Bonaventure raised one finger to the forty-four pairs of dejected eyes that looked on. "That's what people think. And you played 'em off their feet. You know what you did?" Bonaventure asked a rhetorical question. "You made me so proud I can just taste it. You played super." He took off his hat and pointed at them. His voiced raised: "But boy, can you walk tall. Boy, can you feel good. I'm proud of you. And I'll tell you something -- seven and two ain't bad. And I'll tell you, Chicago better buckle 'em on because we're coming."

Bonaventure's speech motivated the team. Although they were still hurt by the loss, Bonaventure forced them to look at the positive aspects of the game. No, there wasn't an extra tally in the win column for them, but they sure received a heavy dose of pride and respect.

During the bus ride home, even though every one of them thought about what it would have been like to win, they still felt excited about their showing. After two nights with little sleep and a hard-fought football game, they all should have been physically and emotionally drained. Instead, each of them was full of energy. Bonaventure was confident that none of them would have trouble saying 'I'm good' when they went to put their heads down on the pillow that night.

The bus got back to the Beloit campus at about 8:30. Even though the past few days were starting to catch up with them, most of the guys planned to go out to the Jungle Safari. Others, since most of the midterm exams were the next week, felt a responsibility to stay in and get some studying done.

When the guys got back to the house, Jandi was waiting in the living room with Jennifer. She and Foster had planned to go out to a movie that evening. Normally, Jandi's mother would have watched Jennifer, but she was called out of town at the last minute and so Jandi brought Jennifer. Jandi searched most of the day for a babysitter, but she couldn't locate one. It came down to either calling the date off or taking Simba up on his earlier offer to watch Jennifer if the need arose. She didn't want to break the date because it was very seldom that they had a chance to go out. Under the circumstances, Simba seemed a pretty good alternative.

Before Jandi presented Simba with the proposition, he was planning on going to the Jungle. However, he quickly changed his plans, not only to help Foster, but also because he was good with kids. But he wasn't the only person to fuss over Jennifer.

Everyone took their turn, either tickling Jennifer or talking nonsense words to her. She loved the attention. She didn't seem to mind at all when Doc took her from Jandi and sat down on the couch next to her. Doc cradled Jennifer and made baby noises to her.

Jandi quickly went over instructions with Simba as she put on her coat. Simba reassured her that he had done all of this many times before and that everything was all right. When Foster came back from his room after changing his shirt, Simba sat back down on the chair while Jandi watched Doc bounce Jennifer on his knee.

"Koochie Koo...Koochie Koo," Doc said as he bounced the baby girl on his knee. He pulled Jennifer close to his face so she could grab his cheeks.

"DaDa..DaDa," Jennifer said as she played with Doc's cheeks.

Everyone in the room laughed. Doc began to blush. With all the excitement, Jennifer was now having more fun getting attention for her sounds. She clapped her hands and jumped up and down, continuing to refer to Doc as her Daddy.

"No, No Jennifer," Jandi said, as she laughed, too.

Doc was flustered. He quickly stood and walked over to Simba. "Here you go, Simba. I've got to get ready to go out." He handed Jennifer to Simba and then moved out of the room in a hurry. Everyone continued to laugh.

25

Simba was at his desk studying when Foster and Jandi came home. It was only a little after midnight. Foster had a long day. After a movie and a pizza, he strained to keep his eyes open. Although it wasn't a long time, it was nice for the two of them to spend a quiet evening alone.

Jennifer was fast asleep on Simba's waterbed. She didn't give Simba any problems. Shortly after Jandi left, Simba brought Jennifer up to his room and let her play on his bed with a three-foot stuffed buffalo he had won at a carnival. As she played, Simba put an Alvin and the Chipmunks album on his stereo. Jennifer was amused as Simba sang along.

The warmth and rippling of the waterbed made Jennifer fall asleep quickly. She still clung to one of the buffalo's legs. Simba turned off his stereo and began studying. He was glad he didn't go to the bar. He managed to get through over half a book he had to read for a mid-term exam by the time Jandi and Foster got home.

Foster brought home an extra pizza for Simba. Jandi also tried to give him twenty dollars for babysitting. Simba immediately took a piece of pizza, but refused any money. Jandi gave him a warm kiss on the cheek. He blushed. To Simba, that meant more than any amount of money she could have given him.

Foster picked up Jennifer and held her tightly to his body. She stirred for a moment and then she rested her head on Foster's shoulder. Jandi led the way out of Simba's room and down to the car.

Jandi placed Jennifer in the child seat and began strapping her in. The front door to the house opened and Simba appeared. He trotted across the front yard and over to the car. He had the buffalo with him. Foster moved forward to meet him.

"Here, give this to Jennifer. She has more fun with it than I do anyway." He spoke softly so he wouldn't wake Jennifer. A smile grew on his face as he looked at the sleeping child.

Jandi had just completed safely strapping Jennifer in. She stood and faced Simba and mouthed the words 'thank you.' Simba only allowed a select few to see this side of him. To him, it was something one had to earn. Jandi had earned it. By having Jennifer stay there, Jandi had done a favor to Simba, not the reverse. For that, he was grateful.

After Simba handed Foster the buffalo, he turned and trotted back in the house. Foster took it and walked around to the other side of the car to put it in the passenger seat. He closed the door and walked back over to Jandi. She waited for him. He gave her a quick peck on the lips and then started to walk in the house. Before he could take a second step, she grabbed him and pulled him back. They engaged in a long kiss and embrace. After their lips lost contact, they looked into one another's eyes.

"Thanks for taking me out tonight," Jandi said softly and sincerely.

"Don't thank me. You paid." Foster smiled and broke the seriousness. She smiled back and gave him a big hug.

They kissed once more and then she got in the car. Foster walked over to the curb as she started the engine. As she pulled away, she beeped the horn twice quickly. Foster waved as she drove off into darkness down College Street.

The TV room was relatively quiet on Sunday. The majority of the mid-term exams were scheduled for the coming week. All the readings, labs, and problems which had been put off for weeks could be postponed no longer. For many, it was time to cram seven weeks of learning into one.

As they had planned earlier in the week, Foster helped Stubby with his paper. Although the paper was due Friday morning, Stubby was confident that he'd finish. After all, Foster had already beaten a path. Foster knew what resources were available, where they were, which ones to use and which ones not to. In essence, Stubby would learn from Foster's mistakes.

Foster didn't mind. Besides, to teach was to learn twice, he always thought. Each time he explained how to use a resource, it would reinforce it in his own mind. The time he spent helping Stubby wasn't wasted. He knew it would pay off on the exam.

At the informal team meeting, everyone tried to re-emphasize what

Coach Bonaventure said after the game. But as hard as they tried, their words were nothing more than just that -- words.

The Lawrence game took a lot out of them. They played a great game, the kind of game they dreamed about playing. However, the game didn't end the way they dreamed it would. They came up short. The game took all their emotional energy. The loss didn't replenish it. There was no reinforcement for their hard work.

Practice in the early part of the week was indicative of what they really felt. They were there in body, but not in spirit. They went through the motions for stretching, drill, scrimmages, everything. They were lethargic. They tried not to be. They tried to concentrate on getting back their mental edge, but their lack of emotional energy made it hard to concentrate. It was just too easy for them to let their minds wander -- to let themselves fall back into the Comfort Zone. They thought about places they would rather be: watching television, lying in bed, being with their girlfriends.

Classes only added to this emotional drain and hindered their concentration on football. Preparing for and taking exams also took a certain amount of energy. And the hours spent cramming for exams replaced the time they usually spent in those places they thought about being. Although mid-term break was coming at a good time, it was still too far off to provide any motivation.

Bonaventure knew that the team couldn't be up all the time. These periods of low enthusiasm served to replenish their supply and gave more meaning to the times when they were spirited. Besides, he and the other coaches were feeling it, too. However, by Thursday, Bonaventure felt it was time to take them out of this low state. He hadn't said much about it, until then. But now it was time to start getting ready for Saturday.

University of Chicago wasn't a particularly good team. Beloit had no problem beating them in the past. However, Chicago couldn't be taken lightly. Bonaventure knew that and he had to get that across to the team. But more important than a loss to University of Chicago, he had to get them to focus on what a win in that game and continued winning might mean. Although they hadn't beaten last year's champion, they were still in the race for this year's title. Before practice started, Bonaventure huddled the team at the center of the practice field and started explaining a scenario where the Beloit College Buccaneers still could be Midwest Conference champions.

The Midwest Conference was comprised of eleven teams which were divided into two divisions. Six teams made up the South Division, and Beloit was one of five teams in the North Division. At the end of the season, each division would name its winner, and then the two divisional winners would play one another for the conference championship.

Conference games were played against teams in each respective division. The first four games Beloit played were nonconference. North Central College and Northwestern College were in separate conferences and Knox College and Grinnell College were in the South Division and, therefore, didn't count as conference games. Lawrence was the first conference game. They had three others along with another nonconference game.

So, at this point, they were O and one in conference play, but if they won the remaining conference games, they would finish the season with a three and one conference record. Bonaventure was sure they could do that, which meant that all that had to happen was for Lawrence to lose one conference game. That was possible, too. The North Division was a competitive one. At any point, anyone could beat anyone else.

If Lawrence lost, then the Bucs would be assured of a share of the North Division crown. Who would go on to play the South Division winner for the conference title would be decided by a vote of the coaches in the North Division. At that point, it was anyone's guess. However, Bonaventure speculated that if they beat everyone else, combined with their good showing against Lawrence and the fact that Lawrence played in the title game the year before, then the Bucs would be chosen to play in the title game. From that point, they would only be sixty minutes of football away from being Midwest Conference champions.

Although his logic wasn't complex, it was drawn out. Several contingent factors had to fall in place. Despite all this, the team saw the chances as substantial more than slim. In fact, once they had the opportunity to think about them, the chances seemed good. The only factor that wasn't in their control was having someone beat Lawrence. The other team's hunger to be conference champions would handle that. Everything else seemed to be in their control, even the coaches' vote. They knew if they played convincingly that all the coaches would vote for them.

Bonaventure's logic worked. The team finished out the day with a good practice. Although it wasn't anything like the practices they had the week before, it was the spirit they needed to get by University of Chicago. Bonaventure wasn't going to worry about next week until then. His only concern was that this spirit would carry over through Friday into the game on Saturday.

Wednesday night Stubby finished his paper. On Thursday morning, he went to Peg's room with Foster. Foster picked up his paper and paid Peg for typing it, and Stubby dropped his off to be typed. Peg was finished with her exams and so spent time during the day typing Stubby's paper. By the time she was supposed to go out to dinner with Bill, she had it completed. Before going to Bill's room, she stopped at Stubby's room and gave him his paper. Stubby gladly paid her. Tonight Peg was buying Bill dinner.

After Stubby proofread his paper once, he went down to Foster's room. They had agreed that they would read one another's paper in hopes of catching any flaws they might have missed in proofreading their own. As they read each other's paper, they corrected typos and made notes in the margins where they had a particular question. When they were both done, they started to discuss what each had found.

After a half an hour, they had exhausted their comments and questions for one another. For all intents and purposes, it was mid-term break for them. They both finished their mid-terms earlier that day. All they had left to do was hand their papers in the next morning after class. Stubby bought a Coke for himself and Foster. They sat in Foster's room, just passing time talking, but their conversation was disrupted by a panicked knock on the door.

"Come in, if you're good looking," Stubby hollered from Foster's bed.

The door whushed open and Bert came charging in. He was armed with three pencils in one hand and a half-spent yellow legal pad in the other.

"Where did you find information for this bullshit Econ paper?" Bert was out of breath. He had been at the library, and had no luck locating any information for the paper.

"You mean you haven't even started researching the paper we have to turn in tomorrow morning?" Foster laughed with amazement.

"No," Bert casually responded as if he were right on schedule. He checked his watch. "I've still got over twelve hours before it's due."

Neither Foster nor Stubby was in any mood to go over to the library to help Bert do research for his paper. It was nothing against Bert, it was just that he had poor timing. Had it been a week, or even a day, earlier they would have been happy to help. But now, they were too relaxed, basking in the comfort of being finished.

However, they weren't totally without compassion. Foster and Stubby tried to explain where all the books they had used were by drawing maps of the library. Foster dug through the notes he had generated to write the paper and found a list of call numbers for books he had looked up. He tore the sheet out and handed it to Bert to use. Stubby let Bert have a copy of his paper to give him an idea of what format to use.

When Bert was satisfied with the direction he was given, he went back to the library. Foster and Stubby wondered if he was going to have it done in time. Judging by what kind of time they had to put into theirs, they didn't think so.

Doc hadn't seen Carli in close to a week. He had stopped by her room last Friday night just to watch some television and relax before the Lawrence game. As usual, all her friends were hovering in and out of the room, so there wasn't much time alone.

Since then, they were both getting ready for their mid-term exams. Usually when they went to the library they didn't get much done. The library was more a social event than academic. However, now that it was down to the wire and they had to really get some work done, they each stayed home and studied in their own rooms. Doc called Carli once earlier in the week, but the conversation didn't last long because they both were very busy. Doc was done with his mid-term exams on Wednesday. However, Carli had one on Thursday, so this was the first chance he had to see her.

Doc knew Carli was going to be in her room. She was going home for the one-week break on Friday afternoon. He figured that she didn't have the time so she would probably be packing. After watching television, he brushed his teeth, combed his hair and then started across campus to see her.

Campus was relatively quiet for a Thursday night. People who weren't done with exams yet were studying. Those who were done either had left early for the break, or else were at the bars celebrating the end of the first half of the semester.

Carli's floor was also unusually quiet. A couple of her friends were in the hall when Doc got up there. However, instead of following Doc to Carli's room, they quickly said hello and then went back to their rooms. Doc figured that they still had studying to do.

Carli's door was closed, so Doc knocked. Another one of Carli's friends answered and let Doc in. Carli was in the middle of packing her last suitcase with dirty clothes. She was taking them home to have her mother wash them. Carli stopped packing. She looked surprised to see him.

"Oh, hi. I was coming over to see you in a little bit," Carli said.

"That's okay," Doc quickly interjected, "I wanted to get out of the house anyway."

"Well, I've got to be going. I've got to finish packing, too." Carli's friend stood halfway out the door.

"Hey, if I don't see you, have a good break," Doc said as she closed the door behind herself.

Doc pulled out a chair from under the desk and turned it around so he could sit on it backwards. He couldn't believe that no one was around. He was going to say something, but he wasn't sure how Carli would take the comment. He let it pass.

Carli turned away from Doc and again began packing dirty clothes in the suitcase. She was unusually quiet. For a minute they both remained quiet. Doc broke the silence.

"How did your mid-terms go?" His question sounded sincere.

"Okay," she answered quickly.

By the silence and the shortness of her answer, Doc knew that something was wrong. He figured it was just that she was tired. He didn't want to press her, but he didn't want to sit there in total silence either. He didn't have to worry about either. She spoke.

"Todd," she paused and then faced him. "I don't think we should see each other anymore." She couldn't look him in the eye.

Doc heard what she said, but it didn't register right away. After a moment, his eyes widened and he sat up in the chair. "What?" he said in disbelief.

She rephrased her statement. "I just think that it would be better if..." She searched for the right words. Her speech was labored and her mouth dry. "I just think we should become friends, at least for a while."

"Why?" Doc still spoke as if he couldn't understand what she was saying.

She still didn't look him in the eye as she started to explain. "Todd, I like you. I really do, but I just want to spend more time on school the second half of the semester." She swallowed hard. "This relationship is preventing me from doing that." Doc just sat and listened. "It would probably do us both some good to concentrate more on school."

Doc started to speak irrationally. "You talk as if we spend all sorts of time together. We don't." He started to talk quickly. "We hardly spend any time together at all." He stopped himself before he could lose control of what he was saying.

She calmly started up again. "That's another thing. You're so wrapped up in football that you don't have any time for me."

Doc was on the verge of exploding. "You're not making any sense. First you say that all the time we spent together detracts from school, and then you say that I don't devote enough time to you." He took a deep breath and tried to calm himself. "It doesn't make sense."

Carli knew it didn't make sense. But that's all she had to say. "I just think we should stop seeing one another, okay?" Her tone of voice was insistent.

Doc couldn't remember the last time he felt so angry. However, he contained it. "Okay." He labored to have a calm voice. He got up from the chair and walked over to the door. His head seemed to spin. He knew he had to leave before he couldn't contain his anger anymore. "I guess just have a good break." He gently closed the door behind himself.

After he left, Carli started to cry. She lay down on her bed and whimpered into her pillow.

After Doc left Carli's room, he went for a walk to try and cool down. He replayed in his mind over and over what she had said. He searched for a clue in her words that would reveal what her real reason was. He was too angry to think. Nothing she said made sense.

After Doc's anger passed, the pain of breaking up set in. He fought the tears. Everything seemed to be going so well between them. They seemed to be getting closer. There was absolutely no indication that this was going to happen.

Being alone wasn't helping. He needed to talk to someone to get what was building up inside him off his chest. Doc didn't know where to turn. This was a switch for him. Usually he was the one doing the consoling, not being consoled. He walked back to the house. It was late, and it seemed as if no one's lights were on.

As Doc reached for the door, it opened. Stubby was taking Sue back to her room. She was flying out of town the next day, and she hadn't packed yet either. They immediately sensed Doc's distraught state.

"Doc, what's the matter?" Stubby held the door open for him.

It had been a while since he spoke last. His mouth was dry. He had to struggle to speak. "Carli broke up with me." He sniffled. "I need to talk to someone." He was again on the verge of tears.

"As soon as I walk Sue home, I'll be back." Stubby's speech was rushed.

Sue had never seen Doc so upset. She sensed the urgency. "I can walk myself home. You can talk to Doc." Her voice was concerned. She got on her toes and gave Stubby a kiss goodnight and then walked across the street to the Zeta Kappa Zeta house.

Stubby led the way up to his room. After Doc got in the room, he closed the door. Stubby sat on his bed and Doc sat on the couch. Doc stared at the wood on the side of the waterbed. His eyes were bloodshot.

Stubby was at a loss for words, too. He had never been in this position before. "Talk to me, Doc."

He started to talk, but the words stuck in his throat. He realized that it was futile. He shook his head and began to cry.

After Stubby sat for five minutes helplessly listening to Doc whimper, Doc regained his composure and began to talk. Stubby still didn't know what to say, but by saying nothing at all he did the right thing. Doc needed a sympathetic ear.

The combination of crying and being able to talk to someone made Doc feel better. Although he still hurt and still didn't understand, he was able to accept the fact that she did break up with him. Now he could start to deal with it.

By the time Doc had said everything that he needed to, which ended up being the same things over and over, only reworded, it was three in the morning. He asked Stubby to keep their conversation just between them. Stubby gladly agreed. Doc left his room and went to bed. Stubby took his contacts out and did the same.

At eight o'clock that morning, Stubby awoke. He had slept through his alarm. Although he still had an hour to get to class to hand in his paper, he was uneasy. He made his bed, took a quick shower, got dressed and went down to the living room to meet Foster and Bert so they could walk to class together.

Foster was already in the living room. They sat together and waited for Bert to come upstairs. Stubby disclosed part of what he was asked to keep a secret. He didn't go into any detail of what was said. He at least wanted Foster and everyone else to know that Carli had broken up with Doc, and that Doc was hurting. It was something that people would eventually find out, and it was something that they needed to know in dealing with Doc.

At ten minutes until 9:00, they went down to Bert's room to see if he was up. He was. In fact, he hadn't been to bed yet. Bert was at his desk, still hammering away at the computer. He told Stubby and Foster to go on ahead to class and that he would be along in a minute.

At nine o'clock, Bert still hadn't shown up for class. The professor didn't even notice. He began his lecture as he always did by quickly reviewing the material from the last lecture. Stubby and Foster busily took notes. When Stubby got the chance, he would check his watch to see what time it was. At 9:30, Bert still hadn't showed. They looked at each other and shook their heads in disbelief. Every time they could hear someone walking down the hall toward the classroom, Foster and Stubby expected Bert to come through the doorway seconds later. He didn't.

The rest of the class was oblivious to what was going on. They all sat taking notes with their papers on their desks ready to be handed in. They were intent on listening to the professor. Bert's absence meant nothing to them. In fact, Bert's attendance at this nine o'clock class was so irregular that many of them didn't even know he was supposed to be in the class.

At 9:48, the professor began to summarize his lecture. He had to speak louder than usual because the students in the hall who had been released from other classes were causing a commotion. Still, he didn't cut his lecture short.

Foster and Stubby looked at each other one last time. Their looks were no longer ones of disbelief, but of concern. The paper was worth one half of their grade. The professor rarely accepted late papers, and when he did, the grade usually reflected it.

"Well, that's all for today. Everybody have a good break, and I'll see you in ten days." The professor started to gather his notes. "Please put your papers on my desk on your way out -- thank you."

Just then, the door to the classroom opened and Bert stormed through the door. He didn't even look for a seat. He wasn't planning on staying, even if the lecture wasn't over. He made a B-line for the desk and set his paper down in front of the professor. No one else even had a chance to get to the front of the room.

Bert looked at the professor and smiled. "Remember now. I was the first one to hand my paper in."

The professor had nothing to say. He smiled back with a look of uncertainty on his face. He didn't quite know what to think. Bert turned and left the classroom.

Carli checked over all the stuff she planned to take home one more time. All the late summer/early fall clothes she wanted to exchange at home for late fall/early winter clothes seemed to be there. She lived only about ninety miles away, but she wanted to get it all on this one trip.

She was leaving in about an hour and a half. All her classes for the day were over, and the only other thing she had planned was to go to lunch with her girlfriends on the floor. They were supposed to be there soon. Carli was restless waiting so she started to straighten up the drawers in her desk. As she finished the top middle drawer, a knock came at the door.

"Come in," Carli said with a smile. She expected her friends. Instead, Stubby's girlfriend Sue came in.

"Hi. I don't know if you know who I am." Sue gently closed the door behind her. Carli quickly nodded her head to indicate that she did know who Sue was. Sue continued. "I realize that it's really none of my business, but I'm concerned about a mutual friend of ours."

"Todd?" Carli interjected. Sue nodded her head yes. "What do you want to know?"

"I guess just what you have to say." Sue shrugged her shoulders.

Stubby had filled Sue in about what had happened after she went home. "He's confused. I'm sure we, as two women, can communicate. I could then explain it to him. I know Todd pretty well. Maybe I could help clear up any misunderstanding between the two of you. I don't know. I just know that right now he's hurt and irrational. His defense mechanism is probably telling him that he should be hating you. I'm sure you don't want that."

"No," Carli said sincerely. "Where should I start?" Her heart began to pound.

"I don't know. What happened? Why did you break up?" Sue took a seat in the same chair Doc was in the night before.

"I just want to be able to spend more time on school in the second part of the semester." Carli had trouble talking.

Sue waited for a second after Carli had finished before she started in. "I know that's what you told Todd, but what's the real reason?" Sue spoke calmly and politely. "We both know that he didn't take away from your study time, at least not any more than you allowed." Sue paused and waited for a response. Carli sat quietly. She felt caught in a lie.

"Things were going so well between the two of you," Sue continued.

Carli swallowed hard. "That's just it. Things were going too well for us. It scared me." Carli got up from her desk and began walking around the room. "I really care for Doc. I know that. But I don't know how much I really like him. I don't know what I like. I know that doesn't make sense." She faced Sue and tried to explain. "Todd is the first person I've ever dated. The way I feel scares me. I'm afraid of being hurt and I'm afraid of waking up some day after things get more serious than they are now and figuring out that I really don't like him." She walked over to the window and began looking out as she continued to talk. "I guess I just want some time to date other people, and to find out what I like. Maybe a month or a year from now I'll find out that he's the type of person I really want. Then all this time will seem wasted. I don't know. He may not even be waiting for me then. I may find out that he isn't what I'm looking for. Then this will seem like the best move. I don't know, but it's something I have to find out." She put her hands on the window and continued to stare through the glass.

"What's wrong with that reason?" Sue was confused. "Why didn't you just tell him that?"

"I was afraid that he might take it the wrong way. I was afraid that he'd think that I didn't like him, and that it was something he had done." Carli slowly turned to face Sue. Her eyes began to well up. "I was afraid that I would hurt him."

26

By the time the team started down to Friday's practice, most of the students had left for the mid-term break. Originally, the purpose of the break was to allow students the time to work on special projects or papers, or to catch up on any work that they needed to, but it evolved into a vacation from school.

For the regular student, that was nice. For the football team and other fall athletes, it didn't matter. They were going to be there anyway. And the coaches were going to be filling the spare time they weren't in classes with extra film sessions and chalk-talks.

Bert went to bed right after he returned from handing in his paper. He slept the rest of the morning and most of the afternoon. He wasn't alone. Most of the guys took advantage of this time in the afternoon to catch up on the sleep that they had missed during the week.

Doc skipped all his classes and stayed in bed until noon. Then he stayed in his bathrobe and watched television until it was time to go to practice. The night before he needed someone to talk to. Today he just wanted to be alone. The hurt was running its course.

Stubby went back to bed after class, too. However, he only stayed there until Sue came to his room looking for a ride to the bus station. He felt bad that he couldn't driver her to the airport, but with practice that afternoon, it just wasn't possible. He bid her a safe trip, and she wished him luck in the next two games. She thought how the week would seem like forever, as the bus pulled away.

Prior to practice, Bonaventure went through the traditional awards ceremony. He gave the entire team a star for a win, or a moral victory as he called it. And then he passed out the stars according to the pre-established criteria. Despite the loss, it seemed that more stars were given out this week than after the Grinnell College game.

Finally, Foster was pleased with his performance in the Lawrence game. It was at the level he felt he could play. He wasn't the only one who was pleased. Bonaventure named him 'Pirate-of-the-Week.'

'Buc-of-the-Week' went to Big El. As Bonaventure explained in announcing the award, he was finally back to the El that they knew last year. Against Lawrence, he controlled the line of scrimmage where he played. In short-yardage situations, Doc would sneak the ball behind El for the yardage they needed. It got to the point where the Lawrence men would key off his blocks to determine where the plays were going. That was something that they weren't able to see in the film they had of the Knox game, because it wasn't happening.

It was a tough road for him. He'd been down. He didn't give up and came back. The team showed their appreciation for his efforts. They stood and cheered for him as he went up to Bonaventure and received his award. Bonaventure gave him a firm handshake and said to him, "It's good to have you back."

The atmosphere at practice was relaxed. All the week's tension was gone and they were ready to concentrate on the game. Bonaventure kept both the offense and the defense longer than usual. He hoped to make up some of the learning that didn't get into the early part of the week. However, he didn't keep them too long. When he was confident they were ready, he sent the team into the locker room. The offense went straight in. The defense stayed on the field long enough to run one ten-yard sprint for University of Chicago.

That night, everyone stayed home. Usually during the mid-term break they would all chip in and rent different movies each night. It was a relaxing way to pass the time.

The standards for movie selection were: nothing educational, plenty of violence, lots of nudity, and if it didn't have violence or nudity, then it had to be extremely funny. However, the overriding rule was absolutely no football. They would have enough football films in the upcoming week to last a lifetime. The evenings for the next week would be filled with James Bond, Clint Eastwood, and Sylvester Stallone.

Chicago's team bus went directly to the stadium. At that time, no Beloit players were there yet. Coach Bonaventure was completing his final pre-game chalk-talk at the Morse-Ingersol Auditorium. The

Chicago players didn't know what to expect. They were, without a doubt, the underdogs. All week long, they had seen on film how Beloit manhandled Grinnell College and they had heard about the statistics the Bucs managed to get against the defending conference champions, Lawrence. They questioned whether or not they wanted to be there. It might be the start of a long day and a long bus ride home, they thought.

Aside from a couple of freshmen who got rides down to the Stadium with Jack Benson, Foster was the first Beloit player at the Stadium. He took his usual walk down to the game, listening to the soundtracks from the *Rocky* movies. He was trying to get psyched to have another great game. Motivation from the week before was to keep playing well. All-Conference honors were on his mind.

Just inside the archway that led to the entrance of both teams' locker rooms stood three University of Chicago players. Each was dressed completely from the waist down, and wore maroon sweatshirts to match their maroon and gold pants. They leaned against the wall, stretching their calves.

Foster's eyes met with each one of theirs in succession. Although they only looked at one another for seconds, it seemed to go on for minutes. During that time, neither words nor body language was exchanged. Both parties were curious. It was seldom that they ever got to see an opponent without all his equipment on. Somehow, without the uniform, they all were so ordinary. The helmet and shoulder pads seemed to cast mystical powers over them and transform them into super humans. Foster went into the locker room and the Chicago players continued to stretch.

For Beloit, the home crowd advantage they had in their previous two home games wasn't there today. The students, who made up the majority of their fans, weren't on campus this weekend. The only students who were there were people who lived too far away to make the one-week trip home worthwhile, people on other fall sports teams (women's volleyball and cross country track) and people who were using the break for what it was originally intended -- to study.

The stands were filled with patches of professors, parents, fans from town, and some students who remained on campus for whatever reason. It didn't matter. It wasn't going to be a factor in the game. Recently, the team had been spoiled by having a big crowd, but most of the players were used to having the stands sparse with people at this point in the season. In fact, there was a pretty good crowd compared to other years.

The Bucs looked good in warmups. They went through the pre-game drills with the enthusiasm and precision that the University of Chicago team expected to see out of a team of their caliber. Today they had no new plays in the playbook and no surprise defensive plays. They were the team to beat, and that's the attitude they took. It wasn't a cocky attitude. It was just a mentality that said, we're a good team, not because you have a lot of fancy plays that we can trick you with, but because we play football well. Period.

On the first series of plays when Beloit had the ball, Doc took the offense eighty yards down the field in fifteen plays for a touchdown. There were no special plays run. The Bucs simply executed the basic dives, sweeps, and counter plays well. They nickel and dimed their way down the field, never gaining more than six yards at a time. The extra point was no good because of a bad snap from center. Early in the game, Beloit was up by a score of six to nothing.

The defense followed suit as University of Chicago gained seven yards on their first play from scrimmage. Beloit took the Maroons for a five-yard loss on each of the next two plays. Each play served to fire them up for the next. Deep down inside, they contemplated letting Chicago get a first down, just so they could knock them back again. This was how the season seemed to be shaping up. Every time the defense would start to get ready to really 'stick people,' it was time to come out because the other team was punting to their offense. The defense vented their frustrations by banging each other's shoulder pads on the sidelines.

The next time the offense was on the field, Doc went to a passing attack. It was a nice change of plays. University of Chicago had just adjusted its defense to stop the run. This time the Bucs only had sixty yards to cover. By going to the air, the Bucs were in the end zone in six plays. Doc ran the ball in for the score on the sixth play, after he couldn't find anybody open in the end zone.

He had already completed five of eight passes for 55 yards, run for another twelve and scored one touchdown. The Bucs tried to make up for the missed extra point by getting a two-point conversion, but it failed and they were up by twelve points.

The defense appeared to be the 'immovable object' again when they took the field. Chicago managed, however, to get one first down. It was a pass for thirty yards. After the first play the Maroons ran, for the first time their offense had positive yardage.

Although the defense couldn't continue to hold Chicago's offense to negative yardage, they still played exceptionally well. By the end of the first half, they had limited the Maroons to 71 total yards, five first downs, and had sacked their quarterback four times.

Foster was a big catalyst in the defense's spectacular showing. He had more than picked up where he left off the week before. By the end of the first half, he had more tackles in this game than in any other entire game. This was the best he had ever played. He seemed to be at the pinnacle of his game. All the plays he ever dreamed of making seemed to occur in this game.

But with each play, he wanted more. Everytime he made a great play, he wanted to do it again. Each time he hit someone, no matter how hard, he wanted to hit them again and this time make the hit more solid. His body became addicted to the thrill he got from the street-fight battles he engaged in on the line of scrimmage. His vision became tunneled. He couldn't see the blockers that were in his path. He saw through them to where the ball was, to where he wanted to be.

The next few times on the field, the Bucs' offense wasn't able to move quite as effectively. They would drive the ball for about thirty yards or so and then a penalty or foul-up in the play's coordination would break their momentum. Not until the closing minutes of the first half were they able to score another touchdown. Again, the extra point attempt failed. This time the snap from center went over the holder's head. At half time, Beloit was ahead by the score of 18 to nothing.

In the locker room the team whooped it up as if they had won the game. Everyone was hugging, hand-slapping and hand-shaking, and having a good time reviewing with each other all the spectacular plays of the first half. However, Bonaventure quickly let the wind out of their sails.

"All right men, just sit down and relax. We haven't won this game yet." He took off his hat and wiped the sweat from his brow. The team settled down. "So far I'm not impressed with anything that's going on out on the field."

Bonaventure was pleased that his team finally was able to dominate a game like they had, but he knew he couldn't stop there. He couldn't let them get complacent. They were good, but they weren't that good yet. They had made some mistakes -- mistakes that a good team would have capitalized on. University of Chicago wasn't a good team, but the mistakes had to be cleared up before they played a good team.

"Extra point team, what the hell is the problem out there. Let's get it together. Those points may be a factor later in the game." His face became red from yelling. "Offense, would you please concentrate out there. Mental mistakes. Mental mistakes. Those damn mental mistakes." The other offensive coaches started singling out individual players to criticize as Bonaventure moved over to the side of the locker room that the defense was on. "Are you guys satisfied? Are you really satisfied that you held them to under a hundred yards in offense?" He didn't give them a chance to answer. "You shouldn't be. They're shit. They've got the worst offense in the league. You should be ashamed that you gave them a yard at all." Bonaventure walked over to Foster. "Addison, I expect more out of you. You're supposed to be the leader on the defense. Get these guys going."

Foster's blood immediately started to boil. Bonaventure's words pissed him off. But that's what they were intended to do. He turned to the defense that sat around him.

"Okay, you guys, we've got to take 'em for negative yardage this half. We've got to regain those yards we gave 'em. Right?" Foster's eyes watered, he was so intense. He clenched his fist.

The other defensive players also started to rally with similar words. Bonaventure had succeeded. He changed the team's focus from how good they were, to how much better they could be. After he gave the entire team a few more words of motivation, he sent them back to the field for the second half.

After an abbreviated warmup session, the second half was ready to begin. Beloit had won the coin toss in the first half and had elected to receive. That meant in the second half they would be kicking off to University of Chicago.

With all the enthusiasm created in the locker room, the kicker for the Bucs got excited and kicked the ball deep into Chicago territory. One of the Maroons' deep men fielded the ball and tried to run it out. However, the kick-off team for Beloit swarmed down and tackled the running back inside the twenty-yard line.

The fired-up defensive unit took the field. They congratulated the kick-off team leaving the field. They were ready to regain the yardage they had given up in the first half. The defensive play was called. Loudly, the entire defensive unit yelled "BREAK," in unison as they clapped their hands and went to their respective positions on the field.

Foster was the most intense of all. His body shook with anticipation as the University of Chicago team broke their huddle and lined up on the ball. Foster stared into the eyes of the man who lined up across from him while still watching for movement of the ball out of the corner of his eye.

When the ball was snapped, Foster quickly sprang out of his stance and threw the Chicago lineman aside like he had been doing all day. The runner was sweeping wide. However, the defensive end prevented him from getting to the outside. Foster reached for the runner, but only got a piece of his shirt. Holding onto the shirt, his body was swung around and he was forced to let go. He planted both feet firmly in the ground in hopes of regaining pursuit.

At that same instant, the Beloit defensive end made the same lunging move for the runner. He, too, missed, but he was unable to regain his balance. He fell into an accelerated roll towards Foster's planted leg.

"Aaaaahhhhh," Foster screamed out in pain.

It was like no pain he had ever felt before. It only lasted for a split second, but it was so intense he almost passed out. Everyone on the field heard him, but only Foster could hear the incredibly loud snap in his leg. The defensive end had rolled into his right leg, which was too firmly planted for Foster to fall over. The only give was in his leg.

Immediately after the play was over, Foster removed his mouthpiece and helmet. He had already broken into a cold sweat, and his body quivered with shock from the pain. He was almost hyperventilating as he tried to relax. The pain was gone from his leg, but it was still etched into his mind. He was afraid to move.

Jack Benson was on the field even before the referee signaled him on. Coach Bonaventure was close behind. Both teams huddled around the fallen Buccaneer. Jack Benson urged them to back off in order to give Foster some air. They only backed up a few steps, but they stayed close enough to see what was going on. Coach Bonaventure ordered his team to huddle up ten yards back. The referee told the University of Chicago team to do the same.

Benson probed Foster's leg as Bonaventure looked on. Foster sensed that they were checking his leg.

"Is it broken? Just tell me that. Is it broken?" Foster's voice was scared and panicked. He had never been injured before. The sound he heard when his leg was hit sent visions of a complex fracture to his mind, with bone sticking through his skin and a blood-drenched sock. Foster couldn't bear to look.

"No," Jack quickly answered. Foster breathed a sigh of relief. Jack fiddled with Foster's leg some more and then announced to Foster, "Okay, I want to have them carry him off the field." Jack's stuttering subsided in a crisis.

Bonaventure called to the sidelines for two players to help. Stubby and junior Dave Wilkinson came running onto the field.

Benson grabbed Foster's helmet and followed behind Stubby and Wilk. As they marched Foster to the sidelines both teams clapped along with the fans. Foster looked back at his defensive teammates huddling up to play the next down.

"I'll be back. ... I'll be back," he shouted.

Foster was set down on the training table about ten yards back from the sidelines. Jack continued to fiddle with his knee. He pulled it and twisted it in several directions. By then, even the pain in Foster's memory was gone.

Bert came over to see how Foster was. He stood by the training table and watched Jack examine the leg.

Jack looked up into Foster's eye and said with his most serious face, "I think you've torn ligaments. You're probably done for the season."

Foster's eyes filled with horror and his heart sank. Bert put his hand on Foster's shoulder and pulled him tightly to his body. He wanted to assure him that he wasn't alone. Foster still sat speechless.

Jack started to apply a cold compress to the knee by wrapping ice in an Ace bandage. He again looked at Foster, who stared in shock. He didn't mean to give the news to him so bluntly. However, his policy was always to prepare them for the worst and hope for the best.

Meanwhile, the defensive team was having problems after Foster left the game. They kept looking to the sidelines, waiting for his return. Their momentum escaped them for a short period. Chicago was able to get two first downs before the Bucs could regain their composure. Finally, they were able to stop the Maroons and force them to give up the ball.

University of Chicago punted the ball. They had the wind advantage. The ball sailed. A Beloit player tried to run back and catch it, but the ball ended up hitting him in the head and rolling even farther towards the Beloit end zone. Chicago recovered it on the ten-yard line. This was their best field position all day. They now had the momentum. Two plays later, they scored on a pass. The successful extra point made it 18 to seven.

Foster's heart ached. He couldn't believe that his season might be over. In a million years, he never would have dreamed that it would have ended this way. Other people got injured, not him, he thought. Maybe it was a bad dream. It couldn't really be happening.

After the University of Chicago touchdown, Foster lay back on the table and looked up in the sky. Out of the corner of his eye, he could see President Hardesty coming down the Stadium stairs toward him. All Foster could think of was how he had told Hardesty that the reason he didn't want to apply for the Rhodes was to play football. Now Foster had neither. Hardesty had every right to rub that statement in his face.

"What's the prognosis?" Hardesty set his hand on Foster's shoulder.

"Jack says that it's probably ligaments and that I'm done for the season." A sad look blanketed Foster's face.

Hardesty looked Foster in the eye. "Jack's a great trainer, but he's no doctor. Don't give up hope until the final verdict is in. You've got to stay positive." Foster nodded his head. Hardesty's words were a comfort.

Hardesty helped Foster out of his jersey and shoulder pads and put a warm-up jacket on him so he wouldn't catch a chill. They both turned to watch what they could see of the offense on the field.

Doc had the offense moving the football again. Chicago had kicked the ball back to Beloit deep in its own end. The offense had managed to overcome the momentum switch and now the ball was across the fifty-yard line.

On third-and-long, Doc dropped back for a pass. The offensive line was doing a good job of protecting him, but no one was open. The line couldn't hold the rushers out forever. One by one, they got by and started to pursue Doc. Doc eluded two rushers and headed around end to the wide side of the field. There was plenty of room to run, and the first down was in sight.

Doc made the first down and still had room to run. He made it over to the University of Chicago side of the field and ran down the sideline. From behind, a Chicago linebacker caught him and tackled Doc on the blind side. The linebacker's helmet jabbed into Doc's ribs. Doc heard the air whush out of his lungs as he fell out of bounds.

He pulled his own mouthguard out and began gasping for air. But it wasn't just that the wind was knocked out of him. His ribs seemed to be burning with pain, too. The referee tried to loosen his pants so he could breathe better.

Jack Benson and Coach Bonaventure were again on the field. However, by the time they had gotten to Doc, he was up, with helmet in hand, and walking toward them. His ribs still burned. That made him walk funny. Jack assisted him to the sidelines as everyone clapped.

Jack sat Doc down next to Foster. Carefully, he pulled Doc's jersey and shoulder pads off. Once they were off, he began poking around the area where Doc indicated it hurt.

"Ouch," Doc yelled out as Joe hit a tender area. "Do you think they're broken?"

"No," Jack said, looking Doc in the eye and smiling. "I cccann tttell, bbbbecausse you dddiddn'tt say ouccchhh louddd enough."

Jack proceeded to wrap Doc's ribs in the same manner as he had wrapped Foster's knee. The combination of cold on the tender area made Doc wince in pain.

After ten minutes, Jack explained that he wanted to get both Doc and Foster into the locker room so he could examine them better. First he would walk Doc in the training room and then he would come back out with crutches for Foster.

Hardesty, who had been standing there the entire time, volunteered to get the crutches and help Foster while Jack tended to Doc. Jack led Hardesty and Doc into the locker room. A short while later Hardesty emerged carrying a pair of wooden crutches.

Hardesty helped Foster off the table and onto the crutches. Foster appeared to be wobbly on the crutches. It was one thing he never planned to be good at. Slowly he crutched over to the entrance to the locker room. Hardesty led the way, carrying Foster's shoulder pads and helmet. Just before Foster passed through the doorway of the locker room, he stopped and turned his head around to have one last look at the field. Before he could turn back, a big tear rolled down his cheek.

27

The celebrating that the team did at halftime was all the celebrating they did for the University of Chicago game. Although they managed to hang on and win 18 to 7, the price they paid for victory was high. The evidence of this high price hobbled out of the training room to take part in the post-game prayer. Doc winced as the bending to take a knee made his ribs burn. Foster, whose leg was now in a splint, did the best he could to squat on his left leg and lay the damaged right leg on the ground.

Bonaventure gave the team off until Tuesday afternoon's practice. Instead of watching films on Monday, the film sessions would be spread throughout the rest of the week when they normally would have been in classes or studying. This was their mid-term break. Most people took advantage of it. If a player lived close enough to go home, he did. If a player didn't live close enough, he'd go home with someone who did.

Only a very few stayed behind for the weekend. Foster was one of them. He had been planning on this all along. However, he hadn't planned on being confined to crutches or concerned with when he would get to see a doctor.

The weekend was spent in front of the television watching movies. Jandi came over on Saturday night and sat with Foster as he had to keep his leg iced and elevated. His mind never seemed to be totally focused on the movie. He didn't laugh at the funny scenes, nor did he appear frightened by the scary ones. After a while, Jandi left. She knew he was preoccupied. She kissed him on the cheek and said goodbye. He snapped out of his trance long enough to acknowledge her leaving. He said goodbye, too, as she walked out the door.

On Sunday and Monday, there was nothing Jack Benson could do for Foster, except continue to examine the knee and give unofficial prognoses. There was evidence to support Jack's conclusion that the knee was damaged, but there was equal evidence to show that he might be wrong. Jack was even beginning to have his doubts.

More and more, Foster sided with Hardesty: Keep a positive outlook. He had visions of having the doctor examine his knee and saying to Foster, "There's nothing wrong, you big sissy." He could imagine the elation he would feel when he found out that he would be able to play again. However, he wouldn't know if this dream would become reality until Tuesday, when his doctor's appointment was scheduled.

After the game, Doc went home to Green Bay with his parents. They rigged up the back seat of the car with pillows and blankets to form a bed for Doc to lie in on the way home. Despite these efforts, Doc felt every bump on the road.

Doc spent the entire time at home going between lying in bed with an ice pack on his side and sitting in a hot bath. By now, his ribs had gone from a red welt to a six-inch round bruise. There was no way for Doc to get comfortable. Every way he sat or lay made his side throb with pain. As relaxing as home usually was, he couldn't get any rest this visit.

Adding to the pain in his ribs was the pain that Carli had left in his heart. He wondered if she even knew of his injury. If so, would she even care? It had been a long week for him.

Doc only managed to watch half of the Packers game on Monday Night Football with his dad. It hurt too much to sit up, and he needed his sleep because the next day he had to drive back to Beloit for practice. Besides, the Packers were getting soundly beaten. What else was going to go wrong? he wondered.

At about 10:30 the next morning, his mother made him a large breakfast. It was the first big meal he ate the entire time at home. He felt bad about not eating more because his mother was a great cook, but he just wasn't hungry. By eleven, he was finished eating, and by 11:15 he was on the road to Beloit with three dozen chocolate cookies, and four weeks of clean laundry. If there were no problems, he would be back in time to get ready for practice.

Early Tuesday afternoon, Foster could feel the tension build in his body as he sat in the waiting room at the clinic where the specialist would examine his leg. He paged through magazine after magazine, but none was interesting enough to hold his attention. His mind was focused on what the doctor might say.

OUT OF THE COMFORT ZONE

After a half an hour of waiting, an eternity to Foster, the nurse called him back. He made a joke to try and ease the mounting tension, but it didn't work. With each breath, he had to swallow hard. The lump in his throat was impeding his breathing. Jack Benson followed closely. He, too, had an interest in what the doctor had to say.

The doctor took off the Ace wrap around Foster's knee and began examining it. The doctor twisted it only once or twice before determining that Jack's initial conclusion had been correct. There was 'definite ligament damage and possible cartilage damage.' Foster would be scheduled for surgery the next day.

All the hope and positive thinking were gone in a single sentence by the doctor. Foster fought hard to keep from crying. He retained control, but he couldn't keep his eyes from welling up with tears. Jack tried to console him as they left the doctor's office and got in the car. The entire drive back to campus, Foster couldn't help feeling sorry for himself. Jack spoke to him, but Foster's attention was too far off to listen. He stared out the car window, but didn't watch the scenery. He reminisced about all the glorious days he had played football. From the time he was a tiny freshman for the Houghton High School junior varsity Gremlins up through the first half of the University of Chicago game just this past Saturday, he relived his every glory-filled play.

Jack Benson drove to the fieldhouse and parked. He and Foster got out and walked in to Coach Bonaventure's office. Jack had to walk slowly so Foster could keep up on the crutches. Bonaventure was waiting.

As Jack started to explain what the doctor had said, Foster couldn't keep from crying any longer. He didn't whimper, but tears streamed from his eyes and ran down his cheeks. Foster rested his elbows on his knees and then rested his face in his hands. He looked at the floor. One by one, he watched the tears disappear in the carpet.

When Jack was finished explaining, he left, closing the door behind himself. Bonaventure looked over at Foster. For four years, Bonaventure had watched the love for the game in Foster's eyes. Now he could feel the pain in his heart. He knew that Foster didn't deserve what was happening to him, but that didn't make it any easier.

Still, no sounds came from Foster, only tears rushed down his face. Bonaventure let Foster cry for a minute while he gathered his thoughts. The coach wiped his face with a handkerchief and then cleared his throat.

"Sometimes life just isn't fair. We are taught that if we work hard things will come our way. But we both know now that it doesn't always work that way. And no one can explain God's motives or reasoning for making life like this." Foster looked up at Bonaventure through his teary eyes. Bonaventure was just a blur behind his desk. "Foster, you were a good football player. Your first half against Chicago was one of the best I've ever seen. You went out in a blaze of glory. But sometime now you've got to resign yourself to that, that you were a good football player, but now it's over and you've got to use what football has taught you in the pursuit of the rest of your life." Bonaventure paused.

He didn't know if what he had said was getting through to Foster, who was still spilling tears down both cheeks. Bonaventure moved closer to his desk and leaned toward Foster. He peered over his glasses and started to speak again in a pleading sort of voice.

"We've got a young team. They are very impressionable. You can't let them see you like this. It'll scare them. Please don't let them know how much it hurts. I know it seems like a selfish thing to ask right now, but Foster I need your help." Bonaventure paused again.

Foster responded. He sat up in the chair and sniffled hard twice. Wiping his eyes with the sleeves of his jacket, he said, "Okay." His voice had a slight whimper to it.

Bonaventure gave Foster a ride down to the Stadium. On the way down, Foster asked what the game plan was going to be against Loras College. Bonaventure went into detail explaining it to Foster. Foster listened intently. It not only made him feel that he was still a part of the team to hear how the coaches planned to play Loras, but it also the shaped the frame of mind Bonaventure wanted to present to the team.

Most of the team was on the field and dressed for practice when Foster got out of the car. The wooden crutches he was given at the game had been replaced with aluminum ones. They were adjusted to Foster's height. He seemed to be more proficient on them now.

Doc was the first person to greet Foster. He was only dressed in shorts and a T-shirt for practice. Jack Benson had given him the bad news that his ribs were still too tender and that he wouldn't be playing against Loras College. Doc didn't seem too upset, mainly because he was in a lot of pain and really didn't feel like getting knocked around on the football field. Besides, Loras was a nonconference game. It was better to be ready to play in the final two conference games.

"What's the story with your knee, Foster?" Doc confronted Foster face to face before anyone else had a chance to talk with him.

"I go in for surgery tomorrow morning, bright and early." Foster tried to sound calm about it.

Doc knew him too well. He could see the hurt in Foster's eyes. "Hey, let's go out to dinner tonight. My treat. I'll take you to Shakey's 'All-You-Can-Eat.' I know how much you can eat, and I haven't got a lot of money." Doc tried to lighten the uneasiness. He was wise to Foster's front. Although he didn't know why Foster was putting one on, he wanted to help.

Foster accepted the offer with a smile. He sensed that Doc was trying to help. That made it only harder to keep a 'stiff upper lip.' To avoid any further conversation he walked into the locker room. On the way in, he met up with Jim Francia, the sports editor for the *Beloit Daily News*.

Before Francia could utter a word, Foster started to talk. "How's it going? I just got back from the doctor. I go under the knife tomorrow," he calmly announced. It took all his energy to keep from crying.

"Doesn't that bother you?" Francia asked in amazement at Foster's coolness.

Foster just shrugged his shoulders. He didn't have a response, at least not for the state of mind he was portraying. He wanted so badly to tell Francia just how much he hurt -- not his leg, but his heart. Foster couldn't. He continued to the locker room.

Bonaventure came out of the locker room at the usual time and blew the whistle to start practice. Immediately after warm-ups, he huddled the team and reviewed the situation.

"I'm glad to see that all of you made it back. For those of you who haven't heard, we are going to be missing a couple of players." Bonaventure moved around the inner circle that the huddle created. "Todd Wallace won't be with us this week. He's got bruised ribs. And, Foster Addison won't be playing the remainder of the season. He goes in for surgery on his knee tomorrow morning. So that means that we're going to have to do some adjustments in our line-up. Danny McDonnell will be playing quarterback, and I'm going to move Bill Barton over from the offensive line to the defensive line to take Foster's position." Bonaventure turned to face Bill. "I guess it's back to the defense for you."

Bill smiled and nodded. Although he felt bad for Foster, he was going to get his chance to start.

Bonaventure switched the tone of his voice from announcing to just plain talking. "As I said, Foster is going in for surgery tomorrow morning. That means that 'round about tomorrow night, there is going to be a pretty lonely fellow in the hospital. If Foster means as much to you as he does to me, I suggest that we all try and pay him a visit." Bonaventure then switched back again and started directing players to various points on the field.

Bill was *en route* to meeting up with the defensive linemen for the first time in two years when he took a detour to talk to Foster.

"Hey, Foster," Bill said as he walked in front of Foster, who was crutching off the field. Bill still hadn't put on his helmet. "Ya know, I haven't played defensive line since we were sophomores. The switch back may be tough. I was just wondering if you could maybe help me with some of the plays or even give me some pointers?" Bill was sincere.

Foster knew that Bill would have no problem re-learning the position. However, he appreciated Bill's making him feel needed. "No problem," Foster said as he continued to crutch over to the side of the practice field.

The only thing tougher than practice was having to watch practice. Hours seemed like days as Foster and Doc sat together on the bench, watching the team go through drills. Doc kept ice pressed against his side, and Foster stared off into the trees, wondering what surgery would be like.

As soon as Bonaventure dismissed practice, Doc and Foster went out to eat. Doc continued to load Foster's plate up with pizza and spaghetti. He knew that it would be a while before Foster had another good meal. They tried to talk about anything but football.

After two hours, they'd had their fill and went back to the house. Doc sat in the living room and watched movies. Foster lay in his bed and made phone calls. A lot of people needed to know that he was going in for surgery the next morning. He contemplated not telling anyone, but a nine-inch scar on his knee and a couple thousand dollar medical bill, even if covered by insurance, would be something that just couldn't be hidden. When all the calls were completed, he turned out the light and went to bed.

At 7 a.m. the next morning, Foster's alarm went off. He threw on the clothes he had set out the night before, grabbed a bag of personal items, and crutched out the door, locking it behind himself. He had to be at the hospital by 7:30, which still left him plenty of time. The doctor said he wasn't allowed to eat after midnight and there was no sense showering because they would scrub him up before the operation.

Bert told Foster the night before that he would give him a ride to the hospital in the morning. Foster appreciated Bert's offer. He realized that for Bert, getting up at seven o'clock in the morning was a supreme sacrifice.

Foster stood at the top of the stairs leading to the kitchen and yelled down to Bert to make sure he was up. Foster was relieved to find out that Bert was already up. For one, it would have been a pain for Foster to have to crutch down the stairs to wake Bert. And secondly, if Bert were still asleep, Foster would have his hands full trying to wake him.

Bert threw on a pair of yellow sweat pants and tucked in the T-shirt that he wore to bed. He slipped tennis shoes on without unlacing them. His hair stood up in the back and went every direction in the front. He came up the stairs not looking happy at all to be seeing this time of day. Foster wasn't intimidated at all. This was Bert's morning look.

They arrived at the hospital in plenty of time. Bert didn't park. He planned to get back to bed just as soon as he could. He drove the car up to the patient unloading area. They joked for a moment and then Bert extended his hand.

"Well, I guess we'll see you tonight." Bert's face had a serious look.

Foster put his hand out, too. They shook using the fraternity grip. "Well, I'll probably be here." Foster tried to lighten up the situation. The seriousness made him uncomfortable. His eyes began to glaze over.

"Take care of yourself," Bert said as he pointed to Foster, struggling to get out of the car.

Foster looked back just before closing the car door and said in a long, drawn-out fashion, "I always do."

The check-in process was fairly simple for Foster. Jack Benson had managed to take care of a lot of the preliminary items the day before. Foster was taken to a room and then instructed to strip down and put on a hospital gown. He felt uncomfortable wearing it because it didn't cover anything in the back, and it didn't hang down very far. He felt self-conscious and exposed to the nurses. He decided that he would wear his underwear underneath.

He got away with this until the nurse came in to give him the preliminary anesthetic. She made him take the underwear off before she gave him the shot. After the shot, Foster seemed to be in a daze. He smiled as he lay on the bed. Now he didn't care what part of his body was exposed.

After what seemed like a half an hour, a team of nurses came in Foster's room and transferred him to a movable bed and wheeled him down the hall. All Foster knew was that he was moving. He didn't know where, and he was feeling so good that he didn't care.

When they got him in the operating room, doctors assisted the nurses in transferring him to the operating table. Foster was conscious, but couldn't really control his limbs. They covered him with several sheets and then removed the hospital gown.

A nurse put an I.V. tube in his arm, and then tapped him on the shoulder. She showed him the label of the drug she was administering into the I.V. Foster strained to focus on the label. After a few seconds, he made out the word 'Valium.' Then he lost consciousness.

In the later part of the afternoon, Foster was back up in his hospital room. He was back in a hospital gown, but still unconscious. A bag of saline solution slowly dripped into his I.V. tube. During this time when he was under the anesthetic, he would have no recollection of the passage of time. He had been fully under the whole time. Although he had dreams, none of them registered. It was as if he had fallen into a deep sleep and then re-awakened in the same instant.

The team was still at practice and players weren't scheduled to stop by for two or three hours. Yet Foster had a visitor -- his first. It was Jim Francia of the *Beloit Daily News*. He knew one of the nurses, and she allowed him up.

Francia was almost a part of the team. Bonaventure welcomed him in the locker room at anytime. He seemed to show up at most of the team's practices, and always tried to do an individual article about each senior. Even when Bonaventure's teams struggled, Francia accented the positive. He was known to cheer for the Bucs when the game got tight, and he never printed something controversial without first talking to Bonaventure.

In one hand he carried his usual camera case, filled with camera, lens and note pads. In the other hand he had a newspaper. The *Beloit Daily News* had just come off the presses. Francia got the first good copy for Foster.

"Hey, Foster. Are you awake?" Francia spoke softly. He did not want to call any attention to himself.

Foster began to stir. He twisted his head back and forth, as if he were trying to break into consciousness. After thirty seconds, his eyes slowly opened. It took him a while to focus, and then some more time to get his bearings. Eventually, it all came back to him, where he was and why.

Francia opened up the paper and folded it back. He put it on Foster's chest. "Here. I brought something for you to read."

Foster began to read.

Beloit Daily News - Sports
Jim Francia, Sports Editor

Buccaneers will miss Foster Addison

FOOTBALL IS A TERRIFIC sport and I consider myself an avid fan. But sometimes I can't help feeling guilty about it.
That feeling surfaced Saturday when I watched a pair of Beloit College football players carry defensive tackle Foster Addison off the field at Strong Stadium.
The senior seriously injured his knee in the second half of the Buccaneers' victory over University of Chicago. It was a freak injury -- caused when a teammate trying to make a tackle rolled into Addison's twisted leg. The knee buckled under the strain.
Like McArthur leaving the Philippines, Addison's parting words as he left the field were, "I'll be back." He was wrong. He never returned to the lineup Saturday.

TUESDAY THAT SAME guilty feeling returned when Addison hobbled into Strong Stadium on crutches.

"How's it going?" he said, grinning. "I just got back from the doctor. I'm going under the knife tomorrow."

The Buccaneer co-captain was calm. I was numb. The news, as feared, was the worst. His knee sustained ligament and possible cartilage damage. Addison won't play football again this season. Since he is a senior, his playing days at Beloit are over.

He will be missed tremendously -- by both the team and Buccaneer fans.

"He's always the first player out on the practice field," a teammate said. "He's not a real loud guy, but he leads by example."

When Addison, the only senior starter on defense, left Saturday's game, his teammates worked hard not to let him down.

"We did it for Foster," another player said. "He did so much for us. He always kept up up when the chips were down. We owe him a lot."

Addison, from Houghton, Michigan, is simply the consummate football player. He isn't blessed with great size for his position, weighing less than 200 pounds. But he makes up for any lack of size with strength, quickness, and heart. No one worked harder in the weightroom preparing for the season. And no lineman is faster off the ball.

HIS EDGE IS HIS intensity on the field -- from first play to the last. He is confident of his talents and that rubs off on the younger players. He is the perfect captain.

But there's no need to fret about Addison. He went out a winner and he'll always be a winner. Hopefully successful surgery will put him on the road to complete recovery. We wish him well.

Although Foster wasn't totally conscious yet, he knew that he was somebody, not only when he played, but still. And Francia was doing his best to make sure people knew that. Foster felt touched. Tears began streaming from his eyes. It was a warm feeling inside that made him cry with pleasure, not feeling sorry for himself.

"Thank you," Foster muttered as he turned his head away. He didn't want Francia to see him cry. "Thank you."

Francia took the paper off Foster's chest and set it on the bedside table. The combination of the tears and the thank-you's confused him. He left not knowing for sure whether his article was appreciated. It was -- more than Francia would ever know.

28

Foster cried himself back to sleep. This time he was able to experience his dreams. Although the images were clear, the message wasn't.

Two hours later, he awoke. As he tried to focus his eyes, the first image he made out was Simba at the foot of his bed waving back at him. Foster turned his head to the side and re-closed his eyes. "Oh shit," he greeted Simba in a groggy voice. The pain in his knee was almost unbearable. Suddenly, a nurse turned Foster over to one side to give him a shot of pain-killer in his butt. Just as suddenly, the pain was gone.

Over half the team showed up to visit at one time or another that first night, but Foster's shot every two hours to ease the pain allowed him only intermittent short periods of real consciousness.

From all those visitors, the only conversation he did remember was with Coach Bonaventure. The coach offered to get him an ice cream cone or whatever else he needed in the hospital. It stuck in Foster's mind because it was such an unusual offer. Foster thought that it was probably a ploy Bonaventure was using so he would have an excuse to get ice cream, too. It had been almost two months since Bonaventure had his last scoop.

Although Foster didn't remember the exact conversation, he did remember that Jack Benson explained some strengthening exercises he should be doing with his leg. The exercises were just a series of muscle contractions and leg raises. They were to be done every hour. For someone who hadn't just had surgery, they would be elementary. For Foster, they were incredibly painful. Every motion caused pain to rip through his leg. He did them anyway, cursing Benson with every movement.

Foster tried hard to stick to this regimen, but in the hospital he lost all track of time and soon he forgot when he had done the exercises last. The every hour schedule soon turned into every other hour, and then every third hour, and then finally only when it was convenient. He seemed to lose his drive to work. Getting the leg back in shape seemed pointless. He was still going to miss the rest of the season. It didn't matter if the leg was back in shape in three weeks or three months.

After the first day and a half in the hospital, both cheeks on Foster's butt were too sore to take another shot. The nurse switched him from shots to oral medication. Although the Tylenol IV he was given still made him drowsy, it was a small improvement. He could recall conversations with his visitors. People brought him magazines and food. They told him jokes and stories about practice. Best of all, they brought him smiles. They made the days go so much faster. In fact, the slowest part of the day was when the team was at practice and his visitors were at a minimum. Of course, the hospital served dinner during this time, too -- another disappointment.

At practice the team was sluggish. In fact, practice didn't go well the entire week for anyone. The coaches didn't seem to want to push the team. They simply let them go through the motions. Bonaventure couldn't get the team fired up, which was a rare occurrence. Even Jack Benson's squad of student trainers and managers had problems getting prepared for practice.

It was easily the worst week of practice all season, including the second week of pre-season camp. The difference between pain and injury became blurred for the whole team. Every little ache or nag was reason enough to require Jack Benson or one of the other student trainers to examine the sore spot. Although most complaints were only minor pains, the five or ten minutes of diagnosis was five or ten minutes without practice.

A legitimate injury would normally mean disappointment for the player who had to miss practice. However, this week it was hard to find any disappointed looks on injured players. Not practicing was a relief. Just sitting with ice strapped on their body was about all their emotions could handle. Even the thought of having to run thirty-six 80-yard sprints at some later point didn't spoil their enjoyment at being sidelined for practice.

Nobody had any spirit. Their lack of spirit caused depression, which caused lethargy, entirely eroding their spirit.

The weather was gloomy all week. The dark cloud cover was low and threatened both snow and rain. Although it did neither, a cold mist filtered down on the practice field on both Wednesday and Thursday. Autumn was in full bloom. All the leaves had changed colors and were beginning to fall. But the gloomy weather spoiled all the color of the trees. And despite Bonaventure's letting the team out of practice earlier and earlier, it seemed to be darker each day at the end of practice.

Another reason for the team's depression was that it was mid-term break. The thought of all the other students being at home and being able to forget Beloit College made people feel sorry for themselves. Freshmen suffered most. Many of them hadn't been home since they came to camp in mid-August. Many had never been been away from home so long. Home, to them, was slowly becoming just a place they could call on the weekends.

Since it was break, the team expected a little bit of relaxation time during the day, but Bonaventure squeezed every available minute out of the team. He knew that no one had any work to do or any classes to attend. Football was their only commitment during break. At least once before practice and once in the evening, Bonaventure would gather the entire team for chalk-talks or a film session. Things were getting to the point where most players wished that school was in session. They figured it would be a little easier.

However, the biggest reason for the lethargic state was that the team lacked its usual catalysts to add spark to practice. Normally it was the captains who got the team's emotions started. The other upperclassmen helped out, but the captains were elected because their team spirit was above that of the rest of the players. Although Stubby was at practice, he didn't have enough enthusiasm to create the spirit needed. Considering the circumstances, it would have been tough for all three captains to get the team fired up. Stubby was trying to do the task all alone. After a short while, he became tired and then he, too, fell into the same general gloom.

Foster remained in the hospital and Doc spent most of the practice trying to nurse himself back to health in the locker room. Jack didn't want him out in the cool, damp air because he felt that it would hinder the healing of his bruised ribs. Doc couldn't understand the logic. He spent most of the time lying on the training table, massaging his rib cage with ice frozen in Dixie cups. He didn't think that outside could have felt much colder.

By Friday, Doc was finally ready, in Benson's opinion, to practice. Just to make sure, he had to run thirty-six 80s. Doc tried to talk Jack down on this number or repetitions or the length of the sprint. He reasoned that thirty-six 80s wasn't going demonstrate either way the condition his ribs were in, and also that it was so late in the season that the running would probably do more harm than good.

Jack wouldn't budge from his position. Although he believed that there was such a thing as too much conditioning, he didn't think that thirty-six 80s would reach that point. Besides, all those who had been injured during the week had missed out on the conditioning everyone else did. This was just a way of helping them catch up.

Jack tried to get Doc to look at it as not a punishment, but a help. Doc couldn't buy this psychology. How could something that was going to make his throat burn and his body ache be good for him? But realizing that he wasn't getting anywhere arguing, he began to run.

Doc started the first of the 36 sprints fifteen minutes before Bonaventure blew the whistle to start the Friday practice. Benson did give in as far as letting him run the sprints without full equipment. Doc ran dressed like he did the first day of practice. Aside from the basic garments he wore under his equipment, he wore only a helmet. After Doc had run his first six, Benson persuaded him to wear a rib-protector that he had rigged up. Although the cover for the ribs was only made of half-inch foam rubber, Benson wanted Doc to get used to wearing it when he moved. Benson directed Doc from one end of the field. He tried to get Doc's impressions of the additional piece of equipment, so he could make adjustments accordingly.

From the opposite end of the field, Doc cursed Benson, but he did everything that Jack required. He cut hard on his right leg and then hard on his left. He ran anywhere from half-speed to seven-eighths speed, forwards and backwards. The rests he took were only long enough to catch his breath.

By the time he was done, he was soaked with sweat. Despite the long Friday practice and his hard work, he was only able to finish in time to run two 10-yard sprints with the defense: One for the University of Chicago win and one for Loras the next day. He figured that after all he had run that day, twenty more yards wouldn't make a difference. Besides, the two sprints were dedicated to Foster, who was still in the hospital.

Most people on campus weren't even aware that Foster had been injured or had surgery, so almost all of his visitors were in some way connected with the football team. These were his closest friends anyway. It was hard to listen to all the stories they told about practice each day. It only reminded Foster of the things he was missing. But he knew they meant well. Foster kept to what Bonaventure had asked him to do. Although there was a time or two when he almost broke down, he kept a cheerful attitude and tried to be attentive to all their stories.

Foster saved his tears for late at night when all the visitors were gone. On one occasion an evening nurse caught him with tears in his eyes. When she asked why Foster was crying, he exclaimed that it was because of the pain in his knee. This was a half-truth. It was pain, but pain in his heart. She seemed easy to dupe. Besides, he doubted that she would have understood his sorrow anyway. Feeling sorry for himself was bad enough. He did not want anyone else's sympathy. The nurse sweetly asked him to try to endure the pain until the next time he was due to receive pain-killers.

Despite the many visitors Foster had in the hospital, his stay was anything but enjoyable. The nurses weren't good looking, he was not allowed to wash his hair, and his body was sore from taking all the shots and from lying in bed all week.

On Friday morning when the doctor made his rounds, Foster pleaded with him to be released that day. The doctor wanted him to stay one more day for further observation. Observation for what? Foster thought. It wasn't like he had open-heart surgery or any other ailment where a relapse was possible. It was routine knee surgery.

Maybe they wanted to see if he would snap because of the boredom. It was break, so studying was out of the question. The television game shows and daytime soap operas never appealed to Foster, so his television viewing was limited.

To pass the time, Foster would listen to the stories his roommate told. Foster befriended the kindly man, named Tovio Maki, when he found out that this cancer patient was from Crystal Falls, Michigan, a city only a short distance from Foster's hometown of Houghton. The tales of the good ole days and copper mining helped get his mind off football.

The doctor kept his word. On Saturday morning, Foster was released from the hospital. The night before, he was unable to sleep. The anticipation of getting home made his heart beat much faster. He got up eagerly and dressed in a pair of sweats. He lay on the bed and waited for a candy-striper to bring him downstairs in a wheelchair. When she arrived, Foster bid farewell to his new friend and vowed to come back for a visit when he got the chance. Foster waved as the candy-striper wheeled him down the hall toward the elevator.

In the lobby, Cort, one of the few non-football players in the fraternity who remained on campus during break, waited to take him home. He walked for the first time in three days. Everything, until now, was done in the prone position. Although the pain from blood rushing into his damaged leg ripped through his body, he couldn't help but smile as he crutched out of the hospital. Sweat rolled down from his armpits. He was so excited.

The team had already left for Loras College when Cort got Foster back to the house. Foster tried to talk Cort into driving to the game, but he had to finish a paper that was due the Monday that break was over. Foster reconciled himself to the fact that he wasn't going to be able to see the game, so he went to his room.

The first thing Foster wanted to do was wash his hair standing up. He couldn't remember the last time he had gone this long without taking a shower. He carefully taped a plastic bag around the cast on his leg and stood on a single leg under the warm water. It was good to be home.

After he toweled off, he started to shave the beard and mustache that had grown on his face in the past three days. When he had the left side of his face cleared of shaving cream, the phone rang. He managed to reach it in three rings.

"Hello," Foster said with a curious tone. He wondered who was calling him.

"Hi. I just called the hospital. They said you had been released, so I figured you'd be either in your room or at the game." Jandi spoke rapidly. She didn't expect Foster to answer.

It had been a long time since they had talked. She couldn't visit him in the hospital because she had to watch Jennifer during the days, and no children were allowed in the hospital. And at night she worked.

"Hi," Foster said again, but this time in a more welcoming voice. "Yeah, I just got home. The hospital sucked. I wanted to go to the game, but I have no way to get there." He took a deep breath. He had so much to fill her in on. He wanted to say it all in a single sentence.

"We'll take you." Jandi's voice was excited. "I've got my dad's car and Lori and I are looking for someplace to go."

Foster was slow to respond. "Okay." He was surprised at the invitation and unsure if he really wanted to go.

"Well, then, I'll be up in fifteen minutes to pick you up. We can talk then." Jandi quickly said goodbye. Then she went with Lori to fill up the gas tank and get Foster.

It wasn't long before the excitement of being out of the hospital wore off and the pain in his leg became unbearable. Foster dug through his gym bag and found the case of pain-killers the doctor had prescribed. The pain went away, but so did his awareness. When Jandi stopped by to get him, his ears were starting to ring and all his movements were at half-speed. He felt as if he were floating.

Jandi had the back seat all made up into a bed for Foster, with a blanket and several pillows so he would be comfortable. He tried to talk to Jandi and Lori, but slowly became a passive listener. Jandi and Lori had a lot to say, mainly conversation between themselves. Foster didn't mean to be rude, but he fell asleep.

The weather at Loras College, in Dubuque, Iowa, was similar to what the team had experienced all week long -- cloudy and misty. Since Loras was located along the Mississippi River, the temperature was much cooler.

The attitude that the team demonstrated all week in practice carried over into the pre-game warmups and then subsequently into the game. It was hard to get emotionally ready. This wasn't a conference game. Aside from their overall record, there seemed to be nothing at stake.

Loras didn't have a great team, but they were solid at every position. Most of the team was made up of cast-offs from the University of Iowa. Under normal circumstances, Beloit would be an equal opponent. Loras had several advantages: no mid-term break; they weren't playing without two of their team leaders; and they didn't have any conference games. Each game had meaning as they tried to earn a spot in the National Association of Intercollegiate Athletics (NAIA) playoffs. The NAIA is an organization similar to the NCAA, but it is considerably smaller and less recognized.

Loras scored on the first play from the line of scrimmage. It was a simple running play around end. It looked like Loras was playing a dummy scrimmage the way their back scooted through the Beloit defense and across the goal line for a 66-yard touchdown. Any spirit Beloit had was now totally gone.

By the time Jandi and Lori found the field, the score was 14 to nothing. Only a short time had elapsed in the first quarter. Beloit had the ball three plays on offense and then punted it back to Loras. Four plays later, Loras had another easy touchdown.

Foster awoke when Jandi parked the car. It was now raining lightly in Dubuque so she found a spot where they could watch the game from the car. Foster, although still dazed by the pain-killer, wanted to get down to the field. He took his crutches and hobbled down to the field while Jandi and Lori remained in the car.

Foster didn't seem to be fully aware of the lifeless attitude the team had. As he walked down the last set of stairs to the field, Doc, who was suited but not playing, spotted him.

"Foster, I'm glad you're here. You've got to say something to try and fire up these guys." Doc pleaded as he met him halfway.

What Doc had said to Foster registered, but somehow he couldn't bring himself to say what Doc wanted. It was as if Foster could say the words, but he couldn't find the enthusiasm that Doc wanted him to use. He returned Doc's request with a helpless look and shrugged his shoulders.

Foster moved down to a part of the field where he could see the game better. Doc somehow understood, moved down by him, and put his arm around Foster's shoulder.

It was hard to cheer on or even yell at their teammates when they weren't playing. For the first time since their freshman year, they felt helpless. There was nothing they could do on the sidelines to help the team. The words and enthusiasm weren't there.

The helpless feeling turned to guilt. Somehow they had let their teammates down by not being able to play. They were blaming themselves for the loss. Doc could fix this feeling in a week, but Foster knew that he was stuck.

Foster was coming to the realization that football was over. It wasn't a good feeling. All the if's and might's he had formulated in his mind through the years would always be left unanswered. He could see all the mistakes and missed opportunities on the field. For each one, he imagined how he would handle them now. His heart pounded with excitement. But there was no way to fulfill these desires. He was totally depressed with frustration.

In addition to Foster's hurt at watching the game, it also hurt his teammates to see him on the sidelines. He was a symbol that the only guarantee in football was the next play. After that, the future was just a roll of the dice.

Foster's presence reminded them of the goals he had set. They knew how hard he had worked to achieve them. It was evident now that many of those goals would never be achieved.

Instead of playing with the intensity that each down may be their last, they competed with apprehension. They expected each play to be their last. Instead of welcoming it with all they had and ending their careers the way Foster had, they lacked vigor because they were afraid of how it might end.

Bert was able to overcome this fear early. After several plays of thinking that every little pain he felt signaled the end, he realized that his attitude was ridiculous. Play the game. What was going to happen, was going to happen. No amount of worrying was going to change that.

As the game wore on, one by one, members of the team regained their courage to play football the way it was meant to be played. However, by the time there were enough players whose attitudes had changed, it was too late to make a difference. Loras College was winning by a score of 44 to nothing, and both teams were starting to substitute their second- and third-teamers.

Foster didn't wait for the game to end before he went back to Jandi's car. Halfway through the fourth quarter, he started to ascend the stairs to the parking lot where she was parked. Although it didn't rain terribly hard at any point, the constant drizzle and mist soaked Foster's hair.

He felt as if he had played in the game. His movements were sluggish, and the look on his face was dejected. He felt humiliated like the rest of the team.

He got back in the car, only saying "thank you" to Lori for helping him with his crutches. After that, he was quiet. It was if he were back in high school, when the coaches didn't let the team talk on the bus trip home after a loss. His somber attitude contaminated Jandi and Lori, too. The only words that were spoken until Foster fell back asleep were those that were essential for getting out of Dubuque, Iowa, and back toward Beloit, Wisconsin.

Bonaventure was quiet as the team filtered into the visitors' locker room. He removed his hat and brushed back his rain-soaked hair with his hand. This was the low point of his coaching career. Even in his first year at Beloit, when the team was winless, he didn't feel this bad. Never had he taken a team into a game so ill-prepared, both mentally and emotionally. He tried to be fair, but somehow he couldn't help but dump the blame on himself.

The only sounds in the locker room were the thumps and scrapes of players removing their equipment. Bonaventure sat squatted against the wall and stared at the floor. He began to play a series of hindsight games in his mind. Every game situation was run through a maze of "could haves", "should haves", and "would haves" to try and determine what might have changed the outcome of the game. He could reach no conclusions, only frustration.

Players occasionally glanced over toward Bonaventure to see if any expression had returned to his face. It was almost five minutes before Bonaventure snapped out of his trance. Quickly he stood and gathered the players around him. They moved slowly. They had been beaten up badly in the game, but nothing was more injured than their pride.

Bonaventure spoke softly. "Men, I don't know what to say." Bonaventure pulled his hand through his hair again. He couldn't look anyone in the eye. "It seems this week we sort of fell back into the Comfort Zone. And I guess we all know why." Bonaventure looked at Doc and thought about both him and Foster. "Men, we got to try and get back out. Somehow we got to get back out." His voice choked up. He ended the post-game comments by directing everyone to take a knee.

Before Foster fell back asleep, he had directed Jandi out of Dubuque and onto Wisconsin Route 81. Dubuque, Iowa bordered Wisconsin so Highway 81 was easy to find. From there, Beloit was due east. Once

Jandi and Lori were certain that he was sound asleep, they resumed the conversation they had been having during the game.

Foster slept most of the way back. Almost coincidentally he awoke as they crossed the Beloit city limits. Before he became fully conscious, he winced in pain. It had been hours since he had taken a pain pill. The last one had worn off. The doctor suggested that Foster keep the leg elevated. Instead Foster decided to stand all afternoon in the rain on the sidelines of a football game. This defiance resulted in an aggravation of the pain.

In addition to the throbbing of his knee, Foster's throat was dry and scratchy, and behind his eyes he could feel a headache developing. He felt feverish. Spending the afternoon standing in the rain hadn't been very sensible.

Foster rapidly blinked his eyes to clear them. He didn't dare move his aching body. Trying to relieve the pain, he stared at the ceiling and took light, deep breaths. However, the throbbing of his leg wasn't a pain that he could simply block out of his mind, especially with a headache. As hard as he tried to relax, his body only became rigid as the leg seemed to throb in unison with his heartbeats.

When Jandi looked in her rearview mirror, Foster's eyes were open. She smiled. He seemed happy to be awake, and she felt good seeing him awake.

"Hey, good morning, sleepyhead," Jandi said as she laughed. She still looked in her mirror, while periodically glancing back at the road. "We thought we were going to have to carry you into your room when we got back."

Foster had nothing to say. He ran his fingers through his hair and expended a lungful of air. The pain in his head was starting to mount. Jandi's high-pitched voice seemed to aggravate it. He lightly tried to close his eyes and relax. He had almost blocked the pain from the headache out when Lori broke his concentration.

"Hey, you were snoring so loud that the police pulled us over and said that we needed a new muffler." She started to laugh.

Jandi joined in once she caught on to the joke. Their laughing became more violent as Lori started to make exaggerated snoring sounds. Foster wasn't amused. In fact, he was rather annoyed. All the noise only made his head hurt worse.

In their joking, Jandi wasn't paying attention to the road. Her foot inadvertently pressed on the accelerator, causing the car to creep up on a truck they had been following. When the truck slowed to make a left-hand turn, Jandi had to quickly slam on her brakes to avoid hitting the back end. She and Lori had their seatbelts fastened but Foster, leaning back with his eyes closed, went crashing against the back of the front seat and onto the floor.

"Jesus Christ. What the hell are you doing?" Foster screamed as he tried to pull himself out from between the back and front seats.

Jandi was in shock. She knew she had made a mistake, but she had never heard Foster become so angry. She felt bad. "I'm sorry. Are you okay?" She and Lori waited for a response as Foster got back in the seat. Silence filled the car.

"Just get me home," Foster snarled. "Alive ... in one piece." Foster breathed out heavily in disgust. He shook his head for a moment and then tried to relax.

Jandi and Lori were quiet for the remaining five-mile trip back to the Beloit College campus. The tension in the car was heavy. Jandi drove as carefully as she ever had.

When they got to the Sig house, Foster quickly got out of the car. He stood on one leg on the driver's side and reached inside for his aluminum crutches. Lori, who appeared panic-stricken, turned around to help him.

Just as Foster was situated on his crutches, Jandi turned to ask if she could stop by later that evening. Before she could finish, Foster slammed the door shut.

She thought about rolling down her window to ask, but he seemed too intent on crutching into the house. She turned back and faced the road, swallowing the words that rested on the tip of her tongue, very hurt.

Lori sensed her friend's distress. She knew Jandi too well not to notice.

"It's okay, Jandi. He's probably just tired. It's hard to get any rest in the hospital." Lori put her hand on Jandi's shoulder and smiled.

Jandi smiled back. What Lori had said was reasonable, but it still hurt. Her smile disappeared.

The trip back for the team was equally somber. Everyone seemed to enter into an unofficial pact to limit their conversation to sentences under three words and head nods. Normally after a loss players would look back and try and examine what they could have done to change the outcome. On this trip, they tried to avoid even thinking about the game. Mid-term break seemed like a waste of time. They didn't even care to chalk up to experience the beating they took.

The bus got back to Beloit an hour after Foster had returned. The players who lived close enough went home for one day of home-cooked meals. Those who were stranded in Beloit gathered around the television to watch one more evening of movies. Their laughs did not seem as hearty nor did they seem as engrossed in the movie as the night before. They mainly wondered what it was like to be on the other end of a 44 to nothing game.

When Foster got home, he hurt too much to eat. He went straight to his room. Out of the medicine cabinet he got two pain pills, two aspirin, and four 500-milligram vitamin C tablets. Taking all those pills wouldn't do much more than half as many, but the thought of taking eight pills provides a placebo effect. With a mouthful of water and one swallow, all the pills were on the way.

The pain pills for his knee worked first. However, not only was the pain eased, but Foster also began to drift again. He lay on the bed and fixed his eyes on a single point on the ceiling. Slowly he could feel the other medication take effect. The headache and the sore throat faded.

But as the physical pains left, emotional pains of the injury took their place. Foster relived all the great plays he had made against Lawrence and University of Chicago. That's how he always dreamed about playing football. He wondered, had the injury not occurred, if he would have continued to play as well. If so, what would it lead to: All-Conference, Most Valuable Player, a 100-tackle season. His imagination had no limit.

The elation this daydreaming brought Foster turned quickly to depression as he looked at the full-length cast on his leg. Tears began to stream from his eyes down onto the pillow. Yes, it really was all over. Foster needed to have a good cry. Bonaventure only asked that he hide emotions from others, not himself.

From the elation of daydreaming Foster dropped to the depression of reality, to the bitterness of why was he the one chosen by the good Lord to suffer this -- there were so many others who hadn't worked nearly as hard as he did. This cycle drained his energy, but it wouldn't let him sleep.

Jandi came back about three hours later. This time gave her a chance to get cleaned up and into a new outfit she had bought because Foster said he liked it when they went out two weeks earlier. She felt much better now.

She parked her car and walked up to the house. Most of the guys were in the living room watching movies. Jandi went in the side door by Foster's room without their noticing. In her hand she had a football-shaped planter she had bought for him earlier in the week, but couldn't deliver.

She let the outside door close slowly and then she leaned against Foster's. She wasn't sure if he was there, but this would be the first place to check. A big smile appeared on her face as she thought how surprised he would be to see her. She lightly rapped on the door in her familiar manner.

At first, Foster thought he was hallucinating. That evening he had imagined so much, it was hard to discern the difference between reality and fantasy. Jandi waited a moment and knocked again. Foster knew now that he wasn't dreaming. Someone was there.

"It's ...," Jandi tried to get out as she knocked.

"Go away. I don't care who it is. I don't want to talk to anyone," Foster growled.

He was in the angry phase of his cycle. Every time he went through the cycle, as his energy drained, the anger became more intense. It didn't register that Jandi was at the door until after he had spoken. But at that time it didn't matter. He wanted to sulk alone. No one knew exactly what he was going through. It made him bitter to think that someone might try. His sorrow for himself left no compassion for anyone else.

Jandi didn't wait around to knock again. She didn't wait for an explanation. She knew one wasn't coming. She was seeing a side of Foster that she hadn't seen before. The hurt she now felt was worse than the earlier one and Lori wasn't around to console her.

Jandi ran to her car carrying the planter. She got in, revved the engine, and squealed the tires as she pulled away. After a block or two, she could no longer continue driving haphazardly. In fact, tears filled her eyes so much that she couldn't see anymore. She pulled over and began to cry.

29

Jandi had cried for close to a half an hour. In her mind, she replayed the good times that they had had, and she, too, wondered where the relationship would be had the injury not occurred. It was hard for her to understand what was going through Foster's mind. This was her first exposure to the football mentality. Nevertheless, she wanted to understand.

When she was through crying, she searched for a Kleenex. She didn't have one so she gently wiped her nose on her sleeve as she drove. When she got home, her mother could tell by the eye make-up that ran down her face that she had been crying. Foster's silence had rubbed off on her. She didn't want to share her pain with anyone. She went to her room and cried herself to sleep.

Foster wasn't troubled by what he had said to Jandi. He had become self-centered. In the hospital, he didn't feel quite so sorry for himself, but after he was out, he realized that the game of football was going on without him.

He stayed up for another two hours, going from elation to depression to anger and then back again. Finally, the emotional exhaustion allowed him to fall asleep. However, his mind continued the cycle.

Sunday was quiet around the house. Everyone tried to enjoy their last day of what could hardly be considered the break. Players on the team did as little mingling among the returning students as possible. It was nice to talk to people about the games they had won, but explaining a 44 to nothing loss wasn't. They were certain that they were being ridiculed behind their backs.

The first thing in the morning, Foster unplugged his phones from the wall outlets. He knew that as soon as people returning from break heard of his injury, they would start to call. He didn't want to have to explain over and over about what happened, nor did he want their sympathy. If Foster had to make a call, he could easily plug the phone back in and dial.

In blocking out calls from the rest of campus, Foster also blocked out calls from Jandi, which was the first thing she did when she got up. Jandi wanted to apologize. She felt that Foster's anger was her fault. Although this was totally untrue, she was placing the blame for everything on herself. She shouldn't have driven so crazy on the way back from Dubuque and she shouldn't have stopped by unannounced, she thought. No matter whose fault it was, she wanted to re-establish contact.

She called both his numbers to his room and let each ring at least twenty times. Either he wasn't answering or else he wasn't home. She was afraid to face him for fear he might react the way he had the last two times, but she had to communicate with him. Her only hope was to write him a letter. She started the first of several drafts of a letter to him.

Sunday night no one had any reason to go to the library and study. Any work that needed to be done had been done earlier in the week. This was the first week that the team didn't have its informal meeting. Most of the local players were at home so the meeting would only be held with a small percentage of the team. It probably wasn't needed anyway. Everyone knew what was on everyone else's mind -- the loss. There was no sense in talking about it.

Doc, Bert and Simba took advantage of the free evening and went down to the Jungle. On Sunday night, the Jungle was generally empty. Its patronage consisted mainly of senior citizens who had frequented this bar long before it was the Jungle. Even the bartender wasn't the same one who was there on Saturday nights. They had to pay for their drinks. That night, it wasn't the Jungle that they had come to know.

A week and a half ago, Doc had planned to take Carli out this evening. Instead, now he was slowly getting drunk, and bad-mouthing the girl he really still cared for in his heart. Only in private would he dare mention that he still had great affection for her. Sitting alone with Foster or Stubby without the macho image that had to be portrayed in the barroom setting, he could easily admit to how strong his feelings were toward her. However, it was the socially acceptable thing to talk bad about one another once the breakup had occurred. He was certain she was doing the same.

Bert and Simba offered plenty of sympathy. They had always had their complaints about the women on campus. Now they could voice these feelings more openly. Carli was one of the 'all right' women up until now. In any breakup, it was common for friends of the parties to choose sides. It was a given that they would side with Doc. She was blacklisted for what she had done.

Together they enumerated what they disliked about women in general. Once they were drunk enough, they jokingly formed their own version of 'Our Gang's' Women Haters Club. Doc was Alfalfa, Bert was Spanky, and Simba agreed to be Buckwheat.

Carli's friends naturally took her side, too. However, Carli did her best to squelch any bad talk that was generated about Doc. She was really the only one who understood the true reasons behind the breakup. She still had feelings for him, too. The breakup was only a test to see if those feeling were real.

Her only anger with Doc was that he didn't try hard enough to understand. This only created a slight bitterness. However, despite what had happened, she vowed to always speak fondly of Doc, no matter what she thought of him. Without a macho image to uphold, it was easier for her to disclose these feelings.

Monday on campus, whenever Doc came across Carli's friends or Carli came across Doc's, tension filled the air. The groups passed one another as if the other didn't exist. No one ever established eye contact. Both sensed the lines that had been drawn and the walls that had been built between the parties. Each had paranoid delusions that the other side was plotting against them.

Doc and Carli crossed paths once in the Mailroom. They tried to avoid one another, but when it was evident that they would inevitably meet they delayed acknowledging one another until the last possible moment. Each then greeted the other with a "hi, how are you?' that would indicate that they were surprised to see one another. But they both felt uncomfortable being in each other's presence. For now, at all costs, they would avoid having contact with one another despite their mutual feelings.

After Jandi wrote her first letter to Foster, she tried to call him again. The results were as unsuccessful as the first time. She couldn't get the events of the weekend out of her mind. She decided to write another letter.

On Monday morning, Jandi drove up to Beloit and deposited the letters at the post office. She wanted to be sure that they would be delivered in one day. On the way home, she thought of some more things she wanted to say. After trying to call again, without success, she started to compose another letter once she got home. She hoped he was writing her, too.

Bonaventure spread the word to the team that Monday afternoon's session to review Ripon's game film would be Monday night, and that the team would not review their own game film from the Loras College game. Had Bonaventure not had to send the film to another team for film exchange, he probably would have destroyed it. The Loras College game was one nightmare he never wanted to re-live.

The team was happy that there would be no review of the Loras College game film; however, they were on edge all day when Bonaventure said that they were to report to the Stadium and dress in helmets and shorts in lieu of the film session. They figured that Bonaventure was going to run them like he had the first three days of practice. Although running a team this late in the season was an ignorant thing for a coach to do to his team, everyone had been around the game of football long enough to know that this didn't mean it wouldn't happen.

However, their worries were unwarranted. When Bonaventure gathered the team around to start practice, he divided the team into eight sub-teams. The purpose of this was to set up a touch-football tournament. Each team would be able to play three games as the tournament Bonaventure set up had a winner's bracket, a loser's bracket and a pair of consolation games.

Despite the fact that there was only one champion, and that one team had to lose all three of its games, everyone had a good enough time to forget about the game of the past weekend. Bonaventure's plan to boost their spirits worked, and it carried on through the week. Although practice wasn't of the quality that they had had in the week preceding the Lawrence game, it was far above the practices they had the week before.

Bonaventure only dwelt on the Loras game long enough to remind the team that it was a non-conference game, and that the Beloit College Buccaneers were still in the race for the North Division title. In fact, part of the contingencies that Bonaventure laid out two weeks earlier to make this possible had already occurred: They had continued to win in conference play, and Lawrence lost to Lake Forest.

Now Lake Forest was the team to beat, and Beloit would have their chance at them in the last week of the season. Although Bonaventure didn't want the team looking beyond the Ripon College game, this information provided an incentive to keep the team's spirits alive.

Foster received two letters from Jandi on Tuesday, and then one each on Wednesday, Thursday, and Friday. In each letter, Jandi emphasized how much she appreciated their relationship, and she expressed an interest in wanting to understand his feelings. She pleaded with him to call or write.

Despite her wishes and pleas, Foster made no contact with Jandi. He didn't do it intentionally. He really appreciated her thoughtfulness. However, he lacked the courage to disclose his feelings to her. It wasn't that he didn't trust her. It was just that he was never one to be real emotional. Other than a few people on the team, there weren't many people who really knew what mattered to Foster. This emotional wall had been built over years. Although Foster had an urge to reveal his heart to Jandi, he didn't know how to overcome this wall.

The wall was a defense mechanism for Foster to avoid being hurt. If someone doesn't know where your heart is, then it can't be hurt. However, Foster never realized that in protecting himself he might hurt others.

Jandi wasn't aware of Foster's wall, but she was aware of the pain it caused her. Each day she waited by the window for the postman to come down the street. Each day she sifted through letters and bills to other members of her family, but found no letter from Foster. She was confused. She continued to call with no success. At one point she got out of bed at five in the morning, knowing for sure that he would answer, but he didn't. She was inclined to call in sick at work and go up to see him, but now she no longer had the courage to endure such a threatening situation.

Foster was having enough trouble playing the role that Bonaventure had asked him to – to be unaffected by his injury. To play the part, Foster had to block out the pain. It wasn't easy. It required being aware of what he felt at all times. To open up to Jandi might break his concentration.

Foster did a good job. Most people were amazed at how well he seemed to have taken the end of his football career. He came down to practice each day and went through the warm-up drills with the team. He retrieved water bottles and blocking dummies for the players and held play cards for the coaches. It was if he hadn't left the game at all.

Bonaventure's philosophy worked. The younger players didn't seem worried at all about the potential final outcome of their careers. As much as it hurt Foster to play this role, he was glad he was still of value to the team.

Although this play acting benefited the team, it didn't do much for Foster. He stopped working out altogether and he seldom studied. When he wasn't playing his role for others, he sat quietly in his room and felt sorry for himself. There wasn't any energy left to motivate him to study or work out. The strain of hiding his emotions caused him to lose the discipline he had. Everything seemed to be falling apart.

Early Saturday morning the team headed north for Ripon, Wisconsin. This was their second away game in as many weeks. The novelty of the road trip had long passed.

For Foster, it was really the first week in which he had not traveled with the team. Although he did not travel or play against Loras College, he had been in the hospital all week and so it wasn't a game week for him. It was tough not to be going on the bus. For four years, he had made every travel squad and played at least one down in every game. It was like the end of an era. He was missed on the bus, as much as he missed being there.

However, he still vowed to make it to the game. He had the royal blue Chevy waiting by the bus just before it was to depart so he could caravan with the rest of the team to Ripon College. Traveling with him were two other players, Dave Wilkinson and Paul Guicik. Wilk, as he was known, was on the team but did not play much. Nevertheless, he and Foster were friends. Guicik was one of very few who hadn't traveled with the team all season. Foster thought it might be nice if he could make this last trip with the team. After getting the okay from Bonaventure, the arrangements were made.

To drive with his cast, Foster had to push the seat all the way back. This way, he could accelerate the car by extending his foot, and also work the brake with the same foot. Most people are accustomed to driving with their right legs. For Foster this was true and a lot safer than using his left foot.

The bus ride up was unusually quiet for the team, despite the fact that everyone stayed awake most of the trip. Stubby and Doc sat in the back seat together. Stubby tried Foster's tactic of listening to music before the game. Although the Charlie Daniels Band was nothing like the soundtracks to the *Rocky* series, he hoped the effect would be the same.

Doc studied the cards that the offensive coaches had drawn up during the week. He tried to determine what defensive formation the Ripon College Redmen would use given the offensive formation he called in the huddle. When would they blitz? Whom did they key on? When would they go to a zone or man-to-man coverage? Doc jotted some notes in his playbook, and then tried to find some patterns. Although no real clear pattern was evident, there were some tendencies that would be worth gambling on.

Everyone was aware of what this game meant. It was an obstacle that had to be overcome in order for the team to still be in the race for a spot in the conference championship game.

Bonaventure's scenario unfolded perfectly. Both Lawrence and Ripon had one loss apiece, and Lake Forest College was unbeaten in conference play. If the scenario continued, then Beloit would give Ripon its second loss and knock them out of contention like University of Chicago already was. Then, the next week, when Lawrence played Ripon, Ripon would win. Lawrence would no longer be a factor. It would all come down to the Lake Forest game for Beloit. The only conference game Lake Forest had left was Beloit. And if the Bucs could beat them, both teams would have a one-loss record. The trick here would be that Beloit would have beaten Lake Forest, and therefore proved itself the superior team. It would be hard for the coaches not to vote Beloit into the title game.

However, there still were a half dozen "ifs" between now and then. Ripon was the first. In Bonaventure's career at Beloit, he had never beaten

Ripon College. In fact, up until the previous week, Ripon had handed Beloit some of its worst losses through the years.

Another factor the team, especially the seniors, had to consider was that they had never beaten a team that they weren't supposed to beat. Through the years, Bonaventure's teams had won almost as many games as they lost, but the games they won were games they were supposed to win. It was never any surprise to anyone that the Bucs beat University of Chicago, Northwestern College, or Grinnell College. They had never won as the underdog, however. It was something they had to overcome. Today they were, at least in the media's eyes, the underdog.

The pre-game warmup went as it always did. They seemed to be ready for the game. Their spirits were high.

Beloit won the coin-toss and decided that they would receive the ball. On the first three plays, the Bucs moved the ball like they had against Lawrence. However, on the fourth play, Doc dropped back for a pass and was hit on his blind side by a Ripon defensive back blitzing through the line.

Doc was hit in the area where he was hit two weeks earlier against University of Chicago. Despite the extra padding Jack had rigged up for him to wear, a burning sensation hit him hard. The pain was so intense that everything appeared blue. However, he didn't dare leave the game for fear that he might not get back in. He held his side and walked back to the huddle.

Bonaventure sent in the next play for Doc to call in the huddle. Because Doc was sacked on the last play, it set up another passing situation. Doc faded back again for the pass. He tried to ignore the pain. This time, no one blitzed. Instead, Ripon switched from a man-to-man coverage to a zone. Doc didn't pick this up. He should have. It was one of the tendencies he noted on the bus trip. However, he was too concerned with throwing the ball well despite pain throbbing in his side.

Doc threw the ball to what he thought was an open man in the flats on the wide side of the field. It was intercepted by a Ripon defender, who ran it back to the fifteen-yard line before Simba made a touchdown-saving tackle.

When the defense took the field, they were back playing like they had against Lawrence and University of Chicago. Bill was finally getting the hang of playing defensive tackle.

The Bucs' defense held them for no gain on three plays. On the fourth, however, Ripon decided to try to get the touchdown instead of kicking a field goal. They threw a pass which fell incomplete, but the referee threw a flag. He called a pass interference penalty on Beloit in the end zone. Bonaventure and the rest of the players protested the call.

It didn't matter. Ripon was still given a first down with the ball on the two-yard line. Although the defense played tough, the change of momentum and the field position allowed Ripon to score on the second play from the line of scrimmage. The extra-point kick was no good. Ripon was ahead by a score of six to nothing.

Before the Beloit offense could regain possession of the ball, Ripon recovered inside the ten-yard line when the ball was fumbled by a Beloit player on the kick-off. Bonaventure ran his hand through his hair and thought, 'Loras revisited.'

The defense was back on the field, but the spirit they demonstrated in the first series was gone. Ripon scored another touchdown the next play on a pass in the corner of the end zone. There wasn't a defender anywhere near the receiver. Ripon tried to make up for the failed extra-point kick with a two-point conversion. It failed also, and the Redmen led by a score of 12 to nothing.

"Okay, Okay men, it's time to play catch-up ball." Bonaventure clapped his hands as he spoke. He turned to face the stunned offense. He knew that yelling at them wouldn't help. Besides, there was plenty of time left.

"Let's go," Bert yelled. He tried to catch Bonaventure's enthusiasm.

The offense took the field after the kick-receive team returned the ball to the thirty-yard line. The defense stood on the sidelines blaming themselves for the team's 12-point deficit. Bill started to cheer them out of this mood. The defense was playing great and that's what he tried to tell them. He was doing his best to fill the leadership void Foster had left when he got hurt.

The offense started to play like they had in the first three plays. Although they didn't score, they had proved to Ripon, and more importantly to themselves, that they could move the ball. After a missed attempt at a field goal, Ripon, for the first time that day, didn't have the ball in striking distance.

The defense forced Ripon to punt the ball back. Now the Bucs' offense had better field position. This pattern continued for the remainder of the first half. Beloit would march forward two steps and then get marched back one. Eventually, in the last part of the half, the Bucs were able to score. After the extra point, they went into the locker room at halftime only down 12 to 7.

In the second half, there was more of the same. Beloit would gain ground and then give some of it back. Gain ground, give some back. Every inch of turf was hard fought. There would be no easy touchdown or a decisive winner. Both teams stuck to a conservative nickel/dime approach to moving the ball.

Up until then, both sidelines were tense. It was evident that with each series Beloit was gaining ground. The question on everyone's mind was whether Beloit had enough time left to gain the necessary yardage to score the go-ahead touchdown. The third quarter was scoreless, and so was the fourth quarter until the closing minutes.

With a minute left, the question on everyone's mind was answered. Beloit had finally worked the ball down close enough to score. On a short run up the middle behind Big El, the Bucs went ahead for the first time in the game. Although the margin was only a point, it was enough.

The coaches held a quick sideline conference and decided that kicking the extra point would serve no purpose. Now they were only ahead 13 to 12. An extra-point kick would only extend the margin to two points. They decided to go for a two-point conversion. They had nothing to lose. If it failed, they would be no worse off than if the kick was successful. A field goal by Ripon could overcome a one- or a two-point margin. With the two-point conversion, the Bucs would have a three-point margin and Ripon would need at least a touchdown to win.

The referee lined the ball up on the three-yard line. Beloit quickly set on the ball. Doc faked a dive to the fullback up the center, and then raced around end. He was almost across the line for the two points when he was dragged down from behind. They would have to settle for a one-point margin. This didn't hurt their spirit at all. They'd tried.

On the Beloit sideline, everyone waited to greet the offense. The entire team was involved in back-slaps, hugs, and high-fives to celebrate. Nothing felt better than to 'blood-n-guts' out a win. It was better than beating someone decisively.

OUT OF THE COMFORT ZONE

The offense flopped on the bench and tried to catch their breath as the the ball was about to be kicked to Ripon. The defense got ready to take the field.

Ripon recovered the ball and quickly got their offense on the field. They had to travel 55 yards for a touchdown, and not quite as far if they wanted to kick a field goal.

As expected, they came out in a passing formation. Beloit went to a man-to-man coverage and rushed five people. The defensive rush was heavy on each play and a considerable amount of pressure was put on the quarterback, but each time he managed to get the pass off.

The clock stopped after each play, but Ripon made no forward progress. After three plays, it was fourth and ten yards to go for a first down. Only 15 seconds remained on the clock.

The Ripon quarterback dropped back for what would probably be the last play of the game. The defensive linemen swarmed on him more intensely than on any of the previous three plays. Bill got a hand on him and started to drag him down. The quarterback threw the ball as hard and as deep as he could. He didn't see where it went.

Two people were in the area where the ball was thrown -- a Ripon receiver and a Beloit defender. It was a foot race for the ball. The Beloit player had a head start, but the Ripon player was close behind. Just as he was about to reach the ball, the Beloit defensive back lost his balance and fell. The Ripon player extended his arms and grabbed the ball. There was no one around to pursue him. He easily ran in for the score. Ripon went ahead 18 to 13. No time remained on the clock.

The elation of the Beloit bench raced over to the other side of the field. Replacing it was shock. It was almost impossible to believe what had just happened. The Beloit defender who had tripped remained on the ground with his face buried. He felt worst of all.

As the teams lined up to shake hands, the Beloit players were dazed and stunned. They could hardly grasp the Ripon players' hands as they passed them in the center on the field. Every Ripon coach, player and fan jubilantly celebrated.

Bonaventure kept his composure as he searched out the Ripon coach to congratulate him. It wasn't supposed to be, he thought, it just wasn't supposed to be.

In the locker room, many eyes were filled with tears. A chance at the conference title and a chance to be the victorious underdog for once vanished with a freak pass. The season had one disappointment after another. Until now, the team was able to contain them.

No one noticed as Bonaventure entered the locker room. The speech he gave after the Lawrence game would have been appropriate had not everything else happened that season. Bonaventure didn't know what to say when he huddled the team around him. To give himself time to think, he had everyone take a knee.

During the prayer, there was no whimpering. Several players, however, could be heard sniffling. Everyone, including Bonaventure, had trouble concentrating on the prayer.

Bonaventure let the prayer extend considerably longer than normal. In that time, he was still unable to think of something to say. There had to be something to say. He had to think of it quickly. Everyone's eyes were now focused on him.

He cleared his throat. "I don't know what to say." There was a long pause as he still tried to think. "I'm proud of you...You battled like champions." Bonaventure paused again. "I'm damn proud of you," he said with a solemn voice. His fist was clenched. He turned and left the locker room.

30

Bonaventure came back to the locker room after about ten minutes and said to each individual the same thing he had said to the team collectively. He shook their hands and patted them on the backs. Sure, it would have been nice to win, but the important thing was achieved. That was that the team learned a little something about what they were made of. Although one cannot be precisely certain at what point their limit is reached and their potential determined, everyone today knew that that milestone was a little farther than what they had thought before.

For Foster, sitting on the sidelines was again difficult. When the team was staging its comeback, he felt left out. It was being done without him, and he had no hope of making any contribution. When the team ultimately lost, Foster felt guilty. He thought that maybe if he had been there the outcome would have been different. He felt he had let the team down by being hurt. It was a no-win situation.

After everyone had showered, they loaded their equipment and went to the bus. The team's loyal following was, as usual, there to greet them. By now most players were greeted with a hug and a kiss by the mothers of other players on the team. The guys, now that the season was nearly over, knew enough about each player to enter into a meaningful conversation with them. Even Bonaventure and the rest of the coaches mingled with the friends and families of the team.

However, the post-game gathering didn't last long. There was still a long trip back to Beloit and the team had to stop to get something to eat, too. Bonaventure signaled to everyone that they had to be getting started back. Players said their farewells for another week and climbed aboard the bus.

Wilk was riding back with Foster. Simba was the second person in the car. Paul Guicik rode back on the players' bus in Simba's place. Foster persuaded him to do this by making it look like he was giving Paul a real opportunity for fun, but in essence Foster wanted Simba to come back in his car so he could let him drive. Simba was one of the few Foster trusted with his car.

The team stopped for dinner near Ripon, Wisconsin, where McDonald's, Burger King and Kentucky Fried Chicken were all within a short walk from one another. This way no consensus was needed by the team, and each player's indecisiveness was his own problem.

Foster, without having to worry about fifty people, picked a Ponderosa. They had to drive a little farther out of Ripon to get to the Ponderosa, but both Simba and Wilk agreed that it was worth the wait. It wasn't elegant dining, but it was a step up from fast food and they could gorge themselves on the salad bar for very little money.

After the team got back on the bus, there was some playfulness among the players. There was an exchange of jokes and teammates ribbed one another about women they had taken home on particular occasions. Although the game still weighed heavily on their minds, they weren't going to let it make the trip back seem any longer than it already was. Besides, there would be plenty of time to dwell on the Ripon game in the next couple days before they had to get ready for Lake Forest.

Once the bus got rolling, however, the team quieted down. Players finished the remainder of food they had brought back on the bus, then tilted back the seats the small amount that they would recline and looked out the window as dusk took over the lonely plains of northern Wisconsin.

Bert, Doc and Stubby sat three abreast in the far back seat. The seat was designed for three people, but those three accounted for at least three and a half. Although they were shoulder to shoulder in the seat, this kept their exhausted bodies upright as they talked.

"Four and Four," Doc remarked about the team's record. "That doesn't sound too fuckin' familiar."

Stubby shook his head and rolled his eyes in agreement. There really wasn't much that could be said.

It had been over fourteen years since Beloit had a winning football team. In that time, the college had gone through close to a half dozen coaches. Bonaventure got the job as head football coach when Beloit football was at its lowest point. He didn't mind. It was the challenge he was looking for, to build a nothing team into a champion. His first season he had only 19 players to work with. That season, the team was 0 and 9, but he recruited more than 30 freshmen and the next season the team went .500, the first non-losing season in ten years.

The next year was this senior class's freshman year. Again, the team went four and four. In fact, every year they had been at Beloit their record was the same at this point in the season. Their sophomore season, Bonaventure added a ninth game. The team thought this would ensure that they wouldn't be four and four. However, going into the last game they were four and four. They tied this game and so their record was four, four and one, still only a .500 record. The last season they lost the ninth game after going into it four and four. They finished with a losing record and the winning season eluded Bonaventure and Beloit College again.

Bert lay his head back and and gently shut his eyes. He didn't want to sleep, but his eyes stung each time the lights from an oncoming car came through the window. He began to speak even though the shaking of the bus garbled his words.

"Yeah, about four games ago I really thought this was going to be 'the' season. But a couple injuries and some dumb luck and then shit turns to black." Bert laughed and shook his head in disgust.

"When you think about it, we really only lost two games this season -- Loras College and North Central College. Stubby leaned forward to share the observation. "That sounds great. I can hear us ten years from now. Yeah, we only really lost two games our senior year in college. The other losses we decided not to count."

Doc laughed. Then he got serious. "It's hard to believe that at one time this season we had three straight victories."

"Yeah, I know. Whooping it up in the locker room, like we did, seemed to happen so long ago. It's like a dream." Stubby made one more observation and then tilted his head back and shut his eyes.

Their exhaustion was overcoming their desire to feel sorry for themselves out loud. Doc pulled his body out from between the bulky offensive linemen. He found a vacant seat to sit in. Bert and Stubby shifted their bodies to take advantage of the extra space. Neither opened his eyes in the process. Within ten minutes, they were all asleep.

After Foster, Simba and Wilk finished at Ponderosa, they got in the car and departed for Beloit. Simba drove, Wilk sat in the shotgun position, and Foster was sprawled in the back. Foster's leg didn't hurt much anymore. When he drove, the cast protruded up into his behind. It was nice to be able to sit comfortably.

Neither Simba nor Wilk knew the way back to Beloit, so Foster had to give directions from the back seat. When they started out, Foster directed Simba the same way the bus had come to Ripon. However, after they had driven about ten miles while Foster was studying the Wisconsin map, he claimed that he had identified a shortcut back to Beloit. Five miles farther down the road, he directed Simba to take a right on a county dirt road. This would lead them to the shortcut.

By now, it was dark. For miles on each side of the road were harvested farm fields. They continued down the road for almost twenty minutes before Foster determined that they had gone down the wrong one. Simba used the entrance to a farmhouse to turn around and backtrack the distance.

When they finally got back to where they started, Foster got them on the right county road. Already, the purpose of the shortcut was defeated. The shortcut now, if it existed at all, would only ensure that they got home at the same time as if they had stayed on the original course.

On the back roads, Simba could only drive about half as fast as he did on the main highways. But according to Foster's shortcut, the back road would get them to the main Interstate quicker.

They listened to a country/western radio station. It was the only station they could tune in with any clarity. There was little conversation as they concentrated on where they were going.

Simba and Foster began telling short stories about funny incidents they knew of or had experienced in their years at Beloit. As a general rule, if the stories weren't very flattering, they were tales that they knew of but weren't involved in. When any story enhanced their images, they quickly took credit for it.

Wilk, only a junior, supplemented the conversation whenever he could. Although these stories couldn't compare with the best Simba and Foster had accumulated over the years, they added to everyone's amusement.

Their laughing and carrying on made the miles seem to go faster, so much faster, in fact, that Simba drove past the turnoff they had to take to pick up the Interstate. Considering the state of their temperaments, they all laughed. Simba pulled over and turned on the dome light. Foster opened the map and began to determine where they were and where they had to go.

They were close to fifteen miles west of where they were supposed to turn south to pick up the Interstate. One option for them was to backtrack again. However, Foster figured that they would be better off traveling west another five miles or so. Another road intersected there that would take them south to the Interstate. Simba proceeded. This time, although the joking didn't stop, they were careful to locate the turnoff.

They headed south and looked for signs that would direct them to the Interstate. There were none. Foster thought that was peculiar. He had Simba pull over again so he could check the map. Sure enough, the road they were on intersected with the Interstate. It couldn't be but a few more miles. Simba continued.

Eventually they did reach the Interstate, but the road went over the Interstate with no on-ramp in either direction. This explained why there were no signs.

"I quit," Foster said as he threw the map up in the air.

Simba and Wilk laughed. They were already an hour late. By the time they had taken the side roads and done the necessary backtracking to get to Beloit, they were close to two and a half hours late.

"We aren't going to tell anyone we got lost on the way back are we?" Wilk inquired. "We'll take so much shit."

"Got lost. We got lost four or five times." Simba laughed. The lights of Beloit were just ahead. "You better believe if someone finds out, we are going to take shit."

Foster sat up between the seats. "Well, let's come up with a story we tell everyone to explain why we're late."

There was a silence. "I'm waiting," Wilk said as he turned to the other two. "You two seem to have all the great stories."

Simba and Foster were quiet. They seemed to be stumped.

"I've got an idea," Foster said. "Pull over in that bar."

Simba parked the car in the parking lot of the bar and the three went in. They received the usual stares that strangers receive when they enter an establishment that has regular clientele. Foster crutched up to the bar.

"I'll have a beer and a shot." That's the way his grandfather would have asked.

The bartender returned with a foamy glass of beer and a shot glass filled with whiskey. Foster took the whiskey and dabbed some of it behind each ear like cologne. The bartender, as he straightened the crumpled dollar bills, looked at Foster as if he were crazy. Foster smiled back. Foster then took a mouthful of beer and swished it around his mouth. After a moment, he swallowed. He poured a little beer down his front and then he dumped the remainder of the shot on his jacket. He took one more mouthful of beer and gargled it as they left the bar. Once outside, he spit it out on the pavement.

"Okay, Simba. Now drive home quickly," Foster said as he messed his hair and lightly smeared dirt on his face.

Simba looked at Foster as if they weren't quite sure what he was up to. However, Simba followed his directions and drove directly to campus.

Simba sped past a self-serve gas station where Jandi was filling her gas tank. Lori pointed out Foster's car to her. She quickly topped off her tank, paid the attendant, and then pursued the car. By now, she was close to a half-mile behind. However, she was certain that he was going back to campus.

"Hey, you fuckin' pussies," Foster slurred his speech and drew out the pronunciation of his words. He staggered on his crutches up the front lawn of the Sig house. "Come on out here, you pussies."

Foster's plan was to explain their lost time by making everyone believe that he was at the bar getting drunk, sort of drowning his sorrows because he couldn't play football anymore. In other words, the Ripon College game was the breaking point for his emotions.

The alcohol he poured on himself was just for effect. He wore sunglasses so no one could see that his eyes didn't have the glossy, drunk look. Simba and Wilk were told to follow his lead. Immediately, they caught on.

The first person to step out of the house was a woman who was there to see one of the guys. She went to Beloit College, too, and knew Foster well enough to know that he didn't drink, or at least hadn't before. She approached him laughing as Foster swayed back and forth.

"He's drunk," she said to herself quietly. She continued to approach. "Hey, you guys, it's Foster, and he's drunk." She turned to yell back in the house.

Before she could turn back toward Foster, he grabbed her by the wrist and pulled her in close to his body. Just then, Jandi turned the corner onto College Street. She stopped the car immediately when she saw Foster grab hold of the woman.

"That's right, I'm drunk, you sex machine." Foster squeezed her tight. "Now I have the courage to do all those wild things to you that I always fantasized about." He dropped his crutches and tilted her over his good knee. He tried to kiss her on the lips, but she wouldn't let him. He started gnawing on her neck.

Jandi's heart sank when she saw this. She couldn't bear to watch. She backed her car down the one-way street and then squealed her tires as she drove off. She felt angry this time, not hurt. No one bothered to look. Tires squealing on a Saturday night around campus were common.

When Foster let go of the woman, her instincts made her slap him in the face. He used the opportunity to fall to the side, face first in the mud. As Foster pulled himself to his feet, she ran behind her boyfriend, hoping that he would defend her honor. He wasn't going to mess with Foster even when he was on crutches and intoxicated. Besides, watching Foster was too funny. Foster still had a leaf stuck to the side of his face as he started into the house. He ignored the woman.

Simba and Wilk laughed the hardest of all. Foster's act was funny, but the fact that he was fooling all those people was even funnier. Even Foster could hardly keep from laughing.

By now, most of the people who were at the house were in the living room to see Foster. It was like a carnival sideshow. This was one of those things that they always wanted to see, but they never thought they'd have the opportunity.

Bert led the taunting of Foster. It made Foster feel best of all that he was fooling Bert. This was the acid test. Bert was the self-proclaimed team champion drinker. He knew every drink ever made and then some. He had a dozen cures for hangovers, and he denounced other people as fakers when they had claimed to be drunk.

He left his crutches in the front yard as he staggered through the living room. Twenty people gathered around to closely examine his every move. The woman, whose neck was still red with gnaw marks, followed behind her boyfriend. They wanted to be accurate when they reminded Foster of that evening for years to come.

"What prompted this?" a younger player on the team inquired, a question to the general populace.

Simba, playing along with the joke, had the answer. "Foster was depressed that Jack Benson wouldn't let him play anymore, so he made us pull over at a bar. Before we knew it, he was like this. It didn't take much." Simba's acting was as good as Foster's.

"Jack Benson? Where is Jack Benson?" Foster played off of Simba's lead. "I'm gonna kill that skinny motherfucker." Foster punched his fist into the wall. He had to do it hard enough to be convincing, but not hard enough to hurt himself.

Like most intoxicated people, Foster switched his attention rapidly. He made nonsensical remarks out of everything people said, and made belligerent comments about what people wore or what he actually thought of them. Foster liked the role he was playing. It was his license to say what was on his mind with little chance for repercussions.

He slowly moved toward his room. After fumbling with his keys for a minute or two at the door, he let himself in. The multiple pairs of eyes that continued to follow also went in.

Foster went into his bathroom and locked the door behind him. Quietly, he filled a large glass of water as he continued to talk nonsense. When the glass was full, he knelt down by the toilet and began making noises like he was going to be sick. He threw part of the glass of water in the toilet. To the people outside the door, it sounded as if he had vomited. They looked at one another and began to giggle.

Foster then became quiet. He flushed the toilet and began to straighten himself up. The people outside his door became curious. They were worried that he had passed out. Although they still joked, they started to tap lightly on the door, requesting a response from Foster.

Foster couldn't help smiling. He didn't know how much longer he could keep this up. He figured that now was as good a time as any to end it. Without warning, he quickly swung the door open and confronted the numerous curious faces.

"Fooled you all," Foster said in his most sober voice. He was leaning against the frame of the door with his arms crossed. He had his sunglasses off so everyone could see his eyes. After about ten seconds of standing with a serious look on his face and taking in the foolish looks everyone else had, Foster began laughing. He relieved himself of all the laughter he had accumulated.

"Real funny joke." Stubby stepped forward. He spoke as if he was almost angry that he was fooled, but there was a slight hint in his voice that he wasn't serious. "Well, one good joke deserves another." Stubby grabbed Foster by the wrist. "You're going in the shower." Other people moved forward and grabbed Foster by his other limbs and picked him up.

Foster continued to laugh until he realized that they were serious about putting him in the shower. Someone had turned the water on and pulled the curtain back. "No, no, no, I've got a cast on. It can't get wet." Foster was serious enough to utter those two sentences. When he knew that they realized that their revenge was foiled, he started laughing again.

"Okay then," Stubby said as he reached back into Foster's medicine cabinet and retrieved a can of shaving cream. He began squirting it in Foster's hair while others rubbed it in. The woman he had molested stepped forward and did the same with his tube of toothpaste. Before they were through, Foster was covered with shaving cream, toothpaste, shampoo and conditioner.

It took over an hour for Foster to clean himself and his bathroom up. By now it was late. He was tired and ready for bed. He lay down and smiled. This was the first time in over two weeks that he didn't feel sorry for himself. Although the injury still bothered him and he knew it would be a scar on his heart for the rest of his life, it felt nice to have a good laugh. Quickly, his body started to relax as he began to fade off to sleep.

Just before he went from the point of deep relaxation to sleep, a loud knock came at the door. He got up and hobbled to the door without his crutches. As he put on his bathrobe, he said to himself, 'this better be good.'

Jandi stood on the other side of the opening door. Immediately, she pushed her hand against the door as if to prevent it from being shut in her face. She was intoxicated. This was no act.

"Jandi," Foster said with surprise. "What are you doing here?"

She could barely stand. Foster held the door halfway open so she wouldn't fall inside the room. Lori stood in the background. She had a concerned look on her face.

"I want to know," Jandi started to speak. "I want to know why you don't like me anymore."

Jandi's speech was slurred. She couldn't focus her eyes; she stared straight ahead with her big glossy blue eyes. Her body swayed back and forth. Both Foster and Lori were ready to catch her at any moment.

"Jandi, I still like you. Really, I do." Foster protested.

She didn't listen. "Why don't you like me anymore?" She started to pound on his chest to emphasize each of her sentences. "You won't talk to me. You don't write, and you don't answer the phone when I call. I saw you with that girl tonight. Do you think I'm dumb? Just because I'm not in college I'm dumb. That's it, isn't it?" She pounded hard once more on his chest. "Tell me. Why don't you like me anymore?" she yelled.

Foster realized that he wasn't going to be able to communicate with her in this state. "Jandi, just go home," he spoke softly. "We can talk when you're not drunk." He started to move her toward the outside door.

She was strong. In his cast, Foster couldn't move her. She pushed him back in the room. "No, I'm not drunk. And I'm not going home until you tell me why you don't like me anymore." She was demanding.

Feeling frustrated, Foster got mad. "Jandi, just get the fuck home," Foster said, raising his voice.

Jandi was stunned by his tone of voice. Lori was too, but she didn't keep her silence. Up until then, she was willing to give Foster the benefit of the doubt with respect to the way he had been treating Jandi. She scowled at Foster over Jandi's head.

"Come on, Jandi, let's go. He's just a jerk like all the other guys." Lori continued to stare at Foster. Foster stared back. He was equally angry.

Jandi turned back at Lori for a moment. "No, I'm not leaving until he tells me why he doesn't like me anymore." She turned back toward Foster. He was still staring down at Lori. His teeth were clenched.

"No, we're going home right now," Lori said in an angry voice.

Lori grabbed Jandi by the arm and spun her around. The momentum was aimed toward the door which Lori had opened with her other hand. Jandi lost her balance and fell head first against the frame of the opened door. Her body became limp as she rolled along the inside wall and slid down it to a sort of seated position. Her body appeared lifeless.

"Jandi," Lori cried as she ran inside to Jandi's aid. There still was no sign of life from Jandi. Lori started to cry as she shook her, yelling, "Jandi, Jandi, please speak to me."

Jandi's head slid along the wall to one side leaving a large smear of blood on the back wall. Lori became frightened. She backed up against the other hallway wall and looked on with horror.

Foster's heart pounded. With the cast he couldn't kneel, so he crouched down on one leg beside her. He examined her head. There was a deep, inch-long gash on the top of her head, bleeding heavily. He tried to apply pressure to the area to stop the bleeding. As he tended to her, life seemed to come back to her limp body.

"Get away from me," Jandi said, as she pushed Foster back.

"Jandi, I'm just trying to help you." Foster pleaded with her as he tried to get closer.

"I don't want your help," Jandi said softly as Foster continued toward her. She noticed the blood that covered both his hands. "I just want to know why you don't like me anymore." She started to cry midway through her sentence.

Foster moved back in and gave her a warm hug with one arm and applied pressure to the cut with his other hand. She continued to cry. He kissed her on the forehead and then rested his cheek against hers.

31

After Foster got Jandi's head to stop bleeding, he had Lori hold a cloth filled with ice on the bump that was developing. He then went upstairs and woke up Doc. Lori was still so shaken by the incident that he was unsure about having her get Jandi to the hospital and then home.

Lori drove Jandi's car and Doc followed in his VW. Foster continued to hold Jandi in the back seat of her car as Lori drove to the emergency room.

Jandi's cut looked worse than it actually was. As the nurse explained, any cut to the head bleeds a lot because there are so many veins so close to the surface. Because it wasn't so bad, the emergency room priority system pushed Jandi in line behind all the accident victims who happened to be at the hospital that night. They had to wait almost two hours to get Jandi stitched up.

During the wait, Doc slept on the floor with a three-month-old issue of *Sports Illustrated* over his face. Lori smoked cigarette after cigarette, trying to calm herself. She blankly stared at the wall through the window. Jandi's fall replayed over and over in her mind.

Foster sat on a couch with Jandi in his arms. He gently stroked her blood-stained hair. The T-shirt he had put on before he left his room had a faint outline of blood on the shoulder. He was tired, but he forced himself to stay awake and alert. He was afraid that if he fell asleep, she would be gone when he woke.

Jandi quietly slept. Occasionally she stirred to scratch her nose or adjust her position, but her head remained on Foster's shoulder. The warmth from his body made her feel comfortable.

When it was time for her to get stitches, the nurse informed Foster, and he gently woke her up. After she received four stitches, she was released. Again, Doc drove his car and Lori drove Jandi's. Jandi went back to sleep in Foster's arms. Foster rested his eyes, too.

By the time they finally got Jandi home, it was five in the morning.

Her mother was up waiting. From the look on her face, she was worried sick. She had already had two sons killed in accidents. Nights like this made her re-live that horror.

Lori opened the door while Doc and Foster helped Jandi in the house. She was groggy. They awoke her from a deep sleep. She was still a little drunk. As Jandi was passed to her mother, Foster and Doc introduced themselves. Jandi's mother remarked that she had heard a lot about Foster, but that was the extent of the conversation. Foster and Doc left while Lori and Jandi's mother put Jandi to bed.

Doc started to drive Foster back to Beloit. It had been a long night. Foster yawned, but by now he was overtired. His body was telling him that it was time to starting getting up. It started to wake for the day.

"Thanks a lot, Doc. I really appreciate the help." Foster rubbed his eyes. He continued to look straight ahead down the road.

"No problem," Doc said with sincerity. This was just something they did for one another. Maybe someday the favor would be returned. Maybe not. Maybe it already had. Their friendships didn't keep track of such things.

"So, what's the story, Foster?" Doc inquired as he took his eyes off the road long enough to look at Foster in the passenger seat.

Foster looked back puzzled and said, "What do you mean?"

"I don't know. What's going on in your mind? It just seems like there are a lot of things you're feeling that you're not telling or showing." Doc waited for a reply.

"What makes you say that?" Foster was defensive.

"Come on, it's not like we just met. I've known you for four years now. I know you." Doc paused as he shifted the car's gears. "You haven't been yourself since your injury. In front of us it appears as if not being able to play football anymore doesn't bother you. That's not you. I know how much football meant to you. It means a lot to me. Christ, if my career ended like yours, I'd have scars on my emotions. I haven't seen you study once since we got back from break. That certainly isn't you." Doc looked back over toward Foster, who stared straight ahead. He had a guilty look on his face.

"I know your injury is bothering you. I just don't know in what way. But I think you should talk about it." Doc spoke in a serious tone. Doc wasn't expecting a response. He just wanted to give Foster some things to think about. "Don't keep it bottled up. It'll tear at you forever." Doc lost his serious tone. "You might as well let us know this. We know everything else about you." A smile came across Doc's face, as he looked toward Foster, trying to lighten the situation.

All Doc expected out of his lecture was thought-provocation. It worked. Although Doc's joke broke the seriousness for a moment, serious thoughts still occupied Foster's mind.

When they got back to the Sig house, they both went to their rooms and to bed. It wasn't long until they were sound asleep. However, Foster could only sleep a couple of hours. The combination of his body not being able to sleep at this time of the day and the thoughts that continued to churn in his mind forced him to wake naturally. Although awake, his body felt heavy. He concentrated on trying to get back to sleep. After an hour of rolling in bed, however, he determined it was futile.

Sleep wasn't the only thing Foster couldn't concentrate on. Doc was right. He hadn't studied in a week. Although he had a lot to do, he couldn't seem to concentrate on his work. He tried studying in his room, in an empty classroom, and then finally the library. Each place yielded the same results. His mind kept focusing on Doc's words.

Maybe Doc was right. Maybe he should let everyone know what was going on in his mind. But then again Bonaventure's request had merit, too. Foster didn't want to be responsible for making the younger players 'gun-shy' with respect to football. It wouldn't be fair, not to Coach Bonaventure, or to the younger players.

There was no clear right side to this issue. Foster debated back and forth with himself for the rest of the afternoon and into the evening. He wasn't sure if it was because he was so tired that everything seemed so confusing. However, by the time the informal team meeting came around, Foster still was unclear what he should do. If he were to disclose his feelings to the team, then this was the best forum to do it. Since tonight was the last meeting of the season, and therefore the last one of his career, this would be his last chance. If he were going to keep his feelings a secret, then this was the last obstacle he'd have to overcome. He was certain that his injury would be a topic of people's comments.

As the ball moved around the circle, Foster could feel the pressure build. He was right. Aside from commenting on past games and future wishes, everyone seemed to have a comment to make about his injury and how well he was taking it. The general consensus was that they were impressed at how well Foster was handling the injury and that they wouldn't be able to take it as well.

A few players went into detail on how it would feel for them to have their football careers cut short. Their description of how their own pain would be was almost identical to what Foster had felt at one point or another. Foster wanted to stand and say, "Yes, oh God, yes, that's how I feel." But he contained himself even though the pressure continued to build inside. He wanted to explode.

Doc was the last person to speak before Foster. Foster tried to swallow the lump that had developed in his throat, but each time he did, it returned -- bigger. Foster was concerned that Doc would give him the same lecture he had on the car ride back from Jandi's. Foster didn't need that.

Doc had a list of comments he wanted to make. None of them pertained to Foster. When he was finished, he handed the ball over in Foster's direction. Their eyes met for, as it seemed to Foster to be, an eternity. Doc could see the emotion beginning to well up in Foster's eyes. He nodded to him as he let go of the ball to signal him to let go of his emotions. Foster took the ball and started to tremble. The room was quiet as Foster seemed to study the leather grain on the ball. He began to speak with a quiver in his voice.

"I guess I have some things to say about my injury." Foster spoke softly. He looked down at the ball and then up at everyone's anxious looks. "I want you to know that it hurts." He could barely get the last words out as tears began rushing from his eyes. He worked hard to wipe them away with his sleeves. He spoke in a whimpering voice. It was as if all the emotion he had concealed for days was being released all at once. "Football meant a lot to me just like it means a lot to you. We work hard at it in hopes that all our wishes come true, but now I know and you should, too, that that isn't always the case." He glanced around the circle and tried to look as many people in the eye as he could. "But that doesn't mean we should stop trying. I guess what it means is we should try a little harder, because if we try a little harder then just maybe those wishes will come true a little sooner and then just maybe we don't have to worry about something like this." He pointed to his cast. His emotions moved everyone.

Although tear tracks were still on his face, he had stopped crying -- for the moment. "I want to take this time to resolve myself of something before all of you. Each of you someday will have to resolve yourselves of the same." Foster, almost word for word, recited what Bonaventure had told him, when he found out he would have surgery, what he must resolve. "That is that I was a good football player, but football is behind me now. I have to use in the rest of my life what I've learned in this game. It's taught me a lot. I hope I've given it something in return." Everyone listened to Foster attentively.

Foster looked down and then quickly back up as he switched topics. "Coach Bonaventure didn't want me to let you see me like this." Foster sniffled to indicate he was crying. "He was worried that you younger players might be afraid to play. He didn't mean to shelter you so it wouldn't hurt his team. He did it because he wants to give you every opportunity to live your life to its potential, on and off the field. He wants your every dream to become reality. He did it because he cares about you, because he cares about me, because he cares about all of us, because he doesn't give a damn about having us win football games for him compared to how much he cares about us getting the most out of life for ourselves. "

"As for being scared, don't be. It's all been worth it, every pain and every ache. I'd do it all again, even if I knew that it would end this way." Foster paused for a moment to think. "Yeah, I'd do it all again in a minute just for the chance to know you people, to call you my friends, and to play by your side, to have you share in my glories as well as my heartbreaks."

"Win or lose on Saturday, I'm damn proud to have played football at Beloit College."

Foster sat the football down, ending the last informal team meeting.

32

It was a little after 9:00 in the morning on Monday, the first week in November. Over the night, a trace of snow was left on the ground. Not enough to shovel, just enough to say it had snowed.

Jandi had just finished feeding Jennifer and was ready to put her down for a nap. On the way to Jennifer's room, Jandi heard a car pull into the driveway. It was hours before her mother was supposed to be home and no one normally stopped by. Jandi was curious. With Jennifer still in her arms, she walked into the living room and looked out the picture window.

Her heart began to pound when she saw Foster's car. She didn't know why he was there. He didn't call to let her know he was coming. In all fairness, Jandi still had a right to be mad. However, she felt threatened that he was there. Somehow Jandi assumed that her actions late Saturday night gave him a right to be angry. Maybe he's here to tell me off or tell me that he doesn't want to see me anymore, she thought.

Foster's heart also pounded. He had the same worries that Jandi did. Maybe, after all that had happened, she didn't want to see him anymore. Maybe she would tell him off. He knew that despite her actions, he was still well in the wrong.

He wanted to explain himself in person. If he called to ask if he could come out to see her, she might say no and then he would be forced to explain himself over the phone or in a letter. Neither of these mediums was effective. Foster could never tell if his message had been received the way he wanted it to be. Although saying what he had to in person would be more threatening to him, he felt that Jandi deserved that much.

Jandi rocked Jennifer in her arms as she watched Foster carefully get out of his car. A serious look covered her face until she saw Foster fall on the slippery driveway. Crutches were never designed to be used on ice and snow. At first, she was concerned, but when she saw Foster get back up laughing at himself, she started to, also. Her laughter quelled the pounding of her heart. However, only for a moment as she realized that he was still coming to see her and she didn't know why.

Jandi greeted Foster at the door. She opened the door and indicated he could come in without saying a word. He waited to go in the house until he had all the snow brushed off his pants. She chuckled inside. It made her think of how he looked when he fell.

Once Foster was inside, Jandi shut the door. Her first words to him were that she had to put Jennifer in bed for her nap. She left the room to do so. Foster remained in the entryway. When she returned, they both had looks of uncertainty on their faces. Foster spoke first.

"I don't know where to begin." He smiled nervously. "I know I haven't been real nice to you lately. Lori is right. I've been sort of a jerk." He smiled nervously again. He hoped Jandi would, too, just to break the tension he felt between them. She didn't. He swallowed the lump in his throat and continued. "I want to say that I'm sorry."

He paused and waited for Jandi to say something. She remained quiet. He had to search for something else to say. The silence was torture.

"It was nothing you did to cause me to act that way. Don't blame yourself at all. I know this is hard to understand, but football meant a lot to me. A lot of my dreams were wrapped up in it." Foster swallowed hard to keep himself from crying. "When I found out I couldn't play anymore it hurt. It was like a part of me died. I didn't want to share the pain with anyone, but I guess I sort of did." He again paused and waited for her to respond. Nothing. Her expression didn't even change. "I don't mean this as an excuse. It's not. It's just a reason."

Jandi still waited for Foster to continue. The silence made him uneasy. He shifted his weight on the crutches. Sweat rolled down his back. He continued just for the sake of breaking the silence.

"When I played football I felt important. I stood out on the field and really believed I was somebody. Now that it's over, that feeling is gone." Foster stared at the ground as if he were flashing back. "I sense that I'm being forgotten. I stand on the sidelines and feel like a nobody. I never felt that before. At least when I sat on the bench there was always the hope that someday I'd get my chance. That feeling isn't there anymore. I know it's all over. It's sort of breaking my heart to know that I'll never be the somebody I once believed I was." He looked back up into Jandi's eyes. "But you know, now after I've spent time with you, I can honestly say that I'd rather spend the rest of my life being a nobody with somebody, than being a somebody with nobody."

"I don't know where we're headed from here, though. I want you to know that the times we had together were some of the best I've ever had. I'll always cherish them." Each word was becoming harder to speak. As the lump in his throat grew larger, his mouth grew drier. "I'm not expecting that things will ever be the same again between us. I only hope that you can find it in your heart to forgive."

This was his final pause. He had exhausted everything he could possibly think of saying. After a long moment of silence, he lowered his head. His face became somber. He had failed. He started to shift his weight again. This time he meant to move towards the door.

Jandi rushed forward and hugged him. She almost knocked him off balance. Tears quickly filled her eyes and ran down her cheeks. Foster took his hands off his crutches and hugged her back. He didn't have any tears left, but the sentiment was there. Jandi began to speak through her tears.

"I forgave you." She sniffled. "I forgave you on Saturday night when you held me in your arms. I just didn't know how to tell you."

"It's okay." Foster kissed Jandi on the top of the head. The area was still very tender from the fall. She didn't mind. The affection overcame the pain. "It doesn't matter now."

The storm of their relationship was over. Jandi squeezed Foster as hard as she could. Whether they had children together as husband and wife or whether they had children with other people they married, their friendship would be passed on to their children, Foster hoped.

"Hey Jandi, I've got to get back to campus." Foster's eyes were shut as he rested his chin on her head. She squeezed him tighter as if she didn't want him to leave. "I'll try and write this week. But I can't promise anything, because I've got a ton of work to catch up on." Foster alluded to all the work he put off the week before. Jandi was still crying. She swung Foster in her arms like she had swung Jennifer. "But let's go out Saturday night after our game."

"Okay," Jandi said with a whimper.

"Tell you what, too ... I'll pay. It may only be fast food and a cheapy theater.." Foster kissed her again. "So don't get your hopes up. But I'll pay," Foster kidded.

Jandi started to laugh through her tears. They squeezed each other tightly once more, and then let go.

Foster crutched out to the car even more carefully than when he came in. Jandi watched from the open door. She felt too good to sense the cold. When Foster got to his car, he shouted back to Jandi.

"Hey, you better put some sand or salt down on your driveway. It's dangerous." He smiled. She smiled back.

Jandi shut the door and watched Foster get into his car. Then she remembered that she still hadn't given him the planter she bought for him. She ran out the door with it just as he began backing down the drive. He saw her and stopped. He put the car in park and rolled down the window.

"Here. I got this for you." She handed him the planter through the window.

He thanked her and turned to put it on the passenger seat. When he turned back she leaned in the window and gave him a big kiss on the cheek. Foster didn't expect it. He blushed.

Jandi turned to start walking to the house, but before she could take a step, Foster grabbed her by the front of the shirt as if he were a bully picking on her. He pulled her down and gave her a long kiss on the lips. She responded.

When they broke, she slowly stood back up. As she did, Foster looked her in the eyes and said, "That's just something to think about until Saturday night." He winked as he put the car in reverse and backed out of the driveway.

She waved from the front porch as he drove off.

Since the team had had eight or nine film sessions before, the film session to review the Ripon College game was rather subdued. In the first three or four weeks, Coach Bonaventure had made it clear that film sessions were not for fooling around. However, once he had that established, he didn't have to be quite as hard-nosed in his approach. Instead of carrying on and laying into people, all Bonaventure had to do when he identified a mistake a player had made is to say their name. The tone of voice he used and the silence he created made the player own up to his own mistakes.

"Wallace." Bonaventure enunciated the names in a fashion that made it draw on forever.

"I know. I should have checked the flat area first for the wing back before I went deep to the wide receiver." Doc recited what he had been taught in practice and what he had failed to do.

Besides, now each player took it upon himself to make films a learning experience. The players watched attentively their every move on the screen. They identified things that Bonaventure didn't point out. The good plays they made brought them satisfaction and reinforced what they should have learned. On the bad plays, they cursed themselves and went back over in their minds what they should have done.

In addition to these two reasons, the fact that the Lake Forest College game was a good game for the team helped add to the calmness of the film session. Aside from the first two series of downs, Bonaventure had no complaints about the game. Even the play that scored the winning touchdown for Ripon College was a fluke, Bonaventure admitted. Those were part of the game, and although one never really knew when they were going to occur, one could be sure that at some point they would, and so provisions had better be made for them.

By Tuesday, the snow that had fallen during the early part of Monday was gone. Since it was only early November, the snow would fall and melt away several more times before it would ultimately stay on the ground for the winter.

But the end of fall meant the end of football. New enthusiasm stemmed from the fact that this was the last week of practice. Up until now, practice was a chore for everyone on the team. They all loved to play the games, but practices they could have done without.

Now, however, the team was in its last week. For some, it might be nine more months until they could put on the equipment again. For the seniors, this was the last week ever. It was a sobering thought. There's an old adage, 'you don't know what you've got, until it's gone.' At least with football, the team could see what they had before it was all gone.

Each drill and each play was done with crisp perfection. The recency effect would ensure that this would be the way they remembered football practices -- for the next nine months or the rest of their lives. They tried to practice the way they wanted to remember it.

Even though Foster had long since reconciled himself to the fact that he would not be playing in the last game, he could sense the energy that this last week brought. He did whatever he could to be a part of it.

He lifted weights before practice, then crutched the half mile down to practice, and tried to do as much as his limitations would allow. Several times, Bonaventure had to scold him for getting too involved. He couldn't help it. He had to satisfy the physical and mental urges his body imposed on him.

These urges or feelings were innate in football players. Each fall for the rest of a football player's life, that feeling returns and their body experiences all the senses that it had during football. Even Bonaventure, who hadn't played a down in close to twenty years, felt these. The body's metabolism becomes increasingly active and the heart cries to be fed the endorphins that once poured through the blood. Muscles crave the exertion and violent physical contact that go along with the sport. There are even times when the nose will savor the smell of sweat.

Like the sign that hung in Stubby's room, during this week, 'football was their lives; everything else was bullshit.' Football became the number one priority. School, work, and relationships all were put on the back burner for this one week. A player's attitude was: 'you can flunk me, you can fire me, and you can break up with me, because all that really matters right now is football! Nothing pierced this mind set. Nothing. A player becomes possessed by the game. Fortunately, this fixation with football only lasts a week, a short enough period for any professor, employer, or girlfriend to endure. Eventually things return to normal.

Just as Tuesday's practice seemed to get going, it seemed that it was time to run the single sprint for Lake Forest College at the end of Friday's practice. This time, the sprint was not limited to just the defensive unit, but the entire team. As Doc signaled them to go, each man powered out of his stance as hard as he could, trying to expend the last trace of practice energy he had in his system.

The first practice of the season ended with welcoming handshakes. The last practice ended with hugs to say 'we're done; I'm so glad I could share this milestone with you.' It was as if they had climbed a mountain together. In essence, they had. At the end of each season, the feelings were the same, but the names and faces changed. Although partings would eventually bring new friendships, things would never be exactly the same.

A big lump formed in senior throats as they left the practice field for the last time. Although they knew this day was coming, they never really believed it would arrive. Only one game stood between them and the end of a career with a sport they had learned to despise and love all at the same time. Even though they still had the Lake Forest game to play, they couldn't help wondering what life would be like without football.

Daylight Savings Time and November made light scarce at this point in the day. The other side of the field could barely be seen now. Players hurried into the locker room to get out of their practice equipment for the last time.

Stubby was the last player to leave the field. He ran an extra lap to enjoy the field's company one last time, all by himself. It seemed like just yesterday that he had first stepped on this field as a freshman, a few hundred pounds of sweat and a lot of tears ago.

As he walked through the archway that led to the locker room, he turned to face the field one last time. It was now quiet. It would get a rest now for nine months. It would get a rest from Stubby forever.

He raised his arm and gently waved goodbye, with tears in his eyes.

As Foster stood inside on Saturday morning, the sunlight shining through the window made the day seem almost hot. When he stepped out on the front porch, he found that crisp, cold weather was developing. Even though Foster's nose immediately began to run and he could see his breath, the weather wasn't going to stop him from crutching down to the Stadium.

From there, he was going to get into a uniform just like all the other players. He wasn't playing, but it was still his last game, too. He wanted to seem as much a part of the team as possible. Although he didn't put on the pads or helmet, wearing his game jersey and pants made his status official.

Despite the weather, many fans filtered into Strong Stadium to watch the game. Usually, at this point in the season, only the most loyal of fans would be at the final game. But then, this year was not a usual year. In the past, this last game had often made the difference between ending the season with one or two wins, or no wins at all. Except for two years earlier when the team was four, four and one, the final game meant that the Bucs would have a chance to be .500, a feat that was highly anticlimactic.

This year, however, the Bucs had a chance of ending the season with a winning record. Everyone knew that Lake Forest had a good football team and that they could be the conference champions. But they also knew that the Bucs had a chance, which was something that wasn't there in previous years. No matter how small, no one wanted to miss out on this chance.

Although seemingly lost in the crowd, all of the loyal Bucs fans were at the game, banded together at mid-field directly behind the team. Good chance, bad chance, or no chance -- they would be at the game.

Doc, Stubby, and Bert each bought their mothers corsages to wear at the last game. It was just a small token of appreciation for years of having to put up with dirty football uniforms and late dinners. Although it had been four years since they put their mothers through these drudgeries, only now did they realize how much they appreciated it. Without their mother's support, they knew that they wouldn't be there now.

As usual, President Hardesty and Professor Ames were in attendance at the game. However, they didn't come alone to this game. Hardesty brought his wife to see what had occupied him every other weekend or so in the fall. Ames brought his young son. Although Ames' son was too young to totally understand the game, he knew that football was the natural course to follow for a boy.

Bonaventure didn't change any of the pre-game routine even though it was the last game. Everyone got dressed, and was taped by the trainers, and took the field as they always had. A change at this point in the season might have been beneficial, but then it also might have been detrimental. It was best to leave well enough alone. The kickers, quarterbacks, and receivers took the field early to go through their special routines, while the remainder of the team suffered the wait in the locker room.

Doc went through his pre-game ritual as he always had for four years. He slowly warmed up his arm by throwing the ball to receivers running short patterns. However, halfway through the routine, his shoelace broke. He asked a second-team quarterback to drill the receivers as he went to the bench to get a new lace for his shoe.

Heidi helped him quickly get the old lace out by cutting it at each eyelet with a pair of scissors. As Heidi went to discard the old lace, Doc began putting in a bright, new, white lace in the shoe. He couldn't remember the last time he had put a new lace in his shoes. A year ago, maybe longer. It didn't take long to replace the lace. After two or three minutes, he was applying the final bow to the shoe.

As he reached for his helmet to return to the pre-game drills, he felt a tap on the back of his shoulder pad. Without thinking, he turned. Carli stood behind him with her hand extended. A surprised look covered Doc's face.

"I just came down to wish you good luck today," she spoke softly. It was evident by the tone of her voice and the look on her face that she was uncertain of how he would react.

Doc's surprised look was replaced by a smile. He took her hand and shook it firmly. He spoke softly and sincerely saying, "Thanks, thanks a lot."

They continued to look at one another for a moment. There were no other words to be said. This was evidence that their friendship was always there. It was only hidden for a while by a misunderstanding. Doc started to put on his helmet.

"Thanks again," he said, looking back as he ran on the field.

Soon, the entire team was on the field going through its warmups. The crowd marveled at Foster, who helped Doc and Stubby lead the team in calisthenics as if he were going to play in the game himself.

Foster wanted to believe that he would play. The thought of not playing brought tears to his eyes, but then, so did the actual possibility of playing. If there were to be tears, the tears of high-energy emotion were needed more than those of self-pity.

After they did ten jumping-jacks together, the calisthenics broke the team into smaller groups according to positions. As Doc practiced taking snaps from Stubby, Foster cheered on his fellow defensive linemen as they worked on pass rush techniques.

The team's emotions were high. Football was all they could concentrate on. It was the only thing they had concentrated on for a week. Their hearts beat a little harder, and their breathing became a little deeper as the official clock started to wind down from fifteen minutes to indicate how much time was left until kick-off.

When 9 minutes and 35 seconds remained, the referee signaled to both coaches that he needed their captains at the center of the field.

Bonaventure shouted: "Captains," to the team. Although he didn't know where Doc and Stubby were, they got the message and came running over to where Bonaventure was standing. Before Bonaventure gave any instructions to Doc or Stubby, he yelled again.

"Foster." Bonaventure had no problem spotting Foster on his crutches. He waved him over to where the other two captains were.

Foster got over to Bonaventure as quickly as he could. Still using his crutches, he managed to get a running stride in between the time his crutches touched the ground. Before Foster came to a full stop, Bonaventure spoke again.

"Foster, I want you to go out with the captains for the coin toss." Bonaventure's voice commanded, only partly masking the thoughtfulness that emanated from his heart.

Foster was speechless. He wanted to say thank you and give Bonaventure a big hug for not forgetting about him on this last game. However, that wouldn't be appropriate for the moment. Besides, if he started to say anything, he knew he wouldn't be able to hold back the tears he was concentrating on keeping back. He nodded to Bonaventure in agreement and listened to the instructions he gave the captains for the coin toss.

On the way to the center of the field, Foster kept tucked behind Doc and Stubby. He was worried about how the other team or the referees might react to an injured player in this pre-game ritual. He remained quiet and did his best to keep up with Doc and Stubby as they trotted to where the referees and the Lake Forest captains waited.

After the referees introduced themselves and then had each side's captains introduce themselves, the head referee began instructing the parties on the fundamental rules of the game. Both sets of captains had heard these rules several times this season. They were inattentive as they stared one another down like prizefighters in the center of the ring.

When the referee was finished with the pitch he was required to give, he produced a Susan B. Anthony silver dollar and showed both teams' captains that the coin had two sides. Then he backed up and turned to the Beloit team.

"Okay, Beloit, who is going to call it?" The referee waited.

Doc turned to Foster. "It's your call, Foster." Doc pointed at him. Doc, Stubby and Foster took turns calling the toss. It was actually Doc's turn, but he wanted Foster to have it. Stubby also indicated that Foster would make the call.

The referee turned to Foster as if he didn't even notice the crutches and said, "Okay 43, call it in the air." The referee flipped the coin.

All this came too fast for Foster. He was still engaged in a stare down with one of Lake Forest's captains, who also happened to be a defensive tackle. Their commonality made them natural enemies. However, Foster hurried to catch on to what he had to do. If this was all he could do for the team that day, then hell, he thought, 'I'm going to do it the best I can.'

"Heads," Foster uttered without breaking his stare.

The referee caught the coin and turned it over on the back on his hand. "Heads it is," the ref exclaimed as he tried to make an act out of the coin toss. "It's your choice, Beloit. Kick, receive, or defend a goal."

Doc took control of this decision. He was the only one who really understood what Bonaventure meant in his instructions. He elected to receive the football and let Lake Forest decide which end zone they wanted to defend.

The referee had the captains shake hands with one another one more time and then he sent them back to their respective teams. Once Bonaventure learned the results of the coin toss, he directed the entire team into the locker room for one last pre-game talk.

When everyone was settled in the locker room, Bonaventure began to speak.

"You know, win or lose, Lake Forest is going to play in the title game next week. And you know they probably will win that game because so far they are undefeated." His voice was soft and solemn. "So maybe we can't be the spoilers and prevent them from going to the title game. And maybe we can't be conference champions." Bonaventure's voice got louder. "But I tell you what. We can beat the conference champions. We can beat Lake Forest and cast uncertainty on who is really the best team in the conference. No, we will never be able to claim that we were the conference champions, but then, no one will be able to say that we weren't the best team in the league. Let's take a knee." Bonaventure led the team as he fell to one knee and bowed his head. After twenty seconds, he stood back up. As others sensed him rise, they stood, too.

"Well men, this is it. The time for talk is over." As Bonaventure spoke, lumps formed in everyone's throats. Bert grabbed Simba by the hand to try and fight back the tears. Simba looked back. Tears were evident in his eyes, too. "I've had a great time coaching you guys this season. I just want you to know, especially you seniors, that win or lose today, I'm proud of you. Let's try to go out winners, but more important, let's try and go out having some fun." Bonaventure clenched his fist at the team and then stepped aside so they could exit the locker room.

The team ran around the perimeter of the field in single file. When they got back to their side of the field, they lined up for a quick ten jumping jacks. Everyone counted as loud as they could to demonstrate to the fans and Lake Forest the spirit and enthusiasm they had. After the jumping jacks, the team went to its sideline and waited for the introduction of players.

After the announcer introduced the Lake Forest defense, he began to introduce the seniors for Beloit. The upperclassmen formed a short tunnel for the seniors to run through as their names were called. When a senior ran through, he was cheered and patted by the younger understudies. The announcer gave each player's name, number, position, hometown, and any significant accomplishments they had achieved. As each senior was called, the crowd cheered.

"Dan Simpson. Number 76. Offensive guard from Tampa, Florida. A three-year starter." Simba ran on the field, waving his hand to the crowd.

"Number 77 from Chicago, Illinois. A four-year starter at offensive guard and two-time All Midwest Conference. Charles Ellis." El slowly ran through the tunnel, enjoying his last bit of recognition.

"From Chicago, Illinois. Number 66. Bill Barton. A one-year starter at defensive tackle, and an honor student." Bill raced on the field as hard as he could. He stuck his hands up and patted people's hands as he moved through the tunnel.

"Also from Chicago, Illinois. A two-year starter at offensive tackle. Number 64. Bert Lindsey." Bert casually ran out to join the other seniors.

The announcer then went through four or five more seniors. Finally, the only three seniors left were the captains. Somehow they knew they'd be last. Their hearts pounded. The energy from the crowd made the tears almost impossible to hold back. They said nothing to one another. They just shook each other's hands as they were finally introduced.

"From Chicago, Illinois. Number 55. Four-year starter at offensive center and team captain. Mark Stubner." Stubby swallowed the lump in his throat as he ran through the tunnel.

"Number 12. Three-year starter at quarterback and team captain from Green Bay, Wisconsin. Todd Wallace." Doc smiled as he slapped hands with players moving through the tunnel.

Foster's body began to shake. The emotion was unbearable. He fought hard to hold back the tears. They still welled up in his eyes. Most fans knew of Foster's hardship. They had read the article in the newspaper. They began to cheer as he stood alone, waiting to be introduced. The seniors at the end of the tunnel began to root him on. Foster could not look them in the eye. It took all he had to avoid breaking down.

"From Houghton, Michigan. Team captain and two-year starter at defensive tackle. Number 43. Foster Addison." He knew that this was the last time he would take the field. He had to do it the way he thought it should be.

In the excitement, he threw his crutches in the air and limped forward with his cast. The tunnel cheered loudly as they felt his spirit. He slapped as many hands as he could while still trying to maintain his balance. He could barely see his fellow seniors at the end of the line. They were a blur, his eyes were so teary. 'I'll be damned,' he thought, 'I'll be damned if the last time I take the field I'm going to do it on crutches.'

Foster almost lost his balance at the very end. He made it to the rest of the seniors in time to grab hold of Doc and Stubby and hug them as hard as he could. A tear rolled out of his eye. The rest of the seniors bunched around, and then the underclassmen followed. Not one senior had dry eyes as the entire team chanted "go, go, go," in unison.

The team quickly cleared the field. Emotion was high. Foster didn't have to feel self-conscious about crying because he wasn't alone. Tears continued to roll down his cheeks during the *Star-Spangled Banner*.

When the national anthem was over, Beloit's kick-receiving team took the field. Lake Forest had been waiting to start the game for over five minutes. They took a couple seconds to re-warm themselves as the Bucs lined up.

The ball was kicked and the game was under way. Beloit returned the ball to the forty-yard line. This was a great return, which added to their high spirits. The offense quickly capitalized on these feelings by moving the ball down to the Lake Forest ten-yard line in five plays. Most of this yardage was gained on the ground as emotions overpowered the Lake Forest team. Everyone had the sense that Beloit would soundly defeat the potential Midwestern Conference champions.

On a third and long situation, Doc faded back for a pass. He turned to look right, when he was hit hard from behind by the Lake Forest team captain and senior defensive tackle. The injury in Doc's ribs was aggravated again. The sack also set up a field goal situation.

Doc could barely take the crouched position to hold the snap for the field goal kicker, Greg Denton. As he called the count, he held one hand on his ribs. He winced and held his breath as he caught the ball and it was kicked through the uprights for the score. Beloit led three to nothing.

However, the sack took some of the bite out of Beloit's enthusiasm. Besides, pure emotion wasn't going to beat Lake Forest, a team that thrived on precision execution. After returning the kickoff to their own thirty-yard line, it only took Lake Forest six passes to travel the length of the field to score a touchdown. After the extra point, Lake Forest led 7 to 3.

The touchdown began to sap the Bucs' spirit. When the offense came on the field again, they did their best to overcome the changing momentum. At first, it appeared as if they were going to succeed. Their running game was very effective against the slower Lake Forest defense. However, Beloit was confronted with another passing situation. Lake Forest's defensive line swarmed Doc as he tried to pass. Doc got sacked a second time. He was slow to get up. Pain ripped through his body.

On the next play, Doc had yet another passing situation. He dropped back into the pocket, but again defensive tackles infiltrated the backfield and pursued him. In an effort not to be sacked again, he hurried a pass. Doc was hit anyway. The ball was intercepted.

Although the defender who intercepted the ball was immediately tackled, Lake Forest didn't have far to go for a touchdown. Three running plays and five passing plays later and Lake Forest had capitalized on the interception. They now led the game by eleven points.

OUT OF THE COMFORT ZONE

The high emotion that Beloit had in starting the game was beaten down severely, but Bonaventure was able to get them to regroup. Although they didn't score any points, they were able to keep Lake Forest out of the end zone, too. No team appeared to have any sort of advantage. The two teams battled back and forth between the thirty-yard lines for the second part of the first quarter and most of the second.

In the closing minutes of the half, Lake Forest was able to sustain a drive inside the thirty-yard line. The Bucs' defense had been on the field for a long time and was tiring. Lake Forest looked as if they would be able to score another touchdown, but Bill rose up. He stopped their backs twice for a loss and then sacked the quarterback to set up a long field goal situation. Lake Forest barely got the ball through the uprights. Nonetheless, they led at halftime by a score of 17 to 3.

In the locker room, the Bucs were quiet. It was a somber quiet as opposed to an intense quiet. It was discouraging to go into a game with so much emotion and still be overpowered. What were they supposed to do now? They could not get any more emotional, and their football ability wasn't enough to overcome the fourteen-point deficit. Their minds were starting to concede the loss.

"What are you men so long-faced for? Jesus Christ, we're only down by two touchdowns." Coach Gibson stormed into the locker room. He was Bonaventure's right-hand man when it came to firing up the team. "Are you going to lay down and die and let these assholes beat you? Because that's exactly what they are going to do if you let them. They aren't going to put in the second-stringers today. No sir. They want to run up the score on you." Gibson had fire in his eyes. This was as intense as they had ever seen him. "They want to show this whole league how good they think they are. But they're not. They're shit." He paced up and down in the locker room, looking each player in the eye. "We gave 'em all but three of their points. Shit, it should be a tie ball game. Hey, if they can score 17 points in a half, then so can we. And if we can score 17 points, and don't allow them any, we win."

Gibson got the team's blood moving again. Although they weren't exactly sure how they could do it, they realized that there was still a chance that they could win the game. They started motivating one another. Their minds were now set to listen to the adjustments that the coaches had made to the game plan.

As the teams came out for the second half, it was as if they had returned to a different stadium. Most of the fans had left because Beloit's chance of a winning season was too slim to warrant enduring the cold. There was nothing to miss by leaving the game at halftime. This didn't help the motivation that the team was trying to re-establish.

As expected, the team's loyal followers remained. They huddled together in blankets and sleeping bags, trying to get the cold out of their minds and concentrating on making the team feel as if it wasn't deserted. At times like these, they could identify their true fans.

President Hardesty's wife decided to leave at halftime with most everyone else. To her, it was better to spend Saturday afternoons engrossed in a medical journal, than not being able to feel your feet at a football game. Hardesty understood. He knew that football was like coffee -- an acquired taste.

Professor Ames and his son also remained. The cold had gotten to his son. However, Ames persuaded him that he could endure it by slowly sipping a cup of hot chocolate. It seemed to work as the young boy was no longer shivering but grew excited as the Buccaneers returned to the field. Ames put his arm around the boy to help keep him warm.

To start this half, Lake Forest had the option to kick, receive or defend a goal. They chose to receive the ball and Beloit chose to defend the north goal.

Gibson's speech worked well. After the kickoff, the Beloit defense stopped the Lake Forest offense in three plays and forced them to punt the ball back to Beloit. Beloit was not able to score a touchdown, but they got the ball down close enough to Lake Forest's end zone to attempt a field goal. Although the field goal attempt failed, the offense had confidence that it was able to move the ball against Lake Forest.

Lake Forest took the ball on its own 20-yard line the next series and began to march down the field. Their yards were all hard fought. Beloit made them earn every inch, but however tough the yards were to gain, they were gained. Lake Forest was moving the football. Although it took them fifteen plays, Lake Forest went the 80 yards down the field to extend their lead by seven more points. Beloit now trailed 24 to 3.

Using Bonaventure's terms, the defense battled hard. They gave nothing to Lake Forest, and the Beloit offense knew it. The defense's play

OUT OF THE COMFORT ZONE

was inspiring, in fact. The offense took the field after the kickoff with the attitude that they were going to play just as hard as the defense had. Although the touchdown gave them a little more ground to catch up on, they were certain they could do it.

Doc called the play and Stubby led the team to the line. A long count was taken to try and draw the anxious defensive tackles offside. It didn't work. The ball was snapped and Doc rolled to his right to throw a pass.

Beloit was down by 21 points and they only had a quarter and a half to score the points. The team's strategy was obvious. The Lake Forest defense was certain that Beloit would pass the ball and so they lined up accordingly. The defensive tackles raced through the gaps created by the guards and tackles. In the confusion, they broke through the line clean. Doc was running for his life.

He was able to elude the rushers for a while, but eventually they caught up with him. He tried to escape their grip, but it was useless. As he was being thrown to the ground, Doc tried to make a desperation throw to an open running back in the flats. Just before the ball was released, his body was jerked and the ball went high. The back tried to jump for the ball. However, he only managed to get high enough to tip the ball in the air so a Lake Forest defender could intercept it. The defender was immediately tackled, but the ball had changed hands and now Lake Forest was in a good position to score again.

"No," Doc cried out as he saw the interception unfold. There was nothing he could do. The rushers continued to throw his body to the ground. His ribs burned in pain as they rolled on him.

"Bush-league," the Lake Forest team captain said to Doc as he used Doc's body as a support to get up. He gave Doc a dirty look down on the ground and then spat near his helmet.

Simba saw this incident develop. He ran to Doc's aid and pushed the the Lake Forest captain away. Before any retaliation could be made, the referees stepped between the two opponents, and began giving warnings to both men. Neither paid any attention to the warnings. They just stared one another down. Bonaventure rushed onto the field and ordered as many of his players over to the sidelines as he could. Maybe they would lose, but they would lose as sportsmen. They all obeyed, however, reluctantly.

Simba slowly backed off. Doc was now up and there was no reason to continue. However, Simba still coldly stared down the Lake Forest captain.

The Lake Forest captain continued to press. The score wasn't even with Simba, the guy who pushed him. However, sensing that Simba may have been one up on him physically and that he would not be able to even the score, the Lake Forest captain began to shout.

"Hey 76. Look at the scoreboard." He smiled in a sinister way. "You're losing."

Simba could feel the pressure build up. There was nothing that could be said to counter what the other player had said. It was the ultimate insult with virtually no comeback. The bottom line, at least, was on the scoreboard.

After Doc got off the ground, he slowly walked to the bench. He was undetected walking through the players on the sidelines as their attention was focused on the commotion on the field. He was physically, mentally, and emotionally beat-up.

As he sat down, Heidi offered him a towel and Kathy offered a glass of water. He took the towel, but turned down the water. He, like everyone else on the team, began feeling sorry for himself. This was not how he had dreamed it would end, or how he worked for it to end.

He looked at the scoreboard and shook his head at the score. Only about eight minutes and thirty seconds remained in the third quarter.

33

Lake Forest now had the ball inside Beloit's twenty-yard line and they were driving for another touchdown. Coach Gibson was right. They meant to run the score up against Beloit to demonstrate to the conference some sort of football new order. Lake Forest made no substitutions to their first team.

As Lake Forest began to assemble its offense for the relatively short drive to the end zone, everyone conceded the loss. The underclassmen began to look to the next year and what they could do in the off season to ready themselves for a winning year. The seniors, who had no next season to look forward to, quietly sat and felt sorry for themselves. The coach hoped that the time would evaporate, so Lake Forest wouldn't have a chance to humiliate them further. The fans continued to cheer. However, the tone of their cheers went from calls for victory to 'although this game was lost, you had a good season and we still enjoyed following your games.' This couldn't be happening and if it really were, they couldn't possibly have deserved, after all their dedication and hard work, a beating like they were taking.

Professor Ames' son also sensed that the excitement of the game was gone. He began pulling at his father's jacket, pleading to go home because he was cold. Even hot chocolate could trick a young mind for only so long. Ames was hesitant to leave. He didn't want to seem like just another 'fair-weather' fan giving up on the Bucs. However, it was cold and there was a long time to go in the game. He looked at the scoreboard and then back at his son. Although reluctant, he thought it was best to leave. He took his son's hand and they walked to an exit.

As a loss was conceded on one side of the field, victory was assumed on the other. The Lake Forest players on the sidelines lost interest in the game. To them, the quarter and a half left to play was just an obstacle between them and total celebration. They began to joke with one another and shout insults across the field at the Beloit team.

It only took Lake Forest three plays to score their next touchdown. They now led by a score of 31 to three. No one seemed to be conscious of this fact. Twenty-four to three or 31 to three, what was the difference? The game was out of hand.

As Lake Forest got ready to kick off again to Beloit, Doc sat quietly, all alone on the bench. He was well aware that Bonaventure was replacing him with the back-up quarterback, and so there was no reason to prepare to go back in the game. The game was over, as far as he was concerned.

Doc knew he wasn't being replaced as a punishment, but rather as a way of giving the younger players a chance to get some experience. He tried to watch his understudy command the offense. It was nothing against the younger player, but Doc couldn't stand to watch the game.

Nevertheless, McDonnell slowly moved the ball down the field for the Bucs. The rested second-team offense was a match for the tiring Lake Forest first-team defense. Although they didn't score, they had managed to move the ball and kill some of the time that remained on the clock.

As Lake Forest's offense took the field, Foster came over toward Doc. Foster was again on his crutches. Jack Benson, who almost went into shock when Foster ran on the field, made it clear that he was to use the crutches at all times. Foster was sick of the crutches by now. He merely hung on to them in an attempt to avoid any further controversy with Jack.

Foster sat next to Doc and set the crutches down between them. He sat and watched the game with his friend. Doc stared at his feet. Foster felt Doc's pain; however, he didn't come over to quietly share the last part of the game with his fellow captain.

Foster continued to look at the game, and Doc looked down. "You know, they say that it's your last game that you remember most." Foster spoke softly. Doc didn't acknowledge that he heard Foster, but he was listening. "I never believed it. I used to think that the memory of each game would be just as vivid as the next. I was wrong. It is the last game you remember most. All the other games I played in I remember, but not like that last game. The University of Chicago game is like a movie playing over and over in my mind. I can remember exactly what was said and what I was feeling, expressions on other people's faces, even the taste in my mouth."

Foster turned and looked at Doc. He was still looking down as if ignoring Foster. "Yeah, I got injured that game, and that hurts me. I'm still wrestling with that disappointment. It's a scar on my heart I'll have to carry for a long time. But up until then I was having a great game. It was the game I always dreamed about playing." Foster turned back toward the game and started to stare off into nothing. His mind flashed back. "There was a point during that game when I felt like I was invincible. I couldn't have been any stronger; I couldn't have been more intense. It was like I was on the edge of something wonderful. I guess Coach would have said I was outside the Comfort Zone. That game gave me a glorious feeling about myself as a football player. That feeling ... that feeling of glory is what I'll always remember about football. Nothing else."

Foster turned to Doc. "You can't let it end like this. You can't go through the rest of your life remembering football like this. You've got to try to leave this game with some glory, something to look back on and feel proud about, something that you can look back on and tell yourself, God damn, I was good. Coach Bonaventure owes you that. The team owes you that. You owe it to yourself."

Foster wasn't sure if Doc had heard anything he said. He didn't want to belabor the point or be a pest. Doc had to make his own decision. Foster got up and grabbed his crutches. He crutched forward, right in front of Doc. Doc still looked at the ground. Foster gently pinched the back of his neck.

Foster almost whispered, "Go out with some glory. Go out with some glory."

Foster said nothing more. He continued to crutch down the sidelines. He didn't look back. As he moved away, Doc looked up and watched him. 'Go out with some glory,' echoed through his mind.

The Bucs were on defense now, and Bonaventure also had the defensive second-teamers in the game. Lake Forest was able to gain a considerable amount of yardage on these younger Beloit players. However, eventually the Bucs were able to stop the Lake Forest offense. Lake Forest continued to play its first-teamers. The almost three quarters they had played could not out-endure the rested second-teamers.

Lake Forest readied its punt team to kick the ball back to Beloit. Coach Bonaventure wasn't paying any attention to the punt-block team he had in the game. He was busy going over some instructions with the back-up quarterback, Dan McDonnell. Just as Bonaventure was almost finished giving McDonnell directions for the next series of downs, Doc interrupted the conversation.

"Coach, I know that Danny needs the experience, but I can't have the last pass I ever threw be an interception. Can I have one more series?" Doc felt like a little kid pleading to be able to play.

Bonaventure thought about his request. Before an answer could be given, Doc turned to Dan McDonnell. "Do you understand?"

McDonnell nodded. It was only a short while ago that he played his last game in high school. He had the same feelings then.

The ball was punted. It didn't go too far. Beloit was given good field position. The ball was just short of mid-field. The second-team offense was half leaving the sidelines onto the field when Bonaventure began shouting.

"I want the first-team offense in the game."

The second-teamers were puzzled leaving the field, and the first-teamers were puzzled going back on. In fact, only Foster, Doc, Coach Bonaventure, and Dan McDonnell really knew what was happening.

"Thanks," Doc said to Bonaventure as he put his helmet back on and entered the game.

Although he did not think it would make any difference, Bonaventure granted Doc's request. He remembered his last game, still vivid in his memory. He realized that it would be unfair to let Doc or any of the seniors finish their careers the way the last series on the field ended.

Doc was the last man into the huddle. He could see that everyone was uncertain as to why they were back in the game. He didn't have time to fully explain but did the best he could in the short huddle.

"Okay you guys. Let's show them what we're made of. Let's give it all we've got for one series. Let's end this season," he nodded at underclassmen, "and our careers," he nodded to the seniors, "like winners." He paused and then called the play.

The huddle broke with everyone still uncertain about the situation; nevertheless, they lined up and readied themselves to run the pass play Doc had called.

As Doc approached the line, Lake Forest's captain badgered him. "Number 12 is back, good. Time to dole out some punishment." The defensive tackle snorted like a bull. The cold air made his breath visible.

Doc tried to ignore him as he called the count. However, the pain his body had experienced from the numerous times he was sacked by the man made it hard. He trembled as he prepared to take the snap.

The ball was snapped and Doc dropped back in the pocket. He didn't even have time to set up before the Lake Forest player came crashing through the line after him. Doc's eyes widened as the man closed in screaming. Doc cradled the ball as he was hit. The Lake Forest player squeezed Doc's body as hard as he could as he tried to break through the already tender ribs. He continued to hold on to Doc as he rolled over and crashed him to the ground a second time.

Pain raged through Doc's body. The second smash to the ground was unnecessary and turned his fear to anger. Doc quickly got up. The Lake Forest player was only half to his feet. He reached inside the Lake Forest player's mask and squeezed his face as hard as he could. "You fuckin' dick." He pushed the Lake Forest player back.

The defensive tackle almost fell to the ground, but retained his balance. At first he was startled by Doc's actions, but that only lasted a second. He started after Doc. Doc didn't back down. He pushed him again. "You're not so fuckin' tough, you big dick." Doc looked him square in the eye.

Before the two men could confront one another again, each team pulled their own men off. The referees quickly stepped in and warned both sides. The tension was starting to build. The Lake Forest captain was irate that he wasn't able get Doc back. He pushed at his teammates. As he was pushed back to his huddle, he yelled to Doc.

"That's okay, number 12. I'm coming to get you next play." He spat in Doc's direction.

"Well, I'll be here, you dick. Come and get me." Doc took out his mouthguard. It was red with blood.

Eventually the Bucs got huddled. Doc was still sore, but he hardly noticed it as excitement ran through his body.

"I'm glad you guys gave it all you had last play," Doc's tone was sarcastic. "Same play as last down."

Doc broke the huddle with a clap and Stubby led the team to the line.

As Doc readied to take the snap, his heart pounded. He felt several emotions -- fear, anger, excitement. His hand trembled even more this time as Stubby hiked the ball back to him.

Again, Doc dropped back into the pocket, and again, the Lake Forest captain came surging through the line. Beloit's offensive line still wasn't feeling the excitement that Doc was. They weren't looking for that final taste of glory. Their play showed it.

The defensive tackle lumbered toward Doc like a big train. His mouth was wide open. His scream was deafening. His intensity was focused on hitting Doc as hard as he possibly could.

Blood drooled out of the side of Doc's mouth. His eyes weren't widened with fear this time. He calmly stood and waited. The ball was gripped in one hand at his side. It appeared as if he were going to let the man take a free shot at him, as if he awaited the punishment due him.

Just as the defensive tackle was about to make contact, grabbing Doc by the shoulders and throwing him to the ground, Doc ducked down and avoided the tackle. He almost fell to the ground, but he kept his feet by using one hand on the ground to retain his balance. The defensive tackle stumbled, unable to recover from the evasive move, and fell to the ground.

After Doc got back to his feet, he started to run around to the wide side of the field. His ribs were riddled with pain as he headed down field in the open area. Despite the pain, he tried to open his stride as much as possible, while still being alert to the approaching defenders.

The offensive linemen, who were busy blocking the defensive players who didn't rush in, did not notice Doc until he was past the line of scrimmage. They stopped blocking their men and followed Doc. The receivers Doc had sent out for passes were confused, like the linemen, but once they realized what was happening, they began to block the Lake Forest men who had been covering them.

Doc's run sparked the Beloit sideline and fans. A new electricity was developing for the team that was down by 28 points. Everyone remaining in the stands rose to their feet and began to cheer. The players and coaches on the sidelines moved as close to the edge of the field as possible and followed along with Doc as he raced down the far sidelines.

Doc only had one man left between him and the end zone. He still hugged as close as he possibly could to the opponent's sidelines. As the defender approached, Doc quickly remembered what had happened to him in the University of Chicago game. He had to avoid that, he thought.

When the defender neared contact, Doc cut hard on his leg and changed his direction toward the center of the end zone. His would-be tackler was unable to adjust and he ran out of bounds. Although there was no one left to challenge Doc, he increased his speed and went in for the score.

He tossed the ball to the referee after he had scored. He did no celebrating but started back to the sidelines. Although the clock was stopped, he still had the sense that time was running out. There were only about 17 minutes left. The Bucs had a lot of points to make up. Comeback was in the foreground of Doc's mind.

Most of the players on the field were well behind Doc so they waited for him as he ran back from the end zone to the sidelines. Doc wasn't concerned with congratulations. He pushed through all of them to the coach. Bonaventure could see the intensity in his eyes as Doc approached.

In the excitement, Doc grabbed Bonaventure by the front of the shirt and shook him once. "WE CAN BEAT THESE SONS-A-BITCHES," Doc shouted in his face.

Bonaventure was startled. He grabbed for his hat which was almost jarred off. He could sense the electricity in the air. Bonaventure knew that Doc wouldn't grab him like that unless he were really serious.

After a couple of seconds of clutching Bonaventure's jacket, Doc realized what he had done. He slowly released, expecting reprisals. There were none. Bonaventure moved aside to watch the extra point kick. It was good. The score now was 31 to 10. However, Doc's words and tone were firmly implanted in Bonaventure's mind.

As the kick-off team went on the field, Bonaventure grabbed the kicker as he came over to get the kicking tee. Bonaventure gave him instructions as they both slowly walked onto the field. When the instructions were given, Denton, the kicker, trotted to the huddle, and Bonaventure walked back to the sidelines. His face was straight. He appeared deep in thought, as if his mind was calculating every possible scenario they might face. 'We can beat these sons-a-bitches' still echoed in his mind.

As the kicker approached the ball on the kickoff, everyone expected to see the ball sailing deep into Lake Forest territory. The ball, however, was lightly kicked toward the sidelines. The eyes of the front line of the Lake Forest kick-receiving team widened with surprise. Beloit was attempting an on-side kick.

The trick in this maneuver is that it must go at least ten yards. If the ball is kicked too far, then the kicking team doesn't have a chance of recovering it. This tactic is mainly reserved for late-game comebacks.

This decision was a spur-of-the-moment one for Bonaventure. He let no one know about it except the kick-off team. Keeping a secret from your own side ensured that it would also be kept from the other side. Bonaventure had a good poker face. It always hid what he was thinking.

The ball bounced and rolled the required ten yards. The Beloit players aggressively pursued it and the Lake Forest players nervously awaited it. As the ball bounced high, a Lake Forest player jumped for it. It appeared that it was in his control. However, Bill, who had been placed on the kick-off team early in the season as a second-teamer, also made a jumping grab for the ball. As the two men fell to the ground, they wrestled for the ball. Bill outwilled the Lake Forest player. When he hit the ground, he rolled away from his opponent with the ball.

The referee signaled that the ball belonged to Beloit. Bill got up off the ground and danced in place with the ball held high above his head. Several players rushed on the field to congratulate him as the offense came back onto the field.

Doc called the play quickly and Stubby hurried the team to the line. Although Beloit now had the momentum, time was of the essence. Doc no longer approached the line with fear and trepidation. His face radiated the new confidence. He looked over to the Lake Forest captain. There was a look of concern on his face and he was quiet. Doc wasn't concerned with having a personal grudge match with him. He just looked long enough to let the man know that he remembered what he said the last play. Doc smiled gently.

After the snap on the 43-yard line, Doc took the ball, stepped back from the line and handed it off to his wing back. The offensive line, now alive with excitement, opened a hole in the line and the runner scooted down to the five-yard line before he was tackled.

That was the last play of the quarter. The referee had the teams switch ends as they changed the ball from one five-yard line to the other. Beloit was now facing north, toward the scoreboard, a definite advantage.

OUT OF THE COMFORT ZONE

Three plays later, the Bucs managed to score. The touchdown was needed, but they took too much time with the last five yards. After the extra point attempt went wide of the uprights, the Bucs trailed 31 to 16 with 13:03 left to play in the game.

On the next kickoff, Denton kicked the ball deep in the end zone, just as everyone expected. Lake Forest was unable to make a return. They started with the ball on their own twenty-yard line.

Lake Forest appeared as if they were going to have extended control of the football. On the first two plays, they got fifteen and sixteen yards. However, the Bucs held them for no yardage the next three plays. Bill blocked one pass and stopped a Lake Forest running back at the line of scrimmage. A Beloit linebacker knocked the ball out of a receiver's hand before it could be caught. Lake Forest was forced to punt the ball back to Beloit.

However, Beloit wasn't content with just getting the ball back. Bonaventure sent in a play to the punt-receiving team designed to put enough pressure on the kicker to cause him to punt badly. The play was more successful than Bonaventure had anticipated. The punt was blocked by several players, and the Bucs recovered the ball on the 35-yard line of Lake Forest.

The Beloit running game was going well, probably too well. Lake Forest quickly learned that they could easily key on the running backs to stop the Bucs' offensive momentum. They were correct. On first and second down, Beloit tried to run the ball. On both downs, they were stopped for little or no gain. This brought up a third down and long-yardage situation. The distance was still too far for a field goal, so they had to move closer. Besides, there wasn't enough time to try and overcome Lake Forest's 31 points three at a time.

Doc still wasn't confident that he had enough time to set up for a good pass. His ribs hurt too much to throw on the run. The trick he had pulled on the Lake Forest captain would make him think twice when he rushed in, and hence slow him up. But would it be enough? The Bucs had no other choice than to pass the ball. It was evident that they weren't going to get ten yards in one play running.

Doc dropped back. He quickly checked the edge of the field for an open man. There were none. By now, the Lake Forest rushers were through the line. Doc scrambled for an open area to throw. It wasn't to be found. A tackler grabbed him by the jersey just as he saw an open receiver. Doc winced in pain and he threw off balance. He was slammed to the ground as the ball sailed toward the receiver.

The receiver outran his defender across the middle of the field. With his arms outstretched, he caught the ball and ran in for the score. Denton, the kicker, wasn't sent in for the extra point. Bonaventure wanted to make up the missed field goal with a two-point conversion; however, this failed. Doc was stopped at the line of scrimmage when he tried to sneak behind Stubby for the two points.

Beloit now only trailed 31 to 22 with ten minutes and fifty seconds left in the game.

Many of the people who left the game at halftime continued to listen to the broadcast on the local radio station. When they realized that Beloit was staging a comeback, they didn't want to miss out. Quickly they re-dressed themselves in long underwear and sweaters so they could stand to be out in the cold weather again.

Ames also was listening to the radio broadcast on the way home. He was convinced after the second touchdown that Beloit was going to make a game of what earlier appeared to be a rout. First, however, he had to get his son home.

The tires on his car squealed as he pulled into the driveway. He left the engine running as he parked the car. He raced around to the passenger side of the car and took the seatbelt off his son. He picked his son up and ran him in the house. His wife was curious why he was home so early from the game, but he didn't have time to answer. He set his son down on the couch, kissed his wife on the cheek, and then went back to the idling car. He squealed his tires again as he pulled out of the driveway and headed back toward Strong Stadium.

Beloit kicked off again. This time, Lake Forest was able to manage a return, but they only got the ball out to the 25-yard line. There was a lot of field and a fired-up Beloit defense between them and any more points.

Lake Forest started to move the ball. The Beloit defense, although fired up, was tired. They spent most of the first half of the game on the field. This extra duty was reflected in their slow responsiveness. Lake Forest was quicker than they were at the line, allowing Lake Forest to move the ball down the field. More critical, however, was the fact that their conservative play was eating up the crucial time that remained in the game.

Lake Forest was at the center of the field before the defense was able to group. Only about seven minutes remained in the game. It was second down and three yards to go for the first down. Bonaventure had Bill, who acted as leader of the defense, call a timeout and called the entire defensive unit over to the side of the field. Bonaventure had no wonderful insights or powerful words for the defense. The timeout was just a chance for them to catch their breath.

The time was well spent. On the next two plays, Bill stormed through the line and took the Lake Forest offense for an eight- and a two-yard loss, stopping the Lake Forest momentum and forcing them to punt the ball back to Beloit.

Bonaventure again sent ten men rushing the punter in hopes of getting another block. No such luck. In fact, the punter was able to get off a good punt, and the lone deep man was forced to down the ball on the 17-yard line. Beloit took over first and ten.

The Bucs had a long way to go to score. Everyone's hearts pounded. There was only a little over seven minutes left in the game and the Bucs were down by nine points. That meant they would have to score at least twice more to win.

Doc quickly adopted the 'if it works once, try it again' philosophy. He called the same play that had scored the touchdown last series. This time it didn't score a touchdown, nor did it gain them 35 yards. It got them 25 yards, however. This was enough to get their backs away from the walls.

On the very next play, Doc dropped back again. The Lake Forest defense called out 'PASS.' That's what it appeared like to them. After a two-second delay, a hole opened up in the line and Doc handed the ball off to one of his speedy backs, a delay. The back took off through the hole. No one was able to touch him. He raced the entire length of the field for the score. The whole way down, he put distance between himself and the defenders.

Again, Bonaventure opted to go for the two-point conversion. Lake Forest expected another run. They lined up heavily on the ball. Doc took a step back and faked the handoff to the same back who had just scored the touchdown. The Lake Forest defense converged on the back. He sacrificed his body as Doc dropped back. Quickly, Doc tossed the ball in the corner of the end zone to his receiver. The ball was caught; the conversion was successful. Beloit only trailed by a point. The scoreboard read HOME 30, VISITOR 31, TIME 5:49.

Foster and Doc stood thirty yards from one another on the sidelines. They hadn't had any contact since Foster's talk. Doc was too busy planning the next strategy with the other offensive players and the coaches. Even now, they did not speak. The two just happened to catch one another's eye. Doc broke with his intensity long enough to smile. Foster smiled back.

By now, the cheering crowd for Beloit was growing. Students packed into cars, rode bikes and walked the half mile from campus to Strong Stadium to see if the comeback was for real.

Professor Ames roared through the gate just as Beloit scored its last touchdown. He could see the referee raise his arms to indicate that the points had been awarded. He beeped his horn.

He parked his car on an incline near the entrance to the Stadium. As he excitedly ran out of his car, the force he exerted on the door wasn't enough to overcome the incline and shut the door. Looking back, he slowly saw it re-open and the dome light come back on. He waved his hand to indicate that he would just ignore it. There was more important business to tend to.

Everyone now, including Lake Forest, knew it was a game. Emotions on both sides of the field were high. Lake Forest hoped to hang on to win. Beloit had come back too far to lose.

Lake Forest rallied its offense. Their team needed more points as insurance for their dwindling lead. Lake Forest was a good team; they didn't get this far undefeated on luck. Pure emotion wasn't going to beat them. Part of being a good team is rising to the challenges that emotion swings bring from time to time. Beloit provided an excellent proving ground to test their boast that they were the best team in the league.

OUT OF THE COMFORT ZONE

On the other side of the field, the Beloit defense paced back and forth behind the other players on the sidelines. They awaited the outcome of the kick-off to Lake Forest. The intensity was like nothing they had ever felt before. Their mission was self-evident: to stop Lake Forest from scoring any more points. Their nerves were increasingly tightened by the endorphins that flooded their bloodstream. Their vision was tunneled. The cheers of the fans didn't register.

The kick went out of the end zone. Lake Forest would take over on the twenty-yard line. As the defense took the field, they had to swallow the bile that rose from their stomachs. The lumps in their throats made it hard to breathe. These symptoms would disappear once the action started.

Lake Forest's game plan went from a wide-open passing offense to a conservative ground game. They were no longer concerned with moving down the field a large chunk at a time. Now they were content with slowly gaining ground four or five yards a play.

By moving the ball on the ground, they would ensure that they would retain control of the ball. They didn't want to chance an interception. In addition, the ground game kept the clock moving. That way, if they didn't score, at least Beloit would have limited time in which to move the ball down the field. If they scored too fast, Beloit would have plenty of time to strike back and possibly go ahead.

The change in strategy worked. As hard as the Beloit defense played, they couldn't prevent Lake Forest from getting the needed first downs. The clock continued to tick.

Bonaventure was frustrated. He knew that his offense could move the ball, but that wasn't going to help as long as they weren't on the field. He couldn't be angry with the defense. They were playing tough. They were giving nothing away that wasn't earned. Lake Forest continued to move down the field.

However, when Lake Forest crossed inside Beloit's thirty-yard line, the Bucs received a break. Lake Forest got a five-yard penalty on first down. They were offsides. Now it was first and fifteen yards to go for another first down.

On the next play, Beloit stopped Lake Forest for no gain. Another break. It was second and fifteen, a passing situation, the first one Lake Forest was faced with this series. However, the clock continued to run. It was inside three minutes.

At this point, the Lake Forest sideline was beginning to relax a bit. They were, however, nowhere near the celebration they enjoyed earlier.

Tension remained on the Beloit sideline. The entire team lined the edge of the field as Lake Forest marched down the field. Their cheering was still loud and enthusiastic. But seeing Lake Forest finally get inside their thirty-yard line, no one could help getting that sinking feeling that all they had done to come back was for nothing. Nevertheless, their spirits remained high. After all, the situation had been worse.

Their perseverance sparked the fans, who were now moving down out of the stands onto the track that surrounded the field. It was as if being closer to the action would somehow change the outcome of the game.

The Lake Forest quarterback faded back for the pass. It had been a while since he threw his last pass. His arm was cold and so was his confidence in his throwing ability. Even the Lake Forest offensive line wasn't ready for a passing down. The last ten plays had made them used to the short surges of the running game.

Beloit took advantage of these two factors. The defense rushed the quarterback like Doc had been rushed earlier in the day. Under the pressure, a weak pass was thrown. Bill jumped to try and block it. He only managed to get his fingertips on the ball, but that was enough to make the ball wobble. It was falling short of its target.

Two Beloit linebackers left their zone coverage and raced for the ball. They both had a hand on it. Their combined eagerness almost caused neither of them to get the interception. Without a word, one let the other have the ball as he led him returning the ball in the other direction down the Beloit sidelines.

As one of the linebackers took himself out of the play by blocking two men, the other ran as hard as he could. He gritted his teeth and strained his vocal cords, growling. He hugged the sidelines. It was evident that he wasn't going to make it all the way for a touchdown. As he neared center field, he could see three or four Lake Forest players on a collision course with him. That was all right. He had done what he could. It was up to the offense now.

Foster stood on the edge of the field, cheering as the Beloit linebacker approached. In the excitement, he neglected to move back. He wanted to be as close to the action as possible. The game's intensity felt good.

The linebacker was gang tackled out of bounds. The mass of bodies rolled where Foster was standing. He sensed he should move, but the crutches and cast hindered his reaction time, and they all plowed into Foster. His crutches were mangled beyond repair. His body flew over the pile, and he landed on the ground shoulder first.

For a second after Foster hit the ground, he was still. Everyone stopped breathing as they watched the lame body come to rest on the ground. However, with a quick jerk, as if life had been injected in him, Foster got up to his feet. He had the same look in his eyes as when he played. The football thrill returned to his body, 'God, that felt good,' he thought. It was good to get a small taste of the action.

In the split-second everyone knew Foster was all right, they began to pull the linebacker from the wreckage of bodies. As he was pulled loose, he was congratulated. Everyone crowded around to get a hand on him. The Lake Forest players had to struggle to sneak away.

The remainder of the defense felt sort of left out. Their contribution deserved as much praise as the intercepting linebacker. However, this lonely feeling only lasted a second or two. At this point, it didn't matter who received the praise. All that mattered was that there was a reason for praise.

The sideline tension turned to elation for a moment. Then it turned back. They still had fifty-five yards to get to the end zone. Two minutes and forty-nine seconds remained to play. If it were any consolation, Lake Forest was feeling the same tension.

34

The sidelines, now jammed with players and fans, cheered for the offense as they stormed the field. They were glad to get a chance to be there again. Their nerves were tense.

Doc's voice was rushed as he called the play. It was impossible to relax. In these situations, endorphins were both a salvation and frustration. Each man had to quickly learn how to use the former and ignore the latter.

As Stubby led the team to the line, Lake Forest waited. Their looks were intense, too. They had as much to lose as Beloit had to gain, mainly pride.

Now Doc's nerves caused him to tremble as he called out the count. He tried to notice how Lake Forest might be adjusting its defense for what would probably be the last series. It was hard to concentrate on anything. His heart beat too loudly.

He took the snap and quickly went back to the pocket formed by the offensive line. However, the pocket didn't last long. Lake Forest players sifted through from all directions. Doc couldn't allow himself to be sacked, nor could he fall to his knees to save himself. They would lose some time, a down and some yardage. All three were precious.

Doc ducked to the outside and scrambled toward the Lake Forest sidelines. He did his best to look downfield. He could see no men open, but to get a good look, he would have to stop. That meant that the pursuing tacklers would have the chance to catch him. He had no other choice. He was running out of room to escape.

Doc pulled up and took a quick look downfield. A receiver was wide open. He threw the ball just as a swarm of tacklers hit him.

Although beneath a pile of players, Doc watched the ball fly to the receiver. He was wide open. The ball was perfectly thrown. However, the receiver's nerves caused him to drop it. Doc quickly pushed his way out from under the pile. He ran down field to meet his dejected receiver halfway.

"Catch the fucking ball," Doc screamed. The tension overtook him. Everyone heard his words.

On the way back to the huddle, Bonaventure called onto the field. He signaled to Doc to settle down and regain his composure. The dropped pass was important, but not crucial. When Doc got to the huddle, he quickly apologized to the receiver in front of the rest of the offense. It was nothing formal or fancy. There wasn't time. No harm was done.

Doc then called the same play. He directed the same receiver to do the same thing. When the ball was hiked, Doc followed the receiver's course across the field. The rush came again, but Doc didn't have to do any moving. The receiver got open early. Doc threw the ball and this time it was caught.

The receiver was immediately tackled. Doc started to rush everybody up to the line. The clock was still running, but the referee called time out. A man was hurt.

Big El was on his hands and knees with his face in the ground. He moaned in pain. On the last play, his helmet was pushed down over the bridge of his nose, gashing it open. Blood rolled down his face. The pain prevented him from opening his eyes.

Jack Benson rushed to his aid. Bonaventure was close behind. Jack removed the helmet and quickly decided that the wound was superficial, not superficial enough, however, to have El return to action. It would take longer to bandage him up than there was time left in the game. Bonaventure turned to the bench to look for a replacement.

There were three back-ups for El. Each waited by field's edge for his name to be called. Each was a freshman or sophomore with limited playing experience. Bonaventure couldn't risk experimenting to see if any of them were game-ready.

"Barton." Bonaventure shouted for Bill.

After the interception, Bill figured that he had been on the field for the last time. Nevertheless, he was on the field and at Bonaventure's side seconds after his name was called.

"Bill, I know you've played all game on defense, but I need you to play El's position. I know you're tired, but can you do it?" Bonaventure waited for an answer.

A smile grew on Bill's face. A straight yes-or-no answer wasn't

OUT OF THE COMFORT ZONE

forthcoming. "Coach, up until about three games ago, all I did was rest." Bill turned to the huddle. Bonaventure patted him on the ass as he started in that direction.

Doc came into the huddle last. He had just received the play from the sidelines. It was a screen pass, where the quarterback dropped back for what looked like a long pass, and the offensive line let the rushers through the line as if they would get an easy sack. If all went well, at the last minute, the quarterback would loft the ball over the heads of the attacking rushers into the hands of a back. From there, it was all a question of how well the offensive line could block.

"Okay, we're going to run a 10-27 screen pass. Now, you offensive linemen make your blocking look real, but make sure that those rushers come through the line hard. Got it? 10-27 screen pass on three. Ready... break." Doc broke the huddle as everyone clapped.

For the entire game, El had been playing against the Lake Forest captain who was giving Doc trouble in the backfield. Now that El was injured, Bill was supposed to line up across from the defensive tackle. However, since the screen pass had no real structure, Simba persuaded Bill to switch sides for this one play. As Simba approached the line, his new opponent began to badger him.

"Ah, number 76. Looks like I'm going to get a crack at you after all." The man remembered the incident earlier in the game.

Simba didn't say anything to him immediately. He just smiled. Something was up his sleeve. Halfway through the long count, Simba looked up and caught the defensive tackle's attention.

"Hey 98," Simba called his number and waited for his attention to turn from the ball. "Your mother was good last night."

Simba could see the anger fill the man's face as the ball was snapped. Simba could hardly keep from laughing. The defensive tackle fired off the line as hard as he could. He was intent on ripping through Simba and Doc. Simba let the man run right past, as he was supposed to.

Doc backed up as four rushers approached him. Just before they reached him, Doc lofted the ball over their heads. He couldn't see beyond them. He hoped the back was there. He was.

The ball was caught and the back started to run behind the wall formed by the advancing offensive line. The back could move as fast as the blocking line, slow. The back made it to the nine-yard line before he was dragged down from behind. He was tackled in bounds. As soon as the linesmen moved the yard markers, the clock continued to tick. It was now inside a minute and ten seconds.

Doc quickly huddled the team and called a simple dive play up the middle, but the Lake Forest defense was tough. The back only managed to get a yard.

The clock continued to move. Less than a minute remained.

Lake Forest was slow to get up. They wanted as much time as possible to pass between plays. Beloit had no timeouts left to stop play. The only time they had to gather themselves was during the few seconds between plays. This added to the tension, especially on each sideline where players and coaches were now helpless.

It was second down and one on the eight-yard line. This was an ambiguous area for calling plays. It was too close to pass and yet too far to run. Doc paged through the playbook in his mind. There had to be a play for this situation. He was stumped. It was obvious, though, they had to run the ball. They couldn't risk losing ball control. That was critical. Doc huddled the team.

"This is it. It's down to the line." Doc exhaled. The excitement almost made him hyperventilate. Sensing the finality of the moment, everyone in the horseshoe-shaped huddle held hands.

Doc called the play. "We are going to give the ball to Scooter to sweep right. Now if Scooter doesn't get out of bounds, line up quickly. I am going to have to throw the ball out of bounds to stop the clock so we can get the field goal team in here." Everyone nodded.

Doc looked each player in the eye. In his most serious voice, he said, "Let's just fuckin' win." He broke the huddle and Stubby led them to the line.

As Doc approached the line, the clock read forty-five seconds. His mind was so focused on the game that he didn't even hear the cheers of the players and fans on his own sidelines chanting, "GO, GO, GO!!"

He breathed deep and called the count. He handed the ball off to Scooter and watched him head for the right side of the field. Before the play could be turned up field, a Lake Forest linebacker darted through the line and tackled the ball carrier.

Again, Lake Forest was slow getting up. The clock continued: 29 ...

28 ... 27. Doc shouted to have his own players line up on the ball. Then, he shouted to the referees, complaining that Lake Forest was delaying the game by getting up too slowly. The referee ignored the appeal.

There were fifteen seconds left in the game when Beloit lined up. The ball was in the center of the field. Doc didn't say a word. He just signaled to Stubby to hike the ball. Doc took the ball and stepped back from the line twice quickly. He intentionally threw the ball over the head of one of his receivers and out of bounds. The clock stopped with ten seconds left.

Bonaventure immediately sent in the field goal kicker. It was now fourth down on the ten-yard line. All of a sudden, the elements of the game didn't matter anymore. There was only time for one more play. One more play was all Beloit had. Beloit was too far for a touchdown in reality, but in a perfect position for a field goal. A field goal was all that was needed. The only element that remained was scoring. And there was only one chance.

Beloit lined up in field goal formation. Everyone on both sides of the field toed the edge of the playing area. Their hearts pounded. They all knew that nothing was for sure. It was a fifty-fifty proposition. Either the ball would go through the uprights, or it wouldn't. Past kicking abilities didn't change those odds.

Doc sat on a single knee with his arms outstretched to receive the snap. As he tried to catch his breath to call out the count, he also had to shout to be heard over the jeers of the Lake Forest team and the mumbling that came from their own fans. Both these objectives couldn't be reached at the same time. It was one or the other. Doc told himself, 'just a little longer,' as he began shouting out the count.

Stubby looked at him through his legs. He waited for the word to tell him to hike the ball back to be kicked. His heart pounded so hard he could feel the blood rush to his head.

Doc gave the word and the ball was hiked. However, in the excitement, Stubby hiked the ball a little too high. Doc tried to get it but instead it bounced off his helmet and began to tumble away from his grasp.

The Lake Forest bench relaxed. It appeared they had held on to win.

The hearts of the Beloit players and fans sank. They had come so far, so close, so many times. Everyone seemed to breathe disappointment, everyone except the players on the field. They abided by the number one rule of football: the play isn't over until the whistle blows.

As soon as Doc realized that the snap was bad and that the kick would not be made, he yelled 'FIRE!' This indicated to the rest of the players, who weren't looking back, the essence of what was going on. The linemen were supposed to hold their blocks and the receivers were to release into end zone patterns. Everyone heard the call and reacted.

Denton, the kicker, instinctively ran to where the football was rolling. He only had a chance to pick the ball up before he realized that almost the entire team of Lake Forest players was converging on him.

Just before he was hit, Denton flipped the ball back to Doc, who also was pursuing the stray ball, but several steps behind Denton. Two or three players took Denton to the ground. The rest altered their course and went after Doc.

Doc began to run to the other side of the field. At the same time, he looked in the end zone for an open man. Lake Forest had a zone pass coverage. No one was open.

Bill turned back from the line to head off the first of Doc's pursuers. This gave Doc a little more time. Simba and Stubby also each made blocks on would-be tacklers. However, the time they bought for Doc was of no value, since no one was open.

Doc had no other choice but to try and run the fifteen yards in for the score. This choice wasn't much better than passing, because just ahead of him as he ran was the Lake Forest captain. He was on a collision course, and he had getting even on his mind.

Doc started to bury his head and try to run through the man. In his mind, he knew this was futile. In his heart, he knew he had to try. It was Beloit's only hope.

As he approached the man, out of the corner of his eye Doc noticed Denton, the 130-pound team kicker, wide open in the end zone. After his tacklers had left him, he made his way to the end zone undetected.

Just before colliding with the Lake Forest captain, Doc leaped into the air. He lofted the ball on what he hoped was a perfect course. Doc watched the ball for about ten yards before his body made contact with the defensive tackle.

The man hit him with an incredible force. Doc heard his grunt and then felt the pain rip through his ribs. The pain was so intense that Doc blacked out momentarily.

He was unconscious from the time he was hit until the time he landed on the ground. As he lay on the ground, he raised his head just enough to see Denton catch the ball and the referee signal that a touchdown was scored. He lay his head back down on the ground and let his body relax.

His relaxation lasted only long enough for the tension he'd been feeling to leave and an exhilarated feeling replace it. Go out with some glory, he thought. God damn, he had. He went out with more glory than he had ever dreamed of.

Bert was the first to reach Denton. He held the little kicker up as high as he could in his arms. He hugged him around the waist tightly. He squeezed his eyes shut and tears began to roll down his cheeks. Damn, they had done it. They had come back. "We're winners," he said, straining through his tears.

Denton raised both arms over his head and let out a yell. The time had come, as Bonaventure put it, to whoop it up. He clutched the ball tightly in his left hand. Never had he felt so big. Never had he felt so proud. Never had he felt so mighty.

Immediately, the fans who had come down from the stands to watch the final minutes of the game came rushing onto the field. There would be no extra point try and no two-point conversion. They created a commotion so the Beloit players on the field couldn't find one another, leaving the Lake Forest players to slip away in their humiliation.

Stubby went over and helped Doc to his feet. They slapped their hands together as hard as ever before and shook. This handshake then became an embrace of equal magnitude. Arm in arm, they each raised their free hands, clenched into fists, toward the sky. "Yeah," they both yelled with strained voices, "we did it!"

Bill ran toward the bench, where Bonaventure was. On his way there, he recalled what Bonaventure had said to him through teary eyes: "If you stick with me, I promise you you'll be a factor in something big this season." I didn't know how he did it, but the son-of-a-bitch did, he thought. Bill's opinion of Bonaventure was the same that it always was -- high.

Bill and Coach Gibson grabbed Bonaventure by the legs and lifted him up. Other players filled in to make it appear that a mob of people carried him. They extended their arms to carry him as high as possible.

The players who didn't lift Bonaventure ran toward the end zone to join in the celebration. They weren't concerned about shaking hands with the Lake Forest players, only congratulating the offensive unit.

Foster was among these players, but his cast prevented him from keeping up. Halfway to the end zone, he stopped and raised his hands over his head in triumph. An incredible energy seemed to stream through his body, the feeling of ultimate glory.

As Foster stood in insulated celebration, he was tackled around the ribs. It startled him. Pain ran through his body, but he didn't care. It wasn't enough to overcome the feeling the endorphins in his system gave him.

When his body came to rest on the ground, he realized that it was Simba who had tackled him. The two began to laugh as they wrestled around on the ground, celebrating.

The exhilaration of the accomplishment and success turned to tears. For so long, it seemed that nothing could go right and they were destined to be heartbroken. Then, all at once, their every dream came true. All the disappointments, all the hardships and all the setbacks were overcome in one glorious moment brought about by perseverance and discipline. They felt proud. They walked tall.

Each player, whether he played a lot or not at all, had tears streaming down his face, as the team gathered in the end zone. The coaches and fans joined them in exchanging handshakes and embraces.

Through teary eyes, players greeted the fans. It didn't matter how loyal they were. The fans were thanked for sharing this moment. Without them, it wouldn't have been as wonderful or glorious.

Bonaventure and the other coaches were surrounded by players offering congratulations on the season and thanks for giving them the opportunity to be a part of it. This moment was like none they had experienced before; they might never experience one again.

Most of all, players embraced one another, saying whatever they could through their tears. The essence of what was said was, "We did it, damn, we did it; and now we're winners. We're winners."

For the seniors, the tears were especially heavy. It was a long, hard road to proclaim this winner status. But the road they traveled and all its hardships did not matter now because it had come to an end and they had made it together. What a way to end a career. What a way to always remember something you loved so much. What a way to feel about yourself.

Out of the corner of his tear-filled eyes, Foster noticed Jandi standing all alone watching him from the archway of the Stadium. He stopped, in the midst of all the commotion, to look back. She fought hard to hold back her own tears. Her eyes started to glisten as tears began to accumulate. She was so happy for him. She nodded to him and gave him the thumbs-up sign.

Foster cleared the tears from his face with the palm of his hand. Streaks of dirt were left on his face. He smiled at her. He was so glad she was there.

Sue waited for Stubby with his parents at the edge of the field. Stubby took time out from the frolic to greet her. She met him halfway, jumping into his arms and squeezing his neck. She could sense the strong feeling in his body. It made her warm, too.

"I'm so proud of you," she said, still tightly clinging to his body. "I love you so much." Stubby was unable to say anything in return.

Sue wiped the tears from her own eyes. Smiling, she pushed him back. "Go on. Go be with your teammates."

She pointed to the players in the background still enjoying their moment of glory. She knew that this was his moment to share with his football friends. She understood. There would be other moments for them to share together.

Stubby gave Sue a hug and then returned to the other players.

Denton gave the game ball to Doc. As soon as Doc had it, he searched out his parents. They stood together near the edge of the celebration. Doc wiped his eyes on the way over. He felt funny about crying in front of his parents. He extended the ball to them as if it were a gift.

"Thank you...for everything. Thank you both very much." He could no longer hold back his tears. He rushed forward and gave his mother and father a hug and a kiss. They held him tightly, too. They were so proud.

Coach Bonaventure was stuck in the middle of all the commotion. It was nice to win. It was great to win the way they did, but that wasn't where his heart was just then.

As soon as he spotted his wife, he pushed his way through the mass of well-wishers. When he finally got to her, he didn't say a word. He gave her a warm hug so she could share the emotion he was feeling.

He put his head over her shoulder and squeezed. As he gently closed his eyes, a small tear overflowed from his eyelid and fluttered down his cheek.

35

Almost forty minutes after the game, the scoreboard still glowed HOME 36, VISITOR 31, and TIME 0:00. The team wished it could stay illuminated until the first home football game next fall.

The Bucs carried on their celebration out on the field for close to twenty minutes. After that, the party was moved inside the locker room, where admittance was limited to players, coaches and staff.

After the team took a knee, there was no lecture or post-game. It was time to enjoy the moment.

The team's loyal following sent several cases of beer into the locker room. The team used this as their champagne. Every player had beer poured over his head. Simba went so far as to chug a beer that was poured inside his shoe. His size 14 feet held an even 24 ounces of beer, foam included.

Bonaventure, who even on such a celebration didn't drink, wasn't left out. His wife quickly went to the local supermarket to get what her husband had given up for the entire season: ice cream. A full half gallon was brought in. Although he did not eat it all or even half, he made a sizeable dent in the half gallon.

Everyone gave the celebrating a rest after a while. They had to save some for later that night. Players began to ice down their wounds and shower up their sweat-stained bodies.

Doc could do neither until he and Bonaventure had completed an interview with the local radio station and Jim Francia from *The Beloit Daily News*.

Bonaventure stressed how wonderful it was for the seniors to finish their careers the way they did. He also emphasized what this game meant to the football program at Beloit. The team had a lot of young players who would be returning next fall with the taste of this winning experience. In addition, for the first time, they could be recruiting new players with the boast of a winning season.

The press tried to get Doc to talk about himself. Doc kept ducking these questions, giving credit where it really belonged: to everyone. Every chance Doc got, he mentioned the value of the contribution of guys like Joe Whitman, who went from an immature and self-centered individual to a team player; or, guys like Bill Barton, who stuck with the team for four years even though the prospects for playing weren't good. Or, guys like Dan Simpson, whose easygoing personality and sense of humor always kept the team cheerful. Doc could have gone on for days talking about each individual's contribution to the team and the season that made this moment possible. Doc never said that their victory was anything short of a team effort.

As everyone started to shower, Foster went out to the field and helped the managers put equipment away. Because of his cast, his assistance was limited. Now without his crutches, both hands were free to re-pack first-aid kits or empty water bottles.

When the job was complete, he started to hobble on his cast across the cinder running track to the locker room entrance. When he was halfway across the track, Doc and Stubby came running out of the locker room. They had their shoulder pads off, but they had put their jerseys back on.

"Come on Foster, let's go for a victory lap," Doc said with a smile on his face. He motioned to indicate that they should start to run right now.

"Yeah, just one lap. The three captains," Stubby added.

Foster knew they were trying to use his own words against him. "Fuck you," Foster said in a joking manner. He smiled back and waited to see how they would counter.

"Come on. We'll let you set the pace." Doc laughed, knowing that he mimicked Foster's very words.

"Finally, after all those games, and when I'm in a cast -- no doubt -- you want to run a victory lap. Something doesn't sound right." He waited for a counterargument.

"But Foster, all those other games weren't the last game." Stubby smiled because he knew his logic was the counterargument to Foster's point. "Just think, this will be the last chance you'll ever have to run a victory lap with us. Think about it." Stubby winked.

Foster's face indicated that he was giving in. "Okay. I'm still going to kick your asses."

As Foster started his momentum in the direction of the lap, Jack Benson came out of the lockerroom. "Hhhhang onnn." Jack had heard Doc and Stubby convincing Foster to go for the run. "Yoou arren'tt rrunning anywhere." The pressure exerted on the leg while walking in a cast was bad for Foster's knee. It hindered recovery. Jack had an image to uphold. Of the players he trained who had knee surgery, 100 percent recovered.

"Come on, Jack. It's only one lap. We'll go slow." Doc didn't understand Jack's reasoning, but he pleaded anyway.

Jack paused. He thought about Doc's plea. The sentiment of the game got to him. He held up one finger to indicate that they should wait. He then dashed into the locker room. Doc, Stubby, and Foster looked at each other, puzzled. Not five seconds later, Jack emerged again with the pair of wooden crutches Foster used when he first got injured.

"Oookkay. You ccccan gggoo on the lllapp, bbbuttt you gggott tto pppromise to use ttthese." Jack tossed Foster both crutches.

Foster grabbed the crutches and put them under his arm like they were supposed to be used.

"Don't break 'em, either," Stubby added.

Everyone laughed as they began the lap. Initially, Foster had to work hard to keep up, but Stubby and Doc then slowed the pace.

It was getting colder, but they didn't care.

Made in the USA